Medicine Song

CELESTE LOVICK

SHELTERING TREE BOOKS
LONDON

Published in 2017 by Sheltering Tree Books, London.

Printed and distributed worldwide by IngramSpark.

Cover image painted by Dorrie Joy. www.dorriejoy.co.uk

Drawings of the alchemical elements by Glennie Kindred. www.glenniekindred.co.uk

*To **Chris**, an extraordinary musician*

and the first one to show me that music could be medicine.

*And to our beautiful son, **James**, one of my greatest teachers.*

Contents

"And so I am not at all different from you,
these windows I look from are also your own,
and when you catch sight of the infinite pattern
and wonder what moves you,
you are not alone.
It's the peace of the action,
the heart of the matter,
ki and the buddha,
the medicine way,
the water of life in its flowing and growing,
the skull and the fire
and the love of it all"

From the song, 'Peace of the Action', by Brian Boothby

GLASTONBURY FESTIVAL 2013

A FEW DAYS AFTER THE MIDSUMMER SOLSTICE

1. Water

"These things you keep
You better throw them away
You wanna turn your back on your soulless days
Once you were tethered
Now you are free
That was the river
This is the sea"

from the song, 'This is the Sea', by Michael Scott [1]

It's the centre of its universe. From the higher vantage point on the hillside, Cedar can see the old oak clearly, standing amidst a sea of tipis and tents. In the ten years that he has been coming to this festival, the vista has shifted a little each time, but for the most part the tree has been the same. It has become a friend to him.

Cedar's didgeridoo rests on his lap. It's his favourite one – the big D. Harder to carry up here, but worth it. It's become part of his Glastonbury ritual, as has communing with the old oak. Over the years, Cedar has had his share of extraordinary experiences in these fields. *And they're not over yet*, the sense comes to him.

His eyes rest on the strands of multi-coloured lights which have been draped across some of the oak's lower branches, marking the path that runs alongside it, taking people from one field to another. The birds which usually settle in its branches have fled, finding temporary shelter in the trees beyond the large silver perimeter fence a few yards further up the hill from where Cedar sits.

---

1. *Dizzy Heights Music Publishing, Ltd. All rights administered by Warner/Chappell Music Ltd.*

He has a feeling that even with all the sub-bass frequencies that are beginning even now and must be resonating in the ground below it, that the tree will continue to feel the sustaining thrum of the earth's humming as its roots reach deep, a mirror of its branches above.

He thinks of Moon.

From here, Cedar can see the centre of the Tipi Field down below with its sacred fire burning all the time, and from this fiery centre how it reaches out to the four directions – North, South, East and West – with each direction presided over by a banner of one of four Great Chiefs: Sitting Bull, Chief Seattle, Red Cloud and Chief Joseph.

Somewhere in the East, with Chief Joseph, is Moon's tipi. Cedar had helped her set it up yesterday. At least the first part. Although many things have changed between them, this part of their Glastonbury ritual has remained the same. They had lashed together the first three pine poles and lifted them up, erecting them into a tripod. Into this they had placed the 15 poles which would form the bones of the structure.

As Cedar had watched Moon lithely flipping the lashing rope round the tops of the poles to secure them, he'd caught a look in her eye – something unsettling. He can feel it now in his solar plexus like a message.

Something is up.

Moon has been a faithful companion throughout the past year, seeming to accept the conditions of their relationship, even though it hasn't been easy for her. So often she had stopped herself from following a flow that would have been so natural before.

But it can't continue this way, he knows. *Something has to change.*

It is changing.

He can feel it in the breeze rushing up across the expanse of the festival site below him, and the energetic shiver that moves through his body.

In the weeks leading up to the festival, Cedar has had a growing sense that there would be a significant meeting here. Something of importance would happen. His eyes rest again on the old oak, and he smiles.

It's simple for the tree, he thinks. *The tree doesn't judge, so it doesn't suffer like we humans do.*

Cedar realises how full of thoughts his own mind is, and reminds himself to breathe and bring his awareness down lower, to that centre inside himself. He imagines his own roots sinking deep into the soil, earthing him. He feels himself growing calmer, his mind becoming more still.

He hasn't yet made his intention for the festival. He lets his gaze rest softly on the oak and then soften more, to take in the festival beyond it as a whole, knowing the answers don't come from trying to think too hard. They have to come into a space that's open for them.

As he lets his vision shift into soft focus, Cedar begins to see the subtle glow of the tree's aura – a clearer than clear lightness surrounding every part of the tree, sometimes gold and green and shifting colours. He can see how this energy field is touching those who walk by on their way from one field to another, giving them just a little more energy – whether they realise it or not. Most don't even notice the tree there, let alone experience the energy that surrounds it.

He runs his hand along the smooth cedar wood of his instrument.

To find the key. To deepen the journey. That is my intention.

There is a song humming around the edges of Cedar's consciousness, asking to be sung. He listens.

You are Love, the words come to him. They have been spoken so many times by so many people, especially in these green fields. *But to really feel what that means...*

He lifts the didgeridoo to his lips, and riding on his circular breathing, he sings into the shaft of the instrument.

You are Love... You are Love... You are Love...

He offers the song to the wind and the oak tree, across the tops of the tipis and out to all the people beyond. To Moon – wishing her well on her journey through this festival which has a power to be so intense for those who are open to transformation. And like a wave of warmth washing through him, he has the strongest sense of someone else. Someone he wants to send this song to, whose path is so close. Someone who, like him, has a dream of awakening.

She feels as insubstantial as the dust rising around her feet. Like she could, at any moment be blown over by a breath of wind. To Anna, nothing matters right now in the face of losing all she has been working towards. Numb, she stares blankly at all the passing people, seeing right through them, a million miles away from it all into nothing. Both her guitar case and the full box of CDs she had placed such faith in feel like dead weight in her arms. The midday sun is blinding.

Where do I go now? Where is there to go?

As if in answer, a breeze from the far hills with just a hint of coolness brushes across her face. She closes her eyes, feeling the brief relief of it, as if it is all that is left to her.

In the distance, a didgeridoo vibrates the air.

When Anna opens her eyes, her gaze is resting on a maroon-coloured tent across the way, one she hadn't noticed before, nestled just off the main arena of this part of the festival. Above the entrance is a large, hand-stitched fabric sign reading: *The Chai Chi Tent.*

As she steps beneath the shade of the tent, Anna is greeted by the pleasing aroma of incense and sweet spices. Upbeat reggae music plays on a stereo, which somehow doesn't completely clash with the other beats coming from the various stages and cafes in the area. Anna recognises the song. It's Bob Marley's *Three Little Birds.*

Colourful woven mats cover the floor and small, knee-high round wooden tables are dotted about the front of the tent, each surrounded by small cushions. The walls are lined with batik-style throws of reds, oranges and yellows and the wooden shelves are filled with different musical instruments from around the world: drums, wooden flutes and shakers made from gourds. At the right side of the tent, large handmade wooden tables create a serving area, laden with plates full of delicious looking brownies, cakes and flapjacks, along with a coffee machine and two large metal pots filled with Chai – one dairy, one vegan.

Looking very chilled out behind the counter, and moving his head to the beat is a young man with long, nicely cared for ash blond dreadlocks tied up in a red hairband. He wears an orange t-shirt with a red mandala-type design on it. Anna guesses that he's probably just slightly younger than she is, maybe in his mid-twenties. As he stacks more brownies on one of the plates he's singing along with the music.

Kai has been working with chi energy for many years now in the form of qigong and reiki healing, amongst other things, and wanted to start a chai tent where all the food and drink were made with conscious intent and life-force energy put into them. Also a practitioner of t'ai chi, Kai decided to call his cafe The Chai Chi Tent.

The pot on his back stove has come to a boil. Kai's making a new batch of his special Chai recipe. He peels fresh ginger root and grates it into the pot. With his mortar and pestle he grinds the cardamom pods, cloves and black pepper and drops them into the simmering water. Now for some fresh grated cinnamon, with a few larger pieces dropped in for extra flavour. With a small handful of his favourite spice, the flower-shaped star anise for that hint of liquorice sweetness, he's nearly done.

And of course, there is the last ingredient – the most important one of all.

This is when Kai notices the young woman with the guitar standing at the entrance to the Chai Chi tent. He can see that she has had a serious shock of some kind. There is a lost, vacant look in her eyes, and her shoulders are slumped forward.

He can also see right away that she's one of those beautiful young women who doesn't know they're beautiful. She's wearing a dress that's too tight for her, and shoes that look so uncomfortable. Her auburn hair has been hairsprayed in place so that it doesn't move about her shoulders as it would naturally, and she's hiding behind that heavy layer of make-up. To Kai, all women are beautiful. It's just that most of them don't know it. Kai wants to say to these women sometimes: *Please! You're beautiful as you are! You don't need to cover it up!* Sometimes he does say that to them, but also he is trying not to judge, because they are on their journey, too. And maybe they really like wearing make-up. Who is he to say what's right for another person?

Kai notes that this young woman is carrying a guitar case and a box of some kind that looks far too heavy for her. The picture all falls into place. She's a musician, she's come from a gig and her ego has taken a hit.

So Kai decides to give this one a little extra energy. He finishes his blessing of the chai and turns to give her his full attention.

Anna notices the young man behind the counter is smiling at her. It's such a bright, friendly smile that Anna thinks he must have confused her with someone else.

"Hello!" Kai beams at her.

"Hi," Anna replies, not sure how else to respond. *Who does he think I am?* She steps closer, so that he can see clearly that she is not the person he's confused her for. But even as she does, his smile stays as bright and constant and full of recognition as ever.

"Just had a gig?" he asks.

Anna looks down at the guitar in her hand, which she had almost forgotten she was carrying. It feels utterly strange in her hand. She feels utterly strange herself, like she's at the bottom of a pond. Nothing makes sense.

She lets her guitar drop onto the mat by her feet and places the CD box on top of it, just to be free of the burden of them for a little while. She doesn't know how to speak about what's just happened, because she can hardly believe it herself. To speak it aloud would somehow make it more real. At the moment, she would prefer to hide in the stunned stupor of numbness. But this young man is being so friendly, Anna feels she owes him at least some kind of reply. So she just nods.

Kai's eyes show immediate understanding. "It didn't go how you wanted it to?"

Anna is surprised to see such an expression of care there. The tenderness and understanding in the man's face are enough to cause a sob to rise up into Anna's throat. She wrenches it back down.

Standing there with his friendly gaze on her, Anna wonders briefly if perhaps this young man is actually trying to hit on her, and that maybe that's where the extreme friendliness is coming from. When men she doesn't know are friendly with her, it is usually when she's dressed in something like this, and it usually means they want something from her. Of course, it had been her intention to cultivate the look of the sexy singer-songwriter for her big Glastonbury moment.

However, in this instance, looking up into Kai's exuberant, almost child-like face, Anna decides that this must be different. It doesn't feel like this young man wants anything from her at all. Quite the opposite. She can't figure it out, though. If he doesn't want anything, why is he being so nice? She gives up trying to understand and lets out a shuddering breath.

"No. It was... not what I had expected." Barely holding her face in check, she opens the lid of her CD box, showing Kai the neat rows of CDs – 50 in all – without a single empty space in it.

"Anna Leigh Mayes..." Kai reads her name. "You write your own songs?"

She nods. It had all seemed like a grand plan at first. When Anna had been offered this official gig at Glastonbury Festival – albeit on one of the slightly smaller stages – it had seemed to be her chance to make her big break. With encouragement from her boyfriend, Damien, and funding from her father, Anna had recorded her debut album *Your Love is the Answer*, in readiness for this big moment.

It had involved many months spent in the studio going over and over the tracks, falling down with exhaustion in the night and telling herself that even if it was no fun at the time, it would all be worth it in the end. When the CD was finally complete and packaged in plastic, Anna had lifted the first one and held it between her fingers, staring at the face on the cover. For some reason she couldn't fathom, rather than feeling a sense of accomplishment, she'd felt like crying. She had made herself smile then for Damien as he told her how professional it looked, but all she could think about was how it looked like somebody else on the cover, and how inside all the vocals had been auto-tuned, and so many parts separated out from one another to avoid bleed between tracks. According to the sound engineer, they had achieved their aim; it was radio playable.

And when it had finally come to the gig, standing up there on that stage with her Martin guitar, in front of that sweaty microphone, wearing an uncomfortable dress that didn't actually sparkle under the stage lights after all, in shoes that made her stumble, Anna had tried her best. She had tried her best to sing over the noise from the larger stages nearby and to gain the attention of the people who sat at the bar and talked throughout her whole set. Then at the end, she had tried to stand tall when people had politely clapped and nobody had approached her to buy a single CD. Perhaps worst of all was the absence of the Very Important Music Industry Man who Anna had envisioned would be there to hand her his golden business card and tell her she has what it takes to make it in the music industry.

Kai nods understanding. "Well, my hat's off to you, Anna Leigh. I have a deep respect for anyone who can write songs like that."

"Even songs that nobody wants to buy?" Anna effects a laugh at herself. The sob pushes its way back to the surface again. It's harder to quell down this time, lodging itself like a large ball in her throat.

The young man looks at her with such compassion that she half expects he's going to lean over the counter and hug her, but he doesn't. He's thinking about it though, she can tell. If he did, she really would break out sobbing.

Instead he just says, "It can be hard, I know, putting yourself out there, and if you've got a lot riding on what you're selling, then that can make it feel all the harder."

His face is kind as he says this, but Anna hears something in his words which irks her... *if you've got a lot riding on what you're selling... He makes it sound like I'm a salesperson!*

This connotation bothers her. It's as if he's insinuating that she's not primarily a musician, but someone toting wares. Yet, even in her half-numb state, she realises that in a way he's right. With all her marketing materials and the dress and everything, what has she been doing all this time but creating herself as a product to sell? Suddenly, seeing herself this way doesn't sit so well as it did before.

Before Anna can question it further, her attention is caught by the giant plate of moist and decadent organic chocolate brownies on the counter in front of her.

Kai notices the direction of Anna's gaze and grins.

"Why don't you let me give you a drink and a cake on the house?" he says. He wants to offer her something. He doesn't normally give things away until the end of the day, but he can feel this moment calls for some kind of an offering.

"Really?" Anna can't really believe this man's generosity, and wonders again whether he has an ulterior motive. "Why?"

"Because, Sister, we've got to stick together. Help each other. Besides, we always give away loads of stuff here at the end of the day anyway. It's part of the ethos of the place. We sell and we give. It all comes around. Giving and receiving are two sides of the same thing."

Anna still feels a little confused about accepting anything for free, but also she is aware of just how little money she has with her – only a £5 note and some small change. She had been so certain she would have a significant amount of cash from CD sales by now. She had even imagined selling them all. That was why she hadn't bothered to stop at a cashpoint on her way to the festival or to wait for an hour in the queue at the festival's cashpoints.

"That's... so kind of you. Thank you." She casts her eyes across the array of delicious-looking creations on the counter.

"There's nothing... special in these brownies is there?" Anna asks, thinking about the people she'd passed earlier, who had been wearing faery wings and selling hash faery cakes. "Of course, in my current state I could probably use some of that... but still." Anna attempts to smile at herself, and is pleased when Kai laughs.

"You mean is there any herb in it? No. But special, yes. They're protein-only brownies, made with almond flour, organic fairtrade chocolate and... Love."

Anna feels a smile curving the edges of her lips. For some reason this man's cheerfulness is starting to rub off on her. "I'll definitely have one of them, then. I certainly could use a little more love today. That's for sure."

"The more the better," he agrees, selecting the largest brownie in the pile and placing it on a napkin.

"Here you are." He offers it to Anna in a way that reminds her of how the priests in her parent's church offered holy communion; the sacred sacrament of the chocolate love brownie.

"And a cup of our special Chi Chai?" Kai asks.

"Yes please."

"Cow or soya?"

"Uh... I don't know. You pick."

"I'll give you the soya. It's been... steeping longer." His eyes twinkle with a hint of mischief. He spent a good long time on this earlier batch. It's particularly good; he's had three cups of it already.

She watches as he carefully dips the ladle into the larger of the two pots, drawing out the creamy, steaming light brown liquid and pouring it into a brightly coloured mug with elephants painted on it.

"What makes it Chi Chai?" Anna asks.

"A liberal dose of love and good intentions," Kai grins.

Anna laughs, surprised to find genuine humour in herself. This whole situation all seems so silly suddenly. It's like she's in a strange dream, having walked into a multi-coloured landscape of Bob Marley and Love Chai.

"And hey, by the way, don't worry about your CDs not selling," Kai says. "Because

I heard that's happening to alot of musicians here. People are all into downloads now. So don't let it get you down. The number of CDs you sell at a gig is not a measure of your true worth. The truth is, your true worth is not about what you sell, or what anyone else buys. Your true worth has NOTHING to do with ANY of that." As Kai speaks these words, he feels the power of them. This is something he's meant to say to her. It feels good to say it. He doesn't know whether she completely gets his meaning, though.

"Thank you." Anna accepts the mug of steaming chai and carries it and the brownie over to a sheltered table at the corner of the tent, where she can have the protection of the canvas at her back and a view of the sun-streaked crowds walking by. Kai kindly follows with her guitar and box of CDs, placing it against the tent beside her.

"Thank you," she says again. *Wow. Good service here.*

Service is one of Kai's intentions. "You are most welcome." He offers her one more grin and returns to the counter to serve the next customer who's come in.

Anna takes a shaky breath, feeling how good it is to be sitting down. Her feet are really throbbing now. With relief, she kicks off her shoes and reaches for the big colourful mug of hot chai. Inhaling the spicy stream, she feels an immediate sense of calm settling around her. She touches the mug to her lips and the sweet, milky drink slips over her tongue and down her throat, creating a warmth inside her that seems to be spreading throughout her whole body. Her throat completely relaxes. This is without a doubt, the most soothing drink she's ever had. She looks up at the young man and wants to ask him again, *are you sure you didn't put anything funny in this drink?*

Just love, he'd said. *Love.*

Made with Love. People just say that, don't they? It's a figure of speech. Or so Anna had always thought. But as she sips this drink and feels the change inside herself, Anna is beginning to wonder if maybe there is something more to this love thing after all. Because if you could put the warmest, cosiest hug ever into a cup, this would be it. Love Chai. She closes her eyes and drinks it slowly, savouring each mouthful. There is nowhere to be, but here, having this drink. For a moment Anna forgets her feelings of failure and the gig – and she hasn't even tried the brownie yet. It's a haven of chocolate gooeyness.

Funny how simple things can bring so much pleasure, Anna thinks, savouring every last crumb. As she sips the last drops of chai, she marvels at the young man's ability to show so much kindness to strangers. She can see him giving that same generous smile and attention to every single person who comes in, as if each one of them really matters. *He made me feel that way*, and following on from that thought – *He can't possibly want something from all of those people. Maybe he really is that kind. Maybe he really is.*

Anna sits with this realisation for a while, that a person could be generous and kind with no hidden motive. A sense of something comes to her, something about selflessness. She furrows her eyebrows, searching for it and catching a brief glimpse of something that both surprises and disturbs her. There has always been a hidden reason for pretty much everything she does. She furrows her brows again, but then sighs and looks out at the crowds which appear to have doubled in size since her gig.

And now what? I can't sit here drinking chai and eating brownies all day. On one level, she is tempted. But something inside her feels stronger now; she is buoyed up by the energy she's received and feels like taking action somehow. She decides that she's not ready to give up yet.

He's probably right, she tells herself. *How many CDs I sell isn't necessarily a mark of how good I am as a performer.*

With this thought, determination ignites in Anna again. She slips her tight shoes back on, wincing at the blisters forming on the back of her heels. But she wouldn't dream of walking barefoot through this public arena. So on with the shoes, pain and all.

Okay. Don't lose faith Anna. You're still here. This is Glastonbury Festival. All is not lost. There are still things you can do.

Earlier this morning, when she had been queueing for the loos in the artists camping area, she'd overheard some musicians talking about how they had signed up for gigs once they'd gotten here. One musician had said he'd reached a personal best of 11 extra gigs at Glastonbury this year.

I could do that. Anna tells herself. *I could find myself some more gigs.*

There are no customers for a moment, so Anna seizes her opportunity and with her guitar in one hand and CD box under the other arm, she approaches Kai again.

He can see a change in her as she approaches. There is colour now in her cheeks and her hazel-green eyes have more life in them.

"I just wanted to say thank you again," Anna is genuinely smiling. "That was literally THE best chai and brownie I have EVER had. I'm actually starting to really believe you about the love thing."

Kai grins again. "Well, in my experience, love is the most important ingredient in anything."

Love is the most important ingredient in anything.

Something about this idea tickles Anna, as if love could be put into something.

As if you could actually choose to add it, like you would sugar or milk. Or soy for that matter.

"Absolutely," Anna nods in agreement. But she does wonder exactly what Kai means when he says that. *How do you actually put love into something?*

Besides, what is love anyway? She ponders this briefly and then remembers the real reason she's come up to speak with him.

"I was wondering... You mentioned you know some musicians. Do you by any chance know about any stages at this festival where people can sign up for extra gigs?"

He thinks for a moment. "Yeah, I do actually. One of my buddies has got a few gigs over in the green fields. Green Futures I think he said. He was telling me there are quite a few stages up there that leave open slots for musicians at the fest to fill. But it's pretty late into the festival, now... what day are we on?... Thursday. But you never know. It's worth a shot."

Yes. It is worth a shot, she tells herself.

"Thank you... and thanks for everything else." Anna can feel how much this man has helped her with his cheerfulness and his Love Chai. She even feels a little flutter of excitement at what she might discover in those green fields.

It's even hotter than it was before. It doesn't take long before Anna is dripping with sweat again in her synthetic dress, and coated with a thin layer of dust rising off the track. The blisters are getting worse, but there's still no way she's taking off these shoes.

Up ahead, standing cheerfully at the edge of *The Park* arena is a patch of large wooden flowers, taller than Anna's head. She winds her way through the colourful bluebells, marigolds and violets and passes beneath an archway made from the wings of two impressive teal-green dragons with golden horns and red wings. Just beyond that is the dust track that leads past the public camping field and towards the artist and crew camping. When Anna had arrived yesterday, these fields had still been green, but less than a day later thousands of feet have trampled it into hard dirt and dust. To her right, as far as she can see there are hundreds, maybe thousands of tents covering nearly every available patch of grass, or what's left of the grass. Litter is already beginning to accumulate in the minimal spaces between the tents and along the edges of the path: beer cans, empty beer can boxes and plastic bottles.

Anna is breathless as she reaches the tall metal fence which keeps the artist and crew area separate from the general punters camping. She flashes her Glastonbury Performer's wristband to the stewards at the gate and is allowed into the compound. Her first stop is the water point. She holds her mouth underneath it, gulping. The taste of the blue alcathene pipe is a far cry from the sweetness of the chai, but she feels somewhat refreshed by it nonetheless. After this, Anna drops her guitar and CDs in the artists lock-up. She grabs a couple of CDs just in case she wants to hand them out to any of the venues.

Back at her tent, she refreshes herself and changes out of the sweaty dress and heels into sandals and a light cotton summer dress with a floral pattern. Over her shoulder is her small brown leather satchel, into which she puts her Glastonbury Festival pocket map and what little money she has. One more retouch on the make-up and hair, and she's ready to embark on her quest to find more gigs.

Stepping back out onto the track, Anna is struck by the chaos of people moving around her in all directions. As well as those who are already well-embedded in the festival, there is a steady flow of people still arriving and trying desperately to find a space in this already crowded public camping field. She stays close to the fence, which leads towards a larger dirt road, one of the main thoroughfares into and out of the festival and will take her to the Green Fields.

According to her little Glastonbury pocket map, the arena immediately to her left is called *Arcadia*. On her way past she peeks in through the gate and her eyes widen at the sight of the thirty-foot high metal spider, made up of what looks like jet engines and other reclaimed scrap.

From here, the Green Fields are only on the other side of the hedge to her right, but there is no entrance into them yet. She joins the stream of people moving along the road through an avenue of cherry, oak and hawthorn trees, looking along the hedge line for an obvious way into the next field.

After only a few moments, her mind begins to wander, creating stories about what she might say to the venues when she approaches them. As she imagines these scenarios, a knot of nervousness forms in her solar plexus. She thinks about Damien and how he always tells her that to get ahead in life you just have to go for it. So even if you feel that fear, you have to step ahead, and put yourself out there.

Anna is so lost in her daydream that she doesn't see the man with the giant brown feather duster until it's too late. Coming after people and trying to dust them with his giant feather duster is Lewis' gimmick for this year. Every year at Glastonbury he chooses some kind of trick to play on people, usually young women. Mostly people find it funny, and some even find it hilarious. He likes making people laugh. Lewis is actually quite a shy guy, but with these gags, he comes out of himself and finds he's able to meet people. He caught sight of Anna only a few moments ago and targeted her as someone he'd quite like to meet.

Realising she is being accosted by a feather duster, Anna barks ferociously at the man responsible, furiously batting him away. "Get off! Don't EVER do that to people!" She surprises herself at how forcefully this comes out, but for her it's a desperate self-defense. Mostly she's horrified by the idea that A, he's going to mess up her hair and she wants to look nice for the venues, and B, that this feather duster may have already been on the heads of who knows how many other people, and who knows what other body parts. Lewis is in a state of shock about this response to his attempt at humour and feels like a chastised child. He's too stunned to realise he should apologise, and then when he thinks to do so, it's too late. Anna is already running off through the crowds.

In her effort to escape the feather duster, she dashes through the first little gap in the hedge she can find. This is how she finds herself in the *Permaculture* area, standing at the edge of a grove of leafy ashes, willows, oaks and chestnuts. On the entrance gate is a large, circular poster with the heading: *The 12 Permaculture Principles*. Anna is about to disregard the importance of this, thinking Permaculture has nothing to do with her when something at the centre of the circle catches her eye. They are the three Permaculture Ethics: *Care for the Earth, Care for People, Fair Share.*

She stares at the words for a few moments and then reminds herself what she's supposed to be doing. She takes a few shallow breaths to steady herself and runs fingers through her hair, trying to undo the worst of the damage done by the feather duster. She looks around her for something reflective to check her appearance in. There is nothing. So she smooths down her hair as best she can by feel and tries to get her bearings. Her little map indicates that the path heading through this little grove of trees should lead her out into the Green Fields. She turns into the trees, following the maze of winding paths, through little archways made from willow and low bending branches.

The sunlight filters through the leaves creating a sparkling dappled world. It is a pleasant surprise to find such a place here in this busy festival. In the shade it's cool, and being among the trees is so different from where she has just been. Already Anna feels herself becoming calmer.

As a little child, if Anna had come across a little forest glade like this, with all its winding pathways, she would have run about and whooped with delight. Something of this delight stirs almost imperceptibly inside, causing her to look just a little more attentively at the surroundings, at the little garden plants which stand out in the foliage at the sides of the path, each with their own little sign describing the healing properties of that plant: Wild Rose, Borage, Thyme, Marigold, Meadow Sweet, Nasturtium, Nettle, Lemon Balm.

One of the pathways opens up into a kind of a clearing, where people are sitting in little nooks on wooden chairs and tables made out of round, polished slices of tree trunks. Between two trees an occupied hammock sways gently. This is when Anna catches her first sight of the *Rainbow Wishing Well.*

The circular well appears to be made of stone bricks, but as Anna reaches out to run her hands along the edge of it, she sees the blocks are actually soft and foam-like, and expertly painted to appear as grey stone. Inset into the surface of the faux stone are fragments of mirror, in circles and triangles, reflecting the extraordinary colours of the rainbow stained glass panels in the well's sloping roof. There is one panel for each colour of the rainbow, made into intricate patterns of green leaves and flowers, orange swirls, a yellow starburst, red flames, blue undulating waves and purple seeds like dandelion clocks.

Above this is a large multi-coloured glass panel showing two people dancing for delight. Anna looks down at her performer's wristband and sees the Glastonbury logo showing a similar image.

At the centre of the well there is a circular hole, a couple of feet across and a few feet deep, lined with silver foil and covered by a metal grate. Through it, copper and silver coins catch the sun's light, sparkling as she moves around it. A sign on the side of the wishing well reads: *Throw a coin and make a wish. All profits go to Greenpeace and Global Justice.*The sun shines through this creation, making the sparkles of coloured light dance. Anna is momentarily mesmerised.

"Pretty isn't it?" A little voice chirps beside her.

Anna looks down to her left and sees the girl, who looks to be about ten years old, with her hair done up in dozens of tiny braids, each woven with a different brightly coloured yarn. Anna has the thought that she seems to match the well.

Matching the rainbow well is deliberate. Freya sees herself as a *'Rainbow Well Helper'*, making it her personal mission to encourage people to make their wishes. Freya leans forwards against the wishing well and tilts her face up at the stained glass roof, the rainbow light catching her face and transforming her into a little faery creature.

"Yes, it is," Anna answers. "Very."

"My Mum's friends helped to make this," Freya says with a hint of pride. "Are you going to make a wish?"

Anna hadn't thought that far. She considers for a moment. *What would I wish for?* The first thing that comes to her is that she should wish to find more gigs and to be successful at this festival, but following on from this thought her inner skeptic scoffs at her, saying, *You really believe in wishing wells?*

"I don't know," Anna replies.

"You should." Freya begins to skip around the well. "It's magic."

As she says the word 'magic', her eyes grow huge and reverent.

Anna smiles a little at this girl's exuberance and the fact that she actually believes in magic. "Is it really?"

The girl nods. "That's what my Mum says. She's over there." She points to one of the tree-lined nooks to where a young woman with similarly braided hair sits, dressed in green flowing trousers talking to a young man in an elf hat. To Anna, that woman and the man both look like absolutely the stereotypical hippie folk you might expect to find in a small forest in the middle of Glastonbury Festival. The woman, whose name is Sophie, is a school teacher and in her every day life she dresses completely differently. Glastonbury Festival is the one time she lets herself be the free spirit she is. It's the same with the man in the elf hat. His name is Charlie and he gets home each year from the festival and hangs up his hat until the next festival.

This year, Sophie has vowed to bring a little more of this free-spirited part of herself back into her regular life at home. Her daughter Freya is loving this whole experience. Partly for Freya it is about seeing how happy her Mum is here. How free. She's loving experiencing her Mum this way. Sophie looks up when she realises Freya is pointing to her. She smiles first at Freya and then at Anna, as if she knows exactly the conversation going on around the well. As if Freya has this conversation with everyone she meets around the well. Which of course, she does.

"My Mum says that when you make a wish at the well, you have to make an offering. You have to give something of yourself, and that's why people put a coin in. And you have to say thank you as you're wishing. It's called Gratitude. That's what makes the magic happen." Freya peers into the well. "You can see yourself if you look in."

Anna approaches the well and places her hands on the stone-foam edges. They feel rough against her palms, but warm from the sun. Freya dances away from the well momentarily, giving Anna a little space. Anna ducks her head under the rainbow roof of the well and peers through the grate into the glistening water. It's not deep. There have been quite a lot of wishes so far, judging by the number of coins lining the bottom. On the surface of the water, Anna can just make out her own face, almost in silhouette, peering back at herself, a halo of rainbow light surrounding it. Then she catches a flash of her face in the tiny mirrors and is surprised at how sad the eyes staring back at her seem to be.

Who am I? The thought passes through her mind.

At that moment, Freya leans into the well again, the light catching her hair and bringing out the colours. "We're rainbow faeries," she says.

Anna laughs at the ridiculousness of this whole thing and steps away from the well.

No, I won't be making a wish, she decides. Freya is regarding her seriously, with a concerned brow as if hearing these thoughts. In fact, Freya does frequently pick up on the thoughts of those around her. She is a sensitive child, and has always been this way.

"You should make a wish." Freya regards Anna.

"Have you made a wish?"

Freya rolls her eyes as if this is the stupidest question Anna could have asked. "Of course I have! I do it every day!"

"So what did you wish for then?" Anna asks.

"World Peace," Freya says with an absolutely straight face. "And that people would stop doing damage to the Earth. Mum says it's good to wish for things for other people sometimes, and not just for ourselves."

Anna almost laughs out loud to hear a little girl speaking this way. *Such big wishes. If only she knew,* Anna thinks, *the impossibility of those wishes.*

Freya looks Anna square in the face. "It's possible, you know. Magic is real."

A shiver moves through Anna's body, as she finds herself stared down by this young girl with such clear eyes. For a moment, she is speechless, and everything around them both seems to stand still. Anna becomes aware of a small, subtle whisper rising inside herself, a desire for it to be true, for there to be such a thing as real magic. That there really could be a possibility that one day peace could exist in the world. In the certainty of these eyes, Anna almost begins to believe her.

Freya turns away and skips around the well again. "I also wished for a boyfriend."

Anna can't help smiling at the thought of this faery-like little girl wanting a boyfriend. "How's that working out so far?"

"Good, actually. It's already starting to happen, I think. There's this boy in our camp I like. The World Peace one might take a bit longer though."

A chuckle escapes Anna's lips and she stops herself, not wanting to hurt the girl's feelings. At this moment, a middle-aged man wearing a straw sunhat and overalls arrives at the edge of the wishing well. His name is Dave, and he's been working all week in the Permaculture gardens. He reaches into his pocket and pulls out a silver coin. He grins at Freya. "I finally figured out what to wish for."

Freya skips over to him. "What?"

His eyes twinkle. "It's a secret. But it's good."

He pauses for a moment, looks at the coin meaningfully and then tosses it in, making a small splash. He casts a cordial smile at Anna before walking on. It strikes Anna that this man looked like he was seriously making a wish. A grown man, believing in wishing wells.

"So are you going to make a wish?" Freya asks Anna again.

Anna finds her eyes drawn by the way the breeze moves in the branches of the willow tree above, changing the pattern of sunlight on the stained glass, creating new, shifting colours.

"I don't know," Anna replies. She thinks again about whether or not she should wish for her Glastonbury success. She wouldn't admit this aloud to the girl. For some reason she feels an embarrassment about admitting this aloud to anyone. When compared with World Peace. She decides again that she doesn't believe in wishing wells. "Maybe I'll come and make a wish later."

Freya gives Anna a knowing look, and then smiles cheekily. "Okay. See you later then!" she chirps and dances off to where her mother is, and crawls onto Sophie's lap in the way a younger child might.

Anna takes one final glance at the well and a sigh fills her body. She doesn't even know what the sigh means, but she feels a wistfulness. Like she's lost something. Like she's forgotten something that really matters.

Never mind, she tells herself. *Remember why you're here.* With her task in mind, Anna takes decisive steps, leaving the well behind and following one of the little winding pathways out into the open.

As she steps out into the *Green Futures* field, Anna is greeted by a scene of dozens of tall, colourful flagpoles, with billowing multi-coloured flags flapping against the blue of the sky.

The breeze plays in her hair and brushes past her cheeks and Anna feels her spirits lift. There is a sense of aliveness in this place, of possibility, as if maybe there is something special to be found here after all.

The field has many open green spaces, bordered by tents of all shapes and sizes and colours. Some of them are surrounded by solar panels. Some have small wind turbines whizzing round above them. In the centre of the field there is an abundant recycling centre, with bins for every conceivable item, plus one small bin labelled 'hazardous' for landfill items. Next to it, she is amused to see *The Tetra Shack*, a small house constructed from used tetrapacks.

Carrying on her explorations, Anna discovers a bicycle-powered mobile phone charging tent, the *Groovy Movie Picture House Solar Cinema*, gardens made from willow, an eco-themed crazy golf course, pedal-powered laundrette and mobile phone charging, a travelling observatory and the *Little Burmese Tea Tent*, among other things. There also seem to be several decent looking venues dotted about, and Anna feels a rising excitement and nervousness that she may find a gig at one of them.

She sets her sights on three stages for starters – *The Mandala Stage*, a funky solar and bicycle-powered stage, *The Small World Solar Stage*, a cosy cafe venue with little round tables and bright paintings of dancing people, and *Toad Hall*, the largest of all the solar venues with a cheerful painting of a toad out front. Some of the venues have more time for her than others, but the result is the same for each one.

Sorry, but we're already fully booked.

With each successive attempt, Anna feels her resolve weakening, and the critical voice in her head growing steadily louder.

You're deluding yourself. This isn't going to work, the voice taunts. But she thinks of her father and Damien and that box of CDs and what they would say if she told them of her failure.

Don't give up, she urges herself. *Don't let them down*. She thinks of everyone who's waiting to hear about her Glorious Glastonbury Experience. *I can't come back empty handed. There's got to be something that makes it all worthwhile. Keep trying.*

The next venue is the *Speaker's Forum*, which doesn't take musical performers. Anna stops for a moment to listen to the man onstage, who is speaking earnestly on the topic of 'The Orwellian Guide to Sustainability'.

She scans the area for any other venues she's missed, and notices one tucked away in the far corner of the field, overhung by leafy oak and ash trees. *The One Earth Stage*.

As she moves closer to it, Anna feels her spirits lift. There is a sense somehow of being in the right place finally. Everything about this venue seems bright, and in ways she can't quite name, exactly what she's looking for.

Though Anna can't hear the music onstage yet, she can see that whatever it is, people are flocking to it. Inside the tent is full and people are even spilling out onto the grass, many of them laying back with the sun on their faces as they listen, clearly enjoying themselves. Brightly chalked blackboards list the performers for the day and there are colourful paintings of flowers, trees and musical instruments decorating the walls. Large solar panels to one side of the tent catch the sun. It's both friendly and professional at the same time. Like The Chai Chi Tent, there are low tables dotted about for people to sit at, and little cushions on the floor.

A single gentle guitar melody drifts out from the stage.

Wow, that performer has a similar picking style to me. Perhaps they would like my music here.

At the same time as thinking this, a wave of jealousy passes through Anna, that someone so similar is already playing here. As if because they got here first that somehow takes something away from her.

This is the moment when she hears the voice of the person in question, sailing out over the crowds – the voice that sends the floor out from beneath her. It is a young woman's voice, pure and strong, and in every way Anna can tell, beyond her own ability. As she steps closer, joining the crowd at the edges of the large, colourful marquee, she's nursing a guilty hope that this woman onstage isn't also physically beautiful too, because that would just be too much.

Peeking inside the tent, the first thing Anna sees is that there are easily twice as many people in here than had been at her gig, even though this tent is smaller. And even though this one too, is a cafe, and this field has significantly fewer people in it than the field in which Anna had played. Perhaps the hardest comparison of all is that every single person here is listening with their complete and total attention.

Added to all that, Anna catches her first sight of the person responsible for the extraordinary voice. As well as having an earthy kind of physical beauty, this woman is also beautiful in other ways Anna can't quite name – she has a kind of natural radiance, as if generated from within. She stands on the stage at the far end of the tent, slim and dark-haired, wearing a simple teal blue dress and bare feet. The bare feet bother Anna most of all.

What's with the bare feet? Is she trying to be some kind of super-hippie? Anna knows it's irrational, but it feels like the woman is somehow deliberately rubbing in the fact that bare feet are so much better than the completely non-practical high heels she had chosen to wear for her own gig earlier. Everything about this woman says ease, effortlessness and naturalness. For Anna, her experience onstage earlier was almost entirely full of strain, discomfort and nervousness.

Nina Marshall is not trying to be anything other than what she is. She has a good, practical reason for her bare feet. It's easier to feel the ground beneath her feet with no shoes on. She feels more grounded this way. It is purely a practical thing – necessary for her music, and it just feels good.

Nina's fingers move lithely over the strings of her guitar. What had first seemed to Anna like a similar style of picking to hers, now she realises has a very different quality. Like the voice, Nina's playing seems to flow, without any struggle. It's as if she isn't even trying. For Anna, being onstage is always about constantly trying not to make a mistake, to keep from flubbing notes on her guitar, to try and reach the perfect vocal trick.

As Nina plays, she is wide-smiling, her head moving with abandon as if experiencing some divine bliss. There is such joy in this woman's face that Anna can hardly believe it, especially when contrasted with her own experience of music, which has been mostly absent of joy for some time. Certainly, Anna can't recall ever feeling anything like this sort of extraordinary happiness. She can't fathom how anyone could possibly be standing up there on stage in front of an audience and looking like that, feeling like that, like everything in the world is perfect, like she's got everything she needs, like all is as it should be.

She must be on drugs. Anna tells herself. *How else can anyone be so happy onstage?*

There was a time when Nina herself stood in a very similar place to the one where Anna stands now. There were things in Nina's life that challenged her to the point of devastation, and so became a catalyst for transformation. Three years ago, Nina left her job, her relationship and went travelling around the world to find herself. On her travels to South America, Australia and India she discovered the magic of life, the power of love, the capability of the human being, and the medicine of music. Through those experiences she began to make music again, and to find the true joy that comes with being in the flow, from being in Love. Sometimes she doesn't find it so easy, but she has techniques she uses for bringing herself back into flow. Some days are more challenging than others. Today is not one of those. Today, Nina feels free.

There is a small memory trying to lodge itself free inside Anna, of a time before she first went to school, when she used to sing to the trees in her garden, and knew they could sing back to her – how joyful that was. Back then she smiled and laughed without thinking. Back then she kicked off her shoes all the time. Anna skirts the edges of this memory, but it feels so distant she can't quite bring it into her conscious awareness.

Anna turns her attention to the crowd around her. There is a deep joy on these faces too. It is as if they have all been cast in some kind of spell. It's as if the joy radiating off the stage is enveloping them all in a bubble and they have no choice but to be in it. Some of them have their eyes closed with smiles of absolute contentment on their faces.

One man is swaying in delight at the back of the tent, and Anna decides that this man, at least, must be on drugs of some kind. Because it just doesn't seem possible that a member of an audience could be that intoxicatingly delighted.

The man in question has, in fact, taken a number of substances, and while they are certainly contributing to the velocity of his swaying, they are not the primary reason for it. In his state of drug-induced openness, he is genuinely moved by this music, and he's not the only one here to be so. It's impossible for Anna to ignore that this audience is responding very, very differently than hers had.

Why? What is it about this woman? Anna moves further in, drawn partly by her own jealous curiosity and partly because although she doesn't want to admit it to herself, this music is having an effect on her too. She steps carefully through the crowd gathered at the edges, picking her way around the clusters of people who are sat inside on carpets amidst tiny tables and finds an unoccupied cushion. With her arms wrapped around her knees, she surrenders to the listening.

Nina's voice is rising and falling like the waves she is singing about.

"It's here in between... In the seen and the unseen...

In the sky up above... and the earth that we love...

The flow it is flowing... through knowing and not knowing...

A wave in the ocean... of energy in motion..."

Without warning, a sob rises up from right inside Anna, spilling out in silent tears. She can't fathom why she's crying, except that there is something here she wants more than she has ever wanted anything. She can't even name what it is. She hides her face under her hair, so no one will see her.

"It's moving through... all we do...

Every thought creation... pure vibration...

The hum it hums... as the song it comes...

A wave in the ocean... of energy in motion...

Awakening... Awakening...

Awakening... Awakening...

To know itself... to know ourselves...

As this sea..."

Anna is relieved as the first wave of silent tears subsides. As it does, she just listens quietly, allowing the music to continue moving through her, until the song comes to its end and all that remains in the shelter of the tent is a deep pervading silence.

She waits for the thunderous applause that this singer is so obviously going to get. Still the silence stretches on. After a while, Anna lifts her head to see what people are doing and is amazed to find that they are still listening. Most of them still have their eyes closed, softly smiling. They are listening to the silence in the room.

After what seems to Anna an inconceivably long time, a hum of murmurs begins to arise from all around her. "*mmmm... mmmm...*" These are the sounds of pure pleasure, echoing about the venue. From out of these sounds emerge the first gentle clapping of hands. The clapping builds and builds until it is the huge thunderous applause Anna was expecting and even more. Nina is humble onstage, bowing her head, with her hand over her heart.

"Thank you," she says. With a final bow of her head, she steps gracefully off the stage, and the applause continues.

Anna can't even begin to compare the applause she had with this – and now they are calling and whistling for "More!... More!... More!"

The MC for the afternoon, a cheerful man by the name of Stanley steps up onto the stage and takes the mic briefly. "The wonderful Nina Marshall, everybody! Shall we have one more song?"

"Yes! Yes!" they cheer.

Nina approaches the microphone again. "Thank you so much. It's been such a joy to be here with you today. I'll play you one last song. This isn't one of mine, but it's by a songwriter by the name of Carrie Tree, who has inspired me greatly. If any of you know it, or feel like singing along, please do." There are some claps and whoops of recognition throughout the tent. "And please, feel free not to clap at the end if you don't feel like it. I'm happy if people want to take the stillness away with them."

Nina closes her eyes and is quiet for a moment, turning her attention inward. This is one of the things Nina does before she plays. It helps her to centre herself and allow the music to come from the right place. She has to remind herself to come back to her centre now and again, because she sometimes finds herself drifting into thoughts. She's not hard on herself about it, though. She's learned about that through her meditation practice. Thoughts come, they go. Just bring yourself back. As she feels the clear, silent space inside her, Nina opens her eyes and begins to play. She is letting the music take her again. These words she sings are not her own, but that doesn't matter. The song is singing her anyway.

"*Here I stand with a quest on my heart... I'm here to hear my ancestor's song...*
I'm here to find out where I come from...
Mama Kita Makaya... Mama Kita Makaya... Mama Kita Makaya...
Whispering wind says to follow it...
My aching heart says drop everything, return to fire...
I love this ground...
Mama Kita Makaya... Mama Kita Makaya... Mama Kita Makaya..."

Nina knows the meaning of these words – *Mother you are my home.* It is a song about joy and love for life, a song which echoes her own journey, a quest for something deeper. The search for that Fire within. The desire to experience a true purpose. To find the soul's path. To return home.

A sense of this is calling to Anna, though she doesn't consciously understand it, and yet even so, there is a response – surprisingly strong – arising from within her.

Yes... I want that... yes, that's what I want...

Please, help me. She becomes aware of herself repeating this over and over in her mind. *Please, help me.* She doesn't know who or what she's asking. *Please. Please help me.*

Eventually, the song comes to its close and the last note of Nina's guitar rings out across the tent, out into silence – and even with the fear Anna can still feel twisting somewhere inside her, she is in the silence too. This time, with eyes closed, she stays in it with the rest of the audience, with them, still listening, not wanting to break the spell and have to face what comes after.

Again, the silence stretches on and on. And on. This time, nobody claps. Eventually, Anna opens her eyes and gazes around her. Everyone looks so happy and peaceful. While the stillness still seems to be everywhere in the air around her, Anna feels like it is not really hers, and at any moment it could just slip away from her.

Slowly, there is movement in the room, as people begin to stand and stretch their bodies. Murmurs of appreciation bubble up from all around Anna and a steady flow of people begin moving towards the front of the stage, where Nina is standing, face shining. Seeing the queue which is starting to form in front of Nina, Anna feels a knot forming inside her stomach again. With every successive person joining the queue, the knot winds tighter. At first there are only a few people, which Anna tells herself isn't so bad. But now there are ten, and fifteen. And twenty. And still more. Anna stares, aghast, unbelieving. *No. Not this! Not this too!*

She thinks about what the young man at the Chai Chi Tent had said to her about people not buying CDs because of being into downloads. As nice as he was, she feels a sense of betrayal, because not only are people buying CDs from Nina Marshall, they are buying them in the dozens.

This is it. Something cracks and shatters inside Anna. In her desperate attempt to escape what she feels is threatening to engulf her, she runs. She has no conscious idea where she's going, but she just has to keep going, as if by moving, she will be able to outrun this thing that's coming. She dodges her way around people trying to make their way toward Nina, and more happy looking people stretching and talking about how wonderful it all was, until she finally escapes out into the open. She doesn't know where she's going, but as her feet pound along the grass, Anna's body seems to know what her mind does not. Without thinking about why she's doing it, in a kind of daze, Anna takes the first right turn she sees, past a big white geodesic dome called *Her Temple*. Inside, a group of women dressed in red are chanting.

It's a blur to Anna, as she stumbles by crowds of people walking along this narrow grass alley, lined by stalls which are asking people to save the dolphins and whales, and to sign the petition to stop Trident, the UK's nuclear deterrent. Beyond these, Anna vaguely notices the Traveller camp, people whose home is always on the move. They are offering a tent with shelter and company, but Anna can't stop here. Not yet.

At the end of the path there is a wooden bridge leading over a small stream and through a tunnel made of purple ribbon into a new field. Here, the grass is even greener.

> *"So if we are to love then let it be without*
> *Thoughts of tomorrow in the seas of doubt*
> *And we sway on the tide still trying to find*
> *Our whisper on the wave rolling in*
> *Heartbeats in a cave echoing*
> *From the cradle to the grave*
> *Let life sing*
> *Bring it on, bring it in*
> *Let life sing"*

from the song, 'Cradle', by Tina Bridgman

Anna stands at the edge of this new field, scanning the expanse of green, which is bordered by many tents of different shapes and colours, including yurts, tipis and bell tents. People are moving past her, wandering about and sprawling themselves on the grass in the sunshine. The atmosphere here is even more relaxed than in the last field. To her left, a dozen or so grinning people are hoola-hooping them-selves into a delighted frenzy, next to a sign reading: *Hoola Revolution.*

Where am I? Where do I go?

In the centre of the grassy space is a circular garden created from woven willow withies. Inside it, Anna can see dozens of potted trees giving shade and green, and handmade wooden benches set around little ponds. At one side of the garden there is even a little dome-like bender shelter made from a patchwork of light and dark blue canvas.

She dashes across the grass towards the garden and passes through the entrance archway, which is made from the curved necks of two giant white willow and tissue paper swans. As Anna enters the sanctuary of the garden, despite the peacefulness which clearly pervades the place, she is filled with an uncontrollable panic. Every bench is taken, and in every little shady nook beneath every potted tree someone is resting. There is no privacy to be had anywhere here, especially in the little patchwork dome, which is already sheltering half a dozen people. Anna is about to give up on this garden, when out of the corner of her eye she sees that a bench has become vacant. This particular bench is tucked away at the far side of the garden, nestled beside the dome and sheltered by overhanging boughs. If peo-ple weren't looking at it directly, this might just offer some semblance of a private space. In front of the wooden bench is a raised pond made of clay, with upward ris-ing sticks arranged around the outside of it, giving the effect of roots rising up out of the earth. The water on the surface glistens in the sunlight. A few white stones lay at the bottom.

Anna curls herself into the deepest corner of the bench and clutches her knees to her chest. Everything feels like it's whirling, as if the ground is no longer beneath her feet. Each thought seems to create generate a new storm of pain beneath her ribs and in the centre of her chest. *If I'm not good enough to be a songwriter, if I give up, what's left of me? Who am I if I'm not the person I've been trying to be?* She feels like she's running out of air, as if something is pressing down on her from all sides, like suffocation. Nothing makes sense anymore.

Within the span of a few minutes, the sun completely disappears behind the fast moving clouds and the air temperature plummets. Anna lifts her eyes in surprise, and sees the low weather front that has moved in overhead. The sky is filling with grey clouds and there's a new chill in the wind. She shivers, pulling her knees even closer into her chest, wishing now that she had thought to bring another layer with her, but it had been so hot before.

Now it's beginning to rain. First the tiniest drops on Anna's bare arms, fleshing her skin with goose pimples. The wind blows, making her colder still. But as the rain mists her, something unusual happens to Anna. She becomes aware of her body, and its place within the garden. The wind rustles the leaves which overhang the bench. It makes ripples on the water of the pond. As Anna turns her attention to these simple, natural things for a moment, like a passing storm, the emotions inside her begin to quieten for a moment. She lifts her eyes to take in the space around her. Across from where she's sitting, on the other side of the garden, there are two more ponds, one which features a blue clay figure in a meditating posture. Two clay dragons with painted blue scales weave their tails around the edges of the other.

Dragons, thinks Anna. *That's the second time I've seen dragons today.* This brings to mind the dragon archway she had passed through earlier, and beyond that how the day had progressed from her failed gig right through to Nina's performance and now to being here in this garden. *I don't understand...*

There is an older man Anna has not yet noticed, sitting by one of the far pools. Johannes likes to come here to the Water Garden to clear his head between readings. Of all the quadrants in the Healing Area, he is happiest here in Water. He finds it a tranquil place. Usually. But for some reason this time he keeps being drawn to look over at the girl sitting on that bench over there, with her knees curled up to her chest and looking so much in pain. A sense of anguish is coming off her in waves.

I can help her, the thought comes to him. But then, *Really? Can I? Would she want me to?*

Johannes is a man who has been practising listening to his heart for a number of years now, and he's getting used to understanding and responding to the prompts he's given. Sometimes he still second guesses himself, but it's happening less often now.

Go and speak to her, the message comes to him.

Johannes thinks again about letting this young woman be. He doesn't want to disturb her, but with these thoughts, he feels the now familiar tightening inside, and knows this is his body's way of directing him to think again. He's learned over the years that a thought which is not in harmony with the heart's guidance creates tension in his body, and a thought which resonates with truth moves through the body and brings energy. So as Johannes accepts that he will go speak with this young woman who looks so sad, he feels the affirmation of energy rising and flowing through his body.

After only a few steps towards her, Johannes can tell she's seen him and clearly doesn't want him to approach. She isn't looking up, but everything about the way she is holding herself screams to Johannes, LEAVE ME ALONE.

He pauses, but again feels that tightening inside, and so continues to move forward. Arriving at the raised pond just beside the young woman's bench, he asks in as gentle a voice as he can, "Excuse me Miss, Are you okay?"

She lifts her face to reveal red eyes and an expression bordering on terror. She really, really doesn't want him to be here. He takes a breath, steadying himself.

"I'm so sorry to disturb you. I don't mean to pry, but I noticed you were crying, and I wondered if you were okay – if I could be of help in any way."

Anna doesn't know how to speak to this man. At first, when she saw him walking over, she hoped that if she ignored him, he would turn and walk away. But now he's here and talking to her, and she can hear the kindness in his voice. And while on one level she wants him to leave her alone to her misery, there is something else inside Anna drinking in this kindness.

She briefly looks up into the eyes of this man, wild and kind blue eyes that gleam out from under grey and unruly eyebrows. She almost smiles, because with his tufts of grey hair flying out to either side, he reminds her of a tall and moderately young looking grandfather elf. Something about his face makes her instinctively want to trust him, but she's not in the habit of trusting men she's never met before, even ones that look like friendly grandfather elves.

Anna notices a hint of a Germanic accent, and there's something else about the way he's speaking to her. It feels familiar. He's speaking like he would to someone he knows and cares about. Strangely for Anna, it reminds her of the young man in the Chai Chi Tent. It's a feeling of being cared for by somebody. A sense of genuine compassion. With all this simultaneous familiarity and strangeness, Anna almost gives Johannes an honest answer – *I feel like my life is falling apart. Nothing makes sense anymore* – but at the last moment the judgemental thoughts step in. *You don't know him. Why would he care about your troubles? And why would you want him to know anyway? He's a stranger.*

"I'm fine, thanks." Anna forces a smile, in an effort to convince him that she really is fine.

"Okay." Johannes nods understanding. He begins to step back, feeling a mild confusion. *Why was I supposed to go up to her if she won't speak to me?* But after a moment, he lets this concern go. He's learning to trust the ways of things. They don't always make sense at the time, but when you go with the flow, and trust, the flow always takes you where you're meant to go. So Johannes just smiles and immediately moves off to give her space.

Through the damp tendrils of her hair, Anna watches him go. She feels his absence with a sadness that she has deliberately driven him away. *Could he have helped me?*

Well even if he could, it's too late now. She tells herself these things, but still she is watching him, alert suddenly in a new way.

The grey-haired man is walking over to a yurt at the edge of the grassy area. There's a sign next to the door, but Anna can't read it from here. A shiver runs through her as she realises he must be a healer of a kind. This is the moment it becomes clear to Anna that she has accidentally wandered into the healing fields. She notices now that in the tents and yurts which border the edge of the grassy space, there are therapies of all kinds on offer – shiatsu, massage, acupressure, and a plethora of other things she's never heard of before. She turns her attention back to the grey-haired man's yurt. *What kind of healer is he?*

Right now, he is speaking with a cheerful-looking young man and woman in front of his yurt. The grey-haired man pulls back the flap of fabric that covers the entrance to his yurt and the young woman follows him inside. The flap closes behind them and Anna watches the man – who seems to be the woman's boyfriend – walk happily off, trusting his partner to whatever is about to happen inside the yurt.

The wind is growing more restless, blowing up in little gusts, flapping open the fabric from time to time and offering Anna tantalising little glimpses of the scene inside. The grey-haired man and the young woman are sitting cross-legged on something soft and white, facing each other and holding hands. Or rather, it looks like the grey-haired man is clasping her hands with his. There is an intimacy to it, but it doesn't look romantic. It's as if he is examining her.

The next time the curtain shifts, Anna sees the grey-haired man speaking to the woman with intense focus and the woman listening and nodding with a kind of excitement. Now she's laughing.

The wind whips up, becoming even wilder, as if this really is a storm. The rain falls harder, and harder still, until it is pelting Anna relentlessly through the shelter of the trees, and she is forced to dive for the shelter of the patchwork bender, along with everyone else who had been in the garden. She crouches in the corner, arms wrapped around herself, watching the deluge. They all seem surprised at the sudden change in the weather, all except the one man who checks his watch to see if the Glastonbury weather app had been accurate. It had.

Anna wonders how long the rain will go on for. She notices that at the back of the bender there is a large bronze bowl filled with water and surrounded by ferns and water plants. It seems like a kind of shrine to water. It is now that she realises this whole garden seems dedicated to water somehow. And now the water is pouring everywhere. She clasps her arms around herself again, shivering uncontrollably. There appears to be nothing to do but wait for a break in the rain. She keeps returning her gaze to the grey-haired man's yurt, occupying herself with thoughts of what he and the young woman might be doing in there, and trying not to be too uncharitable.

Some while later, the curtain across the yurt door opens and the young woman emerges, an expression of delight on her face. She stands out for a moment in the rain and laughs. She and the grey-haired grandfather elf man exchange a few more words, both smiling. Anna wishes she could hear what they are saying. It's obvious from the woman's body language whatever has gone on in that yurt has been immensely satisfying for her. The delighted young woman walks off into the rain with a bounce in her step.

What has he done to her? What has he told her? Anna asks herself. *Can he tell me something about myself that makes me that happy?*

She notices now how the grey-haired man is braving the rain to check a whiteboard outside his yurt, as if he is expecting someone. He glances around, and not seeing anyone approaching, ducks back in behind the fabric into his shelter.

Go. Go now, the thought comes to her. *Now.*

Anna can't understand why she feels such a compulsion to go over there, but she really does. She battles with this, finding excuse after excuse not to go there. *It's raining too hard*, she tells herself.

In perfect timing, the rain stops pelting down and becomes more of a fine mist. For a few moments, it's really not rain at all. Anna watches as some of the other people who had been sheltering in the dome take the opportunity to dash out and find new places to go. Rain is no longer a viable excuse.

Go. Now.

An energy moves through Anna's body, and without thinking, she stands straight up. She tells herself it's because there really is nothing else to do, and because she's getting so cold she can't stay still any longer.

I'm just going to have a closer look, she tells herself. *That's all.*

She moves across the wet grass to the yurt, hoping that the man won't come out, but also at the same time hoping that he will. Bending down to read the sign next to the whiteboard, Anna observes a picture of a hand with lines and symbols drawn on it and the words below, reading: *Johannes Bergen. Chirologist. Hand Reading by donation.*

Hand reading? Anna shakes her head. *That's what he does?*

She tells herself she doesn't believe in that stuff. *Besides*, she reminds herself, *even if I did, I don't have enough money to pay for it anyway.*

The drizzle is beginning again. She's just about reached her limit with the cold and decides to go try find somewhere to get warm when a hand pulls back the curtain and Johannes' kind face appears.

"Oh! It's you from the garden. Hello again." He smiles at her.

I see. Johannes nods to himself. *This is why I was meant to speak to her. I'm meant to give her a reading. Of course.*

Anna can't understand why the grey-haired man looks so pleased to see her.

"I uh... I was just looking at your sign..."

"Would you like a reading?" There is a natural warmth and openness in this man's face which unguards Anna. For a moment, she finds herself wanting to trust him and wondering if maybe she would like a reading after all.

She glances past the man into his yurt, taking in the natural wood floor covered with sheepskins and cushions. It looks so invitingly warm and dry. At this moment, the rain begins to pelt down again, even harder than before. The drips are trailing down Anna's nose and dripping off the ends of her hair. Her dress is almost wet through and she wraps her arms around herself, feeling a mild gratitude that she didn't choose to wear her white summer dress.

Just as she is coming to the decision that she would probably like a reading after all, she remembers again how little money she has with her. "I'm... I'm not sure I have enough money to... to... I've only got..." She reaches into her bag and pulls out the crumpled £5 note and some coins.

Johannes puts up his hand and smiles. "Don't worry about it. Money is not the primary reason I do this. Sometimes I get a feeling that something's just right. Like now. I just have this sense that I'm meant to offer this to you. So, I'm happy to take whatever donation you feel able to make."

Really? Why? Why are you meant to offer this to me?

Anna doesn't think she believes in ideas like 'meant to be', let alone that a person could actually have a knowing about such rightnesses. All the same, she recognises that he is offering her something. Again, for the second time today, someone is offering her something – with such generosity – and again, she questions this generosity, searching for the hidden motive.

But even as she does this, she's looking at the warm and dry inside of the yurt, and feeling like she really does want to go in there. The other woman had come out looking so happy. Surrendering to the inevitable, Anna nods her head. "Thank you."

Inside the round, wooden yurt it is simple, cosy and warm. As well as the sheep-skins and cushions, there is a small wooden table and a bedroll up against the far side. Sweet incense burns in a clay incense burner near the door, not quite cover-ing the scent of sheepskins that have been used for years and a man who has been at a festival for days.

It isn't completely unpleasant, but Anna finds herself nursing a growing feeling of claustrophobia, especially as Johannes lets the doorflap fall shut. But as she lis-tens to the heavy sound of rain on the yurt roof, she resolves that whatever strange things she might encounter in here, they are probably better than being out there. Probably.

"You're making a puddle," Johannes says, looking down at where the water is dripping off the hem of Anna's dress and pooling around her feet.

"Oh! I'm sorry."

He smiles again, compassion warming his face and bringing out the lines at his eyes. "Don't worry about it." He reaches for a towel and offers it to her. "You can use this to dry yourself off, if you like."

"Uh... okay. Thanks." She accepts the towel and is relieved to find that it has the starchy feeling of clean laundry. But it's still infused with the various scents of the yurt, and this feels too personal. She doesn't really want to use it.

"Don't worry... it's clean," Johannes assures her. He can see she's trying to hide her discomfort.

He takes a breath and exudes as calm an energy as he can. He's curious about her, as he is with every person he meets. For Johannes, each person is a completely unique and beautiful combination of things. He always feels a certain amount of gratitude when people offer their hands to him, because they are offering a win-dow into their innermost selves, and what a privilege it is to see that. For Johannes it's one of the most fascinating and humbling things he ever experiences. He loves to see how each person is special in their own unique way, each like a perfect snowflake. And yet, at the same time – he is able to see this more and more – at the heart of everyone he meets, there is the same light. In their truest essence, they are all the same, and made of exactly the same stuff.

Johannes can usually guess what elements will be prominent just by looking at a person. He likes to play this game, to see if he's right. He usually is.

Water, he guesses, looking at the way she holds herself. *Water, and Fire, and both out of balance.*

She has the fine features of a water person, and a slender build, but not as wil-lowy as Water on its own would be. Johannes can tell this is a body type that could have both strength and flexibility, and he can see she has developed a modicum of musculature, but at the same time, she seems lacking in vitality, and doesn't appear to have the confidence to stand up straight. She is an attractive young woman but Johannes can see she is withdrawn, as if all her energy is collapsing inwards. It's like her fire is hardly being expressed at all – and yet he can just see it now, if he looks with his inner eye – that there is something there, just beginning to break through. It's there in her hazel eyes, a barely smouldering ember, that might be coaxed to life if she so chose. And there's a sweetness there too... She has small, spritely ears, like his daughter – very Fire.

Anna's finding it awkward to dry herself with the towel, both trying to dry the parts of herself that are dripping, but also trying to avoid touching her face with the towel. He feels a softness for this young woman. Perhaps it is because she reminds him a little of his own daughter. And just like his daughter, this young woman has no idea how wonderful she is.

Well, perhaps, Johannes thinks, *I might be able to offer her something there.* That's the heart of what he seeks to do for people in his readings. To show people something of the marvellous that resides within them.

"Thank you." Anna hands the towel back to Johannes, offering him a forced smile as she takes another glance at the door.

"You're most welcome," Johannes says, getting the feeling that even though it's raining outside, he should open the curtain just a little wider to let some air flow in. As he does this, he sees a perceptible relief in Anna's face. "I'm Johannes by the way." He holds out his hand to her. Handshakes tell him a lot about a person.

"I'm Anna." She hesitates for a moment and then reaches out to shake his hand. In it, Johannes can feel her tentativeness, but so many other things as well. Hidden strength. Determination. These are hands that can heal.

"Pleased to meet you, Anna. Make yourself comfortable." He gestures to the sheepskins.

The scent of them still bothers Anna, but at least they're warm and dry. The wool sticks to her damp legs, tickling her. She turns her face towards the fresh air.

Johannes pulls out some paper from behind him and places it on the wooden table, scrawling her name on the top of the page. A tea-light burns inside a little glass jar, which sits on the table between them. For some reason the flickering candle makes Anna feel a little better. It gives her something to focus on, to calm the rising feelings of anxiety.

"So do you know much about Chirology?" Johannes asks her.

"Not really anything. But I'm guessing it must be like palmistry?"

"Insofar as palmistry and Chirology are both about reading hands, then yes, they are similar. But Chirology is not like traditional palmistry in that it doesn't predict futures. It dispenses with a lot of the mumbo jumbo and is actually a lot more simple and straightforward than traditional palmistry."

Anna nods, as if she understands.

"You see," Johannes explains, "your hands are like a map of your brain. A huge portion of your brain's processing is devoted to your hands... more than to any other part of the body."

"Oh." Anna opens her fingers and gazes at the lines on her palms, wondering if this could really be true.

"That's why so much of how we process information and respond to the world around us and within us is reflected in our hands," Johannes explains. "Some things are genetic and don't change throughout your life, like your fingerprints, your hand shape and your skin type. But other things like the lines of your palm can change a lot over time, especially the minor lines. So as you change the way you think, so too your lines change. So as I said before, this is not a fortune telling session. It is about discovering your unique blueprint. To help you learn about your natural tendencies, about what is most harmonious for you, to discover your best path."

My best path? At the use of those words, Anna feels a pull inside herself, connected with that raw longing she experienced in Nina Marshall's gig. It rises up and catches in her throat. She's surprised by the intensity of the feeling, and also by how much she wishes that it was true that she did have a path.

Do I really have a path? Something I'm meant to do? A future?

"Your destiny is not fixed," Johannes explains, as if hearing Anna's thoughts. "Now, what I tell you is based on what I see in your hand, and any information I give you about a potential future outcome is based on where you have been, how you are now and where you are currently heading, if you do not alter your course of action."

"Okay." Anna feels a wave of nervousness pass through her at this statement, even though she still hasn't consciously decided to believe in any of this yet.

Johannes places a head torch on his head but doesn't switch it on yet. "The purpose of Chirology is to help you to become conscious of how you are living your life and thinking, so that you can make choices to act to embrace your life, to choose those things which are in harmony with your nature, rather than in discordance with it."

As Johannes says this, he is thinking about the flow of energy and how discord creates tension, and harmony creates flow. *Sometimes tension is necessary. Like the pulling back of a bow, in order to release the arrow. Like the pressure of the wind on a sail.*

This thought causes him to stop for a moment, because suddenly something makes sense to Johannes more deeply about the challenges human beings face. There's a reason that every person he gives a reading to always has significant challenges etched into their lives. *They always have some elements stronger and some weaker. For it is the striving for balance which propels us forward in the world. It is that which creates growth. It is what gives us the chance to experience what it is to be a human being, and to wake up to our true nature.*

Following on from this, another extraordinary thought occurs to Johannes. *Our challenges are as much a blessing in our lives as those gifts which flow easily to us. For this reason – without them, how would we set our sails flying? It is the challenges in our lives which give us something to push against, to build our strength. They are the catalysts for change.*

Johannes thinks about how this young woman before him has certainly been having a challenge of some kind today, and whatever it is, it has been the catalyst for many things, no doubt, one of which has been that it has lead her here, to experience the message Johannes has for her, to whatever it is he can offer her.

"Sometimes our challenges can be the things that are the catalyst for new growth, and in this way, they become blessings in our lives."

Anna stares at him, not understanding. She realises with embarrassment that she's been sitting and clenching her fingers so hard that she's made little nail marks in both of her palms, and that her palms are clammy – a giveaway about how nervous she is about being here. She wipes her hands on her damp dress and holds them out to him.

Johannes notices both the clamminess and the little semi-circle nail marks right away, but feels no judgement about this – only compassion. He takes a breath and makes the conscious intention to let lifeforce energy flow through his hands into hers. He finds that it usually helps people to relax.

Anna feels the dry warmth of these hands that are holding hers. It's as if they've been warmed by a fire, and they're getting warmer all the time. As much as a part of her wants to resist this, she recognises it is a pleasant feeling. More than that – it's deeply comforting.

So this is what he was doing with that other young woman, Anna realises.

Johannes is now testing the flexibility of her fingers and the thickness of the mounts on her palms. Watching him, Anna is surprised to discover that being here with this man she's only just met, rather than feeling apprehension, there is instead a sense of being with a friend, of being with someone who cares about her. It brings up a memory for Anna that she can't quite recall, of the way her father might have held her hands when she was a girl. She looks up into Johannes' intent face, observing how he is pouring over these hands, as if they are some extraordinary resource. With each thought or realisation, his eyebrows – with all their rogue white-grey hairs – do a little rise and fall dance, as if they have a life of their own. For some reason, this strikes Anna as funny, and she restrains herself from laughing out loud.

He gently pokes and prods, nodding to himself. *As I thought. Water. But, interestingly, as I suspected, she has a lot of Fire too. A lot of Fire. Yes. Fire and water together, and both extremely out of balance.*

At this moment, a band kicks off in the Toad Hall stage just over the hedge in Green Futures field. There is a sound of a powerfully rhythmic djembe and other instruments like a bass, and a guitar and now a man's voice ringing out strongly, and soulfully, the words carrying out through the rain.

"*I am not a somebody*
I am not a nobody
I'm a cell in one body
Filling all space
All I ever could be
And all I ever should be
And all I ever will be
Is here in this place..."

And now many voices rise up to join with the one...

"*I am as old as the Universe*
I've been here before and I'll be here again
I am a child of the universe
A part of all women and a part of all men..."

"Ah," Johannes nods, listening too for a moment. "Seize the Day. They do a good thing there."

Anna wonders what he means and then realises that Seize the Day must be the name of the band. *Seize the Day. Carpe Diem.*

Johannes turns his attention back to Anna, switching his head torch on to better examine the subtleties of her hands under the light.

Under the brightness, she feels even more awkward. She can't see his face, and she feels on display now, in some ways like being onstage in those times when you can't see the audience but they can see you. Those are the times Anna feels most on the spot, most judged. She stares at her hands, still being held by Johannes, and wonders what on earth he could possibly be seeing there, on these hands that for Anna had only been useful thus far as a means for helping her achieve her goals in life. They had been so familiar to her up to this point, as a means to an end, and yet now, they seem to hold some great mystery, some untold secrets.

Maybe he can show me something about myself after all.

Please let it be something good.

And without realising she's done it, she has actually begun to allow herself to believe in this. Sitting there, waiting for the verdict, Anna is aware of the emptiness still threatening, that big, scary monster that is the collapse of her life. The black hole. And while it is waiting at the edges, ready to engulf her, for the time being, whatever it is, it appears to be waiting outside the yurt. It doesn't seem to hold so much power in here. For something in the glow of the candle and the warmth and friendliness of Johannes, and the feel of his sure hands holding hers, gives Anna the feeling that for now, she's safe.

Johannes switches off the head torch and regards Anna for a moment. He takes a breath, wondering where to begin. "You have... hands filled with the most wonderful, beautiful potential," he says, feeling like the words fall so far short of what he wants to say to her, and yet it is the truth. He wants to use the word extraordinary, but he tries not to use that word with people. For to say one person is extraordinary implies that there are other people who are somehow less than extraordinary. To Johannes, each person is a wonder and a blessing. He believes that we are all equally special, with equally wondrous and amazing gifts. Yet, even so, he has to admit that when he sees the hands of certain people – and it's just happened for him a few times in his life – he gets the feeling he wants to use the word extraordinary, because for him, what he sees evokes such an excitement and a delight.

For on this young woman's hands are two of Johannes favourite things – Music and Healing – and he's never had the opportunity to see these two things so clearly together in one hand before. No doubt there are many others with this same potential, but he hasn't had the chance to see those hands yet.

Anna takes a shallow breath, almost daring to believe that Johannes might have something positive to tell her about herself. *Potential? What does that mean?*

"Chirology works with the elements," Johannes explains. "We are each made up of a combination of all the elements. Earth, Air, Water, and Fire. Our unique combination of more or less each element is what makes us who we are in this physical incarnation. And when these elements are in balance in our lives, we feel happy and in harmony with the world around us."

"And when they're not?" Anna asks.

"When they're not... well, we find ourselves in situation where we must change and grow. Or continue being unhappy. And since human beings naturally evolve in the direction of happiness, it is in our nature to strive for this balance."

"And you can show me how to... balance my... elements?"

"I can offer you suggestions for how to improve the quality of your life, and how to act in ways which are in harmony with your nature. And I can offer you suggestions for how to cultivate those elements which are weaker to create balance in the whole. But what you do with those suggestions is ultimately up to you. You're the one who sits in the driver's seat of your life. I can't change your life for you. Only you can do that."

Am I really in the driver's seat of my own life? Anna wonders. Her experience of life in the last few years is of being a perpetual passenger, riding shotgun to everyone else's driving. Of course, she had contributed to the decisions, helped make the plans, but when it had become clear that the plans didn't work for her somewhere below the surface, she had been at a loss for how to stop them, or change them, or even feel that she was allowed to, somehow. She's surprised suddenly to feel a flash of anger rising about this. *No, I don't want to do that anymore.*

"Looking at these hands, I see someone who performs and shares her creativity with others through performance. It is a hand capable of such flow. That's the Water in you. Also there is such potential for action, spark, transformation. That's the Fire. I would say, if I was to hazard a guess... that you are involved in performing music of some kind. Am I right?"

Anna opens her mouth in surprise. *How does he know that?* She nods. But barely a moment later, hardly missing a beat, her inner skeptic jumps in. *Well it's obvious, isn't it? You've got callouses on your fingers from playing the guitar. Anyone could look at your hands and tell you that.*

"You have a great, deep capacity for music," Johannes says. He's trying to convey this to her somehow. To show her what he means. He can see the doubt on her face.

"You also have the mark of a writer." As Johannes says this, he feels the familiar flow of energy. He's on the right track. "So, I would also suggest that perhaps you are a songwriter?"

Anna's inner critic has trouble dismissing this one so quickly. Anna nods again. "I... I do write. I'm... a... a singer-songwriter." As she says the words, they sound empty of meaning. *Am I? Am I really a singer-songwriter? Really?* After the events of today, she's not sure she believes that anymore. She had placed so much of her identity on those words. Yet now, spoken aloud, they feel barren.

Johannes nods in confirmation. "Yes. But even though all this potential is here, I don't think you've found your true path with music yet. Your line of fate, or purpose, here, is not very strong." He runs his finger along a faint and broken line, which runs up the centre of Anna's right palm and disappears a third of the way up.

Johannes looks up and sees the panic on Anna's face. *Gentle, Johannes,* his heart reminds him. *Be Gentle.* Now he knows what it is that he's meant to tell her, but he reminds himself to go slowly. Sometimes it can all pour out so quickly, because Johannes has a quick and intuitive mind, and he often sees so many things all at once.

Anna's thoughts have already run away with themselves. For her, in this moment, Johannes has just confirmed the very thing that Anna has most been fearing he would say. That she has no strong fate. That she has no purpose. That she is not really anyone special. That she is without value.

"Please, don't worry, Anna," Johannes says. "This is one of those lines that can change over time. As you find your path, it will grow stronger and deeper. You're still quite young. How old are you? Twenty six... seven?"

"Twenty-eight. Almost twenty-nine."

He nods. "Well, you've got time to figure this out. And in fact, if I am correct, I think you will do so quite soon." He feels a shiver move through him with this statement. *Yes. Very soon.*

Anna shivers too and wonders if it's because she's cold, because the curtain is still open a little and she can see the wind is blowing outside.

"Is it okay if we close the curtain?" Anna asks.

"Certainly." Johannes smiles and reaches over to drop the flap. He turns his attention back to her, wondering how to convey the importance of this to her.

In the background, Seize the Day are still going strong, this time with a powerful female voice soaring out. Anna listens to the words, which are just audible through the rain.

"Stop feeling small
You're a part of it all
Everything you say and do
Every time you let the truth come through
It makes a difference
Believe in your significance..."

"Anna, what I am trying to say to you, in my long-winded way is... that you are capable of doing something that very important. You have the ability – albeit hidden at the moment – to create music with the potential to bring true healing to others. Or rather bring the opportunity to others to heal themselves through the resonance of your music. Through embodying yourself that which brings healing."

At this, Anna feels another shiver move through her. *What? What does that mean?* She tries to read Johannes' face, trying to understand this with her mind, but she can't. *Potential to bring some kind of healing to other people through my music? Me?*

Yet, even with this doubt, she can feel a perceptible change in herself at this idea. Something's bubbling up inside her, wanting to overflow. It's an excitement, because this feels like a puzzle piece she's been missing her whole life, that fits exactly into the hole that she didn't even realise was there, labelled: My *purpose in life.*

"By true healing," Johannes elaborates, "what I mean is this – by finding your own connection, and bringing that to your music, you could help people to find their own connection to the whole. To the divine, to inner peace, to Love."

Anna hears herself laugh out loud. "It sounds like you've got me mixed up with a woman I just saw performing on the One Earth Stage just now. If you'd seen my gig earlier, you might well revise your statement." Even as she's trying to make light of this, the knot is forming in her stomach again with all the memories and all the comparisons.

Ah, thinks Johannes. *So that's what it is. That's what's causing her energy to collapse in on itself this way. She's comparing herself to others.*

He shakes his head. "No, Anna. Had I been at your gig, I am absolutely sure that whatever it was I'd witnessed there, I would still be saying the same thing to you now. You have a powerful potential here. A potential you have not yet realised. And, you know, that part of you which is comparing yourself to that other person, that part... is the very part of you that by its very nature cannot see who you truly are."

"What part is that?"

"Your ego."

Anna bristles. "Are you saying I have a big ego?"

Johannes laughs. "No. That's not what I mean. I'm talking about the veil of illusion. Have you ever come across this idea?"

Anna shakes her head.

The beat of a djembe breaks through the air again as the band over the hedge belts out:

"I am strong as a tree on a mountain
Full and fresh as a free flowing fountain
Bright and pure as the stars beyond counting in the night
I am their light
I am the light that shines in a thousand people
In my sight every life is equal

No one's slave

I am no one's master..."

"Essentially, we are all made of Spirit," Johannes explains. "That is our true essence. Love. This is true of all human beings on Earth."

"Yeah, right. I know some people who are certainly not made of love." Anna thinks of Damien's friend Eden, and the feeling she gets every time Eden is around.

Johannes faces her with all seriousness. "I mean everyone, Anna. This is what I'm talking about. Those you describe... and also the aspect of you that sees them this way... this is all part of the veil of illusion."

Anna is starting to question this again. *Veil of illusion?*

Johannes reads her expression. "As souls, we made a choice to come here, to be incarnated on Earth to experience physical reality. And for most of us, that comes with taking on the veil of illusion, which is a kind of forgetfulness, a kind of sleep which makes us forget who we truly are. Of course, babies when they are born, and very little children – you can still see the light in their eyes – they still have an innate knowing of who they are. The veil of illusion settles around them as they grow, faster or slower dependent on the adults around them. Or in some rare cases with very conscious parents, children can keep this openness to life, this knowledge of their innate magnificence. But for most of us it is not like that. It is by emulating the adults around us, learning about the world of form through them, that we learn to see this veil as reality, and we learn to believe this voice in our heads that judges and criticises. The voice I'm talking about is the human ego."

It's a lot for Anna to take in. Her own ego is standing up and demanding that she not listen to this. It's *ridiculous*, the thoughts in her mind tell her. *This is fantasy. Don't believe this.* And at the same time, there is another feeling inside her which seems to say *Yes, that feels true.* She feels the pull in both directions.

"The ego is not a bad thing," Johannes explains. "It is a necessary thing for us to experience our true purpose, which is waking up to our true selves. For without the forgetting, how could we experience the remembering?"

"I don't really understand what you mean."

Johannes takes a breath. He has to slow it down. He finds that he downloads things so quickly and he can see the whole picture and wants to just pass it on to people. But as he listens to Anna, to her innermost being, he knows she is not really getting this. The window of acceptance and openness he saw in her is closing.

"Okay. Try and see it like this." Johannes moves the tealight on the table closer towards her. "How is it that you can see this flame burning?"

"I don't know. Because it's there in front of me?"

"You see the light because of the dark around it. How bright the candle appears to us is completely dependent on the amount of light and shade around it. The darker the environment around the candle, the brighter the flame will appear. It is the contrast which enables us to see it fully. If all there was was light around us, we wouldn't be able to see the flame at all. Do you see what I mean?"

"Um... not really."

"The ego is like the darkness. We need the ego to be able to see the light that we are. To contrast it, so that it becomes visible to us."

"I don't see any light inside myself." But even as Anna says this, she wonders if it's true. There is a glimmer of something there... a flickering...

"Maybe not yet," Johannes says. "But you will. You will. And as we begin to see the light that we are, this is what we call an awakening."

"An awakening?"

"You wake up to your true self. You remember how I said the veil of illusion is like a kind of sleep? It's this sleep, this forgetting, that we wake up from. So as you begin to see this light that you truly are, you have these experiences of waking from that sleep, waking from illusion. Hence, awakening."

"Oh."

"And as you begin to awaken, what you will experience is a kind of silence inside you, an inner listening. A presence. And as you become aware, you begin to recognise another voice. One that you probably already hear and has been with you your whole life, but you have been ignoring or discounting up until now because your ego's voice has been louder. This is the voice of your true self. It is the Voice of the Heart."

"The Voice of the Heart?"

Johannes nods. "These are messages from our Higher Self, which is that part of us, or rather, that whole which we are an aspect of, which knows itself as God, or consciousness."

At this point, Anna balks. This is too much for her. Because ideas of God for her have an unpleasant resonance. It makes her think of hard church pews next to her mother and the enforced hours spent listening to the droning words of a man in a priest's robe, describing a male God, full of judgement. A personification of something decidedly outside herself.

"If the word God feels strange for you, Anna, you can substitute 'Love' or 'Source'. It is that which gives rise to everything, exists in everything. The Unified Field of All Possibilities, as my friend who practises Transcendental Meditation says. I am talking about the part of you that knows itself as Love. Any message from your heart, is always a message of Love."

Now a new female voice is rising out from beyond the hedge, leading the band.

"Deep within the heart of every creed
There is a part that fills the need
In you and I to feel the Earth and touch the Sky
And it's a timeless truth that life's a dream
And here's the proof
Close your eyes and realise that your awareness never changes
We are Big, Big Love
We are Big, Big Love
So life is all about the dance between the you that's in the dream
And the bigger you that's watching and enjoying every scene
And the awareness is the key
For showing you and showing me
How to dance life's dance together
And set our Spirits free
To live in Big, Big Love
We are Big, Big Love..."

"You may at times experience it as if there are two voices inside you. Ultimately this is just part of the illusion, because there is really only one of us. Even our ego is part of this consciousness. This is the dichotomy. We are many, and yet we are one," Johannes explains. He can see she is still sitting on the fence, being pulled both ways.

"You see, you always know it's the ego speaking to you because the ego always resonates with fear. If you're judging yourself, thinking any thought about yourself or another person that is less than loving, that is always your ego. Always. If the thought makes you feel bad, sad, contracted... That's the ego. That's not truth. The ego judges, criticises. It believes everything to be separate. It will always see itself as either better or worse than others. It cannot see the truth. That we are all part of the same light."

Anna can feel that there is a part of her that wants to believe what Johannes is saying, but she's been believing the negative self-criticisms for so long that it's hard to reverse that way of thinking. But even so, a little hope opens up inside Anna that maybe this voice she's been believing all these years could be wrong about her. That maybe she isn't so completely unlovable after all.

"So Anna, I know I'm waffling on a bit here, but let me try to get to the point. It's about the voice of your true self. The voice of the ego is not the voice of your true self. Its nature is to keep you in illusion, so you cannot see the truth. So if you ever have a thought that is unkind about yourself, that tells you aren't good enough, don't listen to it. Don't believe it. Because it's a story made up by the ego, and it's absolutely not true. Your ego resonates with fear. Your true self, your Heart-Self, resonates with love."

"But who is this person you're talking about? This Heart-Self?" Anna asks, confused. "Because it doesn't feel like me. I can't see that person inside me. At all." *Or can I?* she wonders, momentarily looking inwards.

"That's because you are still living in the veil of illusion. You still believe that you are your ego. So you believe what it tells you. But you can make a choice right now to place your attention – your awareness – on your heart, and listen to this other voice. The voice of the heart."

"How?"

"Notice your body. Fear contracts. Love expands. When a thought is in alignment with Love, you feel flow and expansion in your body. You feel energy. A message from your Heart may come in the form of a picture in your mind, or it may be a feeling that translates into words in your mind. Whatever it is, it will give you that feeling of energy. Just notice your body, notice how it feels. Your body gets messages much more quickly than your rational mind does."

"So you're saying that if my mind tells me that I am not as good as Nina Marshall, that I shouldn't believe it?" Anna asks.

"That's exactly what I'm saying. At your core, Anna, you are the very same as that person you think is better than you. Exactly the same."

Anna furrows her eyebrows. *Really? I'd love to believe that. But really?*

"Yes, really," Johannes feels to say. "It's a life's work for some of us," he explains, thinking about himself. "Or more likely, a work of many lifetimes. But if you can learn to see with the eyes of your Heart-Self, this Love that is at the centre of you, you will see that there is nothing to compare. Because you would know that really, that other person IS you, that there is no separation between you."

This concept is too much for Anna right now, he can see that. *You're getting ahead of yourself Johannes*, he tells himself. She hasn't had her first experience of awakening yet. Until that happens, no amount of describing can come close to conveying the truth of it. Experience is the only thing that will show this to her. Yet, still the energy is flowing as he says the words. Perhaps she needs to hear it now, so that when the time comes, she will remember it later.

"Perhaps we'll come back to that," Johannes says. "Where were we before I went off on that tangent? Oh yes. We were talking about purpose. Which I guess is not such a tangent actually. Because this brings me back to what I was saying about the deeper purpose of your music being about enabling people to experience this truth of who they are. But of course, before you can offer this to anyone else, you must find this truth in yourself. And as you find this truth in yourself, you become an example for others. You radiate that out into the world."

Anna stares at Johannes, disbelieving. And yet, what he is saying sounds familiar somehow, like a lost message returning home. She shakes her head.

"I believe you will, Anna. This may all sound crazy to you right now, but I can see this potential in both your hands. Especially the left one, which is your passive hand, the hand of your inner self. The potential is right here. And if you can access this potential, you will find your true dharma in life."

"My dharma?"

"Dharma is a Sanskrit word, which to me speaks about one's deepest purpose. It's that which your soul is born to do in this life. It's the action in the world where you express your greatest joy while at the same time being in service to humanity. Dharma is always about service. Being in service to others and at the same time, doing that which we most love to do."

It is as if by hearing these words spoken aloud, a little seed inside Anna, that had been lying dormant inside her since she was a very little girl, is stirring to life. As Johannes speaks now, she feels a raw longing again, this sense of having been so far away from somewhere she should have been or from something she should have known; something forgotten that could be remembered, and at the same time, beginning to dare to hope that she might reach whatever it is.

Johannes watches a range of emotions passing across Anna's face. She is someone who feels a lot. He can see this in her hand. It is one of the characteristics of Water. Water is Emotion, flow, sensitivity.

"These are hands with great sensitivity," Johannes tells her, clasping her hands again. "This is one of the great gifts of Water. Sensitivity can be one of our greatest assets and out of balance it can be one of our greatest challenges. For you, I feel there is so much sensitivity here that my sense is, you must have created a mask to protect yourself when you are out in the world. There is a real difference between the face you show to pretty much everyone else, and your inner thoughts and feelings. You put on this mask for the world because you don't have confidence in this inner you. You don't have confidence because you believe what your ego is telling you about yourself – that you're not good enough. So you feel you have to pretend, to create a persona that society will accept. Possibly this stems from your relationship with your parents, where you felt your natural behaviour was unacceptable to them. In particular, I see this with your mother."

She feels a pang inside. Yes. Things were more simple with her father. Not always, but mostly. With her mother it was somewhat of a different story. More complicated.

Johannes sees Anna set her jaw, but he continues to speak because there is this energy moving through him again.

"My sense is that you've gone straight from trying to please your parents to trying to please your friends and boyfriends. I can see you often have boyfriends. And friends too, but you keep them always at arm's length. They never get close."

Except for one. Anna thinks of Carolyn, her oldest friend, who she hasn't seen for years now. They had been close. Carolyn was a musician too – a classical pianist. A memory comes now to Anna now of Carolyn on the piano, back before Anna had really begun to play herself. Listening to Carolyn, it had been clear how much her friend had loved playing. For Anna the joy had been infectious and she had wished back then that there was something she could love doing that much.

Johannes takes a breath, as he does when he wants to bring his awareness from his head back down into his body. For Johannes it is especially important to ground himself in the physical world, because he is primarily an Air person, and for him, that means that ideas and the realm of thought and vision and speaking ideas aloud are often where both his gifts and his challenges lay. This time he chooses his words more carefully. For there is something else he feels he must say to her, something delicate.

"This line here – this is the Heart Line, the line of Emotion, also known as the Water Line. I would guess from looking at this line, that you are currently in a relationship, and it is with someone who you genuinely do have some affection for."

He sees a brief moment of surprise pass through her eyes. "Yes. I am... and I do." *Of course I do*, she tells herself.

Johannes takes another breath. *How to say this lightly? Should I say it at all?* But of course, it has come to him. And he is learning that when the energy comes, he must let it flow. So even as he doubts himself, he speaks it. "What I feel strongly is that you have created a persona in this relationship – a persona that you think this man wants – and you have been living this persona out in your daily life. But inside it is not the real you, and it doesn't bring you happiness to live this way."

Anna pulls her hand away and closes it into a fist. She thinks about how Damien has been planning to propose to her any day now. She suspects it will probably happen on her birthday, because he has been alluding to some particularly special present he has gotten for her, and her birthday is only a few weeks away now. She had been planning to say yes. And why wouldn't she? Her family expects it, and he's a really decent guy. Still, there is something about Johannes' statement which is deeply unsettling, because as much as she doesn't want to admit it to herself, she knows he is right about one thing at least. As much as she tells herself she's lucky to have someone like Damien, she certainly hasn't been happy.

"I'm sorry if I've said something that upsets you, Anna. You have to take what I say with a grain of salt, too. All of this comes through the filter of my own experience and my own consciousness. You can take what's useful to you – if anything – and discard the rest."

Unbidden, an image of a man comes into Johannes' mind of a kind, warm man with smiling eyes. And in this vision, the man has said something which makes Anna laugh with real delight. It feels like this man is a lover, but also a true friend of the heart. Johannes wonders if he should speak this vision aloud to her, but he somehow feels that it is important for her to discover this in her own time.

"You see," Johannes says, pointing gently to her hand, "this line symbolises the passion you need to find with someone you can share your whole heart with. You will never be happy in a relationship until you can find a person like that, and be the kind of person who can open yourself up in return."

Again the sob wells up in Anna. It's a shock to realise how much she wants that. *But is that really possible? And could it be possible with Damien?*

"For what it's worth," Johannes says softly, "I do see you being truly happy with someone. Truly heart open and delighted. It may be this man you are with now or it may be someone new." And as he says the words, he knows which one of those feels most true. "It's not my place to say. But I will say this. Before we can find the person we feel truly right about being with, we need to be able to find ourselves first. If you do not find wholeness in yourself, you can never feel whole with another. If you cannot find your own centre, you will forever be pulled this way and that by the whims of others. You will seek to complete yourself within your relationship. People can often find themselves being in a relationship just for the sake of having a relationship, and if they do this instead of finding themselves first, they lose the chance to know who they are, to find their own connection to source. And if you can do that, you will find the person who can truly make your heart sing."

Anna fiddles with the damp hem of her dress. She feels a profound aching sadness rising in her and she doesn't want to look at it. She knows he's right. She's never felt where her own centre is, and has always tried to fill the empty hole inside through having a romantic relationship, through trying to please the other person, always seeking to feel she is worth something through being desired by another. And in every instance, after the initial infatuation stage wears off, relationships have always felt empty for Anna. She thinks about Damien again, and feels a profound sense of loss and anger at Johannes for showing her these things she was hiding from herself. She rubs at the hem of her dress with all the ferocity of that and then looks up at Johannes again, because he's stopped speaking and is watching her. His eyes are so compassionate, suddenly instead of being angry at him, she wants to cry again.

"I haven't been happy," she whispers. "Not really. Maybe, not ever." A flicker of a memory brings the sense that maybe, way back as a small child, she did have moments of true happiness. But the more she tries to grasp the memory, the more it seems to fade away.

Johannes nods. "Whether that's true or not, believe me, happiness is possible for you. It is possible for all of us. You can find this happiness in yourself first, and then I believe you have the potential to experience great heart-expanding joy within a relationship."

Seeing the look in Anna's eyes, Johannes wonders if after everything, she might just leave now after all. Of course, he's nearly at the end. *But not quite*, he thinks, a flash of knowing coming to him about the next part of the message he has to share with her.

"Do you wish me to carry on?" Johannes asks.

Anna takes a shaky, shallow breath. "I... guess what you're saying is... making me feel a little emotional." Her body heaves a sigh. "I feel all these things, but I don't know what to do about anything. It feels like everything's wrong and I have no idea how to make it right."

Johannes nods. "Emotion, that's Water for you," he says lightly. "It's all about flow. I always think of emotion as E-Motion. Like, Energy-in-Motion."

A wave in the ocean, of Energy in Motion.... Nina Marshall's song swims through Anna's mind.

Johannes smiles warmly. "Like I said before, you have this wonderful potential, and to access it, you must allow this energy in you to actually be in motion. Allow yourself to flow. I suppose this is what I am, in my long-winded way, actually trying to tell you. You are a Water person, whose primary gift is about the flow of energy... and you have not been allowing yourself to flow. When water doesn't flow, it becomes stagnant, blocked. So if you wish to be happy, find a way to flow. Flow in your life. In yourself, in your relationships, in your music. Therein you will find your happiness."

"Flow?" Anna asks. She feels helpless with all this information, and doesn't really understand what he means by it. "How do I... flow?"

Johannes considers this for a moment. "Let's come at this another way. Lets look at all the elements as a whole. We speak about the four elements: Water, Fire, Air and Earth. Some people speak of a fifth element, and that is what happens when all four elements are One. That is Spirit, or Quintessence, the fifth essence – what we truly are. What we are looking at is finding a balance with all the elements which brings us connection to Spirit, to wholeness. Each of the elements is not actually isolated on its own. So, if we want to correct an imbalance in one element, we must also look at all the others. You must find a balance with them all, for they are completely interconnected. So let's look at your second major element, Fire. Fire is Passion, Creativity, Sexuality, Wildness. Fire is the spark of life. And just as you do not allow your water to flow, you also do not allow your fire to burn. This is connected because when you experience a passionate feeling, you also do not allow it to flow."

At the word *sexuality*, Anna feels her whole body tense again. She doesn't want to be told by a grey-haired man that she has repressed her sexuality. It's extremely embarrassing for her, and she feels her face colouring just to think of it. But of course, she knows he is right about this too. She has never been free in the whole of her sexual life. She has always thought that was just the way she was. But now, just for a moment, Anna briefly wonders if maybe that's not the case, and that maybe she does have a fiery, passionate self buried somewhere inside her. She's aware of something, just barely tangible, a rising sensation, a little flaring inside, her own spark recognising itself being thought about.

"So... for you, the thing is to allow yourself to be this dragon inside you. This fiery wild passionate creature that you are. It is the most freeing thing in the world to allow the passion in your life to fully express itself. You are a performer. Fire people make wonderful performers. They are the spark. They are the creativity. But you are not harnessing the power of this element in your life. If you could fully be your Fire onstage, Whoa Nelly! There would be some serious sparks up there." He laughs at this.

An image comes to Anna's mind of herself spontaneously combusting into a ball of flame onstage, and for some reason this strikes her hilarious, and without meaning to, she laughs out loud with him.

"And you know, Anna, I believe you will find that spark in your life."

"But how? You're telling me all these things that are wrong. But what, practically speaking, can I do about it?"

Johannes nods. "Yes. Of course. Well, first we have to identify the problems or challenges you are facing, and then we can offer suggestions. I feel for you, the key to balancing your Water and Fire is to be found in the other two elements which have been less strong in your life. The element of Air, for example. Cultivate the strength of Air in your life, and you will find it brings balance to the Water and Fire.

For through the element of Air, we learn about how our thoughts create our reality, and actually regulate and control the flow of energy. Thoughts are made up of energy. They affect not just subtle energy, but physical energy as well. So the first thing for you to learn is to witness your thoughts. Learn to master your thoughts. Create the thoughts you want, let go of the ones you don't. Those thoughts generated by your ego or picked up and supported by your ego cause your body to contract, and stop the flow of chi."

"Okay. So how do I... do that?"

"Meditation. Meditation quiets the mind and helps us to feel the still centre within us, the silence. Meditation is the key to awakening. And for you, it will be a major key to connecting with your centre and being able to be that presence on stage."

"I have no idea how to meditate," Anna says, feeling overwhelmed. At times throughout her life she has seen people sitting cross-legged with their eyes closed, looking impossibly peaceful and had thought that it was somehow out of her reach. She feels a tinge of desperation, wanting Johannes to give her something tangible that she can grasp onto which could save her from the void she still feels is waiting for her outside the yurt.

"There are lots of different ways. Just be open to try new things. Try those that seem interesting to you, and keep the ones that feel right. There are quite a few different meditations in these very fields. Have a walk around. See what you find that takes your fancy." Johannes gestures out into the rain. "So... that's the first two things: thoughts, meditation. And there's a third thing about Air, which perhaps should even be the first and most important thing, because it makes the others possible, and is actually a fundamental part of most meditations. That is the breath. On the physical level, the air we breathe into our bodies brings oxygen to our cells and gives us energy. On a more subtle, energetic level, when we breathe deep, we are breathing in lifeforce energy. We can bring these three things together – breath, thought, meditation. By using the mind to see the flow of energy, and by breathing with that flow, we can create flow. So breath creates flow."

But I can't learn to breathe, Anna thinks, remembering when she had tried to learn to breathe before. It had not been a good experience. She hadn't been able to do it then and can't see why it would work for her now.

Seize the Day are now singing a chant about the Earth, and Johannes can hear the energetic voices of the audience rising with them in the repeating refrain:

"All round Mother Earth
Bring her into birth
Sweet Creatress of the Night and Day

Bring your Spirit through
Rest our thoughts in you
Guide our feet in the natural way..."

"Appropriate." Johannes nods his head in the direction of the next field. "The song they are singing is about Earth, and Earth is also a big key for you. Find your connection with the Earth. Do this on a physical level, and also an energetic level. The Earth is our physical body, the ground beneath our feet. Firstly, your physical body is your instrument. Take care of it. Nurture it. Eat wholesome foods that will give your body energy. Also move your body. If your physical body doesn't move, it becomes stiff and tense. Your lymph doesn't flow. And on an energetic level, if you move your physical body, that will enable your chi energy to flow as well."

"So, you're telling me I should exercise?" Anna asks.

"Yes, but not just any exercise. Movement. Things that really free your body, like dance. Dance your wild self free."

Dance my wild self free? Anna stares at him.

Johannes chuckles. This was a phrase his own daughter had used once. *Dance your wild self free.* "Okay. Perhaps this may not make sense to you right now. But just consider it – something like Five Rhythms or dance meditation. Perhaps you could also look to things like yoga, t'ai chi or qigong – things that are physical and yet also work on the energetic levels."

"Okay," Anna says, feeling unequal to all these tasks he is suggesting to her, and not even sure she really believes any of them will help. "So... let me see if I've got this right. You're telling me that I should learn to breathe, learn to meditate, learn to think properly, and dance, or do yoga or whatever. And if I do all these things, I'll be able to do this dharma you're talking about?"

How can I do all of that? How can I do any of it?

"It's all a process, Anna. You have to take it one step at a time. And be easy with yourself about it. Basically, what I'm talking about is becoming fully present to your life. If you can be fully present, through breath, through meditation, through being in your physical body – whatever it is that works for you – you will be aware enough to make the changes to create more balance in your life, to bring yourself into harmony with your true nature and with the world around and within you. And as you become more present to your life, you learn to listen, to pay attention to each moment, and each moment will become your teacher. You will meet many teachers in your life. In places you least expect and in people you least expect, and if you can be open to these experiences, you can learn everything you need to learn. You will find, as I have found in my experience, that if there is something you need to learn at a given time, the right and appropriate teacher will appear to show you the answer. It might be a person, or a book, or a song. By making the conscious decision to begin your journey of awakening, of self discovery, you will find these things start happening with accelerating speed and seeming coincidence."

Anna isn't sure she wants him to say any more. She feels bewildered by it all. It all seems too strange, too unbelievable. And yet, she can feel that there is some part of her that actually does want to believe in this stuff, and this part of her is still paying attention.

"I'm going to try and draw this reading to a close, Anna, because I can feel I've already given you a lot to work with here." But there is still something left unsaid. Johannes takes a breath and asks his heart the question.

Is there anything else I should tell her? It comes to him, very clearly. "You know, Anna, when you listen to the deepest guidance of your heart, it will always guide you on the path of the highest good. So your actions will be the right ones for you and for those around you, because we're all connected. When you follow your deepest calling, you are following that which is connected to the whole, therefore connected to the deepest calling in others. We are not independent of each other. It's all one. When you are happy, your happiness then can radiate out from you. You are part of the world. Healing yourself heals part of the world and this has an effect on the energetic world around you. So you must start with yourself. Find your heart's path, your dharma. Your way to serve with joy in the world."

My way to serve with joy in the world? What does that mean?

"I know it's not always easy to say the truth, or to hear it," Johannes says. "But in truth there is liberation. To walk your path of truth is to walk the path of love. Only in truth can we have a real, shared experience with others."

Seeing Anna's confusion, Johannes wishes in a way he could offer her a hug and somehow tell her what he sees so clearly. She can't see it yet because she's still living in her pain of the illusion of her separateness. He knows he's said all he can at this time and she must find her own way.

"Anna, something is guiding me to say this to you – Pay attention, because your life is happening right now. Right now is when you can wake up to your life. In this moment. And the more present you can be to your life, the more amazing, life-transforming things will happen. The ego part of you will fight this transformation, because the more you start to live and walk the way of the heart, of truth, the less power the fears of the ego will have. To wake up fully means death for the ego, for that self that sees itself as an individual struggling on alone in the world. You are never truly alone, Anna. Never."

She looks up to him with her eyes wide. How she longs to believe this is true. *But could it be?* She knows that in only a few moments she will have to step out and face the thing waiting for her outside – the dissolution of life as she knows it. She feels like she's stepped into a strange dream; it all seems surreal, and her body is shaky and shivery, but not from the cold. Her hands tremble as she fishes around in her bag for whatever money she has. She holds out the damp and crumpled note and change to Johannes. "I'm sorry... it's all I have..."

Johannes reaches out and closes Anna's fingers back around the money. "Keep it. I'm really happy to give you this as a gift. I am very pleased to have met you, Anna, and to be able to be a small part of your journey. If in some small way, I have been able to offer something to help you find this true path of your heart, then I am happy. Because I have a sense that you are going to do some very special things and make a real difference to people with your gifts. It's a potential, but also I have a feeling about you too. I'm willing to bet that some time in the near future, you will understand what we've been talking about, and it will be more than just potential. You will be walking this path. But of course, I don't make predictions." His eyes twinkle, and Anna can't help laughing a little. She feels a tiny glow of warmth at these last words, humbled by his faith in her gifts.

"Thank you," Anna says finally, her voice catching in her throat.

"You're welcome," Johannes says, opening the flap. It's still raining. He turns to her. "You know, you are braver than you think, Anna. You just have to connect with that courageous part of yourself. Because she is there. And she's..." Johannes has to smile because the image that comes to him is so striking. "... she's a roaring lion."

A *lion?* Anna almost laughs out loud, but then she remembers that her sun sign is, in fact, Leo.

She knows she really will have to face the rain now, which is pelting down harder than ever.

"Here." Johannes hands her a biodegradable plastic compost bag. "If you hold it over your head and run, you might not get completely soaked."

Anna accepts the plastic bag gratefully and steps out into the downpour. "Thank you."

"Blessings on your journey, Anna. It's been a pleasure to meet you."

"You too."

With a smile, Johannes disappears behind the flap of his yurt. Holding the bag over her head, Anna starts to run as fast as she can without slipping on the wet grass.

Despite the small shelter offered by the plastic bag, she arrives back to the artist camping area completely soaked through. Feeling cold to the bone and extremely shivery, she crawls into her tent and peels off her dress. While the air inside the tent feels slightly damp, her sleeping bag seems dry enough inside and so do the clothes in her bag, which is a welcome relief. She puts on the softest, warmest clothing she can find – two layers of it – and huddles inside her sleeping bag. Even cocooned in her bag with layers of wool and cotton around her, it still takes some time for the shivering to stop. As the tremors in her body begin to settle, she feels the exhausted weight of her body. And so, even though it is still light outside and Glastonbury Festival is alive and partying all around her, Anna wants nothing more than to sleep for a very, very long time. As the wind and rain buffet her tent, she lets sleep take her.

"I can see it in your palm
I can see it in your stars
Thank you for remembering
That it's perfectly,
It's perfectly cast"

from the song, 'Perfectly Cast', by Carrie Tree

2. Fire

"Light is Fire
Fire so pure
The Sun is Fire
The Fires of Heaven
Purify me"

from the song, 'Light is Fire', by Vince DeCicco/Praying for the Rain

Anna is in the driver's seat of her car, turning down into her little cul-de-sac, pulling up out in front of her little terraced house in Brighton. It's dark out.

That was fast, she thinks. *Am I back here already?* She sees a light from the corner of her eye and turns to notice that there is a candle sitting in a little glass jar on the passenger seat beside her. It's beautiful, casting its soft flickering light on the inside of the car. It's just like the candle Johannes had on his little table.

Oh, I guess I brought that back with me. What am I going to do with it?

She looks to her house. *I can't take it in with me. Damien wouldn't understand it. I'll have to leave it here. Hide it, so he won't see.*

She reaches into the back seat of her car. There is an old blanket there. She pulls it into the front and carefully covers the candle in its jar. The barest glimmer shines through the fabric of the blanket.

She feels her body contracting, and knows it's not good what she's just done. *But he won't understand. I don't have a choice,* she tells herself, as she steps out of the driver's side and closes the car door. She peers in the window at it one more time, wondering if it will be safe in there and then forces herself to turn away and takes steps towards the gate in front of her house. It creaks as she opens it and she catches a momentary reflection of light on the metal and feels a heat flare at her back.

She spins around and sees what she feared: the blanket has caught fire. The whole interior of the car is aflame. The heat coming off it is intense and Anna backs away, terrified that the fire will escape or the car will explode. Dashing to the front door, she opens it and slams it behind her. Damien is upstairs in their bedroom watching TV, oblivious to her return. She lifts the curtains of a window and sees that the car has become a fireball, and the flames are spreading rapidly, travelling up the pavement towards her, scorching the grass and everything in its wake.

It's coming for me.

You can't escape it, a voice seems to say.

It wants to destroy me!

You can't escape it. It is you.

She lets the curtain fall and edges back from the door until she is up against a wall and can go no further. The fire is right outside of the front door now, licking the wood. A slit of orange light flares through the mail slot.

It's coming. And still Damien has no idea.

The door tips and falls off its hinges, all aflame. The entrance to the house has been subsumed by the fire becoming a flaming doorway. Entering the house, it begins to devour the walls, the curtains, the carpets, everything – surrounding her.

There is no way out. It's going to destroy me! It's going to destroy everything!

There is an explosion outside, and now her ears are filled with a screaming. She doesn't know if it's her own terrified voice or someone else's. The ground shakes with another explosion. Anna's eyes snap open. She is still in her tent.

It was a dream, she thinks, but her heart is still pounding and people are still screaming. *What?* She lies there, frozen, listening, adrenaline pumping through her body. The ground shakes with yet another explosion, and the air rings again with the screams that follow it.

As she comes to wake more fully, Anna realises these are screams of delight and not of terror. Some kind of spectacle is happening outside. She takes a shaky breath, unzips the tent and pokes her head out just in time to see the sky in front of her light up bright orange with another explosion and firebursts shooting sixty feet into the air high over the treetops which border the next field with a giant WHOOMP, in time with the heart-thumping electronic beats.

Arcadia! Of course.

Yesterday she had seen the impressive 30-foot tall metal spider, partially constructed from jet engines and other scrap metal. *So that's what it does. Amazing!*

Temporarily mesmerized by the extraordinary happenings in the sky, Anna realises the rain has stopped. It's late. The reflected light on the low cloud cover is strange and otherworldly, giving the effect of an eternal twilight, tinged with green and orange.

She digs into her bag and pulls out her mobile phone to check the time. 12:02am. Damien has texted her four times. Anna had promised to call him and let him know how the gig had gone, and with everything that had gone on, she had forgotten. Thinking about what to say to him, memories of the day's events flood in, twisting her stomach.

At 4:03pm he'd written: *How'd it go? Bet they loved you my star. D x*

At 6:35pm: *Hey, Annie, call me. Just heard the rain started at Glasto. x*

At 9:41pm: *Okay, A where are you? Call me. Starting to get worried.*

At 11:37pm: *A. Why aren't you calling me back? You ok? Please call me. PLEASE.*

Anna stares at her phone. *What can I possibly tell him?*

She can't bear to break the news to Damien of her gig's failure. Not yet. But she doesn't want to leave him hanging either. After thinking for a moment, she comes up with a reply she feels is reasonably safe.

Hi Love, sorry to worry you. Gig was interesting. Tell you about it tomorrow. So tired I fell asleep. Call you in the morning. Love A x

There is a pain in Anna's stomach which is beginning to gripe, and it occurs to her that she hasn't eaten anything since the chocolate brownie earlier. She steps out of her tent to gaze through the fencing at the throbbing mass of people moving past on the trackway outside the artist's area. Coloured lights are strung from poles which cast the camping field in hazy red, blue and green. It all looks very damp out there. Anna shivers. She wouldn't be braving the night at all, were it not for this hunger, this emptiness wanting to be filled.

There is something else, too. She can feel it now – a sense of some reason to be going out there. As if there is something for her to find, somewhere she really needs to be. *But where could that be on a night like this?*

Anna hoists her wellies out of her pack, grateful for Damien's insistence that she bring them. When she had protested that they would be too heavy to carry, he'd said, "Anna, it's Glastonbury. Bring your wellies." She feels a pang of guilt thinking about Damien, as if somehow she has already betrayed him, as if some part of her has an inkling of what is to come during this night.

She slips on a wool jumper and ties her hair back loosely to avoid it dangling in anything muddy. She does a rough retouch on her make-up, fixing the smudges, just in case she bumps into someone. *But who would I see of consequence this time of night, anyway?*

As Anna pries her boots on she wonders whether the nice man at the Chai Chi

Tent is still working. She remembers her money, and extracts the damp note and change from the wet clothes she'd been in earlier and shoves them into her pocket. Out under the strange sky, she ventures as far as the blue and white striped artist's canteen. The fluorescent lights feel too bright and while it all seemed welcoming enough during the daylight, the rows of wooden trestle tables feel empty at this time of night. Anna has no desire to sit here on her own; it makes her feel even more lonely just thinking about it. Really she wants to be somewhere cosy like the Chai Chi Tent, where she can just hunker down and blend in and maybe feel a little of that special 'love' she had felt there before, maybe to feel the warm attention of the young man with the dreadlocks again – if by some chance he is still working this time of night.

Once back out onto the main track, she finds herself caught in a writhing mass of wet and drunken people. Though the rain has stopped, there is still a cold mist hanging in the air which gets right through Anna's clothes. Her feet slip in the watery mud, but she pushes on, watching the green laser lights splaying across the clouds, like spokes on a giant wheel.

Tonight the dragons on the archway are lit up in vibrant yellow light, and glow down from above as she passes beneath their arched wings. Beyond this is the field of human-sized wooden flowers, magically lit up with coloured light for the evening, Alice-in-Wonderland style.

Anna dodges her way through the crowds in the Park area, past the flashing lights of the bars and the neon signs of traders selling kebabs and pizza to where she remembers the Chai Chi Tent to be. The only obvious light shining from that direction now comes from the huge cut-out GLASTONBURY sign up on the hillside above, made in the style of the Hollywood sign, except that this one is a multitude of patchwork colours.

Moving closer, the Chai Chi Tent just becomes visible, with all its flaps closed up for the night and all its lights out. *Of all the places not to be lit up, why did it have to be this one?* Surrounded by hundreds of people who all seem to be partying with delight, Anna feels utterly alone and adrift.

Above her, the sixty foot observation tower with its Taj Mahal-like bobble on top and long strips of multi-coloured ribbons shines hypnotically in the darkness, glowing with red light. Anna watches it for a moment as it shifts to blue, and now purple, but the crowds are jostling around her and she loses her footing, slipping in the mud. She manages to catch herself just before plummetting into the slick below her.

There must be another way out of here, a quiet cafe where I can sit.

Her sights are drawn to a path, leading gently up the slope of the hill. She can just make out the pale tops of dozens of tipis, like beacons in the darkness. Her feet propel her forward, as if her body knows something about where she is going. She passes a few cafes alongside the muddy path, but none of them make her feel like stopping. They seem crowded and not really cosy. And even if they had been cosy, there is something about the majestic tipis that is pulling her onwards, like a magnet.

Now Anna sees something which makes her heart leap. A *tipi cafe! And it's open!* The first thing that catches her eye is the trail of little glowing candle lights inside paper bags which circle the perimeter. From inside, she can just make out the glow of a fire. A *fire!*

The cafe is made up of two tipis which have been joined together at the middle to make one larger structure. There is a main entrance on the far left side, and on the side closest to Anna is a smaller entrance, through which she can see little candlelit tables, each with its own white lantern. The faces of the people inside are lit by the firelight, and they all seem happy and relaxed.

She makes her way towards the larger of the two entrances, where the serving counter is, and sees to her delight that they are still offering food. The right side of the counter is filled with plates of cakes and raw chocolate truffles. Standing behind the left side of the counter is a pretty young woman with short ginger curls and a blue bindi between her eyebrows, deftly spreading crepe batter onto two pans. Anna feels a sense of familiarity about her, though she can't actually remember having met her before.

The cooking crepes sizzle and the steam carries a delightful mouth-watering aroma of cooking pancakes. While Anna waits her turn in the queue, and to take her mind off the griping hole inside her, she casts her eyes around at the interior of the two tipis. This is the first time she's even been inside a real tipi. The tall poles join together at the top of the tipi up above her head, the canvas pulled taut around them. There is a painting hung up above the counter, strung between two of the tipi poles. It's an image of a smiling Indian woman with a red spot between her eyebrows. Anna gazes at it for a few moments, wondering who she is, and what the spot between the eyebrows is all about.

The tables in the adjoining tipi are low wooden tables like the ones at the Chai Chi Tent, but these are hexagon-shaped and more ornately decorated. Each one holds a white hanging lantern with a warm, flickering flame inside it. In the centre of the space is a circular firepit, bordered by large stones housing a small, but warmly glowing fire. A trail of smoke spirals up to the point at the top of the tipi and out a little gap between the edges of the beige canvas wrapped around the wooden poles. It's a haven of cosiness. Even though the noise from the rest of the festival is still clearly audible here, it doesn't bother Anna so much in the calm of this place. Those settled here on their cushions are speaking softly or just sitting quietly, sipping their drinks and enjoying the ambience.

When it's finally Anna's turn at the counter, she orders an organic spelt chocolate and banana crepe and a chai tea from a slim man with the most extraordinary long, blond beard, which has been made into two neat braids. With the mug deposit, it comes to exactly £8.50 – which is exactly what she has in her pocket.

The man ladles out a mug of steaming chai and hands it over the counter to her. "Your name?" he asks.

"Anna," she answers, and watches him write it on a piece of paper which he passes to the ginger-haired woman.

He gestures to the eating area. "You can go find a seat. Your crepe will be ready in a few minutes."

"Thank you."

There is a sign beside the entrance into the eating area which reads: *Please take off your shoes*, so Anna kicks off her muddy boots and carries her mug across the carpets and floor matting to a free table. She would have liked to sit next to the fire, but all the spaces around it are occupied. Still, it's warm in here and the candlelight is soothing. Anna finds a cushion to sit on, embroidered with little shells and designs in brown and red, and places her chai on the table next to it. She sips from her steaming mug slowly, and feels the shaking in her body begin to settle.

Maybe they make their chai with love here, too, whatever that means.

From the corner of her eye, Anna sees a person rise from around the fire and leave out of the small entrance. Holding her chai carefully, she moves quickly to sit in the free space, as close as she can to the heat from the glowing embers. Even the stones which border the firepit are pleasingly warm. The shivers in her body are subsiding now, as the damp begins to leave her. Anna watches the little spirals of smoke as they rise from the flames and leave through the flap at the top of the tipi. Someone else across the firepit rises and leaves, too. The space is only empty for a few moments before the flames flicker with the swift arrival of a new presence around the fire.

I know her. The thought comes to Anna, along with a shock of recognition. *Don't I?* But Anna can't place where she could have met this woman. Surely she would remember someone so unusual.

Moon is usually bright and keen and sensitive to energy, but tonight she is full with the happenings of earlier, and uncharacteristically for her, she doesn't realise she is being watched. Not yet. For the moment, all her attention is given to the intensity at the heart of the fire which is an antidote to the raging torrent of emotion sweeping through her. She is struggling to maintain a constant vigilance of returning to the breath, again and again, as her thoughts threaten to overwhelm her. She knows all too well what her thoughts are capable of doing to her.

How could he have done that to me? The thought rakes through her mind again and again. *I thought we always said we would be honest with one another. Truth above all things. I thought he loved me.* As the thoughts rage through her body, Moon can feel what they are doing to her. She has been working with her thoughts for some time now, aware of how they can trigger her emotions. Before Moon learned how to witness her thoughts, they used to set off tidal waves of emotion, sending her into unpredictable rages, always with unwanted consequences.

Tonight she had managed to leave the earlier situation before it had turned critical, before she'd spoken out and said something she really would have regretted. As it is, she feels justified in what she's said. At least this is what she tells herself. *Because he deserved it.* The observer in Moon sees these thoughts which are not in alignment with her Heart's Self, but the Moon who is in control at the moment is choosing to allow herself to feel this feeling for now. She could have gone and cried in her tipi, and forgotten about what she had promised to do tonight, but a stronger impulse hadn't let her do that. Instead something had propelled her to this place, to sit by this fire – to see Maddy. She can feel Maddy there, behind the counter, and her presence is comforting.

This is a test for you, the thought comes to Moon. *If you can keep your awareness through this, you know you can keep it through just about anything.*

Again she breathes. She can feel the thoughts creating rough emotional ripples throughout her body, contracting her. So she returns her awareness to her breath, again and again, and to the intensity of the fire, as if it could purify her from all this. As if she could become the light itself. Or that it could somehow remind her of what she is.

Anna watches the intensity in the face of the young woman sitting across from her, still trying to work out whether she's met her somewhere before. The hair is unusual – dark, chin-length and cut in wild, wavy layers that frame her face, making it seem rounder than it is. She appears to Anna to be about her own age, maybe younger, except there's also something about this woman which seems to suggest maturity of a kind: the set of her jaw, the look in her grey-blue eyes.

What is she thinking about? Anna wonders.

Moon is a shapeshifter of a kind. She is as changeable as the tides, depending on the energy moving through her, which is how the medicine name 'Moon' came to her. Moon is both the dark and the light, and she knows it. She knows that for her, the way is to find balance. To reach the centre – where light and dark are one.

There's something else that catches Anna's attention. Even in the firelight, Anna can see that Moon isn't wearing any makeup, and that her skin is clear and tanned as if she has spent most of her time out of doors, which of course, she has. Moon prefers to live most of the summer and the months around it camping out in her tipi and walking in and around the wilds of Dartmoor.

Moon never wears make-up. Not even when she performs onstage. What she does love to do is paint her face, as she has done tonight, with delicate crescent moons in red and brown just above her cheekbones. Anna takes in the androgynous beauty of this face, the curve of the eyebrows, left natural and unplucked and the beautiful facepaint.

The thought comes to Anna that this young woman seems animal-like. It's in the way she holds herself, with a quiet power, sitting absolutely still, just breathing, in the way a wild creature would if they were alert, listening. This is how she appears on the outside to Anna. But inside, Moon's alertness is all about watching the waves of fury moving through her body with each returning thought.

How could he? After everything we've been through together?

And returning to the breath. Again. And again.

To Anna it seems as if Moon has the grace of a deer, but also there is a sense of something more predatory, like a wildcat or a bear, the kind of animal who could look serene and beautiful one moment, and either flee or turn on you in the next. This appearance is enhanced by the sleeveless leather vest Moon wears, that looks like what it is – a completely handmade garment, fur-fringed and embroidered with patterns. Moon sewed it herself, using an animal pelt that a friend of hers in America had given her. Moon derives comfort from wearing it. It reminds her of her animal nature and helps her feel the closeness of her animal spirit guides.

On her wrist, Moon wears two wristbands. Anna is surprised to see that one of them matches hers – a performer's wristband. The other wristband is made of yellow paper and has the words *Find Yourself* on it. Anna wonders briefly what that is about, as her eyes are drawn up Moon's sinewy arm muscles to the tattoo which swirls around her upper left arm. It's a running wolf, its legs and tail extended to stretch half way around her arm, making a kind of arm band.

A wolf. Yes. That's the animal I was trying to think of. This thought sends a wave of nervousness through Anna. Something about the wolf frightens her. The dark-haired young woman closes her fingers around a small, hand-stitched pouch which hangs from a cord around her neck and nestles at the centre of her chest. She squeezes it tightly, as if drawing strength from whatever it contains.

What's in there? Anna wonders.

Moon's skin prickles. She finally takes notice of the sensation that she is being watched. Her eyes refocus through the smoke to meet Anna's. *Oh, it's you.* The knowing comes to Moon before the thoughts can arise to question it.

Catching Moon's eyes, Anna flicks her gaze back into the fire, embarrassed to be caught staring. But as she lifts her eyes back she sees that the wolf-woman is smiling at her. It's a genuine smile, which startles Anna, because it's so different from the intense expression the woman had worn a moment ago when she hadn't known she was being watched. With this smile, her features have completely changed to reveal a bright, human liveliness.

This is one of Moon's shape-shifting moments. She isn't being false. It's just that she's allowing her whole self to respond to the current stimulus, which is her experience of meeting a friend. Moon has had this a few times in her life – an instant recognition. She's come to know this feeling happens with people she will have a significant relationship with in some way, who she has perhaps known before in other incarnations. The sense is of a sister.

Anna smiles tentatively back, wanting somehow to speak with the dark-haired woman, but feeling too tongue-tied. She runs through things in her mind that she could say, like *I like your tattoo...* and is about to speak out across the fire when the woman with the ginger hair and the bindi walks into the room and calls out gently with a soft, Irish lilt, "Anna? A crepe for Anna?"

"Oh! Yes! That's me. Thanks." Having forgotten her hunger momentarily in her fascination with the woman across the fire, it is now back with full force. Anna accepts the paper plate and wooden cutlery as if being handed some great treasure. The chocolate melts delightfully down the sides and pools beside it. Placing the plate on her lap, she digs in. The first mouthful is a heaven of warm sweet banana and melting chocolate.

As she eats, she notices from the corner of her eye that the woman with the bindi is now making her way around the fire, where she kneels down just behind the woman with the wolf tattoo, wrapping her arms affectionately around her as one would do with a special friend.

"Hello you." Moon relaxes into Maddy's arms, as if a weight has just been released from her. Now, instead of the raging heat through her body, Moon feels a wave of grief and her body heaves.

"What happened?" Maddy asks softly.

Moon shakes her head gently, releasing a great, shaky sigh. "I don't know where to begin."

"Is it Cedar?" Maddy asks.

Moon nods. "Who else?"

At the name Cedar, Anna's skin tingles. *Cedar? Who's that?* Her whole body leans forward, listening.

"He's playing tonight. In the Big Tipi," Moon tells Maddy. "Something had come through to Cedar about what we could do with our music – something to do with healing – and he had asked me to sing with him tonight. To try it."

Again, a shiver moves through Anna's body. *What's happening tonight in the Big Tipi?*

"It felt like so much like the right thing at the time we planned it..." Moon releases another sigh. "... but something happened just now and it's... changed everything. And now I don't know if I can go through with it. But I don't want to run away from it either. Maybe if you could come?" She turns around to face her friend. "I might be able to do it if you were there."

"Of course I'll come. I wouldn't miss it for anything. When is it?"

"Soon. At one. I'm just about to head up there, if I can sort myself out enough first."

"Okay. I'll have a word with the guys. I don't think they'll mind me knocking off a few minutes early. I'll come and find you."

Moon wraps both arms around Maddy and holds her, nestling into her cheek. "Thank you," she whispers. "That means a lot."

Anna watches these two women embracing and feels awkward, as if she's intruding on their privacy. She feels the contrast too, because she realises how much she actually longs for a friendship that has such warmth in it. Turning her head to the fire, she focuses on the nearly empty plate and cutlery in her lap, tracing lines in the remnants of the chocolate sauce with her wooden fork.

From the corner of her eye, Anna watches the ginger-haired woman return to the counter and she can hear her speaking in soft tones with the bearded man about getting off early.

They're about to go! I have to go too!

But the critical voice in her head offers its typical response. *You can't go. You don't know them. They'll think you're strange if you suddenly just invite yourself along. You won't fit in....*

Moon watches Maddy for a moment with a soft smile and then turns her gaze back to the fire, noticing the girl sitting across from her again. *She's sitting so tensely,* Moon thinks, observing the hunched shoulders and shallow breathing. Moon finds herself wanting to help this girl – having the sense that somehow she could.

Invite her along tonight, the thought comes. Moon hesitates, questioning the impulse. *If she looks up,* Moon tells herself, *I'll take that as a sign that I should invite her.* But the girl doesn't look up. Instead, it seems to Moon that she is deliberately trying not to.

Anna can feel Moon's eyes on her, watching her, but she's locked inside herself, too afraid to look up. And now, from the edge of her vision, she sees the wolf woman stand, rising with a slow, deliberate movement.

She's going! Say something to her! Anna cries to herself. *You're going to lose your chance!*

But I can't. What would I say?

Now Moon is padding across the matting, towards the exit with her smooth, graceful gait. Anna notices Moon's feet are caked with dirt and mud and watches her completely bypass the pile of wellies, to step out into the night and the mud, barefoot. Anna is so stunned for the moment that someone would actually want to walk barefoot in the cold mud that she almost misses Maddy leaving through the back a few minutes later.

Go! A shiver moves through Anna's body again. *Go. Go now.*

Standing bolt upright, she heads for the door with an urgency that surprises her, exchanging her mug on the way for the 50p mug deposit. But now Maddy is nowhere in sight. Fighting her way through the pile of wellies – which has grown significantly since she's been there – Anna hoists out her own mud-splattered pair and rams her feet into them, nearly slipping in the process. She rushes out into the night, casting her gaze in all directions for a shape that looks like Maddy.

Unrecognisable figures move by like shadows in the night. Anna fears she has lost her chance to find the Big Tipi, but a moment later Maddy emerges from behind the cafe and takes a left, deeper into the darkness of the Tipi Field.

Anna hesitates. *What are you doing Anna? You're stalking her,* the critical voice in her head taunts. But at the same time, she can't seem to stop herself. *I can always follow her for a little while and just stop. At least if I follow her now I won't lose the chance...*

Maddy is now passing by the central fire blazing at the heart of the Tipi Field, made with three giant cedar logs all pushed together at the centre. Standing above the fire is a twenty foot tall totem pole, lit in the dark like a beacon. *How strange,* Anna thinks. *Tipis and totem poles in a green field at Glastonbury. What does it all mean?*

Clusters of people sit around the fire, their faces lit by the glow. A couple of them are playing djembes. *Well, I could always get warm around this fire,* Anna tells herself, even as she knows that this is a far second best to whatever will be happening in that Big Tipi. Heart pounding against her ribs, she follows as Maddy takes a quick right into a cluster of tipis.

There is no question which one is the Big Tipi. It stands several feet taller and wider than the other tipis which surround it and is decorated with patterns of dancing animals. A faint glow of firelight from the tipi's entrance highlights Maddy's silhouette for a moment before she slips inside. Anna moves closer, but holds herself back in the shadows.

Outside the tipi there are a series of rough handmade wooden benches surrounding an outdoor firepit – currently unlit. The benches are just close enough to the Big Tipi to hear what would be going on inside, but just far enough away to be inconspicuous. Or at least this is what Anna hopes. Sitting down, she feels like an intruder, sneaking about in the shadows.

A chill wind blows and she shivers again. Some minutes pass, and she is growing colder. Still too afraid to invite herself in, she knows she will have to give up soon. There is no sign yet of anything significant happening within the tipi, only the soft murmur of the voices of those waiting inside.

Is Cedar in there? Her heart thumps again with the thought.

The sound of approaching footsteps in the wet grass brings Anna to attention. In the strange light, she recognises the figure of Moon, walking with her animal-like stride.

As Moon moves closer to the tipi, her eyes take in the smoke spiralling out the top, and the light of the fire glowing through the open flap. *I wonder if he's here yet.* But she knows the answer. He won't be here yet. He will be waiting for the moment when everyone else is already here, and then he can make his grand entrance. A small smile rises to her lips. She knows this is just his way. As she tunes in and sends her senses through the canvas of the tipi, it confirms to her that he is not here. He's still preparing himself. *Still trying to centre himself,* Moon surmises, realising that he too must have been quite affected by their interaction earlier.

In those moments since leaving Pacha Mama's and arriving here, something has shifted for Moon. She had gone to lie down for a moment back in her own tipi, wondering if she really could pull herself together and do this. Lying on her bed with her hands on her heart, she had willed the energy to flow and shift the painful feelings, but the grief coming up had been too much. It wanted looking at, and feeling. It wasn't going to be shifted so easily. So she had allowed it to take her as she curled into herself, wracking and heaving and feeling like she might never move again.

He will not be the father of your child. This knowledge had hammered inside Moon again and again. Really, she had known this all along, she just hadn't wanted to see it. She now recognises all the deeply held wishes, the fantasies she had created that had made her blind. She'd resisted being with other men – or women for that matter – because a part of her would not let go of that possibility with Cedar. No other person had shone for her the way Cedar had. How could she have considered anyone else? When they had such a deep connection, and such obvious love between them. He was a soulmate. She had been certain of it. Even more, he had said as much too, and one thing Moon knows about Cedar is that while he might intentionally withhold the truth, he would never consciously lie. *Although,* she wonders, *perhaps withholding truth can be as dishonest as an outright lie, if it leads someone else to believe something that isn't true.*

She had lain there in her tipi, convulsed in her grief. The tears had heaved inside her and she'd wanted to scream at him again. Instead, she had found herself hissing like a snake, as if to expel the venom of the feelings. There was nobody she'd been closer to ever. They had shared everything. But he had kept something so important from her. He'd shut her out from the truth in his heart. He'd been her best friend. He'd been her everything. She hadn't admitted it to herself until then, but she had held him up in her heart, even above her own self. And now, it is as if she has been cracked open from the inside, her deeply cherished dreams being ripped out by the roots.

All the while she had lain there, the observer had still been present in Moon, observing, and a quieter voice had softly been asking the questions, *Is it true? Was he the one who was supposed to be the father of your child? Was it selfish and wrong of him to withhold that information? Did he really make you wait? Did he delude you intentionally?*

The feelings were still strong, though, and had Moon found it hard to really listen to that softer part of herself. The feelings had their own thoughts, and as they moved through her, images played in her mind. So the waves of pain had kept coming and she had kept crying, until a kind of quiet exhaustion had settled over her and she felt she might just sleep, and not go to the Big Tipi after all. Just let it all be.

But then something had happened. She had felt a softness, like someone hugging her, holding her – an energy. It was a familiar feeling. Someone was giving her healing. It could have been an angel. It could have been Maddy sending her healing energy. Whatever it was, it had awoken her. She had felt it soothing and soothing until what was left of the pain had dissolved and what had remained was a feeling of calm awareness and of being loved.

Moon had sat up then and remembered herself, and her own techniques for centering. She breathed into her belly. She rooted herself into the Earth. She was able to right herself, and by the time she had stepped out of the tipi under the Glastonbury night, she had felt able to do this.

Now, approaching the tipi, she can see that someone is there on the bench, waiting. Moon can't see who it is, but she feels a shiver of recognition move through her body. It's someone she knows.

Anna watches as the figure of Moon stops a few paces away from her, with the distinct sense that Moon knows she is there.

Moon steps closer. "Who is that?"

"It's me, Anna," she whispers back.

Moon steps closer again, until Anna can just see her face in the soft faint glow of the firelight from the tipi. "I know you... You were in Pacha Mama's just now, weren't you? Across the fire from me?"

"Yes," Anna admits.

There is a pause, which Anna finds much more awkward than Moon does. For in that space, Anna becomes certain that Moon must know she had eavesdropped around the fire and had followed them here. *She knows, I must seem an idiot...*

For Moon's part, she is listening inside herself, for she has the sense that this is important. Finally, the words arrive and Moon speaks them aloud. "Are you waiting for someone?"

Tell her the truth, the feeling comes to Anna.

But how can I? She'll think I'm desperate or strange for following them here. Yet now, with the firelight catching Moon's clear eyes, which seem to expect truth, Anna knows there is no choice.

"I... this is going to sound strange... but I heard you mention around the fire that you would be playing some music here tonight. I was curious... I mean, I wasn't expecting to come in or anything, but I just wanted to listen a little, from out here."

Ahh, so she knows it too. The same guidance comes again to Moon. *Invite her in.* Moon nods, satisfied. "You can come in. I don't think anyone would mind at all. You'd be welcome."

"Are you sure?"

"Of course."

As Anna rises from the bench Moon holds her hand over her own heart in greeting. "I'm Moon."

"Anna." Instinctively, Anna follows the gesture. "I like your name." It does seem to her to be the perfect name for this unusual woman.

"Thanks. I like it too. That's why I picked it." Moon thinks back briefly to that moment a few years ago when she had made the choice to take on a medicine name. That was the moment her life had changed. She had chosen a new path, and the new name had been a part of that. It had come to her in a dream – a dream of a howling wolf and a great full moon, which waxed and waned in one night, showing her all the light and dark of herself, all the ways in which she moved with the tides. For her, Moon was a name to honour the cycles and the sacred movement of emotion. It reminds her to honour all that arises, and to let it flow through her, whatever it may be.

And can I do that tonight? she wonders.

Anna follows Moon towards the entrance. As Moon steps through the flap, she wipes her muddy feet on a towel, revealing another tattoo just below her left ankle, a crescent moon. Stepping in after her, Anna comes into the rounded interior of the tipi where there are half a dozen other people, already sitting there cross-legged around a central fire, waiting. Everyone else seems to have bare feet, so as well as removing her boots, Anna peels off her socks too and leaves them both outside the tipi entrance. The bare soles of her feet feel sensitive against the rough matting on the ground. It doesn't help her numb toes, but at the same time it's not unpleasant. It's been a long time since she went barefoot anywhere. This feels like a kind of nakedness to her.

Moon moves around the fire towards Maddy, who is already settled with a wool blanket around her shoulders and sits cross-legged on a sheepskin at the far side of the tipi. Maddy's eyes are softly focused into the fire, but when she sees Moon approaching, she looks up with a smile of deep affection. After a lingering moment, Maddy turns her eyes to Anna and offers her a bright smile of recognition. The warmth of it takes the edge off the feeling Anna is nursing of being an outsider, an interloper.

Moon settles next to Maddy, right up close to her, hip to hip and shoulder to shoulder. Maddy opens her blanket and Moon snuggles in next to her, feeling the strength of her friend's energy moving right into her own body.

Cedar isn't here yet, but he's close. At the thought of him, Moon reminds herself to breathe, because even with the healing of earlier, whatever it was – she reminds herself to ask Maddy later if it was her – there is still grief and hurt there right beneath her ribs, like a feral animal, ready to knot her up again with a stray thought. This is a moment of truth for her and Cedar.

Sitting next to them, Anna leaves a conscious gap between herself and Moon, so as not to disturb the murmuring closeness of the two women. She can see that Maddy has extended her blanket to include Moon within it, and Maddy's hand is affectionately rubbing the centre of Moon's back. Moon's eyes are closed, receiving this gesture. There is a familiarity and an intimacy between these two women. Next to them, Anna feels awkward and out of place. *I have no right to be here. I don't belong here. I'm not like them.* The thoughts barrage her mind.

It is strange for Anna to see such a strong friendship between two women. They aren't behaving like lovers exactly, just like two people who are extremely fond of each other and not afraid to show it. Anna thinks about how she's never been that close to any of her female friends, and certainly has never cuddled with any of them. Cuddling for her is reserved only for the person who is her current partner. And even then... In that moment, she sees that even with her boyfriends, even with Damien, she's never felt completely comfortable being affectionate. She's always held herself back, always hid parts of herself away. Johannes had said that about her, and he'd been right.

There's always a certain distance between me and other people, Anna realises. Maybe that's just how I am. The aching of that thought hides the quieter feeling that follows it – But I wish I wasn't.

She chooses to focus her attention instead on the softness of the sheepskin beneath her, and how it feels against her bare feet, the woolly strands poking between her toes. The part nearest the fire is lovely and warm. Anna stretches her feet out, closer to the source of the heat, feeling just how cold her toes had gotten in the short time she'd been sitting outside on the bench. The fire has been burning for quite some time, as even the rocks around the edge of it are quite hot to the touch, which Anna discovers when one of her big toes edges too close to them. The embers glow brightly and a small trail of smoke spirals up to the point of the tipi, wending its way out the small opening at the top.

It is much more spacious inside the tipi than Anna had expected it would be. Perhaps it is the result of the glowing firelight in the centre of the tipi and the lanterns lit around the edges, which cast everyone in a warm, golden glow and make their shadows dance on the tipi walls. It doesn't seem to be a space anyone sleeps in, rather more like a ceremonial or meeting space. It is very clear and sparse, with a neatly laid pile of wood next to the fire pit. As well as the faint scent of woodsmoke, there is a pleasing aroma of recently burned herbs or incense. Someone has smudged the space with sage.

Anna lifts her eyes to take in the other people sitting around the fire. In addition to herself, Moon and Maddy, there are three other people there. Looking around, Anna is certain that Cedar – whoever he is – has not yet arrived. There are only two men here and neither of them look like someone named 'Cedar'. One of the men, a quiet-looking, slim and slightly balding man is sitting next to Anna. He wears a red shirt with a yellow mandala pattern on it, like the man in the Chai Chi Tent.

Paul is a friend of Cedar's, and he can feel this is going to be a special night. He doesn't normally like to stay up so late, but for this he will make an exception. Cedar had asked him to be here. Feeling Anna's gaze, he lifts his eyes to offer her a smile of welcome.

There is warmth in the smile and Anna returns it briefly, but as her residual feelings about men being friendly for a reason resurface, she flicks her eyes onward around the fire. The other man there is younger and shorter, with curly reddish hair, a friendly face and a determinedly grown little beard fuzzing his chin. Anna guesses he could be about her age, but the mischievous roundness of his face makes him look much younger.

She notices – while trying not to obviously stare at him – that this man's gaze keeps returning in the direction of Moon. Every so often, when Moon looks up in his direction, he quickly looks away. Moon of course, knows he is watching her. It gives Moon a sweet feeling. She's fond of Alex – or Crow as she calls him. He's the new drummer in their band. He has a kind of innocence about him, and she can see he is opening more each day through the music they are playing. He's a good drummer, and getting better the more present he becomes. She catches him looking at her sometimes in rehearsals. She doesn't want to let her ego be fed by it. For to be desired by one man can sometimes ease the pain of not being wanted in that way by another man. And yet, Moon knows Crow is not for her. But still, she is fond of him. He makes her laugh. So sometimes, when he looks over at her – like he is doing now – she will look up and smile at him, but not with the smile that says yes. It is the smile that says, I *am fond of you, but that's as far as it goes.*

Anna watches the silent interchange between these two, feeling moved by it, for some reason she can't explain to herself. Whoever this man is, there is a sweetness about him. The other thing which endears him to her is that like her, he is unable to sit quite as still as the rest of the people in the space. As if, like her, he is not quite comfortable in his own skin. He fidgets every few minutes, seeming uncomfortable with the silence.

There is a sudden change inside the tipi – from one of quiet expectancy to one of humming imminence.

He's coming. Moon can feel it even before she hears the soft padding of his feet on the grass outside. Others can feel it too; those who were sitting quietly are now shifting their positions and turning their attention to the entrance of the tipi.

Anna holds her breath, hearing the sound of movement outside. The first thing she sees coming through that entrance is a hand – a supple, muscular and long fingered hand – carrying a smooth wooden instrument with a flared end. A didgeridoo. The fingers hold the instrument with such care, manoeuvering it through the opening. The abalone shells inset into the wood are carved in the shape of a bird and glint in the firelight.

Following the didgeridoo is a man of the like Anna has never encountered. Heat moves through her body in response to the presence of this person. A rush of energy, a tingling on the skin. Her body knows what her mind does not. On a soul level, this is a reunion.

She notices Cedar's bare feet, and how like Moon, he must have been walking barefoot outside. This is a further confirmation to Anna of this man's wildness. He tucks the didgeridoo under his arm and wipes his feet on the towel left by the door. As he stands, straightening to his full height, he seems tall to Anna. But then she sees the entrance behind him and realises he must only be slightly above average height for a man. And yet, he seems to be the biggest thing here.

In this heightened state, with his gaze in soft, peripheral vision, Cedar can see the energy around those present, and this tells him who is here. Moon has come. He feels a relief about this, but with it rises an equivalent feeling of challenge. The question is still surfacing – *Can we still do it, with everything that has happened between us?*

The heat of Moon's gaze is on him, but he doesn't look directly at her yet. From the corner of his eye, he can see the swirls of her energy, much more settled than earlier, but still fiery, with little flares like storms on the sun. *And next to her... Who is that?* A flash of recognition moves through Cedar. He can't see the young woman's face clearly because the tousled locks of her hair are hanging down, as if she's hiding. Her aura is withdrawn and close to her body. She seems sad, tense. Yet, there is something about her which gives a lift to Cedar's heart. He can just make out the slender nose and the gentle, feminine hands, with those fingers – so familiar somehow – stroking the softness of the sheepskin.

Who are you? he wonders again.

A memory comes to him of the moment earlier in the day when he had been up on the hill, and playing his didge out towards the old oak tree, sending his blessing out. *You are Love.* Now, he realises looking back, there had been the sense of someone he had been sending that blessing to. Someone he hadn't even met yet. Someone who needed it. He hadn't thought too much about it at the time, but now the presence of the memory here in this moment gives him the answer. *It was for her.*

This feeling of recognition has happened to Cedar a few times in his life. For him, it always means there is a soul connection, that the meeting is significant and life changing. He felt something like this the first time he saw Moon, and before that with a woman back in Australia when he was younger. Both of those meetings had resulted in very intense sexual relationships. The resonance of this places Cedar on alert, because that is not an option right now.

In the past, sex itself had been a spiritual path for Cedar. When he and Moon had become involved sexually, they had engaged in Tantric practices together as a means to experience unity. However, they had never quite managed to reach the state of being they sought. They had come close, but something had always eluded them. Because somehow making love with Moon had been like tousling with a wild animal, being devoured, wanted, eaten and satiated, lifeforce spent. But even so, they had continued to try. Right up until the time when things had changed between them and he had chosen a different path. It had taken all his willpower to do so. *So whoever this girl is*, Cedar tells himself, *it can't be about sex.*

And yet, seeing her sitting there like this, hiding behind those strands of her hair, seeming lost, evokes a feeling of protectiveness in him. He finds himself wanting to take care of her, to offer her something. He takes a breath to clear his mind of this rush of thoughts that aren't about this moment now.

How easily you are thrown my friend, he smiles to himself, allowing his attention to move around the circle, taking in the others who are there, offering them smiles of greeting. There is Shona, next to the entance. A stalwart of the tipi fields, she has arranged for this to happen tonight. She's a sweet lady who is offering him that smile of hers now, a mostly wholesome, but with a hint of desire kind of smile. At Cedar's request, Shona had lit the fire and smudged the inside and outside of the tipi with sage.

You've done a good job, Cedar nods to her. Shona flushes with Cedar's appreciation.

Next to Shona is Alex, who gives Cedar a thumbs up. Beside him is Paul, who nods a greeting. Paul is one of Cedar's oldest friends and an energy worker. Cedar is pleased to see him here, as he knows Paul will be helping energetically tonight. Next to Paul is the girl. Then there is Moon, who has not met his eyes yet. And beside her, dear Maddy. Maddy offers Cedar a wide, friendly smile, which he returns with fondness. Things are simple with Maddy and always have been. In all the time he has known Moon, Maddy has been like a sister to them both.

He breathes in the familiar scents of the tipi and the woodsmoke and drying canvas and earth. Feeling his favourite instrument in his hands, he knows he will be able to play tonight. After his preparation earlier, a strong energy had begun to course through him, and it pulses more strongly with the awareness that something special will happen here tonight, something which involves everyone here.

Anna allows herself another look at Cedar, now that his attention is not directed this way. Hardly breathing, she watches the way his long, straight, blond hair flashes in the firelight as he moves, a perfect combination of wild and yet recently combed. His skin is smooth, too, recently shaved. He wears a sleeveless, beige vest, with russet-red embroidery along the hems. At the centre of his chest hangs a carved bone pendant in the shape of a swirl on a leather cord. His arms are bare too, showing a yellow band on his left wrist – the same as Moon's, with the words *Find Yourself* on it.

What is that? And how do I get one? Anna wonders.

Around Cedar's waist is a belt – also part of his sacred performing costume – which he made for himself from found leather and a hanging feather of his totem animal, found on his last trip to Canada. He picked up the feather one day in a forest of deep silence, and had asked the spirit of that place whether he might keep it. It had felt like a gift left for him. One of the smaller wing feathers, it might be mistaken for the feather of another, smaller bird, but he knew what it was the moment he saw it.

There is a symbol of this bird tattooed on his upper left arm, in the same place as Moon's running wolf. And like Moon's, it is simple and elegant, the outstretched wings of the great bird of prey reaching almost around his bicep to make an armband.

Anna recognises the similarity between the two tattoos. It is clearly no coincidence, and confirmation to Anna of a history Moon and Cedar must have together, which creates an unconscious, contracting wave of jealousy.

But perhaps they are not together now? she wonders, remembering Moon's conversation with Maddy in the cafe. Realising what she's doing, Anna chides herself furiously again. *Anna, how can you be jealous? Get a grip on yourself! You've only just seen this man. And you have a boyfriend! And besides, if he's been with Moon already, how could he want you?*

As if hearing this thought, Cedar turns his head sharply towards Anna. Before she can drop her gaze and hide again behind the wisps of her hair, she catches the look of deep intensity in those eyes, reflecting the fire, flashing with shadow and light. Seeing her. Looking right inside. Then turning away.

Oh God. The shock of it leaves her heart pounding.

The thought comes to her that if she were to really let him look at her for more than just a flash of second, he might lay her bare, and that she would be able to hide nothing. Johannes' words ring in her mind. *You need to find with someone you can share your whole heart with. You will never be happy in a relationship until you can find a person like that, and be the kind of person who can open yourself up in return.*

A desire flashes inside her that this man should see her, all of her. That given the chance, she would bare everything for him. Shocked and disturbed by this sudden awareness, she pushes the feeling back, repelling it. The feeling moves deeper inside her, but her body will not be told so easily. Cedar walks across the mat to the clear space that has been left for him beside Maddy. Anna notices the sway of his hips in those beige cotton yoga trousers. They are a thin fabric and almost translucent in the firelight. She floods herself with guilt. *Stop it, Anna.*

Moon watches Cedar approach, and breathes down into her belly again. *You can do this,* she tells herself. *Please, Wolf Spirit. Please, Pachamama. Bring me strength. Let me serve and not need. Let me have love inside me on this night. Let healing flow. Let me be open, an instrument of love and healing.*

With this invocation, she feels an energy swirl up her body, and knows it will be so. Still breathing, she allows herself to lift her eyes to meet his for the first time since he has arrived.

As Cedar regards the fire in Moon's eyes, for a brief moment his mind slips out of the present, drawn back into a memory of their last meeting.

It began with a simple hug back in Cedar's tipi. They had embraced with their usual warmth. Then she had held him a little longer. So he'd returned the gesture, feeling the love flow towards her, giving her some extra energy. As he did this, he felt her draw herself closer to him. There was a mischief in it at first, as if she was jokingly trying to tempt him to do what they had already agreed many months before not to do. There was a new intensity in it this time, though. He could feel her need for him, and it aroused his need. So he had pulled away from her and breathed deeply into his core like he'd been practising, drawing the sexual energy up his spine, feeling it giving him energy. But Moon had pulled herself closer to him again, predatory, moving her hips against him, her breath on his neck, her lips brushing across his skin, inviting him, saying with her body, *Why not? Why not just this once? We used to do this so easily. Why not let me devour you again?*

Again he had felt himself rise to it. Really rise to it. *Stop it Moon.*

It would have been so easy just to go with it. But no, not with what they had planned for tonight. And not for all the other reasons. No. He pulled back again, this time feeling a flash of anger at her deliberate disregard of their agreement.

"Moon. What are you doing?"

She set her wolf eyes on him, daring him. "You know what I'm doing Cedar. Don't you think it's been long enough?"

That was the moment it had become clear to him what was necessary. What he should have done many months ago. He had to tell her the truth. All of it.

"There's something I have to tell you."

"So tell me then," she whispered in his ear, her breath a shiver up his body. How easy it would have been not to tell her and just forget the whole thing, and go to the bed with her and let all that raw energy take its course, and be devoured again. *And why not?* a part of him was answering her. *Why not this once?*

Because this once would lead to again. And again. And what would your vision mean then?

He pulled gently back from her once more. "Sit with me." He guided them down to the foot of his sleeping pallet and took a deep breath. And told her everything – the whole of the dream vision that had come to him. Especially the part about the dream woman who had come to him, and what she had said.

As he spoke, he could see Moon's whole body changing, withdrawing, seeming to crackle with a charge, fury erupting in her eyes and her opening mouth.

"You lied to me." She shook her head, unbelieving. "How could you do that to me? Me?"

"I didn't lie. I just didn't tell you that part, because I didn't think it was relevant and I figured it would only hurt you."

"Hurt me? You were worried about hurting me? And so instead you lead me here, a year later, a year of waiting for you, to tell me the truth now?"

"I wasn't trying to lead you on, Moon. But I'll admit I probably should have told you before this."

"Yeah. You really really should have told me, Cedar. Holy Shit."

She sat back and shook her head as if trying to clear it. She took a breath, and looked back up at him. "Okay. Let's just look at this for a minute, okay? Maybe your vision was symbolic. You think she was a real woman, telling you that she was going to carry your child, but maybe she was a symbol of Shakti, the divine feminine, the energy of creation, inviting you to create with her."

The thought had occurred to him. At times the woman, with her black hair, almond skin and deep dark eyes that smiled so brightly had seemed the embodiment of the divine feminine. They were interchangeable in his mind. And yet, still, she had felt so real.

"Did she actually ask you to wait for her?" Moon asked.

"No. But she said she was waiting for me, so I pledged the same thing."

"The energy of the divine feminine is always waiting for us to open up to her, to allow her to flow through us, to create through us. It's a metaphor, Cedar. Can't you see your dream was symbolic?"

"I'm sure it was highly symbolic. Like dreams can be."

Moon's face showed her obvious irritation at this comment. Cedar could see she was trying to hold herself together, but the pressure was building.

She spoke slowly. "Cedar, everyone knows that conceiving a child in a dream is symbolic for creativity." Her eyes flashed at him, challenging him.

He knew she was right. These symbols were strong, but even so, the woman was real. He knew it, as much as he'd known anything. He had to keep reminding himself of that. It had been an experience of meeting another soul, like himself – two kindred souls coming together in the realm of dreams.

"What exactly did she look like then?"

Why should I tell you that? He felt a mild irritation move through him. "Why do you want to know? Are you trying to torture yourself or something?"

"No." She glared at him. "Just humour me for a moment, Cedar. You owe me that much at least."

He sighed. "Okay fine. She was tall, beautiful woman, with brown skin, long, dark hair and very dark, wise eyes. She wore a bindi between her eyebrows and looked like she was from India. She was unclothed, except for the bells on her ankles. And she had a beautiful singing voice."

He remembers that it was her voice he had first heard that night. He'd gone on a vision quest and had been out camping by himself under the stars, hoping for some insight about the feelings that had been coming up in the months before that, the sense that something was missing. He'd lit the fire and had sat in meditation for a long time. Some time later, he had lain down and watched the sky and had fallen into a kind of sleep. But it had been an aware sleep; he'd observed himself dreaming. In the dream, he was sitting just as he had been when he was awake and meditating. It was night time, with the stars sparkling overhead, just as they had been when he had fallen asleep, but they seemed brighter now. Everything shimmered. The fire was the same fire he had been sitting by that night, but it too seemed to glow even brighter and more golden. Across the fire from him was a path he hadn't noticed before. He'd watched this path for a while, wondering where it would lead to, when he heard the most beautiful singing, with the sound of gentle, tinkling bells. It had touched his soul. A figure appeared in the distance, hazy at first, but as she drew closer, the fire illuminated the naked body of this extraordinarily beautiful woman. She had come and sat across the fire from him, the firelight shining in her face and sparkling in her eyes. Those eyes were the deepest eyes he had ever seen. For a long time, they had witnessed one another. Nothing needed to be said, for so much had been expressed in that wordless communion.

"Shakti," Moon said. "I know your mind, Cedar. If ever there was a personification in your mind of what Shakti would look like, that would be it."

"Moon, I know as well as you do that while Shakti may well be a Sanskrit name, it does not mean that the creative force in the universe is actually an Indian woman. Shakti is divine feminine creative energy, present in all life, in all beings."

"Oh please. Be honest with me, Cedar. Tonight of all nights. If you were to personify Shakti, what would she look like to you?" Moon's hands were on her hips, her eyes still a challenge.

"You have to let this go, Moon. I'm not going to change my mind. You can't rationalise me out of this."

"I'm not, Cedar. I'm trying to understand something, okay? Can you not just answer my question?"

Taking another breath, letting out the frustration, he turned his mind to her question, and saw that of course she was right – at least about that. If he had to personify Shakti, she would look exactly like that beautiful woman from his dream.

"I can see the metaphor Moon. I can. And yes, I do see the divine feminine in her. But it's more than that. I know you don't want to see this, but she is real – as real as anyone I've met in the flesh, and in some ways more so. Nothing you say will change that. I gave her my word that I would abstain from physical sex with a woman until the point when we would consciously create a child. And I intend to keep that vow." He knew the word 'child' would escalate matters for Moon, but at that point, he was beginning to get past the point of caring.

"A metaphorical creative child," she flared at him.

"No, Moon. A real child."

For a moment, Moon looked like she might sob, but then she turned her face to him, chin set, eyes steeled. "So tell me straight then, Cedar. Just so I have it absolutely clear in my mind. The reason you won't make love with me tonight – was it because you wanted to preserve your ojas, like you said before, or because of this vow you made to this... apparent woman?"

He took another conscious breath, knowing that even with his growing anger, he owed her honesty.

"Both. But the vow to her is what keeps me faithful to that."

That is what had tipped it. Moon's lips had drawn into a hard line. "So that's it, then? You're telling me in no uncertain terms that it can never happen between us? Ever again?"

Cedar breathed down into his belly, feeling the truth inside him. "Yes. I guess I thought that's what I was saying when I first told you about the vision, but I must not have made it clear. The truth is, I love you Moon. We're connected on a soul and a heart level, but I have to honour..."

Moon exploded to her feet, "Give it a rest Cedar, with your fucking honour! You know, you couldn't be clear with me, because you weren't clear with yourself. You didn't want to let me go. You wanted to keep your lofty spiritual ideals, and also keep a woman who idolised you and made you feel good about yourself. And you want to stop yourself from feeling that animal self inside you, that part of you that wants to do it all. That part of you isn't gone, Cedar. You want to deny you're humanness? In case you've forgotten... you do have a dick!"

Moon never would have used this term in the past when she and Cedar were together intimately. She always used to call it *Vajra*, meaning 'thunderbolt' in Sanskrit, or sometimes *Lingham*, for 'shaft of light'. He knew she was just trying to get him to react, to push his buttons. And she was beginning to succeed.

Cedar's own hackles were starting to rise. His own 'shenpa', to use the Buddhist term for being hooked on the dramas of the ego. Usually these days, he was able to catch it before it hooked him and took him over. So, witnessing it in that moment, he tried not to resist the feelings, to breathe into them, to become even more present. He began to feel in control of himself again, feeling that centering of himself and the heightened awareness that comes with it.

"I know what you're doing Cedar," Moon glared at him, baring her teeth. "I can see you doing your deep breathing, trying to be all spiritual and Buddha-like."

Cedar suppressed a laugh, but couldn't avoid smiling. Moon's perceptiveness extended even into these moments of unconscious reaction. In fact, her triggers had often been related to his spiritual exercises.

"I can see you breathing, trying not to be pulled off centre by me. Trying to be all spiritual, because here I am, caught up in my rage and God forbid that might happen to you!"

He kept breathing, witnessing her, witnessing the thoughts that came, breathing into his heart and staying present.

"You're up there on your spiritual high horse, Cedar, but you refuse to accept that when you failed to tell me the whole story, you lead me to believe there could be a future for us. You allowed me to create a story where there was still a possibility for us."

"But I told you not to wait for me."

"But of course I would Cedar! How could I not? After everything? You told me I was your soulmate. How could a soulmate not wait for you? Unless that was a lie too."

"I never lied to you Moon. I still believe you are my soulmate. At least one of them. But you know as well as I do that just because someone is your soulmate doesn't mean you are supposed to marry them. You just have a deep journey with them for a while and become transformed and then..."

"Oh please! You're not being honest with yourself, Cedar. Or me. You didn't want to let me go. You were being fed on what I gave you, on the energy I was still feeding you, on still being desired by me. And even though we stopped having physical sex, you know as well as I do, that you were still accepting that energy from me. You and your flaming ojas."

Cedar felt her last words like a slap in the face as she whirled around to leave. "So what about the music tonight then?" His words stopped her in her tracks, and she spun around again to face him.

"So what about it? It's obviously off."

"For you maybe."

"Well, we're not going to be able to make music together in this state are we?"

"We might not be able to. But I will."

"Oh. Of course. You will because you're so bloody spiritual. You're seriously going to do it?"

"Yes."

"Without me?"

"Well that depends on you, doesn't it? It's entirely up to you whether you can pull yourself together and do some healing or not."

Moon's mouth fell open and he could see that he'd struck a serious nerve. "Pull myself together? Come off your spiritual high horse, Charlie. You're as human as I am." She spat this name out. And this is what had done it for Cedar. The use of his old name as if it were an insult. His conscious self had subsided then in the flare of his triggers, as they got the better of him temporarily. *It's not fair of you to use that name here, Moon.* In his mind she has seriously wronged him by doing this. She'd stepped over the line.

"Be careful, Moon," he growled at her.

She looked like she was going to say more. He could read the rage in her eyes. They regarded one another for a moment in the firelight. Then she turned on her heel and was gone into the night.

He was furious that she had managed to pull that lonely, angry self out of him, the part of him he had always associated with the hardest years of Charlie Pemberton's life. The young adolescent male who, picked on by his peers for his sensitivities had resorted to spending time alone and in nature. Who had become a mysterious loner, and at some point had become attractive to women. And he had needed that attention because inside he had been empty. He was also equally furious that she had spoken of his sacred ojas like that and debased it in that way.

Temporarily out of control of himself, he set off into the night. Just to move his legs. Just to go somewhere. It had been a long time since he had allowed someone to knock him off his centre.

As he tore up the hill, an animal rage was building. He wanted to roar at her, to roar at the sky. *Yes! It has been fucking hard! Yes I am a fucking man!* He thought of the nights he had given himself release in the past year. He had tried to make it a conscious spiritual experience each time, and not just a physical one, but something has always been missing for him. He knows that he is a sexual being. The feeling to express that in physicality with a women has almost been too much for him in the past year, and tonight it had been close. He had almost broken his vow.

What are you doing Cedar? What has she done to you? He doesn't know which *She* he is thinking of. Both of them: She, the woman in the vision, and She, Moon, who has made him question his vision, and who had shown him what he hadn't wanted to look at.

As he walked, feeling his bare feet on the grass, step after step up the hill, Cedar began to become aware of his body again and to remember the earth below his feet. It was enough to remind him of his techniques for centering. So he tried to consciously breathe into his belly, but he became annoyed even at that, feeling there was too much frustration. Each breath seemed to come out like a growl. As the slope steepened, he felt the physical exertion of the speed at which he was pushing himself up the hill, and the breath wouldn't be controlled, so he just let it be, focusing on his feet and his thighs and the rough grass.

There was only one place to go, up to his chosen spot, overlooking the festival, where he had come earlier to play his instrument. It is a place where he could feel nature at its strongest, and seek the guidance and energy of Pachamama to give him strength.

He pumped his way up there so fast his thighs burned, even though they were used to hard walking. He sat on the wet ground, not caring that it soaked his trousers through in seconds. He wanted to feel the earth.

He didn't want to accept that Moon had been right about some things, but he knew she was. He hadn't wanted to let her go. With that knowing came the guilt.

Everything was reeling. He stared out at the sea of lights below him and the flares of searchlights radiating across the clouds. Usually when he was up here he could smell the clear air from the far hills and feel the trees at his back, and the energy of the rolling earth below him, but tonight, with all that had happened, he felt desensitised. A new fury rose again at Moon for doing that to him.

His eyes came to rest on the tree – the tree that judged nothing, accepted all, was part of the flow of life. It hadn't changed. He remembered what he had played out to the tree.

You are Love.

In his memory, Cedar recalls the moment presence returned to him.

There on the hill, the shiver moves through his body, like the wind blowing it all away. He closes his eyes and feels the air against his skin and the blades of grass and the cool earth beneath the soles of his feet. His breath begins to settle. He watches his body, just breathing, each breath a little more still than the last. It takes many breaths, but finally he feels the shenpa dissolving. In its wake is a stillness.

He can see what happened now. Moon hasn't done anything to him. *I've done it to myself.*

Even before he'd had the vision, his inner guidance had been telling him that he was depleting his vital energies through too much sexual activity. He hadn't wanted to listen to that. He had wanted to make sex part of his spiritual path. He and Moon had come across teachings of the ojas in their study of Tantra. They learned about this primary vital energy, which is particularly found in the sexual fluids of a man or woman, and how through spiritual practises like Tantra it is possible to transform the ojas into spiritual strength. But because of the alchemy of himself and Moon, the ojas were always quite spectacularly released. Cedar had told himself that it was because he had not cleared the energy pathways in his own subtle energy bodies enough yet.

He and Moon had continued to work together on this during their sexual encounters, seeking to experience the unity that they'd read about together. And while it had continued to be powerful and transformative, and on many levels good and satisfying, something important had still been missing.

It was this missing thing which had prompted the vision quest over those few days in America. Cedar's visions that final night had shown him that what he needed to find was not through another person, but through deepening his practice with himself. It had become clear that in order to do this, he needed to abstain from sex for a while. He knew without a doubt that Moon would hate the idea on one level, but that she would understand this because of her dedication to the path of Spirit. This was a path they had both pledged to walk. He figured this reason would in itself be reason enough – that Moon didn't need to know the rest of the vision.

Initially Moon had raged about it, but in the end she had accepted it. Had she been listening to her own inner guidance she would have known that there was more he wasn't telling her. But at the time she didn't want to hear it. She wanted to believe that this was temporary, that they could both focus on their spiritual endeavours while still being companions, and that one day when that spiritual attainment had been reached, they would be able to come together on the physical level again. She had let herself believe that. It was her responsibility. And yet, Cedar can also see his own responsibility for what had happened. He had played a part in it too. Moon was right about that. A feeling of guilt passes through him again and he breathes through it.

I did that, he realises. He keeps breathing. Eventually, the feeling softens and releases. He can see now that he had been feeding on the energy she was giving him. It had made him feel strong. He had used it when he should have been making his own connection, and finding his own energy source.

He can see that this past year of celibacy has been harder than he expected it would be, but that it has brought him closer to the centre of himself. He has learned to raise his own energy rather than draw it unconsciously from others – at least he had thought so. Now he can see that there have still been fears holding him back, and he has still been unconsciously drawing energy from Moon. He had feared losing her, and so he had withheld truth from her. This had allowed her to create the fantasy, as on some level he had known she would do.

He had not acted with love with Moon. He had thought he was on a spiritual path, ever closer to enlightenment, and all along, there had been this part of him still acting out of fear and need, a part of him so very much still entrenched in ego. *I thought I was so free of it*, he thinks, shaking his head. Moon would have called that his shadow, the part of him he refused to see. That is why she had called him Charlie. She always used that name when she wanted to point to the parts of him that he was running away from or not facing.

How was it that I didn't see it before? He had thought his awareness had expanded so much, and yet he had missed this critical thing.

But perhaps this is all part of the journey, the thought comes to him. Because all that has happened has brought him here, to this place, to this understanding. Because here at this festival, just in the last day something has shifted for Cedar. He has discovered something new, some part of what's been missing.

It had begun with the tree.

He gazes out at it now, draped in coloured lights and silhouetted against the green and orange sky.

You are Love, he had sung to the tree through the didge. *You are Love.* And beyond the tree, it had expanded into a blessing he was singing to others, to the whole festival. To that someone who might need it.

You are Love.

This was when something extraordinary had happened. It had been so surprising that Cedar had stopped playing and just stared out at the tree. It was a swelling of gratitude. Without trying or intending, his heart had expanded and he had felt this outpouring of love for the tree. He had felt how the tree was part of him, and he loved the tree in a way he had never loved anything. This feeling had then extended beyond the tree and out into the whole festival. Something had begun to flow that hadn't flowed before.

I understand now... He smiles. Perhaps this is why the truth had finally come out now with Moon.

Openness requires truth. Love requires truth.

As he breathes, he feels the familiar tingling in his palms, and that warmth at the centre of his chest opening again. This makes him think of his healing practice. Of all the things he has tried on his search for spiritual truth this year, one of the most transformative has been to become attuned to the ancient healing art of *Reiki*. Initially, Cedar found it extremely useful for doing hands-on healing for himself, but after deeper instruction, he began to practice distance healing for others, and this had been an even more powerful and transformative experience.

He thinks of Moon, and knows what she must be feeling. Moon is very capable of centering herself, but he's never seen her quite so volatile as tonight.

Healing. The intention for their work in the Big Tipi tonight had been about healing. *So let it be.*

As he has been taught, he asks his Higher Self to be present in this healing, and asks to connect with Moon's Higher Self. *So that Moon may receive whatever is in her highest good.*

He moves his hand over the air in front of him, drawing out the distance Reiki symbol and whispering its name three times: *Hon-Sha-Ze-Sho-Nen... Hon-Sha-Ze-Sho-Nen... Hon-Sha-Ze-Sho-Nen.*

Cedar feels the moment when something in the healing energy connects, like the terminals of an infinite battery. The energy has found its path, even as that path has no distance because the two poles are really one. *There is no distance.* This is what the symbol means. Cedar knows that wherever Moon is, this energy is reaching her.

Cedar feels a wave of gratitude for Moon. Her truth tonight had challenged him as much as anything she had ever said to him before, and yet, it had shone a light for him as her challenges often have. They are soulmates. But Cedar also knows that just because someone is a soulmate, doesn't mean they are your life partner. *They come and change your life, and lead you closer to God.*

Or rather, his heart reminds him, *closer to waking up to the God that is already within. You already are God. You can't get any closer than that. You can just get closer to remembering it.*

This is what Moon has done for him. Her challenges have shaken him into deeper awareness, and for that, he will always be grateful to her.

Yes, I am a man, he smiles to himself at all the mystery and wonder of that fact, grateful for the strength in his body and for all that this body is capable of. A memory comes to him of something Moon had said once – *Masculine and Feminine are in every person, whether they are male or female. We are all male and we are all female and we are all neither because we are all one.*

The fire crackles. Cedar brings his awareness back to the tipi and back to Moon, who is here before him. Again here, Cedar feels an outpouring of fondness for her, and gratitude for what she has brought through tonight. He can feel how hard this is for her, but he can also feel her strength.

He looks deeply into her eyes, asking her the silent question, *Will you sing with me?*

Receiving this, she takes a breath into her belly, feeling the affirmation inside herself and nodding. *Yes. I will sing with you.*

So she can still hear me. That's good. The channels between them are still open. They always had an ability to communicate this way. It is a wonder to Cedar that she never saw the part of the vision he had kept from her, with all her ability to perceive him. But he knows that people see what they want to see. Himself included.

Anna sees the potent look which passes between Moon and Cedar and feels a knot inside herself. *They are so close,* she thinks, wondering again at their history.

Moon rises and steps around the fire to kneel beside Cedar. Being this close to him, breathing in the scent of him, brings some of the feelings up again. She can feel the same chemistry they've always had, and just a little wave of grief arises again as she remembers again the finality of that phase of their relationship. She catches herself. *Breathe.*

Closing her eyes, she sees her roots reaching deep into the ground below her. She keeps breathing. After several breaths, she feels it – the quiet stillness deep in the ground, the feeling of being held by Pachamama. With her inbreath, she breaths in that energy, feeling it moving up her body, with a tingling awareness.

As Moon opens her eyes, she notices that her vision has shifted. Everything has a crisp clarity, while at the same time being in soft focus, peripheral, taking in every-thing at once. She can see the luminosity of the fire, brighter and crisper and more alive than before.

The fire needs tending. Her hand reaches for one of the pieces of wood, stacked beside the firepit. Her fingers close around a rough piece, feeling the curves of the bark and the warmth of it. She places it on the fire and blows into the embers, until the flames leap and crackle.

Anna has been watching Moon and notices how she seems a different person again. She appears now to be a kind of goddess, her face glowing in the firelight. Anna is taken by the beauty of her. She's not the only one in the room to feel this way.

As Moon sits back on her heels, the only sounds in the tipi are the breaths of the listeners and the crackling of the fire. The beats are still going on out in the Glas-tonbury night, but in here, there is a bubble of expectant listening.

Cedar is listening too. In a moment the energy to play will rise.

He is each breath; he the sun at his centre; he is the ground beneath his feet; he is the warm expanding energy at the centre of his chest, which is reaching all those who surround the fire. Cedar lifts his instrument with his right hand, his left poised as if to take flight at his side.

The music arrives as a wellspring moving within him, rising up from the earth, through the soles of his feet, through his hands and his heart and into the shaft of the didgeridoo, with a great burst of sound – Wild. Pulsing. Rhythmic.

First it is like the growling of a beast, and now the cry of a great bird, with a beat-ing of wings. His left hand moves through the air, as if dancing to it. Rising to his feet, golden in the firelight, his cheeks expand and contract with the breath and sound. Eyes closed, he is effortlessly, perfectly balanced.

His shadow dances on the wall of the tipi, towering above him like a mystical winged creature, reminding Anna of the dragons she has been seeing around the festival. She has the strange sense, watching him, that he isn't consciously moving – that the didgeridoo is moving him!

The sound becomes a pulsing staccato, and Anna can feel it vibrating right inside her. She can see the contours of Cedar's male body moving rhythmically beneath his light cotton trousers and feels her own body responding again, this time more powerfully, and in a way that is so primal she has no control over it. A heat and pressure is developing in the place between her legs.

The place between my legs. That's what Anna has called it as long as she can remember, being embarrassed by the word 'vagina' or any of the other terms she has come across, being embarrassed by this whole area of her body, and the things it seems to do to her.

Maddy is having a more enjoyable experience. She is feeling a pleasing warmth and energy arising at the base of her spine, and intensifying inside her *Yoni*, which is Maddy's word for this sacred place of power in a woman's body. It is a place she reclaimed when she began to honour the feminine in herself. She calls this place *Yoni* because in Sanskrit it means 'source of life'. She allows the energy to intensify until it rises through her body in waves of pleasure.

While Maddy opens, Anna is fighting her bodily responses, thinking of Damien and then not wanting to think of him, and feeling the guilt, and knowing there is nothing she can do about it. There is one truth which becomes painfully clear to Anna in this moment. *I've never felt this way about Damien.* The knowing comes with a shock – *and I don't know if I ever could.*

It's frightening, this rawness, because Anna can see she is no longer in control, and when it comes to sexuality, she is used to being in control of herself. Every physical movement is always carefully thought out and executed based on what she thought she should do, based on what she thought her partner would want. Never in all her encounters with men had she ever felt anything like this inside her – this whole body response, uncontrollable.

I may as well already have betrayed Damien. With a measure of despair, she gives in, and allows herself to feel all the raw, base feelings, watching this man moving with the thrum of the didge, wanting something so desperately.

Why would Cedar want me, when he could have someone like Moon, or Maddy? Or any of the other beautiful women he must meet every day? Again Anna feels so much less beautiful, less graceful, less serene, less wild than any of the other women sitting around the fire.

Even as the music moves his body and Cedar gives himself to the service of that, there is one resonance in the room which continues to draw his attention. It's coming from the young woman with the lovely hands. With his peripheral vision Cedar can see her face – sweet and tense in the firelight and so familiar to him. She's holding, contracted, afraid of something. The firelight glints copper in the free hanging strands her long hair and for a moment he wants to stop all this and just take her hands and tell her it's okay, like it's something he's done hundreds of times before.

He brings his attention back again to his circular breathing and the fire in his belly. *All I can do right now is offer my love through this.* Cedar won't ever force a healing, so he offers up a quick invocation to his Higher Self and to hers. *Let it be for her highest good, and the highest good of all, whatever happens here tonight.*

Until now Moon has been still, watching the fire and listening, letting the sound of the didge fill her, just breathing, and waiting for moment when the music asks her to sing. It comes now with a rush of energy – the song rising up out of the earth and the fire and the air all around them. With it comes the indescribable joy as her body releases the song, the voice rising up in harmony with the didgeridoo, earthy and rich, riding on the breath.

Anna gasps at the power of this voice and wants to cry for all that she herself can't do. For what Nina Marshall could do. *And now this!* This voice coming from Moon is even more extraordinary – one of the richest, most soulful voices Anna has ever heard.

Well done, Moon. Cedar is grateful, and feels such reverence for Moon's ability to bring this through, this voice that is deeper even than before – perhaps as a result of what had happened earlier. But even these thoughts fade away, because Cedar is shifting into that state where thoughts hold less sway, and he is one with the energy coursing through him. With Moon bringing her presence and drawing the energy up too, the intensity in the room magnifies. For now, Cedar and Moon are being moved together by the energy and the music, and they are listeners, as much as anyone else. They know that they are not the only ones making the music. The presence of everyone here creates it. The music rises out of that listening, from the fire, and from the energy of the earth below their feet.

Mesmerised by the two musicians, Anna almost forgets her own pain for a moment. Moon's eyes are closed and yet her body is completely in rhythm with Cedar's. The rich rawness of that voice soars free, dancing with the didgeridoo, making sounds Anna had never imagined a human voice could make. Even their shadows seem to move as one.

How are you doing this? I can't do what you do! I want to be that beautiful!

Before she can think to look away, Cedar has caught her with all the fire of his gaze and for a blink of a moment, all her thoughts cease in the shock of what she sees there. It pierces her, strips her down. Laid bare by those eyes, she knows he can see her, all her fear and all her desire and all her shame. When he looks away, she is left heart pounding, confused.

What just happened? Her body feels shaky. *Why did he look at me like that? And how can one look do that to me?*

Cedar can feel his body wants to move around the fire now – eventually towards her. But not yet. He moves first towards the woman nearest to him on his right. Shona's eyes are closed, but a smile of private delight fills her face. Cedar lifts his didge so that the flared end is only a few feet from her chest. This is where he often begins – at the heart – and after holding it here for a few moments, he begins to move the didgeridoo around behind Shona, up from the base of her back to her crown and swirling it lightly in circles around her.

The energy of the didgeridoo's resonance and the energy of love moving through Cedar are one and the same. Where the sound travels, the energy of love travels, moving blocked energy and creating flow. Cedar holds the position for a few more moments until Shona's body takes a deep breath. He can feel the completion here and the energy moves him on to the next person.

Anna watches Cedar lifting the didgeridoo towards the young man with the fuzzy beard, who is now doing his best to sit still and serene like the woman next to him, but he can't quite do it, continually breaking out into a grin, and now a stifled giggle as if the whole experience is tickling him.

Cedar knows that what's coming up for Alex makes him nervous, and when he's nervous he giggles. He can't seem to stop himself now, and the more he giggles, the funnier it all seems. And it's contagious. A few others begin to chuckle, and after a few moments, everyone around the circle is laughing, except for Anna. She is bewildered. Even Moon has stopped singing for a moment and is laughing too. Cedar doesn't stop playing, but there is laughter in his eyes.

So it is only Anna now, resisting, but as tears of laugher run down Alex's face, and with Maddy laughing heartily beside her, it strikes Anna how hilarious all this is. To see how laughter is happening here in this sacred place. *And why? Why are they laughing?* Her rational mind doesn't get it. But there is a part of her that is getting it, that understands somehow that divinity and true laughter are one and the same, how humour is the divine delighting inside us.

So even Anna, with all her holding and fear, cannot resist. The laughter gets inside her too, shaking her up, loosening the grip of fear and opening the way for something else – something akin to joy, flowing without thought in laughter's tears. Laughter overrides thought, making presence in its wake.

Eventually the laughter settles, and ultimately even Alex subsides into gentle chuckles and then stillness.

As Cedar steps around the fire moving closer to Anna, the vibration is becoming more intense. From the edge of her vision, she can see him lifting the didgeridoo towards the heart of the man beside her. She closes her eyes, her whole body riveted with nervous excitement in anticipation of the moment when he will turn the full force of his didgeridoo towards her. She wants it more than she can bear, but at the same time fears it, because there is so much he might see, and she doesn't trust herself not to do something embarrassing. An ocean of tears is so close to the surface.

There is movement in the air beside her as Cedar swirls his didgeridoo around the man's body, the ripples of the sound waves just touching Anna, as if he is dancing his fingers just over her skin.

Cedar's own heart beats a little more quickly as he finishes with Paul and turns towards the young woman beside him. *Focus Cedar*, he reminds himself. *This is about healing. This is about service.* He brings his attention back to his his belly and the warmth in his heart and the circular breathing that enables the continuous flow of the sound.

Before he reaches her, he directs the energy temporarily towards the ground, giving himself a chance to offer up another invocation, both to his own Higher Self and to hers. *Let whatever comes through be for her highest good. Let her take only what is in her highest good.*

He feels the energy swirl up his spine and lift inside him in affirmation. *This is for her.* He offers it to her with as open a heart as he can.

It is a tidal wave, a fire storm breaking over and through Anna, a current of energy so big she can barely breathe. It is all vibration and heat behind her. She knows he isn't physically touching her body, and yet he is. The pressure and the warmth of his breath pulse against her through the shaft of the instrument, caressing her back and neck, enfolding her something so warm, as if his very arms are right around her.

For Cedar, each time his thoughts attempt to draw him from his task, into the contours of her neck, the wisps of hair that stray, the wondering of who she is to him, he breathes again, drawing himself back into the healing and letting the energy move through him. Being the instrument, the conduit. He doesn't consciously know what she needs, but the energy does. Images come to him. In his mind's eye he can see her Heart Chakra. Her whole subtle energy system is blocked and contracted, especially around the heart. It feels to him that it has been that way for a very long time, perhaps even since her early childhood. He can feel the sweetness in that heart, and the potential of that heart to love, if it could be open.

The didgeridoo is moving almost of its own accord, and he lets it, flowing with the energy, higher up her spine. Up to that chakra just below the ribs. He imagines the light of a golden yellow sun shining there at her solar plexus, bringing joy and giving strength.

He's pouring all his love through the instrument.

Oh my God! is the thought repeating in Anna's mind. *Oh my God! What are you doing to me?*

Cedar moves higher still, allowing the force of that love to flow to the centre of her chest. Anna gasps, eyes wide. *This is my heart!* She knows now with a striking awareness that this is the heart Johannes spoke of – a non-physical heart that she can now feel as real as anything she's touched with her bare hands. And there is an ache in this heart.

The ache of loneliness.

The ache of separation.

The ache of emptiness.

The ache of not being enough. Not ever being enough.

This ache in the centre of her chest throbs, bringing the ocean of tears dangerously close to the surface, but still she holds herself. *I can't cry. I'm afraid of what will happen if I let it out.*

This pain and the sound and vibration and his breath pulsing against her become all there is. The orange firelight flickers against the backs of her eyelids. It is like being on some strange psychoactive drug, being in an extraordinary dream.

It's so intense she almost wants to beg him to stop, because it hurts, this holding. The fear locked in the place just below her ribs is urging her to run from this, to leave the tipi and wake herself up from this dream before the door holding back this ocean of tears gives out. But this is a turning point in her life, and there is a growing awareness inside Anna that if she runs from this she will never know what's possible on the other side of the door, and she doesn't want the man who is doing this ever to stop, because this is the warmest thing she has ever felt. There is fire before her, behind her and within her, filling her inside out.

This river of energy – Prana, Chi, Love, all these names it could be given – is flowing through Cedar's heart to her, this heart he'd begun to feel in a new way since that moment with the tree up on the hill.

The last vestiges of her holding are dissolving, as this love is inviting her to let go and give in. Until at last the invitation becomes so sweet there is no question of diving in, whatever the consequences.

Now the ocean is here. It is everywhere, in everything, massaging her from all directions, deeper and deeper still, pouring through her and now the tears are rolling out of her in waves, and she is watching this, observing it, bewildered, as her body shakes with the release. As the salty water pours from her eyes and runs down her cheeks there is no more thought, there is only witnessing the movement, the waves of sound, the pulse of the energy moving through her.

This is all there is.

And the sound is *rushing rushing rushing rushing rushing rushing rushing...*

Cedar is speaking to her through the didgeridoo. Anna doesn't hear the words, but the energy of them pulses into her heart.

You are Love. You are Love. You are Love. You are Love. You are Love. You are Love.

She knows he is saying something. It sounds like the call of a wild bird – calling her home, calling her free.

You are Love.

This river is washing away everything that no longer belongs, everything that she is ready to let go of, and as these things release, swept in the current of the river, they are replaced by the sweetest light. The fire is right inside her own heart.

Cedar moves on now to Maddy and though he is physically no longer behind Anna she can still feel the energy moving and vibrating inside her.

This is home, she realises, resting here.

Anna knows the moment when Cedar has finished didging Maddy, because she hears Maddy's deep exhale followed by a soft murmuring hum of bliss.

Cedar is focusing the resonance on Moon now, with the intention that she receive whatever is in her highest good. Moon can feel something is different. She knows now with surprise who was sending her healing earlier, because it's the same energy. It is the same feeling of being held, completely loved, bathed in warmth. *Heart Energy.* Cedar had told Moon earlier – when they had first decided to do this tonight – that something had shifted for him, that his heart had opened in a new way, and he wanted to see what would happen when they played together in this spirit. That had been the seed from which tonight's musical healing had grown.

So this is what happens. Moon feels the smile rise through her body as the song fills her again, this time with even more delight. As she joins Cedar, the voice and the didgeridoo are doing their familiar dance together, a dance they have done so many hundreds of times. And yet now, Moon can feel how the intensity of the warmth is amplified. It is pure love that he is giving her, and it is flowing through her own heart, shaking free the last vestiges of the pain from earlier. She is expanding now, witnessing the love and music as the same thing, moving her body as one energy, singing her. *So this is what's possible with music*, she realises. *This is what happens when Love sings you!*

Anna marvels at the way Moon's voice soars and rises, clearer and even deeper than before. This time there is no pain for Anna in this thought. She is no longer comparing herself, because Moon's voice has become her voice. The joy of that voice moves inside Anna's own body, and Moon's delight has become her own. Anna doesn't know if the joy is inside her or outside of her. It's all the same thing. The voice that is singing is part of her. The thrum and pulse of the didgeridoo is part of her. All the other people in this room are part of her. And outside, beyond the tipi, stretching out across the festival, all the people celebrating out in the night... they are part of her too. It is all part of her. She feels how she belongs to everything.

The circle is complete.

The fire crackles. Cedar lowers his didgeridoo. The healing has happened. The room is vibrating with it, in the air, in all their cells. They are all in it together, in this sweet silence.

Anna feels it still resonating inside her, and she has a sense of the vibration just going out and out, like ripples in a pond, on and on and on...

The fire crackles and whispers *shhhhhhhhhhhhhh*. It seems to Anna to be as alive as she. After a while, people begin to stretch and move, and to murmur, "*mmmm-mmm...*"

Anna stretches her body too. It feels like a new body. More hers than before. She feels comfortable in it. She wants to stretch like a cat, and lets herself. She opens her eyes and gazes into the heart of the fire. It has burned down to red hot glowing embers again, with no flames but intense heat. The fire is not separate from her either. With this knowledge, little bubbles of happiness rise up inside her. She looks over at this man who has brought this feeling of happiness to her, and feels awe.

Thank you, she whispers inside herself. She hasn't said it aloud, but Cedar looks up and smiles. Again their eyes meet. In those eyes, she no longer fears being seen. In those eyes is the deepest ocean. In those eyes, she feels only love and acceptance. Nothing needs to happen. There is no past. No future. This is enough. This being in Love.

Cedar turns his eyes to Moon as she offers him a large plastic water bottle, full of clear liquid. His thirst is deep. He always needs a lot of water when he gives healings and plays music. It's the energy. It transforms the body and the metabolic processes need the water. It's also more than that. It's as if the energy draws and uses the water in the body to conduct itself.

Others are feeling it too, and the bottle is passed around. Anna notes that even though this is a plastic water bottle, it is being handed around as if it were the most expensive of champagnes. When it reaches her, she feels her own deep thirst and drinks. The water in the bottle catches the firelight and shines as she tips it up to her mouth and the image comes to her of drinking light. It's water, but not like any water she's ever drunk – sweet, slightly metallic and full of life. She can see why the others were passing the water to one another with such reverence. There is something special about it. When she feels she's had her share, Anna offers the water to the man sitting on her left.

"Thank you," Paul says, accepting the bottle from her. Anna notices how bright this man's eyes are. His smile is so warm it is shining from his whole face. Anna feels the same warmth in her own smile back to him.

Paul grins as he lifts the drink to his lips. He knows what this is. He offers the bottle to Alex beside him.

Alex swigs quite a lot before stopping to look at the bottle with raised eyebrows. "What kind of water is this?"

Paul chuckles, patting Alex softly on the back. "It's Chalice Well, buddy."

"Did you put something in it?" Alex looks up at Moon. "'Cause this water is doing something to me."

"The earth put something in it," Moon replies simply.

Paul nods. "Indeed. The most healing water I've ever drunk. Perfect drink for an evening of the most healing music I've ever experienced."

There are hums of agreement around the fire.

Yes, Cedar thinks. *It was something special.* Whatever had shifted and healed between himself and Moon that night had created a facility for deeper healing. It had allowed a deeper alchemy to come forth. He can see that he and Moon still have work to do together. A vision comes to him of what that path might hold. Though it may hold its challenges, after tonight, he knows they will be able to do it. He turns to Moon and meets her eyes, feeling such gratitude again, and love for this sister beside him. Moon knows what he is saying to her. She feels the smile lifting in her own body.

This is enough. The words come into her heart, and she knows it's true. Whatever her ego wishes was between them, that is not here now. Here, in this openness, in this Love, this is enough.

Sleep wants to come. All Anna can imagine doing is laying herself down on this soft sheepskin. So she does. She doesn't think about for how long. Others are doing the same. Nearby Maddy is opening her blanket to Moon, who lies down on the sheepskin beside her. Cedar remains seated by the fire, his gaze resting with the embers.

These people are family. With her back on the softness of the sheepskin, and her eyes closed, almost dreaming, Anna can feel the resonance of the didgeridoo still vibrating within her, and the warmth still alive in her heart. She can still feel how she belongs here, how she belongs to all of it, to the fire, to all the people at the festival, all the hills and fields beyond, all the trees and the moon and stars above her. All of it. And with the stars in her own heart, Anna slips into dreaming.

> "Lead me true heart of mine
> Fill me with moonlight and rhyme
> Weave us a love that helps us remember
> Inside this beating heart I sing
> Hold me hear me ring
> Swirl this breath into notes around your body
> Find the courage to keep on softening
> Inside this beating heart I sing
> Hold me hear me ring
> Hands on the ground
> Hearts on Fire"

from the song, 'Hearts on Fire', by Robin Gillmor

As Anna sleeps, Cedar continues to sit, meditating in the stillness, eyes open. His awareness is in the fire and he is in a kind of trance. Images come to him, flashes of knowing, waking dreams. Paul, Alex and Shona have gone, but in his periphery, he can see Moon and Maddy are still here, asleep in each other's arms. And *she* is here. He watches her sleep for a moment. Her face has a softness in it now; her energy has expanded and brightened. It pleases him to see her energy so changed, to know that he had been able to help her. He feels an outpouring of fondness for them all, all three of them – a kind of kinship, as if they are all somehow walking the same journey together. Part of the same soul family.

He wonders briefly again who the young woman is, and what her importance is to him. As he is getting better at doing, he lets go of trying to think of the answer, and just continues to let his gaze rest in the last of the flames, knowing that at some point the answer will come to him. It always does. As the fire crackles gently, he lets his vision drift again into soft focus, and just allows his body to breathe.

After some moments, an image comes to him clearly. He sees just one flash of it and knows they have met before. Not in his last life, but the time before that. In that life, they were lovers. He feels like he knows her that way already and it is a strange sensation, like he could just go and snuggle down there beside her right now, and take her in his arms and it would be the most natural thing in the world. It had been there in the way she had looked at him earlier, with those fiery eyes of hers. *She feels the same way.* With this knowing, Cedar smiles to himself, seeing the challenge unfolding tantalisingly before him.

But this is how it works, he knows. *You think you've cracked it, and you've evolved so far and you've got the lesson and then you find the challenges intensify and the lesson deepens.* He can feel the challenge this girl will be to him, but in this state of peaceful awareness, he feels no concern about it. Only the smile, the knowing that his Higher Self has set this up for him, another lesson, another experience. But for now, it is enough to sit and be with the fire, and breathe and let the heart be open.

He says a silent blessing of gratitude again to Pachamama and to the spirit of the music for bringing them all here, for the healing that has occurred tonight.

A hand brushes against Anna's arm. Something soft and furry tickles her cheek. It has an unusual, earthy smell. She cracks open an eye and finds herself face down in a sheepskin. Momentarily confused, filled with the remnants of dreams not quite remembered, she gazes around her.

Where am I? As her conscious mind wakes up more fully, she takes in the sunlight shining on the outside of the canvas of the tipi and it floods back to her. Someone has placed a blanket over her as she slept.

It wasn't a dream, she realises with a shiver of excitement. *This is real!* Her heart pounds again at the thought and she looks up to see who it was that touched her. *Was it Cedar?*

It's Moon, kneeling down beside her. Seeing Anna's eyes open, Moon smiles. "Good morning."

Anna slowly pulls herself up to sitting and rubs the sleep from her face. "Morning."

"Drink?" Moon asks, offering Anna the plastic bottle which has a few swigs left at the bottom. Anna gulps it down. "Thank you."

She has just had one of the deepest sleeps she's had for years. She feels soft, close to tears and filled with a whole mixture of emotions she can't name. *Where is Cedar? How can I see him again?*

This morning when Moon woke, Cedar had already left. Moon had opened her eyes to find Maddy's arms around her. In her dream, they had been Cedar's arms and she had rested in that warmth, believing that the painful separation had been a dream, and really things were as they had been before. Then when she had opened her eyes and seen the soft ginger curls of Maddy, and smelled the scents of cinnamon and cardamom that clung to her even hours after her shifts at Pacha Mama's, a mixture of feelings had arisen. It was so comfortable to lie there with Maddy – the most comfortable, natural thing in the world.

Then Maddy had opened her eyes too, and they had just looked at one another for a long time, not speaking. They had often gazed into one another's eyes before; it was part of the deep friendship they shared. But this time something was different. Moon became aware of a growing heat between their bodies, as the energy moved between them. As they held one another's gaze, they somehow looked deeper into one another than before, and in this deep place, Moon had seen something surprising. *Maddy loves me.* And not just the love of a deep friendship – something wholly more astounding. And following on from that came the extraordinary knowing – *I love Maddy too.*

This knowledge had sent a ripple of excitement through Moon's body, which in itself had been equally surprising. Because while Moon had been attracted to women in the past – and had even followed that attraction through with physical intimacy a couple of times – she had not seen her friendship with Maddy that way. *But of course*, she realised, she wouldn't have. Since she had known Maddy, there had always been Cedar. As well, the sense had always been with her that she was destined to become a mother, so she had always imagined she would end up with a man in the end. With Cedar she had loved making love with a totality of self. She had believed it possible to be completely fulfilled with a man, and that the love they shared would ultimately create a child.

But this morning, waking in the arms of this beautiful woman, her dearest friend, Moon hadn't known what to make of the child issue. The feeling to become a mother still calls to her, from every cell of her body and with a sense of a soul wishing to incarnate with her, to call her Mama. She knows that even with her body's continuing youthfulness, there is only so much time.

And yet, it feels so right to accept Maddy's love, offered so unconditionally. This is what is now. *Accept what is*, the guidance had come. And so lying there, deep in Maddy's gaze and with this knowing pulsing through her, it had seemed the most natural thing in the world when Maddy had bridged the gap between them and placed her her soft lips against Moon's. And again, an electric current had swept through Moon's body, and without thought, she had returned the kiss; it was so sweet, and so deep, and so confusing to the mind and all its plans.

It still doesn't make sense to Moon. She's trying not to be in her head too much about it, though, because when she tunes into her body, it feels good. To be able to open her heart to someone feels wonderful too, after such a long time of not being able to do so with Cedar. So she trusts it.

Maddy had suggested they go for a sauna, and Moon had agreed. Moon had gotten only a few yards from the tipi when something had pulled her back – the sense of forgetting something. Someone. Anna.

She had followed this prompting back to the Big Tipi, even as her thoughts were telling her she'd rather have a quiet sauna with Maddy, so they could tentatively explore this new territory they were entering, but the feeling to come back had been compelling.

Moon recognised then that the serenity of the night before was no longer with her. She can feel the grief of Cedar again, asking for its due process. The part of her that still grieves is confused about Anna too, because Moon had felt what had gone on between Anna and Cedar last night. She had seen the look in Cedar's eyes.

Last night, in the vibration of love and connection, it had all felt fine. But this morning, it doesn't feel quite so fine. However, even with all these feelings, enough of Moon had been present to the promptings of her heart that she had turned around and gone back for Anna anyway.

"Maddy and I are about to go to the sauna, if you want to join us."

"A sauna? Where?"

"Just across the path there. At Lost Horizon."

The yellow wristband on Moon's wrist jumps out at Anna. She can now see the words *Lost Horizon* printed on one side of it, and on the other, *Find Yourself*.

Cedar had worn a wristband like that, too.

Maybe he'll be there, Anna thinks. This sends a wave of nervousness through her, and she realises, like Moon, that the serenity of the night before is no longer with her. Her old worries and fears are back, albeit slightly more subdued than before.

Was it real? Anna wonders. *The feeling of being part of everything?* It seems like a dream, and yet she is aware of a palpable change in herself. Something really did happen. She lifts her hand to the centre of her chest, holding it there for a moment, remembering all the energy that had poured into her heart the night before. Cedar's love. She can still feel the presence of this new heart in a way she never could before, and while the heart is not so open as it was in those moments after the mysterious healing of last night's music, still the memory remains and along with it, a new softness. Surrounded by the tipi, with the sunlight streaming in, Anna feels held by something special, as if she is being offered an opportunity to continue being part of a magical kind of reality – a reality that people like Moon seemed to inhabit regularly.

Moon is still standing here, waiting for Anna to reply.

"You haven't been to a sauna before, have you?" Moon asks, reading Anna's hesitation.

"Just at the swimming pool," Anna admits, knowing this is going to be nothing like a swimming pool sauna.

Moon can't help laughing. "Then you haven't had a sauna. A Lost Horizon Sauna is something to be experienced. It will cleanse your mind, body and spirit. It's totally rejuvenating."

It was fear that had stopped Anna from accepting Moon's invitation. She had wanted to go with Moon to the sauna, but a familiar nervousness had gripped her, and she had found herself making excuses. One by one, Moon had answered her concerns. Anna wouldn't need to pay because their band performs at Lost Horizon sometimes and Moon would make sure there was a wristband waiting on the door for her. There are towels she can borrow. But the last obstacle was the hardest to overcome. *Festival saunas are naked saunas.*

Moon had tried to answer that one too. She'd told Anna, *Once you get in that space and you're there just as you are and everyone else is there just as they are, you realise nobody's looking at anyone. At least not in a way that's judgemental. Nobody's judging anyone. And then you start to see that no matter what shape people are, that everyone is beautiful. Totally beautiful.* The same questions surface again now in Anna's mind as they did then: *Are you sure? Everyone is beautiful? Even me?*

So Moon had left it with Anna that she could join them if she wanted and as Anna had watched Moon lightly stepping out of view, she had felt an intense sadness, as if she was giving up something incredibly precious.

Anna moves towards the door and slips on her socks and wellies, which are still where she left them outside the entrance of the tipi. The blue sky and the warmth are such a contrast to the mud and wet of the night before that for a moment Anna forgets her dilemma and just closes her eyes, feeling the heat of the sun touching her skin. As she opens her eyes again, it feels as if the world is just a little brighter than it was before, as if things have somehow come more alive everywhere since last night.

Judging by the angle of the sun, it's well past noon. The overriding atmosphere of the festival is one of relative calm, the partiers from the night before finally having gone to bed and the next round of explosions and electronic beats not yet begun. A pop band with multi-voice harmonies has just started up on the Park Stage nearby, and Anna can just make out the sounds of an African band coming in and out from the direction of the West Holts stage further down towards the centre of the festival.

Those who Anna can see moving about in the Tipi Field appear to be relaxing and enjoying the sunshine. To balance out the heat, there is a gentle, fresh wind blowing from the direction of the trees up the hill. The grass is dry already. It appears as if that particular storm has passed.

A lot can happen in a night, Anna realises. Though she has lost that sense of being completely at peace and feeling of belonging to everything, she can still remember it, and that is something. She knows now that it is possible to feel that way. *To not feel afraid. To be content where you are. To feel part of everything. I want to feel that way again.*

She remembers what Johannes had said about being brave. She doesn't feel brave at all right now. She wishes she was.

What do I do? She casts her gaze down the gentle slope of the hill to the sauna enclosure. It is constructed with several tipis and surrounded by long lengths of white canvas, hiding whatever is inside from view. A wisp of smoke rises up into the sky from somewhere within and Anna can hear laughter and splashing. The tree tops inside the enclosure sway gently in the breeze. The whole atmosphere emanating from the place is one of chilled-out relaxation.

But Anna has a more pressing issue – her bladder. *First things first. Go to the loo. Then decide.*

As she walks down through the Tipi Field, with every turn of her head she is looking for him, for that flash of blond hair. She doesn't want to be looking, but it has taken her over, this need to see him again. As she passes the central fire, she looks for Cedar in the figures sitting around it. As she passes the lovely tipi cafe and heads out onto the dirt trackway that borders the camping field, she's looking for him in every blond man that walks by. At one point, she has to remind herself that what she really needs right now is not Cedar, but to find the nearest loos, and quick.

Her Glastonbury pocket map shows her the way to the nearest marked toilet facilities. It just so happens they are female urinals. A large sign above the entrance reads: *WaterAid*, and next to it, 'SHE PEES'.

A kindly grey-haired lady with a blue '*Pump up the Volume*' WaterAid T-shirt offers Anna a conveniently-shaped pink and white folded cardboard receptacle with the words P-MATE on it, which when opened reveal a large opening at one end and a tapered end with a hole in it at the other. It's pretty clear what to do with it.

"You hold it down here and wee into it," the lady explains when she sees Anna's expression. "Trust me. It's very hygienic, and easy to use."

There's not really another option at this point so Anna takes the object into a private booth and following the lady's instructions is pleasantly surprised at how easy it actually is to use. As Anna drops the used cardboard into the bin for biodegradeable disposal and washes her hands, she catches sight of the sign which reads:

783 million people have no clean water to drink.
A toilet is an unimagineable luxury to 2.5 billion people.

Usually with stats like that, she wouldn't pay much attention, she would just move on, but for some reason this morning she can't seem to pass by this one as easily as she might have done before.

At the entrance to the She Pees a group of devoted WaterAid volunteers are talking to people about WaterAid's work to bring every person on the planet clean drinking water and a safe place to go to the toilet, and are accepting donations into their blue buckets.

And now Anna must make a choice: to go or not to go to the sauna. She ponders this as she treads the path back towards the Tipi Field, passing by a lovely mature oak tree she hadn't noticed before, its branches rustling in the breeze.

What do I do?

Now she is standing at the junction. To the right is the entrance to the Tipi Field, leading up the hill towards the sauna, and to the left is the dirt track that leads back past the camping field to her tent. In the middle of the two, right on the corner is the wonderful tipi cafe with the crepes she'd been in the night before. In the daylight she can see the name on a sign over the door that reads *Pacha Mama Cafe.*

Anna's attention is caught by the sunlight sparkling on dreamcatchers and drag-onflies made from cloth and wire hovering over the benches and potted plants of the small garden which surrounds the cafe. The canvas surrounding the back entrance to the cafe has been lifted on one side so that the chai-drinkers sitting inside can have the sun on their faces. A small sign by Anna's feet reads cheerfully: *Have a Magical Day.*

She finds a place on one of the low benches in the garden. *I'll sit here for a moment and decide what to do. I'd love a chai,* she thinks wistfully, fingering the remaining 50p in her pocket. She reminds herself at some point later to brave the queues at the festival cash machines which had been more than an hour long yes-terday. She tries not to think of her misjudgement on how many CDs she would sell, because it gives her a pain in her gut. Or is it hunger?

She distracts herself from the feeling and turns her attention again to the gar-den, watching the plants moving gently with the breeze as it rises and quiets, feel-ing the sunlight on her skin. Her eyes are drawn to a small raised pool to her right, also surrounded by plants and butterflies made of cloth and wire. There is a hand-painted sign on the ground beneath it reads:

WELL OF BEAUTY, WELL OF LOVE
MAGIC WITHIN, FAERIES ABOVE
EYES CLOSED, FEEL ENERGY FLOW
THEN COIN TOSS AND WISH SEW

Anna sighs. Another wishing well. She remembers the girl with the rainbows in her hair and the Rainbow Wishing Well. She hadn't thought then that she believed in wishing wells, but that was before last night. Now, whether they are real or not, she has the feeling that she does want to believe in them. Now she knows what she wants to wish for.

Lifting her last coin, she whispers, "I wish I could be brave," and then lets it fall. The coin makes a tiny splash and sinks, catching the sunlight as it twirls to the bot-tom.

Anna sits back on the bench again, gazing out at the people passing by. Her thoughts turn again to the night before. Something big has happened. On one level, it feels like the biggest thing she's ever experienced. She doesn't even really know what it was. A healing. A transformation. Something tipped the world upside down, and inside out. *Or rather, SOMEONE has tipped my world upside down,* she thinks.

Cedar. The name is on her lips, always hovering at the edge of her awareness. Again, her eyes scan the crowds of people passing along the dirt trackway which runs alongside Pacha Mama Cafe.

She remembers what Johannes said about there being someone who could make her heart sing. *Is it him? But what about Damien? What about our life together? Is it ending?* She doesn't want to think about that now.

Two paths stretch out before Anna – one path heads down the hill into the barren landscape of her tent and one path leads up, through the green grass. The decision seems vibrantly clear.

But I'm afraid.

Go anyway, a voice seems to say.

Anna thinks about what Johannes said about the voice of the heart being a loving voice, and the voice of the ego being a fearful voice. And about how the Heart-Self only speaks truth.

As she thinks about going to the sauna, again the images come into her mind of what she fears – being naked, people looking at her, seeing all the flaws in her body. Maybe even Cedar seeing those things. The fears grip her in their usual way – in knots upon knots. But this time, as a result of last night's healing, something new happens: Anna witnesses herself.

In an instant of clarity, she sees herself hunched over in pain and debilitated by this fear. Something inside her snaps, and a fire rises from within, a fury which propels her bolt upright. She can suddenly see how many times these same kinds of fears have stopped her from experiencing things in life, and she's had enough of it.

Sod it, I'm doing it!

Striding towards the sauna, her middle still feels tight with fear, but the fire that has flared up inside is stronger. The closer she gets to the sauna, the more the energy is returning to her body. There is energy in the flow, and as she steps into it, she moves even faster.

Maybe I can do this.

A sign out in front of the sauna reads: *Find yourself at Lost Horizon.*

And now I'm about to get one of those wristbands, she realises. *Will I find myself too?*

To one side of the entrance they are selling fresh juices, smoothies and raw treats. A man behind that counter with dark curly hair and a goatee beard smiles at Anna. Anna's stomach reminds her that it's hungry, and growls noisily. Her mouth waters at all the healthy treats like energy balls and raw brownies, but without money, she pulls her attention away. On the other side of the entrance there is a table with colourful, natural-looking soaps for sale. A bright-eyed young brunette with a red and gold bandana sits behind the table and smiles welcomingly at Anna. This is Saffi, one of the team who work at Lost Horizon.

"Welcome to Lost Horizon." Saffi smiles at her.

"Hi." Anna glances over at the curtain which separates her from the naked people on the other side.

"Are you here for a sauna?" Saffi asks.

Feeling the fire inside her peetering out somewhat, Anna takes a shallow breath. Having made the decision to go ahead, she steels herself and nods. "I am."

"Have you been before?" Saffi asks.

"Uh... no. I... I'm Anna, a friend of Moon's. She said she'd tell you I was coming."

"Anna! Oh yes!" Saffi loves Moon and her band, *Awakening the Dreamer*. She was happy to oblige Moon's request to let Anna come in.

"I'm Saffi. Here. Give me your wrist."

Offering up her wrist, Saffi deftly wraps a yellow paper wristband around it.

Find Yourself at Lost Horizon, Anna reads. *Now it's on my wrist too.*

"Do you need a towel?" Saffi asks.

Anna nods again and Saffi hands her a pink towel. Anna closes her fingers around it, feeling its clean, fresh stiffness.

"Let me give you the tour," Saffi says proudly, leading Anna around the curtain and into the enclosure.

What a sight meets Anna's eyes. She had known there would be naked people in here. Of course there would be. But there are naked people everywhere – women and men both, as easy with the naturalness of their bodies as little children, just sitting there lounging on the grass or walking around. There is a stage on the left side of the garden area, where a semi-naked young female guitarist, wearing only a slightly damp white t-shirt, is sitting on a stool and preparing to play. There is no sign of Moon or Maddy, or Cedar, anywhere. This brings Anna a brief moment of relief.

She notices there are actually some clothed people here, which brings more relief. They are sitting on some of the make-shift wooden benches and chairs, waiting to hear the music. But most of the audience is naked. And there's a naked soundman with fantastic silver and black curls sitting behind the sound desk. A *naked soundman?* But Anna notes that he seems to know what he's doing, and he also seems genuinely happy. Just like everyone else here.

Anna turns her eyes away to avoid staring too long and sees three people doing naked yoga at the opposite end of the garden. She gawks as they assume the tree posture, and then reprimands herself. *In all this worrying about being stared at, you're doing an awful lot of staring yourself.* The irony of this is not lost on her.

"This is the chill out area," Saffi says, gesturing to a tipi with a cosy fire pit inside. There are several people lounging around the fire on mattresses and cushions. Naked.

"And here is the changing yurt." Saffi gestures to the right, to a good-sized dome, with a large opening at the front, divided into three segments by hanging sheets. People are in there, in various states of undress, some drying themselves off.

This is where I have to take my clothes off. At the thought, fear grips Anna around the ribs again.

Saffi is noticeably chilled out herself, and doesn't seem to be bothered by Anna's discomfort. She's proud of this place she's a part of – a community of people, working together. Nobody makes a profit from this place. It's held in trust, and run by people for the love of it. Saffi loves that Lost Horizon does seem to be a place where people can heal themselves, become rejuvenated, feel more alive. She loves to see the change in people who come in the the sauna looking closed down, or stressed or tired, and by the time they leave, they are clean and clear, with relaxed smiles on their faces. As far as Saffi is concerned, Anna will be no different.

"And here's the sauna. It has double doors," Saffi explains. "You go in one and close it behind you, before opening the inner one. That way the heat stays in." Saffi directs Anna's attention to the raised platform a little way to the right, where a row of four standing silver shower nozzles are connected to plastic water pipes. "These are the showers. We ask that you don't use anything with unnatural ingredients in it."

"Okay."

"There is the plunge pool." Saffi points to the large plastic inflatable pool in the corner of the garden.

Right on cue, a generously-sized man dives into the water, sending spray in all directions. A couple hanging half-naked on a nearby hammock strung between two beautiful oak trees laugh as the spray hits them.

What strikes Anna is how happy all these people look. She's never seen so many happy people all together in one place. *So many happy naked people.* A wide-smiling young man in a beard swings happily on a rope swing hung from one of the oak's boughs.

"You can stay in all day if you like," Saffi says.

All day? Anna wonders how quickly she will be able to get through with this. *If I really am going to do it at all.* There is a part of her still reserving the right to bolt.

"Let us know if you need anything. And enjoy." Anna notices the twinkle in the

Saffi's eyes, as if Saffi knows something she doesn't about what's to come from her experience here.

"Thank you," Anna manages to say, and watches the young woman turn and sashay back towards the entrance table to welcome the next people in.

Anna checks around her again for a familiar face and sees none. *They must all be inside the sauna.* She glances over again at the little yurt with the smoke rising out of the little chimney on top. *I wonder what it's like in there. Could it really be like Moon said?*

Just there by the changing yurt is a small brown plastic barrel of water with a spout marked '*Drinking Water*', surrounded by little potted flowers. A communal cup made from natural, brown clay sits below the spout. Anna feels the intensity of her own thirst, and contemplates using the cup, but the thought of all the other mouths that may have touched it gives her pause. Instead, she bends down on one knee and using her own cupped hands, scoops water into her mouth, spilling it down her chin.

"Anna!"

She knows that voice. *Moon. No going back now.*

She looks so frightened, thinks Moon. *But at least she's come. That's good.* "I'm glad you made it."

Anna can see the welcome in Moon's eyes. Moon's face is a flushed pink, and she looks full of life. Her eyes have a quality a little like Cedar's eyes – they are eyes that can see right through a person. Anna finds it hard to meet those eyes, but equally, she doesn't want to look directly at Moon's naked body either, so she turns her attention instead to the surroundings.

"It seems really nice here," she offers.

Moon takes a breath. She feels like reaching a hand out to Anna, just leading her in, and saying, *It's okay. Really. You're just like the rest of us. You belong here.* But rather than doing this, Moon just smiles as warmly as she can. "It's one of my favourite places in the whole world. I love it here. I'm going to splash some cold water on myself and go back in. I'll see you in the sauna?"

Anna nods. "Okay."

She watches Moon saunter over to the showers and tries not to think about how attractive Moon's figure is. She has the athletic body of someone who could walk for miles, with just enough curves to be feminine.

If I had a body like that, I wouldn't mind being naked either, Anna tells herself.

But then, as Moon steps up onto the shower platform, Anna notices something she had missed before in her effort not to stare at Moon's naked body close up –

something that shocks her. Moon has dark hairs peppering the bottom half of her legs. *Moon doesn't shave her legs!*

Moon throws her head back and squeals with delight as the cold water splashes over her head and runs down her hair. As she lifts her arms to run her fingers through her wet hair, Anna notices something else – Moon has tufts of dark hair in her armpits. *Moon has underarm hair!*

Anna gawks for a few moments and then makes herself turn away, feeling guilty. To avoid just standing there feeling foolish, she does the only thing she can think of, which is to turn and walk towards the shade of the changing yurt.

So Moon is not so perfect after all. She tells herself this to qwell her own fears, but then realises – with a sense of irony – *You've been petrified that people will judge your naked body and yet here you are doing that very thing to Moon.*

She finds a spare space on the wooden frame of the changing yurt to hang her clothes. There are already scores of undergarments and other items of clothing decorating the criss-crossing pieces of wood. One of the garments, a substantial pair of man's underpants, hangs nonchalantly in the rung beside hers. Anna stares at them for a moment, thinking about how soon her own underclothes will be hanging there, too. Slowly, she slips off her wellies and socks and places her bare feet on the muddy ground which has been dripped on by so many wet bodies.

I don't know if I can do this. All the thoughts crash down again about what people will think of her – of her naked body, the body that Damien had often told her was beautiful, but that she could never quite look at in the mirror without cringing. All those trips to the gym so that she could fit into that sparkly dress, so that she could be ready for what she had dreamed might be her Big Break – it hadn't actually changed anything about her self-image. To her there always seems to be too much fat in some places and too little where she'd like to have it.

In lock-down now, Anna is hardly able to breathe with this fear of revealing these things she's worked so hard to hide. And at the same time, there are all these happy-looking naked people all around her, baring everything and really seeming to love it. *And why can't it be like that for me too?*

With a flash it comes again – the witnessing herself suffering over her fears, and again comes the accompanying internal fire, the flaring inside of a self that won't stand for it anymore. Not since last night.

Forcefully, Anna removes one item of clothing after another until all that remains are her white pushup bra and bikini underpants. She knows Damien would absolutely not approve, but right now she doesn't care. With a determined breath, she unclasps her bra and pulls off her knickers, placing them in the empty space beside the nonchalant underpants.

Naked at last – aside from the two bands around her left wrist – Anna steps out of the changing yurt and emerges into the sun, feeling its pleasant heat on her skin, with just a hint of a breeze blowing parts of her that rarely ever feel the open air. She is now in plain view of anyone who cared to look, and of course, nobody looks. Nobody cares whether she is naked or not.

The damp grass beneath the soles of her feet feels good. The mud squishes pleasingly between her toes, reminding her of times long gone, of her delight as a child to play barefoot that way. As she steps across the grass towards the sauna yurt, there is still nobody staring at her. They are all content, all immersed in whatever they are doing – be it naked yoga, naked hammocking or naked lounging.

She reaches the outer doors of the sauna and pulls them open releasing an immediate, but not overpowering scent of wet hot wood and sweat. Remembering what Saffi said, Anna lets the outer doors close before pulling open the wooden inner doors. As she does, an intense, damp heat rushes out towards her from the darkness inside. As she steps forward through the doors, the hot padded inside of the doors bumps against her bottom. She jumps forward, trying not to think of all the bottoms those doors may have bumped against in the dark before hers. She stands there, awkward in the darkness, feeling the warmth of the wood flooring below her feet. The moist air is rich with sounds of deep breathing and sighs of release. She can't see the other people in there, but suspects they can see her.

Is Cedar here? Anna wonders. *Could he be here watching me now? Seeing me naked?* She feels a rush of adrenaline at the thought.

It's taking a while for her eyes to adjust. She feels a mild panic rising which makes it even harder to breathe in the damp air. A hot, moist, unknown hand reaches out for hers.

"Here," a woman's voice says gently. Anna wants to pull her hand away, to not touch someone else's sweat, but then she stops herself, realising that this person is trying to help her. The hand leads her further in.

"Here... there's a seat over here," another voice says.

Someone else reaches out too and takes her hand, leading her deeper in and further along. The unseen hands guide her through the dark, and Anna feels their kindness as they lead her to an empty space.

"Here." Anna recognises the last voice. Maddy's slender hand helps her lower herself down onto a hot, damp wooden bench. It is still too dark to see much, but Anna can hear the breathing and feel the heat of the people on either side of her. The dampness of the bench makes her think of how many people must have sat on that very spot, naked and sweating. The thought makes her so squeamish she almost stands again, except that she doesn't want to appear foolish to the others, who can clearly see her perfectly well. She slides as close as possible to the edge of the bench and makes a mental note to bring something to sit on next time. *If there is a next time.*

Moon observes Anna from the edge of her vision, noting how she seems hardly able to breathe in here. *Breathe!* Moon wants to say. *It won't hurt you!* Moon actually enjoys the mixture of scents here – the earth, the wood, the wet, other human beings, the gentle scent of the orange essential oil they use to cleanse the benches every few hours. Moon inhales the heat into her lungs deep as it will go and exhales, willing the tension she can still feel lodged under her ribs to release.

As Anna's eyes slowly adjust to the low red-orange light, she can now see that they are in a round wooden space, with benches lining the sides in two semi-circles. Six people sit on the bench opposite and about the same number are on Anna's bench. All are naked. None of them are Cedar. This brings both disappointment and relief in equal measure. She can see Moon now, sitting there on the other side of Maddy. One of the hands guiding her had been Moon's.

There is a wood-burning stove at one end of the yurt, which has just been stoked up, and is merrily making all the heat and smoke Anna had seen spiralling up into the sky earlier. Between her and the stove there is only one other person – a man with curly leg hair. Anna tries not to look at him directly, feeling strange being next to a naked man who's not her partner, a man who's sitting so close that each time she relaxes her thighs she can feel the tickle of his leg hairs. She makes herself as small as possible, shifting a little closer to Maddy.

Moon glances briefly in Anna's direction. *How can I help her? She looks so uncomfortable.*

"Anna, this is Crow, our drummer." Moon gestures affectionately towards the man sitting beside Anna. "You might recognise him from last night."

"Hi," the man says, his voice cheerful. Trying to keep her eyes level with his face, Anna turns towards him and sees that it's the bearded man with the child-like cheeks who had giggled so much around the fire the night before – the one who had been staring at Moon and who she had felt a fondness for, since he'd seemed like the only other person there not totally comfortable in his own skin. *He's their drummer?*

"Hi, nice to meet you," Anna says, trying to sound equally friendly.

"You too." He holds out his right hand towards her. She doesn't want to offend him, so she reaches out and allows him to shake it.

Okay, this is awkward, Anna thinks about how strange it is to be introduced to someone for the first time unclothed and sweaty. She extracts her hand as soon as it is socially acceptable to do so and restrains herself from wiping her hand off on something, especially when she realises that the only thing she could wipe her hand on would be her own body, or the damp bench.

"Crow is an interesting name. Did you pick it?" Anna asks, thinking of how Moon had picked her own name.

He chuckles. "Nope. Crowe is actually my last name, spelled with an 'e'. Most people outside of the band call me Alex. It was just that these guys decided to call me by my last name because they liked how it fit with theirs – Cedar, Moon, Crow..."

"And Ed," Maddy adds.

Alex chuckles. "Yeah, Ed... he likes to be original. Truth be told, really, Ed is the one you should call Crow. He's the dark, clever one."

"In mythology Crow is the trickster," Maddy says.

Alex raises an eyebrow. "Ah. Well, there you go."

"Also, like raven, he can travel betweem worlds," Moon says. "It has become a kind of medicine name for you, though, hasn't it Crow?"

Alex doesn't really know about medicine names, but he has to admit that since Moon began calling him that name in the band, something has changed for him.

Moon knows there's power in a name. The vibration of a name affects a person. It had felt compelling for her to call him Crow after a few of their rehearsals, and she had noticed a palpable change in his drumming afterwards. It had become deeper, stronger, but lighter and more dynamic too, as if he had begun to see himself that way.

Alex shrugs. "When it comes to you, Moon, you can call me anything you like."

He says it like a joke, but Anna catches a brief look in his eyes that reminds her of the way he had been gazing at Moon the night before. He means this. Moon catches it too, and reigns herself in. She reminds herself not to draw comfort from the affections of Alex as a remedy for the ache of Cedar. She can feel the ache there now, the grief still held within her energy, still asking to be healed. It will take some time. Being with Maddy is helping, but Moon wants to cry every time she puts her attention on that pain. She knows the only way to let the feelings go is to feel them, to let them flow through her and to breathe through them. Every now and then, she allows the tears to quietly flow, blending seamlessly with the sweat already dripping down her cheeks.

Anna is feeling the heat now, too. Sweat is beginning to bead on her body, which has stayed dry for longer than she expected it to. She realises she should have showered first.

Maddy stands. "I'm going to go take a plunge."

"Oh yeah. Me too," Alex says, following her out.

"I'm going to stay in a bit longer," Moon says softly. She's not done sweating this one out.

Anna stays too, feeling like Moon is a kind of lifeline for her, and she should only leave when Moon does, even though the heat is feeling almost too intense for her already. Moon has closed her eyes again and lets out a breath of relaxation. Glad to not have to think of something to say and with more space on the bench beside her, Anna relaxes a little more too. *Maybe it's not so bad in here after all.*

The six or seven other people also in the sauna have their eyes closed too, and seem to be meditating. This stillness has its effect on Anna, and she is drawn into a more quiet space herself. She closes her own eyes, her thoughts returning to the night before, to the moment when Cedar had given her the full force of the didgeridoo, and how she had felt something move inside her. How she had felt all the pain, and sadness, and loneliness had been washed away, replaced by such an extraordinary feeling of wellbeing, and love. She marvels at the memory of it. She had felt love for everyone in that tipi, for everyone outside the tipi, across the festival and beyond. Her mind travels back to the moment after Cedar had finished playing, and their eyes had met. She had felt truly seen, truly loved, truly understood.

As Anna sees these things in her mind's eye, she can feel the warmth again in the centre of her chest. *Yes, it's still there* – subtle but there. Her heart had opened last night, and some part of it remains open still. She lets her awareness rest in this feeling for a few moments, allowing herself to grow calmer still.

Opening her eyes again, Anna feels her place here with these people, as part of a shared experience, no longer like an outsider. She remembers what Moon had said about how in the sauna nobody is judging anyone else, and you start to see how truly beautiful people are, whatever their shape. Without overtly looking, Anna casts a soft gaze around the space. There are women and men, older and younger, some slim and some more heavily built. Anna realises with amazement, that what Moon had said is actually true. Somehow in seeing everyone together as a whole, she is able to see them all as uniquely beautiful in their own way. And it's not only them. With this awareness, Anna is more comfortable with her own body, too.

In seeing everyone this way, the realisation comes that even the things she had judged as unattractive about Moon's appearance earlier are really beautiful too. In actuality, these things only add to Moon's beauty. For this is Moon, being herself.

Moon lets out a deep breath and turns to face Anna. "So how are you finding it so far?"

"I'm starting to know what you mean. It does make you feel... better." Her rock-hard shoulders have begun to soften, just a little. The warmth is soaking into her bones. As her body sweats, it is as if all the negativity and fear still resonating inside her is ebbing away. She doesn't even mind the scent in the room anymore and is actually starting to enjoy the whole experience, aside from her growing thirst.

"Well, I'm cooked," Moon says, rising slowly. "I'll see you out there."

"I'll come with you," Anna says, following Moon out into the bright sun, which temporarily blinds her. She closes her eyes for a moment. The air feels amazing, dancing over her bare skin. When she opens her eyes again, Anna sees Moon is off in the direction of the plunge pool, where Alex and Maddy are now splashing one another.

Above the plunge pool, the trees are swaying in the same breeze that is cooling Anna's bare skin. It is peaceful here. Anna can feel a lightness lifting inside herself and just a glimmer of understanding about why everyone in here looks so darn happy.

At the water cask, she fills her cupped hands again, drinking and drinking until she is satisfied. As she does, she enjoys the feel of the sun on her bare back. The young half-dressed singer is still crooning her sweet and sultry jazz songs on the stage. The audience seems utterly content, lazing in the sun. Naked yoga is still happening, but now Anna doesn't find it so strange. They look like they are really enjoying themselves.

And why shouldn't they? she thinks to herself.

Moon has dived into the plunge pool with Maddy and Alex and they are all splashing each other now, laughing and seeming very comfortable all together. Briefly, Anna feels a pang of contraction, knowing that she can't quite manage diving into the communal paddling pool. But even that little worry passes in the freshness of this feeling of standing naked on the grass, bathed in sunshine. Besides, she's looking forward to the shower.

As she turns on the nozzle, the spray of water is like ice on her flushed skin. She cries out with the cold, but it is also a cry of delight, because it feels so good! Her body tingles as she lets lets the cold water wash over her and over her, washing off all the sweat and dirt, cleansing her on levels she is not even aware of. In this moment, standing refreshed and naked beneath the open sky, Anna feels free – smiling to herself, for nobody but herself.

Damien will never believe me if I tell him about this.

With the thought comes a contraction in the energy of her whole body. She doesn't know how she can possibly tell him about the sauna, or about last night – *especially about last night.* She feels the gulf between herself and Damien widening, with no way she can think of to integrate it and remembers again what Johannes said about how she hides her true self away in this relationship, and how she can never be truly happy in a relationship unless it is with someone she can be her whole self with.

Could I be my whole self with Cedar? It feels to Anna as if he's seen all of her already. Last night, in those eyes, she had been wholly accepted, wholly loved – and all without words or physical touch.

Cold now, she turns off the water. This time she hurries into the sauna shivering and craving the intense heat. She makes her way through the two sets of doors back into the dark, avoiding the bump of the doors. Her eyes adjust more quickly than before and she can see there are only two others here now – a man and a woman sitting across from her. The others have gone to sit out in the sun and listen to the jazz singer.

"The fire is burning, it's burning, in you and in me..." the singer's voice carries through from the outside. *"...and the world it is turning, returning with this energy..."*

Anna finds a seat near the woodburning stove so she can be nearest to the source of the heat. She closes her eyes and wonders if Moon or the others will be back. She doesn't have to wonder long, as only a few moments later the three make their way back in, giggling about something Alex has said. They stand in the centre of the space, waiting for their eyes to adjust. This time, Anna reaches out and touches Moon's hand, guiding her to the bench.

"There's lots of room now," Anna says. "This whole side of the bench is empty."

They all sit down, one next to each other, with Alex closest to the door and Moon next to Anna. The couple on the opposite bench rises to leave, and it is now just the four of them.

They all sit and just breathe, soaking up the heat, but there is a conversation that wants to happen hovering in the air between them. They've all been thinking about last night.

It's Maddy who speaks first. "That was special last night."

The rest of them murmur agreement.

"Yes, it was," Moon agrees. *For many reasons.* She wonders if Maddy means the music or the falling asleep in one another's arms and what came after. *Perhaps it is both,* she reasons, because Maddy reaches over and squeezes Moon's hand gently.

"I've never experienced anything like that before," Anna hears herself say. She realises she has a longing to speak about these things with others. To somehow integrate what's happened. To know whether they felt the same things – the feeling of being part of everything.

"It's true," Maddy says. "Moon, your voice... I've never heard it like that before. So primal. Both of you were like that. Different. Cedar's didge was... quite an experience."

Yes. Anna thinks. *It was like that for me too.*

"I can only imagine what it must have been like for you, Anna." Maddy's eyes shine. "I felt some of it just sitting beside you."

"What do you mean?" She feels a flutter inside.

"Cedar spent such a long time on you. And he was doing something... singing something through his didge. He did something quite special with you, I think."

Moon takes a breath. She'd noticed that too. Today, thinking about it brings a little more intensity to the pain lodged in her ribs. *More to sweat out then.*

"Was it really so much longer than anyone else?" Anna asks, finding it hard to believe. Time had ceased to have meaning in those moments Cedar's attention had been on her. Her heart flutters to think that perhaps he had offered her something special.

"Oh yeah," Alex chimes in. "He didged everyone around the circle before you for maybe a couple of minutes each and then when he got to you... Wow. I don't know. He just turned up the intensity and something happened. He just kept didging you. And didging you. And didging you."

Oh. Anna feels the flutter again. *Why? Why would he do that?*

Moon can feel the emotions rising up again inside herself as she catches the look of pleasure on Anna's face.

It's not you, Moon wants to say. *Don't think it means he wants you.*

And before Moon can breathe and centre herself again, the words are out of her mouth, in a desire to squash this thing she sees.

"I've seen him do that before. Cedar is very sensitive to energy. He told me once that in moments of real heightened awareness, he can even see energy fields. Like, if someone comes into the group who's maybe a little less grounded or maybe needs some extra healing for some reason, then he'll give them more attention. He sees the connection between everyone. It's not a personal thing. It's just about balancing energy. Clearing blockages, so that everyone can flow together."

Moon's remark feels like a slap to Anna. *You're not special*, is what Anna hears. *The only reason he didged you so long is that you would have been holding the group back with your 'blockages'.*

Anna can't understand this change in Moon, who had seemed so friendly only moments ago. Now there is a decidedly chill air coming from her direction.

Maddy turns her face to Moon. She knows her friend well and can feel what's going on for her now. Moon's body is radiating with a new tension, reflecting the war within her. Maddy reaches out for Moon's hand and squeezes it again. She knows that it will be some time before Moon can fully open her heart and find love with someone else and a long time before she can feel comfortable with Cedar's affections for anyone else. Maddy too could see that something had passed between Cedar and Anna last night. *Strength and love to you Moon*, Maddy beams to her.

Moon witnesses the anger flaring inside herself. As she takes conscious breath after conscious breath, Moon feels the emotions settling inside her and is able to sense the others around her again with her heart. She squeezes Maddy's hand back. Now she can feel what her comment has done to Anna, who is sitting there rigid, with eyes straight ahead.

This time Moon speaks with more softness in her voice. "I'm sorry if I sounded harsh, Anna. What I should have said is that Cedar probably just sensed in your energy some blockage or some imbalance and he just gave you a little extra to bring you into balance with the others in the room. I mean, you probably came right from Babylon or something, didn't you? And the rest of us had been in the Tipi Field for the whole day. That kind of thing makes a difference. It could happen to any of us."

Could it? Somehow I doubt it, Anna thinks miserably, her earlier feelings of well-being evaporating.

"As if you ever get unbalanced, Moon," Alex says.

Anna could have hugged Alex for saying that. This is exactly what she feels like. To Anna, Moon seems like the kind of person always to have everything perfectly under control.

Moon laughs. "Oh I do. Believe me. I do. I get unbalanced ALL the time. And I mean all the time. Like two minutes ago, for one. I'm the queen of the emotional roller coasters."

"She is," Maddy agrees affectionately, still squeezing Moon's hand. "But so am I. We all are. We're emotional beings aren't we? It's just what you do with the emotions that matters."

"Like how?" Alex wants to know. "I mean, you both always seem to have this serenity about you, like you've always got everything sussed."

Maddy laughs, and Moon has to smile. *If only you could see inside me. Then you'd know how often I lose my centre.* But Moon has learned techniques for rebalancing herself. So when she forgets herself, she usually doesn't stay that way long, even if the falling off centre has been spectacular and spark-filled. Her mind travels back again to the evening before, when Cedar had first told her the truth and she had felt like a wild beast, possessed.

"I suppose the thing is, I've learned to notice when I'm losing my centre. Usually. At a certain point, sometimes sooner, sometimes later, I become able to witness myself enough to see that I've fallen off centre and then I have certain techniques I do, that get me connected again and make me feel centered and grounded or whatever."

"Like what?" Alex asks, genuinely curious.

"Well, the most fundamental part of it relates to the breath," Moon says. "Breathing is always where it starts for me."

"Breathing? Like a special kind of breathing?" Alex asks.

"Conscious breathing. With awareness. That always brings me back to the moment. Always. It might take me ten or twenty breaths or fifty, but eventually, if I keep breathing I come back to awareness and whatever thoughts or emotions were knocking me off settle down and I feel my centre again."

"How do you do that... conscious breathing?" Alex asks.

"Just pay attention. Observe internally, each inhale, each exhale. And if thoughts come, bring your awareness back to the breath. It takes practice, but eventually you can get to the point where your mind is still enough to be aware of your breaths without much effort. Only intention."

A few moments pass, as if they are all testing out this theory.

"Shit," Alex says, shaking his head in mock seriousness. "It's not looking good for me. I only got half way through one breath before my mind was off. There's not much hope for me then."

"So did you bring it back?" Moon asks.

"Did I bring what back?"

"Your mind, when you noticed it had gone off and left you."

"Oh. No. I forgot."

Moon smiles. She won't laugh at Crow this time. "Okay, Crow," Moon says, with affection, "I hope you won't take this the wrong way, but I can see something that would help you a lot."

"Do tell."

"You're chest breathing. That's panic breathing. It takes you out of the moment and into fear. To really come back to your body with breathing you need to be breathing properly. Breathe into the belly." Moon pats her own abdomen.

"What do you mean by chest breathing?" Alex asks. "I've always breathed like this. This is how I breathe."

"Let me see," Moon says. "Do a couple of deep breaths for me."

Alex sits forward on the bench and puffs his chest out, displaying all its dripping wet curly hairs and proceeds to take several exaggerated breaths, causing the whole top half of his torso to expand and lift.

"That's not how you normally breathe, Crow."

"When I breathe deeply, I do," he says, in all seriousness.

Moon takes a slow breath, feeling compassion rising inside herself. She can see that he's not joking anymore. This matters to him.

"Crow, those breaths you're taking are exaggerated chest breaths. There's nothing deep about those. They're all up here." Moon gestures from her chest upwards.

Alex breathes again, trying to observe himself doing this. Again, his chest and shoulders rise and fall. Watching this, Anna feels a sinking feeling inside herself, and turns her attention to her own breathing. She can feel the distinctive rise and fall of her own chest and shoulders.

I breathe like that. With these realisations, a sense of loss comes over her. It's becoming more and more clear that there are a great many things she is doing wrong. She has no idea how to do them the right way, but derives some small comfort in the fact that Alex seems to be doing all the work for her, by courageously exposing his own weaknesses.

"So you're serious. I really breathe the wrong way?" Alex says, his usually jovial face taking on just a hint of real concern.

"Right...wrong... I'm not judging you, Crow. It's not for me to say what's right or wrong for you. It's just that I know our bodies were designed to breathe in a certain way. Like, as babies, we were born knowing how to breathe. I'm willing to bet that when you were born, you breathed with your abdomen. And then like most people, you learned from those around you how to breathe with your chest. And you forgot. It's not a big deal. Our bodies can remember. We just have to relearn it. Reclaim it. I did."

"So what am I doing wrong then? Can you show me?"

Moon holds out her hands in a sideways V-shape. "You have to imagine your diaphragm is like a bellows, opening and closing like this... and when it opens... the air flows in. And when it closes... the air flows out. For you, your chest and shoulders are doing all the work your diaphragm should be doing. It's creating loads of tension up here, and it means that you're not accessing the power of being rooted deeper in your body."

Anna can see Alex is struggling heroically to make his diaphragm move, but to no avail. He is jutting out his belly in a comical way, which is not intended to be comical, and still his chest is noticeably rising and falling. Moon knows she shouldn't laugh and she reigns herself in. This is serious for him. She can see that he's really trying.

While Alex continues to exert himself in plain view of everyone, Anna is also trying secretly to breathe properly herself and having desperately similar results.

"Am I doing it right now? This still doesn't feel right."

Moon suppresses a smile. *Of course it doesn't feel right, dear Crow.* "It's not going to feel right until you free your diaphragm. You need to work with someone who can help you. You'll get it, Crow. Honestly, if you work at it, you'll get it. I promise."

Moon can feel what he wants to ask. He's grown silent, and shy. *Would you? Would you be the one?*

"Anyone can learn to breathe. You just need the right teacher, Crow. I don't think I'm probably the right person to help you. Maybe you should ask Cedar. He knows about breathing too. And he'll actually be strong enough to help you with that."

Strong enough? Anna wonders. *For what exactly?*

Alex nods and sighs. "Okay."

No one speaks for a moment, but unspoken thoughts remain potent in the air.

"My God I need to drink some water," Alex says finally, standing up and pushing his way out the doors.

Moon lets out a breath.

"Me too," Anna says, feeling slightly faint from thirst and heat and failed attempts to breathe properly in the damp heat. She follows Alex out into the sun. It's refreshing to breathe the cooler air again. This time, the delight of her senses is mingled with the confusion inside her about all that she can't do, and Cedar and what it all means.

When Alex has finished drinking at the water barrel, Anna bends down and drinks again from her cupped hands.

Alex dives again into the plunge pool, this time seeming more subdued. Anna heads for the showers again, letting the cold water run over her and over her, willing it to wash away all the bad feelings, the guilt and the self-judgement. She closes her eyes and just feels the coolness of the water streaming down her face and over every surface of her body. She stays there like that, until her skin begins to numb with the coldness. When she steps out of the water and opens her eyes, she gazes up at the blue sky above. A thought comes to Anna that lifts her and sends waves of excitement through her body.

Maybe I can learn to breathe. If I can find the right teacher.

Maybe Cedar could be my teacher too!

In her mind's eye, Anna sees an image of herself, alone with Cedar, being initiated into the art of breathing. Her pulse quickens. Standing there, naked under the sky, she feels a new daring, an aliveness tingling in her body that she hasn't experienced before, as if there really is something moving towards her, something new and indescribably exciting.

There is a world these people know about. I want to know about it too.

Moon and Maddy emerge from the sauna, looking flushed and relaxed and moving in the direction of the water barrel. They bend to fill the communal cup, taking turns drinking from it.

They seem happy to drink from the communal cup, Anna realises. *Maybe I should too.*

But she doesn't. Not yet.

Moon and Maddy join Alex who is sprawled out on an open patch of grass, soaking up the sunshine. Anna sits herself down on the grass in an open space beside the others. She knows she will have to find food soon. The thought of leaving here and trudging back across the camping field to wait for an hour or more at the cash machines doesn't feel good at all. She wants to stay here with these people. *And Damien will be worried. I should probably go and call him.*

Moon arches her back and stretches her arms up, flexing the muscles on her upper arm and making it seem as if the wolf's legs really are moving. "I'm ravenous."

"Me too," Maddy agrees, sitting upright.

Me too! Anna's stomach gurgles.

"Who wants a smoothie?" Moon turns to them. "On me. My friend is working in the cafe at the moment. He'll make us something special."

"Oh, yes please! I would love one." Maddy claps her hands with a childlike delight.

"I'll second that." Alex raises a hand from the grass.

"Okay. That's three for smoothies. Anna?" Moon asks, turning toward her.

Really? Me too? There are no traces now of the strangeness of earlier in Moon's friendly face, and yet, Anna feels wary, as if they could reappear at any moment. "I... I would love one. Thank you. I'll pay you back."

"No need." Moon shakes her head. "It all comes around."

Anna watches Moon as she saunters over to the flap of fabric that covers the entrance and disappears behind it, not seeming to mind at all that she has just walked out into public view with everything showing.

The jazz singer is finishing her set now, and people clap. Alex hoists himself up to a seated posture and regards the changeover happening onstage. The sound man is helping the next act on to the stage. Anna does a double take and can't help giggling. It's a band of three musicians who truly are wearing only their instruments – a guitar, a djembe and a violin.

"Where else on site, hey?" Alex grins towards her. "I have to admit, I'll get my kit off for a sauna no problem, but I gotta hand it to those guys. It takes some courage to get up on stage completely starkers."

Anna turns her eyes away from the stage, to avoid staring. Especially at the violinist, who she notes with appreciation must be particularly brave.

"So, Anna, what are you doing at the festival?" Alex asks her. "Are you working here?"

"Working... uh... sort of." Anna falters, not knowing how much to share about herself. She feels so strange about all of it. "I uh... I had a gig here."

"Oh really?" He's genuinely interested. "What do you play?"

"I... sing and play guitar." The words feel false the moment they come out of her mouth, as if she doesn't really believe it anymore. *Do I? Do I really know how to sing and play? Not the way I want to. Not the way others seem to be able to do.*

"So, who are your influences then?" Alex asks.

"Um... I'm not sure really. Lots of people."

"Well, give me one of them. Like... who's your favourite? I mean, who inspires you the most?"

Anna tries to think of an answer that will satisfy him, and not make her sound shallow. She listens to lots of music back home, mostly chosen by Damien. They usually have Radio One on in the car, and sometimes the other chart stations, but she can't really say that she really finds much of that truly inspiring. She recognises the desire she'd nursed for so long that one day she would be one of those women singing on the radio and making it into those charts. She feels a loss inside herself when she thinks about it. It's like a dream belonging to somebody else. *And what is my dream now? I thought I wanted that more than anything, but I wonder if it was really true.* She wonders if perhaps there had always been a deeper desire buried in her for something more fulfilling than that. Something she had just begun to see last night in the Big Tipi.

Anna looks back at Alex. He's still waiting.

Who inspires me? Does anyone? This thought brings a profound sadness to Anna, but then she realises it isn't actually true. A memory comes to her of one of those childhood trips in the car with her father, when he would put on the Band, or Neil Young, or Van Morrison. Or Dylan. Those experiences had made their mark on her. And following on from that, a vivid flash again of the music from the night before. *Yes. There are people who inspire me.*

"I think maybe I was inspired in some ways by music my Dad played me when I was younger," Anna answers finally. "Like... Neil Young. Dylan. The Band."

"Yeah. For sure. Levon Helm, man. That guy was an awesome drummer."

Encouraged, Anna speaks the rest of it. "But... now... I think maybe I'm being inspired by new things too, like... like what Cedar and Moon did last night."

Alex nods vigorously. "I know. I swear, I don't know why those guys let me be in their band."

"Because they know you're on the verge of greatness, Crow," Maddy joins in.

"Well you know..." He feigns bravado. "And anyway, what d'ya mean, 'on the verge'? Greatness is already here." Alex thumps his chest.

Maddy laughs, but then her expression turns intently serious. Maddy knows that Crow sometimes uses humour to hide the fact that he doesn't actually think this about himself, and more likely the opposite. "You joke, Crow. But you are right, you know."

He stares at her. "About what?"

"You are great. We all are." She lifts her face to the sun and closes her eyes. "We just forget we are. Until something helps us to remember." Maddy speaks this, thinking of herself, and of what has transpired between herself and Moon since last night. For years, the feelings she had borne for Moon had no reciprocity. Moon had loved her as a friend, but it was no more than that, and it had been a deep challenge for Maddy, ultimately becoming a powerful catalyst for her to discover self-love – what it is to be able to love unconditionally, to generate love from within the self, without needing it from another. It had become enough in those moments she had been able to do it.

But now after what had happened this morning, something big has changed. She thinks of that look she'd seen in Moon's eyes as they'd held one another, which had made her own heart leap for joy. The look that had told her what she had dreamed of for so long was really happening. *Moon loves me too.* And that extraordinary kiss that sent electric currents to the tips of her toes and made her heart expand to bursting. Maddy has kissed lots of women. She prefers women by quite a long way. But never has she felt a kiss like that. It was electric. Remembering it now sends shivers through her body.

Maddy thinks about the challenge this will bring not to fall into accepting someone else's love in place of the love she has discovered in herself. To keep the flow going. To keep remembering. To keep feeling the centre inside herself, and to not make someone else the centre of her universe, which would be so easy to do with Moon. But Maddy knows that it is a dance, remembering and forgetting. And that remembering is about being in this moment, *for this moment is the only moment that you can remember. As soon as you begin to worry that you might forget yourself in the future, you have already left the present, already forgotten.*

"To remember what exactly?" Alex asks.

Maddy opens her eyes and regards him. "That you have a universe in you. That the universe begins in you and radiates in all directions infinitely, because you are God. Or Goddess, if you prefer. And that love can pour through you if you let it."

Maddy's words send a tingle through Anna's body. *Love can pour through you...*

Alex opens his mouth as if to make a crack such as *well obviously I'm God...* but he closes it again because Maddy's eyes have a fire in them, and he finds himself wordless for a moment, considering her meaning.

"You're God. I'm God. The naked sound man, he's God," Maddy says.

"He's definitely God," Alex nods. "And King Krule over there on the Park Stage, he's God."

"He is," Maddy agrees.

"And the guy at the gate who searched my van and took all my glass beer bottles away. I didn't think he was God at the time. But even him, he's God."

"Yep."

"My dentist, he's God."

"Yep."

"Anna's God." Alex tilts his head towards Anna.

"She is." Maddy nods again.

Anna laughs, feeling like she should respond with something humorous, but she can't find the words, because the idea that Maddy and Alex have just told her she is God is sending flutters of excitement bubbling through her. *It's ridiculous*, she tells herself. *It's a joke.* But there is something in her responding to this as if it were true.

"Hey, Anna, did you know you're God?" Alex turns to her.

"Uh... not recently," she replies, trying to be clever, but then remembers the night before. Had that been anything to do with what Maddy just described? That feeling of having love inside her, of not needing anything because everything seemed to well up from inside. Like the centre of everything was inside her.

"I feel like I knew it last night," Maddy says softly as if to herself. "At least for a moment or two."

"Knew what?" Moon asks, sauntering up with a tray containing four large cardboard cups. Anna's mouth waters at the sight of the green-coloured concoctions.

Maddy allows her eyes to meet Moon's and sees a softness there.

But it's Alex who answers. "We were discussing the fact that I am God, and Anna is God, and the naked sound man is God. And I have a universe inside me, apparently." He shrugs.

"As you do." Moon sets the tray down onto the grass in front of them.

"What's in these?" Alex asks, peering down at the cups.

"Spirulina, wheatgrass juice, banana and apple."

Alex lifts the first cup and brings it suspiciously to his nose, sniffing it and then with a nod of approval, chugs it down.

Anna grabs the next cup and tries to restrain herself from seeming too desperate as she gulps down the drink, feeling it soothe the griping hole in her stomach. It is absolutely delicious.

Maddy and Moon are slower to pick up their smoothies, and drink them slowly, savouring the flavours over their tongues.

"Mmm," Maddy murmurs. "So good. Thank you."

"Yeah. So good," Alex agrees, draining the last of his cup and setting it back down on the tray the way someone would an empty beer glass.

Again, Anna feels the differences between herself and Moon and Maddy. She and Alex seem to be on the same side of something – both desperate gulpers, both unable to breathe properly.

"Hey, you know what's interesting?" Maddy says after a while. "You know how we were talking about who inspires us earlier? That word... 'inspiring'... it literally means 'breathing in'. And we were just speaking before about how important it is to breathe. It seems to me that being inspired must be completely connected to the breath."

"Yes! It is!" Moon nods emphatically. "When I feel truly inspired, it's always connected with the breath. Always. It gets the energy flowing. It brings the creativity through."

Anna's ears prick up with a sense that this is important. Before this weekend, Anna wouldn't have spoken her thoughts aloud, but this new part of her that feels like it's coming alive – this new daring self – makes her say it.

"I know I don't breathe properly." Anna hears herself blurting out the truth. "Maybe I would find it easier to be inspired if I could."

"I'm sure you would. I always do," Moon says.

Anna feels the things she wants to ask sticking in her throat. At the thought of Cedar, her heart pounds harder.

"Moon?"

"Yeah?"

"You mentioned Cedar could show Alex how to breathe. Do you think he could show me too?"

Moon feels the volatile emotions inside her flare up again. *Of course, you'd want him to teach you. Of course you would. He won't teach you.*

Anna notices the strange look that flits across Moon's eyes.

Moon takes a deep breath, and then another, remembering her own earlier comments about how to return to centre. She witnesses herself having these unkind thoughts about Anna and realises she can change them. After a few more breaths she feels able to respond properly.

"To be honest, Anna, I'm not sure Cedar would be the best person to teach you to breathe. I suggested him to Alex because Alex needs someone really strong – a male energy, if you will – and my intuition tells me that he's the right person for Alex. But for you..." Moon lets the intensity of her light grey-blue eyes – all the brighter out in the sunshine – rest on Anna for a moment, considering. The part of her that has difficult feelings about Anna is unsure she wants to offer this. But when she listens to that deeper, loving part of herself, she knows. It's clear – Anna is a sister.

"I could show you if you want."

You? Anna's heart flips, fears gripping her again. It was a woman who had tried to teach Anna to breathe properly before – an intimidating woman – and it had not been a happy experience. The woman teacher had been well-meaning, but she had struggled to show Anna how to breathe correctly because she had not been able to address the real, underlying emotional reasons why Anna was unable to bring her breath deeper in her body. So they had both become frustrated. Anna had felt condescended upon, and beyond that, she had been left with a deeper and more damaging impression – that there was something essentially wrong with her. So she had discontinued the lessons, and had almost discontinued singing altogether, were it not for the encouragement of her father. In the end she did carry on because she hadn't wanted to disappoint him. Rather than seek a new singing teacher, she had devised her own methods, which up until now had seemed to work for her, because it was all she had known how to do.

And now Moon is here with her clear eyes on Anna, offering to teach her. There is a frightening power in Moon. With all Moon's genuine kindness and generosity, Anna can sense the emotional volatility and ruthlessness in her. Last night around the fire at Pacha Mama Cafe, Moon's eyes had been those of a wild, unpredictable creature, who would do what needed to be done, regardless of whether it was comfortable or not. That same look had appeared briefly in the sauna earlier, and a flash of it just a few moments ago.

Can I trust Moon? And what if I can't do it?

Moon is still regarding her, expectant.

Just say yes. The thought seems to arrive in her mind. *Just say yes. Yes. Yes. Yes.*

"Yes," she hears herself say the word, even as her heart is pounding and her solar plexus is tensing and the thoughts are whirling.

"Are you sure? You looked a moment ago like I was asking you if you wanted to go jump off a cliff."

Anna lets out a sigh, accepting that she is not so good at hiding her emotions as she likes to think, at least not with someone as perceptive as Moon.

"I... I've just had some bad experiences with a singing teacher years ago... a woman... that's all... and I..."

Moon nods understanding. "No problem. I completely get it. So how's tomorrow for you? Sometime late morning?"

Anna opens her mouth. It's all happening so fast. "Uh... Tomorrow? Uh... okay. Great."

"My tipi is two down from the Big Tipi. You'll know it because there's a little purple dreamcatcher hanging out front. Meet me there at ten?"

"Okay," Anna agrees. "Ten it is."

Now, having drunk her smoothie, Anna tells herself that there really are no more excuses. It's time to go. She's working up to saying goodbye to them all when Maddy stands.

"I'm going to go back in. Once more for me."

"Yeah. Me too." Moon rises to follow Maddy.

"Yeah. I could do one more," Alex says, trailing after them.

Anna hesitates, watching them go. She can tell by the angle of the sun it's well into the afternoon.

Damien must be really worried by now.

But the other three are already disappearing through the doors of the sauna and Anna doesn't want to leave without saying goodbye.

Just one more, she tells herself, and follows them back inside.

The sauna is pretty much full this time. Anna is guided again by friendly hands to a spare seat. Moon sits to Anna's left, breathing deeply. Anna tries to breathe deeply too, but all she can feel is the frustrating restriction of her limited chest breathing, now that she's aware of it. It's also hard to settle because her mind is whirling with thoughts about this terrifying thing she has agreed to do tomorrow with Moon.

She decides to just stay long enough to get warm again when a man – fully naked of course – steps into the sauna with an armload of wood. George is one of the staff at Lost Horizon. He bends down on one knee and opens the wood burning stove to reveal the glowing orange embers of a fire. Following him is a woman Anna can't help staring at. She appears to Anna like a nymph, with a nubile body and extraordinary long brown dreadlocks, swaying to her waist and woven with beads. The woman stands poised in the centre of the room, just breathing, with sarong-like fabric draped over her left arm and waiting while her co-worker stokes the fire. Anna watches as the flames burn brighter.

"Over to you Ells," George is happy to leave the next bit to Ella. She seems to have a knack for it.

The nymph-woman reaches down to one side of the wood burner and lifts up a ladle, holding it upright, so as not to spill whatever is inside it.

"What have you got in there?" Alex asks.

"Essential oil. We make our own blends. This is the sexy one." Ella gives him a wry smile, pouring the contents of the ladle onto the wood burning stove. With the hiss of the steam, there is a faint, yet delicious aroma filling the room. The heat intensifies, beading on Ella's skin.

Now she gets to do her favourite thing. Ella steps into the centre of the room and begins to whirl the fabric she's been carrying helicopter style above her head, wafting the scented steam around the room. Anna stares at this vision, awestruck.

If this young woman had been goddess-like before, she is even more so now, with her feet planted firmly on the ground and her hips swaying with the movement of the fabric. The scent intensifies so that the sweet, intoxicating scent permeates everything. As Anna breathes it into her lungs, it does something to her. The heat is almost more than she can handle, but it feels good, as if it could burn away everything she doesn't want anymore. She no longer wants to leave, welcoming this.

Satisfied with what she has created, Ella sends a little heart prayer intention of love and healing for those who are here and then steps out.

Anna closes her eyes again and just breathes – as best she can – willing all the tension and pain to leave her body with the sweat. As it drips down her body and through the cleft in between her breasts, it brings her awareness again here to the centre of her chest, where the warmth of the night before still seems to be humming.

From within the circle of breathing, a clear, rich note rises. Anna realises with surprise that it is coming from a large woman sitting beside her. The note is low, rising out from deep in the woman's belly, creating a resonance right inside Anna's own body.

Joyce is a sound healer, and knows about the power of the human voice. She was given a large body to work with in this life, and she knows that one of the reasons she can sing the powerful way she does is because of how she is built. She used to feel bad about it when she was younger, but now she feels a love for this body – shaped like the traditional Mother Earth goddess – for all that it gives her.

Immersed in steam and scent, Joyce's sound resonates around them all in the space – a call to listen. On Anna's other side, Moon joins in, adding a clear, strong note. As Joyce's note shifts, so Moon shifts hers in perfect harmony. And now another voice lifts to join them – Maddy's – and yet another, until there are voices moving together around Anna from all sides. She listens with amazement. These people haven't planned this. They don't know each other. And yet, here they are creating an extraordinarily beautiful harmony of sound.

How do they just know what to sing? Here I am supposed to be a singer, and I'm the only one in this room not singing. But then she realises that Alex isn't singing either. He wears an expression Anna imagines is similar to hers, wondering how this is all happening, and whether he should be trying to join in.

Anna had always just thought it was a special skill to improvise, and not one she had. But sitting here, surrounded by all these people who must not all be singers or even musicians, she is dismayed. They are all creating this extraordinary thing right here without any practice or planning.

I should be able to do it too, she tells herself, feeling smaller, and more inadequate.

So she tries to find a note that fits in with what the rest of them are doing. Unsure if it's quite right, Anna hums it quietly to herself first before singing it aloud. When she finds one that works, she starts to sing it and notices that the harmony in the room has shifted again and now her note stands out, dissonant. Embarrassed, Anna withdraws. She decides to try just singing along with Moon's note, but as Moon shifts her harmony, Anna's note is left straggling. She gives up, collapsing within herself.

You're not like them. You can't do what they do. But even as the harsh voice inside Anna's head carps at her in its usual mode, it seems to be less substantial somehow, less able to draw her into its usual train of logic. Something else is happening here, and its pull is stronger. It reminds Anna a little of the music last night in the tipi. It is in the rising and falling notes and the silences in between moving around her in waves, and she lets go of trying to join in and lets it lap against her, and through her, slowly drawing her back to the feeling of belonging she had felt before.

Now, with surprise, she can hear something. A note. It's inside her. Nobody else is singing it. Anna allows herself to sing this note aloud and to her delight, it is in perfect harmony.

The ability to hear the note inside her comes and goes, with her own thoughts. The more she tries to grasp at the note the more it disappears. The more she just lets go and listens to the room, the more she can hear the note arising within her. And the more she does this, the more joyful it feels to be part of the rising and falling crescendos of sounds.

She is singing with them in the moment when the last note rings out into still-ness and all she hears in that internal listening is silence. The moist air around Anna still seems to be humming with it, and they are all listening, breathing with it. The fire crackles in the wood burner. The silence in here is louder than the wild expanse of the festival outside.

It hasn't felt to Anna that she's been in the sauna that long, but she suspects some time has passed and that she's probably lost track of time. She knows it by the feel-ing in her body. Dehydration. Light-headedness. *I need to drink right now.*

She glances at the other three. They all have their eyes closed, just breathing, still listening. Anna decides not to disturb them to say goodbye. *I'll be seeing Moon tomorrow anyway.* Here in this moment, the thought no longer feels frighten-ing. Excitement is bubbling up inside her again. She feels at the brink of walking through a doorway, a portal, into a new understanding of the world.

Letting herself out into the fresh air, Anna heads straight for the water, and notices that she is picking up the communal cup. She fills it and drinks deeply.

As she walks to the shower, she enjoys the feeling of the grass, cool and wet beneath her feet. She feels her body tingling alive as the icy spray washes over her. In this moment, she knows she is part of something, a note in a symphony, like the beautiful, always shifting harmonies that they had been singing in the sauna.

It feels like a new world! The leaves on the trees seem to stand out more crisply. The kiss of the breezes on her wet skin, each one a delight.

On her way out of the Tipi Field, Anna passes Pacha Mama Cafe again, the sur-face of the wishing well glinting in the sun.

Well, I did feel more brave today. So maybe my wish did come true. Maybe wishes can come true after all.

Stepping back out onto the main trackway leading down through the camping fields, a slight heaviness begins to settle around Anna, brought on by the sur-roundings. And yet it does feel different than before. The mud from the night before has already dried in the wind and sun. The smell of the loos that she passes by is less than pleasant, but even with that and the rubbish being blown against the hedge, Anna doesn't feel so separate from the people around her as she had before.

She doesn't feel like a lost soul. She thinks about how each of the people she passes could be like her, and with amusement, remembers what Alex had said. *Anna's God.*

She smiles to herself. *That man walking by me drinking a coconut through a straw. He's God.*

That woman with the pink wig and fishnet stockings. She's God.

That guy drinking a beer at his tent. He's God.

Really? she wonders. But she likes the game. Maybe like her, any of these people could find someone who could help them feel their hearts. Perhaps they could find themselves in a sauna with music washing over them and suddenly be able to hear the exact right note to sing. Maybe they already have.

Anna looks down again at the damp, yellow wristband on her arm which reads: *Find Yourself at Lost Horizon.*

Yes, I have found something, she realises, feeling a new fire burning inside her. At the edge of her awareness is a sense that actually, this fire is not new. It is an old part of her, as old as her own soul, a fire remembered.

> "Come wind and come rain
> Come time a turning
> Come circle me again
> Come fires burning
> From four corners of the earth
> And meet me in the middle
> Come death and come birth
> For I am light and shadow
> Courage lead me to the flames
> Paint ashes on my skin and
> Phoenix guide me through the fire
> That I may rise again and
> Calling out to the wind
> To teach me to dissolve
> Into this beating heart again
> Come crashing ocean waves
> Salty treasure keeper
> Come singing spirit caves
> Teach me to go deeper
> Wind blow me into dusk
> And plant me in the river

Show me how to trust
For I am gift and giver
Courage lead me to the flames
Paint ashes on my skin and
Phoenix guide me through the fire
That I may rise again and
Calling to the wind
To teach me to dissolve
Into this living earth again
This breathing earth again
This breathing heart again"

from the song, 'Phoenix' by Susie Ro Prater

3. Air

"Wind roars sou'westerly
Thinning out the woods
Dancing air warms the soil
Rattling all the buds
Spring tide stampedes silver horses
Over flotsam shore
It's a salty blow, a wind of change
Tumbling all before"

from the song, 'E.P.N.S.', by Brian Boothby

The Unfairground. Anna knows this isn't the place for her to find any gigs, but still something compels her to enter this arena, to walk along the empty track and just stare – it's so completely bizarre.

At this time of day, the Unfairground is virtually empty of punters. As in some other busy areas around the festival, the grass here has been trampled to dirt and mud and dust, but most of that happened the night before. This is one of the festival's most popular all night raving areas and so at the moment, many of its denizens are still sleeping. Even in the absence of the full carnival crazy wildness that happens only at night, Anna is still struck by the scene here, mildly horrified and disturbed, and yet also curious at the dreams that would invent such a place. From the sounds she had heard emerging from this direction in the early morning hours, it's clear that a lot of people willingly choose to step into this particular dream landscape.

Giant baby-dolls, painted black, with arms and legs missing and pointed at odd angles leer down from atop black upended cars and buildings edged with neon.

There is one giant pink baby-doll, its arms removed and replaced by grotesque metal limbs. Nearby, a spinning wheel with screaming gored plastic heads on the end of every spoke whirls merrily around. As tall as Anna, a giant eyeless and bodiless baby-doll head guards one of the venues ahead of her.

She snaps a few photos on her phone for Damien and stops to gaze up at the venue with three raised carousel horses rearing their heads, or what's left of them, as the original heads have been removed and replaced by sheep skulls and their bodies painted to show internal organs.

Eventually, Anna reminds herself of her mission. *Find more gigs. What were you thinking Anna?*

She looks down at the now crumpled yellow band on her wrist. Only a short while before, with the singing still ringing in her heart Anna had felt like a new life was possible. She had felt such hope walking back from the sauna, as if something really had changed for the better. But surrounded by the chaos of her tent and slipping back into familiar patterns on the phone with Damien, the old feelings of anxiety had begun to get their tendrils into her again. Except this time, it was different, and worse, because of the contrast to how she'd felt only an hour before.

And just when they were saying goodbye to one another after spending an hour integrating why Anna hadn't called him sooner, Damien had remembered to ask how her gig went and how many CDs she had sold. Anna had not lied, exactly. *I didn't sell as many as I hoped, but I have a chance to play a second gig.*

So as before, she had set out on the dusty track to search for more gigs. Except today is different than yesterday. Last night changed everything. On the surface, it seems the same, because Anna is watching herself doing exactly what Johannes had described – wearing the mask and doing what she thinks others want her to do.

You put on this mask for the world because you don't have confidence in this inner you... You feel you have to pretend, to create a persona that society will accept...

Today, the search for gigs doesn't feel good. Or empowering.

Anna makes her way back to the track and carries on to the next arena, *Block 9*, which is a creative post-apocalyptic scene, housing a New York City block complete with a yellow taxi crashed into the roof, spewing smoke. Below the smoking taxi is the NYC *Downlow* venue, out of which loud house music is blaring. Several people emerge from the venue, wearing fake black moustaches. Across the way, there is another venue – a facade of a decaying cement tower block, with a portion of a real London Underground train crashed into the fifth story, also spewing smoke.

Amazing what people can create, Anna thinks, staring at it all with awe. *Damien would love this too.* She snaps another photo and sends it to him, just so he knows she's thinking of him.

There are clearly no acoustic guitars operating here in Block 9 so Anna carries on further along the track into the *Field of Avalon*, where its main venue, *The Avalon Stage* is housed in a massive maroon circus style tent with flags flapping majestically on its peaks. Anna's little Glastonbury programme lists many eclectic and interesting performers playing at this stage: Penguin Cafe, Newton Faulkner, The Urban Voodoo Machine, Sir Bruce Forsyth among them. At the moment, a folk-punk band are playing some unusually vigorous Cornish tunes.

No, Anna sighs. *It's too big a stage to offer a last minute gig for someone like me.*

But not far away is the *Avalon Cafe* venue, where an energetic four-piece folk band are playing. She pushes her way through the enthusiastic crowds to reach the sound desk.

"Excuse me?" she asks, waving her hand at the man with headphones on.

The soundman is so focused on what he's doing that he doesn't turn to look at her. Anna is beginning to see herself now as a desperate character – a waif, a poor struggling songwriter, desperate for a gig, waiting, begging, empty-handed. This image of herself doesn't feel good at all, and it saps what little energy she has.

After waiting five more minutes, she gives up and heads back out onto the dust track, considering giving up altogether on this whole thing, just bingeing on chocolate and hiding in her tent. Hiding from everything. But she pushes herself on.

Don't give up, she urges herself, as she trudges past numerous traders, food stalls, and a tall wooden Helter-Skelter. She is particularly impressed by the two-story wood-beamed pub, *The Avalon Inn,* looking every inch the medieval pub, somehow constructed in the field this very week just for the festival.

This track leads into *Bella's Field,* with its massive yellow and red comedy venue. Next to the entrance is a small stage featuring a line of widely grinning women, swishing their fire engine red skirts as they dance the Can Can.

Anna finds herself walking through a forest of red sonic pylons, with white hand-prints on them. She reaches out and as she passes her hand over one of the handprints, there is a sound of ringing bells, like windchimes, and over the next handprint, windchimes of a different note. Beside her, a little blond boy is laughing with his mother as he squeezes his little hand over the white handmarks on his own pylon, creating a soundscape of bells. Anna can't help smiling. It evokes the feeling of being surrounded by windchimes hanging in forest.

She passes a tiny 8-seater cinema and the world's smallest nightclub, *The Minis-cule of Sound.* Not far away a talented one-man band holds forth in the centre of a large circle of people who are clapping along with his wild rhythms and dancing. There are walk-about acts everywhere. Anna's favourite are the two stiltwalking lady bees in fishnets and frilly yellow and black striped knickers.

And what's this? Anna peers down inside a tiny fenced off area, into a garden of hundreds of tiny clay heads and little naked clay bodies in various postures, dancing and lounging. There is even a miniature pyramid stage and a tiny circus tent and teeny-tiny bunting. It's a vision of a tiny, clay Glastonbury Festival.

Where would I be in all of that? Anna wonders, her eyes alighting on two little clay tipis and feeling a wave of sadness, remembering again the wonder of night before, and feeling so far away from it now. *But I'm not there*, she reminds herself. *I'm supposed to be looking for a gig.* She casts her eyes across this wild and exciting field, looking for anything that resembles a venue.

Two women dressed as white birds dance in a cage atop a food van at the far edge of the field. A giant turtle moves slowly across the field with a man on its back. Anna surmises it must have a car or something under its shell. But there is nothing that looks like a suitable venue.

What next? she wonders. Her eyes keep being drawn to the next field, to the flags which flap atop another huge circus style tent. But she's exhausted. So she finds a bench and slumps on it, feeling the tears moving close to the surface again.

It is the clangy acoustic guitar that alerts her to the presence of an acoustic venue tucked off to one side of the field. It is a small cabaret-style tent with a large bright red painted sign above the entrance reading: 'Imelda's Parlour'. A man is strumming a tinny-sounding guitar on a small stage, which consists of only a wobbly microphone, taped up with gaffer tape in the middle. The tent is very small – large enough for a few chairs and tables and two dilapidated sofas with mismatched cushions. Essentially, it is somebody's living room assembled inside a small tent. *Or rather a living room assembled from all the furniture that's been thrown out*, Anna thinks. It has character, though. *If you can't get a gig here, you're in trouble*, she tells herself.

Behind the counter – which is filled with too-sweet looking cakes, crisps and soft drinks – is a woman is wearing a short, curly blonde wig, with fire-engine red pasted on her lips and a bright pink dress that shows more cleavage than Anna wants to see. *This must be Imelda*, she surmises.

Hatti watches the young woman approaching. Most people think she's Imelda because she owns the cafe, but in fact, there is nobody here named Imelda. She doesn't disabuse people of their ideas though.

"What can I get you, Hon?" Hatti asks Anna. This is around the two hundredth time she's been asked that question today. Hatti is pleased that the business has been decent, but she's very tired and is looking forward to getting off for the night. She's not really paying that much attention to the people that come in. Her mind is elsewhere as she hands them their cake and takes their money. At the end of Hatti's shift she is in the habit of dulling her body's aches and her mind's worries with alcohol and then in the morning, drudging her body into action with extra strength coffee, sugar and occasionally some of the other stimulants to be found on site. Usually by the end of the festival she can hardly move.

"I was actually wondering if you have any spaces left for performers?" Anna asks. The words don't come easily out of her mouth, which has gone very dry.

The woman's eyebrows rise. "Well, it just so happens you're in luck, my doll. We just had our 11 o'clock pull out to go to Sinéad O'Connor. Imagine that. Picking Sinéad O'Connor over playing in this palace. But there you are. So we've got a slot free. Lucky you came in, because we've had people asking for the last three days and we've been full."

On the surface, Anna tells herself she's lucky and maybe she will sell some CDs after all, but underneath, there is a slightly sick feeling gnawing at her, and growing stronger all the time, as if she really should know better. At least it means I haven't lied to Damien, she tells herself. She gives Hatti her name and is informed that she needs to be here for 10:50pm.

As she walks back out, feeling heavy and slightly dazed, a group of tall ent-like stiltwalkers that look like characters from The Lord of the Rings pass by. So what now? A hunger claws at her belly like an aching hole.

Thankful now that she'd braved the queues at the festival cash points earlier, Anna looks for the nearest food vendors. Her eyes alight on a red pizza wagon. Not a good idea. Really not a good idea, something seems to be telling her. Ignoring this particular thought, Anna orders herself a large piece of vegetarian pizza and watches the man, whose name is Harvey, lift – with brown, stained gloves – a soggy piece of pizza, dripping with oil onto a paper plate, which looks only moderately clean. She can see the hygiene certificate on the side of their vehicle is splattered with sauce.

Even though this is clearly a mistake, she accepts the greasy-looking pizza and hands the man her money. He takes it with the same gloved hand he's just used to pick up her pizza, hardly acknowledging her, as if she isn't even there. Like Hatti, Harvey's mind is elsewhere.

Anna feels the keen contrast between this and her experiences at The Chai Chi Tent and Pacha Mama Cafe. She wishes she were back there instead, eating a love brownie or a chocolate banana crepe. There she had felt as if she mattered to those people. For the time she had been with them, they had given her their attention.

Harvey's mind is anywhere but here, full of what he's going to do tonight, what he did last night and counting the minutes until he is off shift and he can go and party. Like Hatti, he too is very tired and fuelled up with instant coffee. He was told to use the glove only for food and not for money, but he's reached such a state of exhaustion that he no longer cares about these things.

Anna stares at him, frustrated by his lack of care and disgusted by how he's managed this interaction with her pizza. For some reason she doesn't quite understand, the words of Johannes slip again into her awareness. *At your core, you are the very same as that person you think is better than you... or, it comes to her – that you think you are better than... exactly the same.*

She almost laughs suddenly remembering that extraordinary conversation at the sauna, hearing Alex's voice in her mind. *The guy serving pizza... he's God.* She finds that hard to believe right now, but at the same time it seems to echo on inside her.

Looking down at the pizza with all the oil pooling around it, Anna contemplates chucking it in a bin, but feeling the empty hole inside herself which disguises itself as hunger and feeling sorry for herself, she decides to eat it anyway. She finds a nearby bench where she can be distracted by the sights of the strange characters walking by.

The first bite tastes just like it looks and smells. Wrong. But still, she continues to stuff bite after bite into her mouth, because it's there in front of her and right now she doesn't care about what she is doing to her body. Before she's even finished her last bite, she feels sick and bloated.

She rises again, intent on walking off the feeling and maybe quelling it down with something made of chocolate. Or at least finding something that could distract her from the gnawing feeling which has gotten worse as a result of the pizza, and not better.

A horde of hairy, grinning trolls wearing wigs and masks with huge noses are heading straight towards Anna, carrying a sign which reads: *Trolls – Free Hugs.* Their leader, the hairiest of them all, can see this young woman is clearly in need. Anna manages to veer away from them just before they reach her, their arms outstretched. As far as she's concerned, the last thing she wants right now is to be embraced by a troll.

Anna doesn't realise that these trolls are providing a valuable service to Glastonbury Festival and would never force a hug on anyone. Beneath all the scraggly hair and dirt-encrusted makeup are human beings with an intent to give love. They know that many people at the festival and the world at large are short on hugs. For the Trolls, they know it is all a good joke and humour can bring its own healing, but there is genuine love in it too. They are creating smiles wherever they go. There is a soft nudge inside Anna, whispering that she could well benefit from the unique medicine the Trolls bring. But she's not ready for it.

As Anna swerves off through the crowd, she catches sight of the Trolls as they find their next willing recipient. With a great show of joy and bibulousness, all three trolls heartily embrace the young man, whose friends are standing nearby laughing along with him. And suddenly the friends too are joining in and it is a hugging free for all. It doesn't escape Anna's awareness that these people look like they are having a lot of fun.

When was the last time I had fun? Feeling the ache throbbing more strongly than ever, she pushes on, deeper into the festival.

Two stilt-walkers in striped red and white trousers with little flat rimmed white hats and riding on seven foot tall bicycles speed past Anna, tipping their hats to her as they fly past. She carries on, past a miniature bug circus, arriving at a stone wall leading to an elegant little wooden footbridge which arches over a small flowing river – *The Whitelake River.*

On the bridge is a bronze plaque, lovingly made with the words:

Bella's Bridge
Arabella Churchill worked tirelessly in these fields for over thirty years
creating some of the best theatre and circus shows in the country.
By building this bridge Glastonbury Festival wants to remember her tremendous
efforts and be reminded of her dedication to our aims and purposes throughout the
years.
Michael Eavis

Anna gazes at the plaque for a moment, thinking of all the people who have given their time and energy to creating this life-altering experience called Glastonbury Festival. So many hearts and minds and hands working together to make something so extraordinary.

On the other side of the bridge are a row of five large spinning metal prayer wheels set into a wooden frame. Anna watches the man in front of her as he runs his hands reverently along them, making them whirl and clack. As she passes by, Anna notices how the shiny bronze wheels catch the light of the sun, sparkling, and contemplates spinning them herself, but then thinks about the number of hands that have touched them and restrains herself.

Now she is standing in another new field. Rising up before her is the *Circus Big Top* tent, with its swirls of dark and light blue rising up to its peaks. The flags atop it flap in the wind, inviting her in.

As the crowd cheers, Anna claps too. It has been a good distraction. For a full half hour she has been immersed in a delightful show of high level acrobatics. She especially loved all the aerial parts where the performers suspended themselves on ropes or ribbons, twirling and holding one another in ways that required real strength. At one point, a man lay horizontal in the air, his thighs gripping the pole while a woman in silver stood atop his legs. Her favourite moment was when two women – one in skin-tight gold and one in a flowing white skirt – dangled at either end of a rotating metal pole like creatures hanging from a children's mobile.

In the delight of these world-class performers, for a little while Anna had forgotten the pains of her own life and the sickness of the pizza in her belly. But now the applause is subsiding and there is a break in between the acts and her own life is calling to her again. She is about to move on but has the sense of a presence beside her. Turning her head, she catches the eye of a very tall, strangely elegant dark-haired gentleman next to her, who is leaning against one of the large wooden poles supporting the tent.

Above the man's larger than average nose are two bright eyes the colour of dark chocolate, twinkling at Anna. "Quite something isn't it?" His voice is pleasant and deep, and accented, as if speaking proper, polite English.

Gangly, is the word that comes to Anna. But the most interesting thing for her about this man is that he wears a perfect gentleman's suit – dark, with pinstripes and tails, an elegant white shirt and a black bow tie, and it's all just a tiny bit too short for him. He looks like a caricature of a gentleman from the past, his dark hair streaked with grey, cropped short and greased back. He even has a dark moustache which curls up at the edges of his smile like a joke moustache, like the moustaches in Block 9. Except that this one appears to be real.

Anthony knows he's tall, but he has come to terms with this over the course of his forty three years. He is happy in his six-foot four frame. As a performer in the circus field, this is a costume Anthony wears, but he loves the feeling of stepping into this persona and finds he feels more at home in this suit than in anything else. He loves to see the awe and delight on the faces of those who come to the circus and he never tires of watching the best acrobats. It lifts his heart, because he knows what they've done to get there. He knows what state of mind they have got themselves into as they perform those feats. Because he's felt that too. And there's a very practical reason this suit is short on him.

It's normal for Anna to feel uncomfortable if a male stranger of any age tries to strike up a conversation with her, but there is something so intriguing about this gentleman that Anna finds herself responding with enthusiasm. "It is quite something," she nods. "I've never seen real circus acts before."

The man casts his gaze back towards the stage. "Yes. Such beauty, such magic in it. When I see them in all their glory, it takes me back to when I first saw people doing that as a lad and was inspired to become a circus performer, myself."

As she imagines this gangly distinguished gentleman before her swinging and dancing around high ropes and ribbons, she can't help but smile. Somehow in her mind, it doesn't quite fit. He doesn't look to Anna like someone who would be able to do those kinds of things. He doesn't look physically strong, or particularly dexterous.

The man chuckles, as if hearing her thoughts. "Sometimes you think you're taking one path in life and realise you're really taking another."

Anna wonders what he means by that. "So did you ever get involved in the circus in the end?"

"In a manner of speaking. Just not the way I expected it."

"What happened?"

"Well, the truth is, at first I was just struck by the glamour of it all. I wanted to be like that. To be able to do these extraordinary things and have the audiences clap for me. But after I joined up with a travelling circus, I began to see things differently. I began to love it for itself. At first, I just did loading and cleaning and setting up, but I was watching all the time, learning all the time. I watched the acrobats preparing, practising. It was a very important time in my life."

"So what kinds of things did you learn from watching them?" Anna can't help being completely intrigued by this man, who is giving her little glimpses into his story.

"One thing I learned is about perceptions." He grandly sweeps his hand across the stage. "This is the part we, as an audience are meant to see, to experience. These perfect, flawless, apparently superhuman feats performed with mastery and grace... but, behind the scenes, each of these performers has spent countless hours, days, months, years practising. That's not so glamorous. They practice the way an Olympic athlete practises."

Anna hasn't really considered this before. "But surely, they also have special skills and abilities which enable them to do those things. I mean, I could never do that."

"Oh, you could. But you'd have to love it, that's the thing. These people are human beings, just like you or me, and maybe they have some natural ability in some area, but the thing that really sets them apart is that they have found what they love to do, and they have the determination to keep at it until they have achieved mastery. So ultimately it's about love. That's what the circus has taught me."

Love. Funny how many times that word has come up in conversation in the last two days, Anna thinks. *What is love anyway? What do I love?*

"So basically, you're saying that these performers got to be able to do this just by practising?"

"That's exactly what I'm saying. For every successful leap and every twirl up on the high ropes, that performer will have fallen more times than you can count. Maybe even broke their legs, or ended up in hospital. And they just kept getting up again and again, until one day they stopped falling. And even then, sometimes they still fell. And each time, they didn't focus on the fall, they turned their minds back to seeing themselves performing the act flawlessly. They return always to the moment. They learn that the fall is in the past. The moment is this step, this act."

"I would find that hard." Anna shakes her head. "I do find that hard. I have been falling, metaphorically speaking, a lot lately. And it's really hard – impossible in fact – not to think about it and be hard on myself about it."

"Mastering the mind takes practice too." The gentleman's eyes twinkle again. "In some cases, as it did with mine, that can take quite a long time."

Anna wonders about this man's story. He seems to possess some kind of wisdom. She is reminded of what Johannes had said to her about becoming a witness to her thoughts, learning to master her thoughts. *How strange that this man is saying the very same thing to me here. And Johannes said the right teacher would come to me at the right time. Is this what he meant?*

"So there's hope for me then?" Anna gives a half-hearted laugh. "That I might get over my propensity to feel sorry for myself?"

"Oh yes. If you choose it."

"So what if I choose it? I don't have a clue where to start... to master my mind, as you say."

"To master your thoughts is about awareness." The man's dark eyes grow more intense and it seems as if the very air around them is somehow becoming more substantial, as if by mentioning this awareness, he is creating it, right here and now. "Presence," he explains. "This is what those people you just watched had to learn – total body presence. You can bet that if at any moment one of their minds left the present, they would fall. But as you saw, that didn't happen."

Anna remembers again the feeling last night in the tipi of being truly present, and again in a less intense way this afternoon in the sauna. *Could a person feel that way all the time?* There is a little lift inside her and the little fire in her heart seems to burn more brightly, as if to say, *Yes. You can.*

"If your mind is working on what you had for breakfast or what you're going to do with your girlfriend later, then you fall. Without question." Anthony knows this from experience. "What they are practicing is presence, more than anything. For them it becomes a form of meditation, like yoga. And it's the love that keeps them doing it."

"But how do I not think about the future or the past? Thoughts just come into my head. All the time. I can't stop them coming."

"Yes. I know what you mean. That used to happen to me a lot. Then I learned to meditate and the thoughts don't come quite so much. And now when they do come, it doesn't bother me. The thoughts themselves are not the problem. It is the entertaining them which takes you out of the moment. You just learn to witness them, and allow them to move on their way while you get on with being in the moment."

"I have no idea how to do that."

"Ah ha. That's the practice, see. You learn that each time your mind wanders from the present, you bring yourself back. Each time you notice. Each time you fall, you bring yourself back. Even if it's hundreds, or thousands of times. Eventually, you will discover you are not falling off so often, and you are staying in the moment for longer. And eventually, you find that you have enough presence not to fall. And that is when you know you have reached a kind of mastery. Not only of your craft, but of your mind."

The next act is ready. Anna wants to keep speaking with this gentleman, but the lights have dimmed again and the next spectacle is about to begin. To great whoops and cheers, five handsome men of African descent dance their way on stage to the sound of lively African beats. Anna giggles to herself to see the way they gyrate their pelvises, wearing little more than golden loincloths. Their bare, muscular chests have been oiled to a shine. Like the rest of the audience, Anna is transfixed. It's not just how they look either. Because almost immediately, they begin to do the most extraordinary acrobatics, which includes one of the men doing 13 consecutive backflips and culminating with another of the men doing a limbo underneath a burning wire which is not more than three feet off the ground. Then Anna watches open-mouthed as one man leaps up to stand on the shoulders of another man, and now pulls a third man up onto his shoulders, so that they are standing three men, one on top of the other. As a climax, the man at the very top flips himself upside down to do a headstand on top of the man supporting him. The audience explodes into delighted applause.

Anna shakes her head, hardly believing such a feat of balance is humanly possible. *How do they do it?*

Love. She remembers what the friendly gentleman with the bright eyes had told her.

The men waggle their hips in time to the music and finish their final acrobatic feat – one man carrying all the other four attached to him in various ways, giving the effect of a strange creature with two legs but many arms and heads. Anna laughs out loud and cheers heartily with the rest of the audience, feeling lighter inside.

As the lights come up, she turns to see if the tall gentleman is still there. She wants to speak with him more, to find out what it was he had chosen to do with his life, what it is that he loves. The space where he had stood is now empty, and Anna feels a little loss. For without him there, and the spectacle finished, she is faced again with herself. Even with the lighter feeling inside, a sigh rises from the depths of her as she remembers what she has arranged for herself later.

As she steps out of the Big Top, everything is cast in the golden pink hue of those magical moments before sunset. The breeze brushes past her, rustling her hair, seeming to draw her gaze upwards. She looks up and gasps.

Suspended twenty feet above her head is a tightrope wire, stretching the entire length of the circus field, and walking across it as if it were the most simple thing in the world is the tall gentlemen with the moustache and the smiling eyes. He holds a long, horizontal pole for balance and steps one foot in front of the other seamlessly, as smoothly as if he had been walking there beside Anna. In fact, more so. For up there, all traces of what Anna had thought of as 'gangly' are gone. In his state of complete presence up on that wire, he has become one smooth movement, graceful and elegant.

So that's what he loves! Anna grins with amazement as he traverses the whole length of the Circus Field, without wobbling even once. *If he can learn to do that, then surely, I can learn whatever it is I am meant to do, to find whatever it is that I love.*

Shari and Eden have come to Glastonbury. When Damien had mentioned that they had gotten tickets in with one of the bands on the West Holts stage, as 'roadies', Anna had felt a sinking inside. She really doesn't want to see them here, especially after everything that's happened. Shari and Eden are Anna's friends by association with Damien, and while Anna likes Shari well enough, she's never felt able to be completely herself with her. And Eden... well, Eden is another story altogether.

There is a text from Shari asking if Anna wants to come with them tonight to see Sinéad O'Connor. Shari has texted Anna several times now. Though Anna would welcome the chance to see Sinéad, she doesn't relish an evening with Eden tonight. Thankful to have an excuse to opt out, Anna texts back to Shari that she can't join them because she's got a gig. As she types the word 'gig', she gets that sinking feeling again. *Oh well, what's done is done. At least I've kept my word to Damien and got a gig.* But Anna can feel that the little fire inside her doesn't like it. Not one bit.

But you are coming to the Stones tomorrow right? Shari texts.

Anna sighs, texting back: *Definitely. See you there x.*

As she hits send, a heaviness strikes her in the chest, but she knows she will do it. When her father had heard the Stones were playing at Glastonbury he had said, "*Go see the Stones for me, Annie*". Then when Shari had invited her to join them to see the rock legends, Anna had felt obliged to accept. Even Damien's parting quip on the phone had been, "*Say hi to Mick for me.*"

Anna thinks about love, and how the gentleman with the moustache had told her you had to love what you were doing to attain true mastery. She shakes her head. *Far cry for me.*

Johannes' words rise up in her mind again, as they so often have since the reading, telling her that she always gives up what she wants to please others and how she always wears the mask. *And here I am doing it again.*

But you don't have to, something inside her seems to say. As she listens to this, the little fire seems to burn brighter again. *You can choose a new way right now. You can choose to follow your heart right now.*

She stops for a moment, as if standing on a crossroads. But no. She's not going to take that path this time.

The sound is terrible. A man with a cigarette dangling from his lips and wearing a bathrobe and a shower cap comes out and fiddles with the sound, mumbling to himself. Rudy is Hatti's partner, and like Hatti, he is in a state of constant suffering. Right now he is suffering about this particular piece of his sound system which is about to come apart. He manages to fiddle it into submission, but there is a persistent buzz afterwards which he gives up on, throwing his hands up into the air and disappearing again behind a dark curtain to the side of the stage. If Anna had thought the sonic environment in her last gig left something to be desired, this isn't a patch on it.

This is the best you're going to get, Anna, she tells herself. *Here you go. This is your gig.*

She strums her guitar, and the sound is bad. Really bad. Feedback squeals through the speakers and Rudy comes out again to turn the volume down, which serves only to make Anna unable to hear her guitar through the monitors. She tries to tell him, but he just shrugs and disappears again.

She opens her mouth to sing, but her voice is lost in the buzz and all the other sounds around her. As the words rise to her mouth, they feel shallow suddenly, in a way they never have before. She thinks about the way Moon had sung the night before, with such power and passion, and how her whole body had felt listening to it. That feeling of bright joy. And in the sauna earlier, she had felt something again when her own voice had risen in song with the others. How different that feeling was to this feeling of trying to get these empty words across to people who aren't even listening. She feels the strain in her throat as she struggles through the first two songs, wishing for the end of her set.

She thinks about her CDs and prays that she might sell some, even as she knows there's no chance anyone will buy a CD from someone they can't hear. *And even if they could hear me, would they want this? Would they really? When I don't even want it myself?*

There are two women sat on one of the sofas vaguely watching, but seeming more interested in talking to one another. At the end of her song, Anna stops playing to re-tune her guitar and overhears something which takes what little wind there is completely out of her sails.

"Do you want to stay a bit longer?" the first woman asks.

"No. I've had enough of this." The second woman looks at her watch. "And Sinéad's about to start. I don't want to be late."

"Yeah. Let's go."

Anna watches them stride out. *Well, if I had to choose between me and Sinéad O'Connor, I know who I'd choose too.* The woman's words run through Anna's mind. *I've had enough of this. That's what they thought of me. Well, I've had enough too.*

"This is my last song," Anna's voice cracks into the microphone. Even though she's got at least twenty more minutes left in her allocated time, she's done. As she says these words, she gets the feeling that she really means them. Like maybe she really won't ever play these songs again. Like she really might just give up on all of this.

" *I didn't know I was asking the question... my heart was out on the floor... but your love, your love is the answer... the one I've been searching for...*" As she sings these words it strikes her – *None of this song is true.*

Anna had written this song for Damien. It's a song about how she felt so alone and then met him, and then didn't feel so alone. The truth she hadn't wanted to admit to herself is that after the initial honeymoon infatuation phase, she had actually felt more lonely as a result of their relationship and not less. This only intensified after they moved in together, because that was when it became apparent to Anna just how much of herself she would have to hide from him.

Your love is not what I've been searching for, she realises. It's something else, something much deeper, and she is starting to wonder if this thing she is searching for is actually not outside of her at all. Last night, the feeling of love had been inside her.

At the end of her song there are a few polite claps. No one approaches her, but really she'd known it would be like that. She just hadn't wanted to accept it.

Let it go Anna.

Shoulders slumped, she stares at her black guitar case and her still-full CD box, not comprehending how on earth she will carry these back to her tent. She had managed somehow on the way here, but now it feels as if all the energy has left her body.

Rudy returns and glares at her. "You've got twenty more minutes."

"I'm sorry... I just can't." Anna feels like crying again.

Rudy shrugs again, and begins to rearrange the stage for the next act.

Though she feels like just dropping everything and running as far from here as possible, Anna knows she can't leave her guitar or the CDs, but she can't fathom carrying them all the way back to her tent either.

"Excuse me," she asks him, "is there anyone here that could help me carry my gear?"

He laughs. "Are you serious?"

But when Rudy sees Anna's expression, he stops. Even with all his suffering, a strand of compassion exists in him. He is a father, albeit a distant one. "You know, all I can suggest is that you go out there and try and hail one of those guys with a bicycle and trailer."

"OK, thanks," Anna says, sucking up the tears that want to come. She contemplates again just ditching the whole box of CDs. She doesn't want them now. But something of what she promised to her father and to Damien keeps her from dumping the box by the first bin she sees.

She hauls her load out into the heaving night, and halfway back finds herself suddenly caught by the outflow from two big concerts that have just finished. Stewards in bright neon pinnies are guiding people into a one-way system to avoid creating chaos at the bottlenecks between fields. Shepherded onto a track leading away from her destination, Anna feels a rising panic. She is surrounded now from all sides, on a path she doesn't recognise, with people bumping into her guitar every few seconds. The floodlights standing on poles which illuminate the area create blind spots in her vision. All she wants is her tent.

Help! She cries out again. It is as if she is crying to that feeling she felt the other night in the tipi, as if somehow that love could hear her and could answer. *Help. Please!*

Strangely, as if in answer, the crowds are parting like waves in the sea and a way becomes clear. With this, just a little more energy returns to her body, giving Anna just enough strength to keep walking. As she picks up her pace, taking step after step in her high-heeled shoes, the blisters on her heels burst and bleed. A new fury rises at the ridiculousness of these shoes, a rage at trying to fit herself into a certain image. She kicks the shoes off with all the energy of that and leaves them by the side of the track for someone else to find. Barefoot and not caring what she steps on, she can feel again that flaring of the little fire in her, with a knowledge that there really is no going back to the way it was before.

By the time she reaches her tent, her whole body is aching, especially her shoulders and fingers. After a thorough foot wash at the tap, Anna climbs into her sleeping bag, shivering, sore and exhausted. The fire and the fury had served a purpose – they had gotten her here. Instinctively, she places the palms of her hands over her heart, questioning all these new thoughts and feelings, a new self tentatively unfurling in the winds of change.

> *"Shake off the dust, you do what you must*
> *Tend to the flame and fire*
> *There's no holding back, back on the track*
> *Come off your tightrope wire*
> *You've traveled so far, guided by star*
> *Stars in your soul*
> *And let yourself breathe*
> *Breathe"*

from the song, 'Stars in Your Soul', by Tina Bridgman

It's hot – heatwave hot. The mud has long since dried and dust is rising in earnest from all the dirt and gravel tracks. By the time Anna approaches the crest of the hill and catches sight of Pacha Mama's, she is dripping with sweat.

Maddy is making pancakes again this morning. She has a rosy glow about her and her eyes are sparkling bright as she catches sight of Anna and smiles a welcome at her. Anna can't put her finger on it exactly, but something about Maddy has changed. She seems radiant, like a woman in love.

"Good morning!" Maddy smiles a welcome to her.

"Good morning." Anna grins back. Maddy's cheerfulness is contagious.

"Moon is waiting for you."

Moon is waiting. Anna's stomach flips.

"Oh. I guess I should skip the pancake then."

Maddy shrugs. "I'm sure Moon wouldn't mind, but if I were you, I wouldn't want to eat anything heavy right before a breathing session."

"Oh, good point."

"I wouldn't worry, though. Moon will take care of you." Maddy's eyes twinkle again.

Take care of me? How? Anna's heart skips a nervous beat.

"The pancakes will be here when you get back," Maddy assures her.

> "What is it that you seek?
> For I am sure there's a goddess inside of me
> Time and again I know how she speaks
> Oh winds come to catch me now
> For I have no idea of these ripples around me
> For I'm off, off to run with the wolves
> To hunt what my soul needs for food
> I'm off tracking, to run with the wolves"

from the song, 'Tracking,' by Ayla Schafer

Anna exits Pacha Mama's through the side entrance and passes by the little wishing well, shimmering in the sunshine as before. The dragonfly over the well dances in the light breeze. The dreamcatchers whirl. *It's all still here*, Anna thinks. *These mag-*

ical things. She remembers her wish. *Could it be that there is magic after all?* That night in the Big Tipi had made her feel that way, and it had happened again in the sauna. She feels a tingle on her skin, a hint of possibilities.

Yesterday I wished I could be brave, and I was. So maybe I can be again today. So with this thought in her mind, and despite the clenching in her stomach, she steps forward and heads up through the Tipi Field, past the totem pole and the central fire where the three large cedar logs are still burning, still tended by a circle of people.

She turns and passes beneath a large banner with an image of Chief Joseph on it, which presides over this section of the Tipi Field, and makes her way through the cluster of tipis. The one with the purple dreamcatcher is easy to spot. Moon is there, leaning back against the canvas next to the entrance, with her eyes closed, basking.

Anna notices that Moon looks particularly at peace with herself, another creature again. Even her clothing appears softer today. The delicate leaf patterns along the edges of Moon's light green cotton trousers are her own design. Moon has a fondness for embroidery and making her own clothing. On the top she wears a light undyed sleeveless vest, her leather pouch resting in its usual place just over the centre of her chest. Her feet are bare, one crossed over the other. These are the weathered feet of one who has spent a lot of time walking without shoes, soles permanently coloured by the earth. Moon's hands are relaxed on her belly, showing the running wolf on her upper arm at rest.

It strikes Anna that Moon, like Maddy, seems to have a particular glow about her this morning. It doesn't occur to Anna that the two might be connected. Because like Maddy, what is radiating from Moon too right now is love. She is basking in the warmth of the sun, and also in the warmth of her night with Maddy. Today, the world feels new. Though the grief is not completely gone, some of the old pain has left Moon, and into its place has flowed lightness and grace. Moon knows that there are parts left to heal, and feelings about becoming a mother yet to be resolved. But this morning, with the openness of her heart and the sweet feeling of being in a body that has been loved and held, she is free of worry. This is one of those clear times for Moon, when the muddy waters that sometimes obscure things have been washed away, and the world is clear and sparkling, each person miraculous.

Moon opens her eyes and smiles at Anna. There is such warmth and affection in that face that Anna is unguarded. This is not the unpredictable, ruthless look Anna had seen back in the sauna. This is a simple, warm greeting.

This morning Moon's senses are heightened. Everything has taken a vivid, bright quality. Things seem to glow. Moon recognises this feeling. When you are in your heart, and that energy is flowing through you, the world looks different. You see the light in things. Moon can see Anna's aura now, shining in the sunlight. It's the aura of a person whose energy has collapsed in on herself. *Something has happened to her since yesterday*, notes Moon. But even so, Anna is still beautiful to her. This morning, everybody is.

"Welcome." Moon smiles.

"I'm so sorry I'm late."

"It's fine. It's all working out as it should. I obviously needed to sit quietly in the sun for half an hour. It's been perfect. Just what I needed."

Moon rises slowly, supple and at ease in her body, while Anna's heart still pounds with the exertion and stress of rushing up the hill, and her worry about what it means to be here, to agree to do this, whatever it is, with all the memories of failures of the past.

Moon stops at the entrance to the tipi and regards her for a moment. *Why are you so scared?* she wonders. But then she reminds herself what it was like when she herself learned to breathe. That had been a profound doorway, and she has a sense that it will be the same for Anna.

"Would you like a cup of tea? Or breakfast?" Moon asks. This is the best way to give Anna some energy, she can feel it. To help her calm down enough to do this work.

"Really? Can you spare some?"

"Of course. I have loads. Come in." Moon leads Anna inside her tipi, leaving the flap partially open so the sunshine can stream in.

It seems to Anna a magical den, perfectly Moon – wild, natural, animal. Rugs and sheepskins cover most of the floor. In the centre there is a small firepit, with just a few smouldering embers still burning and the tiniest wisps of smoke. Beside it are some bundles of sage, partially burned. The scent lingering in the air is both sweet and pungent. On the other side of the fire is a small food preparation area, with a basket of fruits and vegetables and an assortment of leafy plants Anna doesn't recognise. There are also a pair of wooden bowls, one with seeds still clinging to its sides. Beyond the firepit is a sleeping area with woven wool blankets. The bedding looks well slept in. Or well used at least. Beside it is an assortment of beeswax candles, burned down with only the nubs remaining. Something about the scene makes Anna feel as if Moon didn't sleep here alone last night. *Who was here with her? Cedar?*

Moon kneels by the firepit, adding some sticks to the embers and blowing on them until a small flame kindles.

"So are you the only one who stays here?" Anna asks, trying to sound neutral, as she kneels beside Moon on the sheepskins.

Moon lifts her eyes, meeting Anna's for a moment, her lips curling into a wry smile. "Most of the time. But sometimes other people stay here, too." She's not going to say more about that right now. She smiles to herself, remembering Maddy's arms around her, feeling their hearts open to one another, Maddy's lips, her tongue, the energy of the earth and the sky moving through them.

Moon pours Chalice Well water from her large plastic bottle into an iron kettle and places it on the fire.

"It's great you can make your own tea," Anna says, trying to think of what she can say to Moon to cover the embarrassment of that look she'd seen on Moon's face, after asking her such a personal question.

"It is," Moon replies simply.

"It's a really lovely space you've got here. I mean, it looks like you've got everything you need." Anna's nervousness drives her to continue asking questions and making small talk. Moon doesn't do small talk, but she understands Anna's need to do it.

"I do seem to have everything I need," Moon replies after a few moments, a small smile rising to her lips. *Yes. I do.* She lifts the cleaner of the two wooden bowls and drops an assortment of seeds and bits of fresh fruit into it, offering a silent blessing to each ingredient.

From here, Anna can see how radiant Moon's skin really is. There are no wrinkles, aside from the gentle smile lines around Moon's eyes. Anna thinks of her own skin, which has little red blotches on it, and last time she checked, wrinkles were already starting to form around her eyes and mouth.

"Can I ask you something?" Anna asks.

"Of course."

"You have such beautiful skin. And you don't wear any makeup, do you? How do you do it?"

Moon considers this for a moment. "I guess I would put it down to what I eat, mostly. I eat a mainly raw diet of foraged food and food I grow myself. It's living food. I've been doing that for about five years now. My sister says I haven't aged a day since then."

"How old are you? If you don't mind me asking?" Anna is getting the feeling that her earlier assessment of Moon's age is probably incorrect.

"Thirty seven."

Anna's mouth gapes open. Not only is Moon not younger than Anna, she is nearly ten years older.

"Seriously? You're thirty seven? How is that possible?"

"Raw food. Good natural living. Music. Breathing... Sex." Moon shrugs. "It could be genes, I suppose, but somehow I don't think so."

Moon can see what Anna is doing to herself with this information. She is comparing herself, feeling inadequate. And at the word 'sex' Anna's eyes had darted to the ruffled bedding again.

Who? The question runs through Anna's mind again. *Who was it that was here last night?*

"Here. My favourite light breakfast." Moon offers the bowl to Anna, drawing her attention back to the matter at hand. "You don't want anything too heavy before a breathing lesson."

Anna peers into the bowl. There are some pieces of apple, banana, pear, pumpkin seeds, sunflower seeds and some little black seeds she doesn't recognise.

"The seeds are sprouted," Moon says.

"Thank you." Anna is extremely grateful for Moon's generosity, especially since this is the second time Moon has fed her in two days, but she still feels a griping disappointment gnaw in her belly. When Moon had offered breakfast Anna had been expecting something which would fill the gap a little more than this.

This is a breakfast for a bird. As she begins to eat, Anna is surprised by how delicious and satisfying the food is. The sprouted seeds taste different from the unsprouted ones she's used to. The food takes away the ache in her belly, but sits so lightly, it's almost as though she hasn't eaten. And yet she feels a new energy in her body.

The kettle boils and Moon drops a handful of pink and yellow petals and green leaves into it.

"What's that?"

"My own relaxation blend." Moon looks over with a smile. "Rose, chamomile and passionflower."

She lets the infusion steep for a few minutes and then pours them each a mug.

Herbal teas are not usually Anna's thing, but as she sips, a calmness settles inside her. Moon sips her tea too, and feeling the change in them both, knows the time has come.

"Shall we begin?"

Anna's palms are sweating. In fact, most of her skin is sweating. Even as the terror fills her again with all the past memories of failed attempts to learn to breathe properly, a memory comes to Anna of herself by the wishing well at Pacha Mama's yesterday, and the wish she had made. *To be brave.* That fiery self which had risen up and propelled her forward is still here now, still burning. That self will not let her back out of this.

"Okay. So, watch me breathing for a moment." Moon lifts her shirt just high enough to reveal the bottom of her ribs and her belly. "You heard us talking about this in the sauna, right? See how my chest hardly moves, but my belly expands?" Moon breathes in, demonstrating.

Anna watches, and it is just as Moon describes. The part of her belly just below the ribcage expands on the outbreath. Her chest doesn't appear to rise at all.

"And on the outbreath, the belly comes in and the ribcage expands to the sides just a little as the diaphragm comes up. Do you see?"

Anna can see, but fear still tightens in her. *I can see what you're doing, but that doesn't mean I can do it.*

"Do you remember how I described the diaphragm like a bellows? The bellows opens downward as you breathe in, and closes as you let the breath out." Moon makes the shape of the sideways V with her hands again. "The body responds to what you think about. If you can actually visualise this bellows in your mind as you breathe, that will help. Have a go."

Anna tries to see her diaphragm like a bellows, but it only makes her think of the hearth at her parent's house, with their big old dilapidated bellows that's never really worked very well, making its familiar old wheeze.

"The breath is here," Moon says, placing her hands emphatically on her own belly. "Right now, in our bodies. It brings us to the present. That's one of its greatest gifts. See the bellows in your mind. See it opening downward, drawing in the air."

Anna remembers how her old singing teacher had tried to tell her something vaguely like this, except without the being present part, and without the compassion. *What will be different now?* Anna wonders. *If I failed then, why wouldn't I just fail again?*

As she breathes in, trying to see the bellows in her mind, she juts out her stomach in an effort to simulate the movement, but the air is still lifting her chest, and her diaphragm has not been engaged at all.

"If the image of the bellows doesn't work for you, try this." Moon holds her hands like the closed petals of a flower, facing downwards. "Imagine your diaphragm like the opening petals of a lotus flower, expanding and opening in all directions."

Moon breathes in, at the same time opening the petals of the flower, and on the outbreath, the petals gently fold together again. "Because," Moon explains, "The diaphragm doesn't actually just open at the front, it opens downwards in all directions. The feeling is of expansion round the whole base of the ribcage. Try again."

Anna likes the image of the flower much better than the bellows. But despite her effort, she can still feel her chest rising.

"You're still chest breathing, Anna," Moon says gently.

"I'm not sure I can do this." Anna's voice cracks as tears move closer to the surface. *See I knew it...* The words run through her mind. *It's happening again. I can't do it...*

"You can, Anna. Trust me. You can." Moon says this with conviction. She feels the energy moving inside her, and knows she can help Anna. "I'll stay with you on this, allright? Things like this can take time to change, especially if they're lifelong habits. Just don't give up."

An image comes to Anna's minds eye of the gentleman she had met in the Circus Big Top, the tightrope walker, and of what he said about falling, and getting up, and being in the moment, and love. And here is Moon, sitting here, so patient, so loving. So much more than that singing teacher had been those years ago. That woman hadn't understood how to help her. But Moon does.

"Breathe with me, Anna." Moon moves closer. "Watch me, and try to breathe like this. Remember, your chest doesn't need to lift up at all when you breathe in. Feel how your chest expands gently after the breath fills your lower ribs."

Moon holds up her shirt and breaths again. There is an elegance to the movement of her belly, in time with the rhythm of the breath. It's like watching a wild animal breathing – graceful, perfect, effortless.

Again, Anna tries, and again, she experiences failure.

"Don't be hard on yourself, Anna. These things take time. Your body has probably been breathing like this for most of your life. Just take it one step at a time. You'll get it."

Moon observes Anna, who seems unable to even speak, tied up in knots inside herself. In Moon's heightened state this morning, she is more receptive to the messages from her heart and her guides. It comes to her clearly. She feels the truth of it as an energetic shiver moving through her body.

"Anna, there's something I need to tell you," Moon says this carefully, listening as she speaks, knowing this is delicate. "I'm getting this sense that there's something here..." Moon gestures to Anna's abdomen, "... that you don't want to face. And that's partly why something in you is resisting so strongly to breathing deeply. It's because there is some emotion you are not wanting to feel, that's been locked away there. I can hear it in your voice. It's like your voice is... the feeling it gives me is that you're..." Moon takes a breath, searching for the right word,"...hiding. Hiding yourself. And perhaps even hiding something from yourself."

Anna stares at Moon. Johannes had said this very thing when he had looked at her hand, that she wore a mask and didn't show her real self. "You can hear that in my voice?" She's horrified by this. *Can everyone hear it?*

"It's not something to feel bad about," Moon assures her. "There's a lot of people who have suppressed their emotions and breathe shallowly, so as not to feel what's really going on inside them. They don't know that the key to their freedom is really to breathe into it, to lean into it, as the Buddhist master Pema Chodron says. By breathing into these feelings, the feelings move, and transform and we are able to bring ourselves even more deeply into the moment."

The moment. The tightrope walker had spoken about that too, about being present and about mastering your thoughts. Anna had felt it that night in the tipi. With his healing, Cedar had pulled Anna into an experience of being fully present. Before this weekend, she wouldn't have known what being in the moment meant.

"This part of you that's hiding, that is locked up in you..." Moon says, "I'm getting that it's related to a thought... it's a thought that you believe is true, a story you are telling yourself, that your ego would have you believe."

Moon's eyes have a fire in them, like Cedar's eyes – eyes that can see beyond the ordinary. Anna finds the thought unbearable that Moon might be able to see beyond the mask, to all the horrible, unvoiceable thoughts. This is, for Anna, a far worse vulnerability than appearing physically naked.

"Anna, I know these thoughts. I have them too. When I am living in the illusion of my ego – which thankfully, I don't seem be doing so much today – those kinds of thoughts live in me too. It's not who you really are. And what that ego voice is telling you... It's not true."

Johannes had said this about the ego too. The voice of the heart always speaks with love, the ego with fear. *Could it really be that those thoughts about me aren't true?* Anna can't quite accept that – not yet. She can hardly believe Moon would ever have a negative thought about herself, but Moon's admittance that she might sometimes experience these same kinds of things, and that she might also have a human side, opens a doorway for Anna to admit the thing she feels most afraid to admit, to share something of her deepest fears.

"These thoughts... they're about self-worth aren't they?" Moon asks.

Anna covers her face with her hands, unable to look at Moon. *Worthless*, the thoughts say to her. She can hear them even now, like a steady drone. She's spent decades thinking that the voice was her. She's believed this voice for so long, believed it when it told her that deep down, whatever she does, nothing is ever good enough to redeem her.

Moon nods, Anna's silent reply understood. "That's the human ego for you. That's what the ego will tell you. But it's not the truth of who you are, Anna. It's not the truth. It's not."

Anna lifts her hands from her face, daring to face Moon, seeing no judgement there, just calm gentleness. And most surprisingly of all, love.

"So, what is the truth?" Anna asks. "Who am I then?"

Moon breaks out in a wide grin. "A being of total perfection, a Goddess! You're made of Love, Anna!"

Anna feels a startling urge to laugh out loud at the ridiculousness of that notion, and yet at the same time, something of this resonates inside her. For as Moon says it, Anna feels a bubbling up of energy, a recognition. And in Moon's open face, Anna can see that Moon means it, that she believes it, whole-heartedly, completely.

Even with this truth right in her face, the critical, judgemental voice still grips Anna, still disbelieves. "I'm hardly a goddess," she says quietly.

"You are," Moon affirms, her voice resonating with truth. "Like me. Like everyone. We're all made of Love. Your ego would have you think otherwise, but that's its job."

"Its job?" Anna doesn't understand.

"Yeah. How I understand it is the veil of the ego is there so we can see the contrast, otherwise we wouldn't know what we are. You can't know light without dark. So the ego is there with its illusion of separation to give us the opportunity to experience waking up to our connection, waking up to the Goddess or God inside ourselves."

Anna's God... Anna remembers what Johannes said about the candle – surrounded by light, you wouldn't see the flame. She's starting to understand a little more what he meant now.

"So what do I do then with these thoughts?" Anna asks. "They're horrible. I'd love to believe they're not true."

"Well that's the first step. A willingness to accept that they might not be true, and then to choose a new thought."

"Like what?"

Moon listens inside herself for a few moments and then smiles. "Okay. I've got one. Try this out." She pauses for a moment, gazing at Anna squarely. "I am enough."

"I am enough?" No *I'm not*, that same harsh voice in her head replies.

"You are enough," Moon says firmly. "We all are. Say it again, and see how it feels inside you – not like a question, but a statement of fact. I am enough."

"I am enough," Anna says it, mouthing the words and wondering what the purpose of this is. She doesn't feel any different.

"Try it again," Moon says gently. "I am enough."

"I am enough."

And this time as Anna says it, it reaches just a little deeper inside her, and some part of her gasps to realise maybe it might be true? *Could it be? What if it is?*

"Again," Moon urges softly, her clear eyes on Anna.

"This feels silly." *Because how could it be true?*

"Say it again, but really listen to the words. Hear what they mean. See what it does to your body."

"I am enough," Anna says them again, this time listening to herself speaking the words. The words themselves feel strange, but wholesome on her tongue. Anna remembers what Johannes had said about truth. Truth expands. A thought that is in harmony with your true nature brings energy. So she tries it again, this time only in her mind, *I am enough.* She's still not sure she believes it, but as she thinks it, something is happening to her body. A little part of her is waking up. A tiny shoot from a little seed, reaching up, *I am enough.* It's a beginning.

Moon nods. She can feel it's time to try again with the breath.

"Anna these are baby steps. If you feel yourself returning to the other thought, the one that that tells you you're not enough, remind yourself, I am enough."

I am enough.

"Okay, so let's try breathing again," Moon says.

Anna feels another spasm of fear pass through her. *I am enough,* she reminds herself again. Disbelieving, and yet, at the same time not...

Moon guides Anna to a handmade wooden stool with a red felt cushion on it to one side of the tipi. Anna hadn't noticed it before in her preoccupation with the bedding, but now it stands out, as if for her. "Sit here for the next bit, Anna. It's better if your back is straight and your hips can move freely."

Anna looks up at Moon. Why? *What are you going to do to me?*

"What I want you to do is rock your hips slowly and gently backwards and forwards," Moon explains. "Notice your breath. Pause gently as you feel the spine come straight again as you exhale. Enjoy the pause at the end of the outbreath, then let go and allow your breath back in. Allow the breath to breathe you." Moon demonstrates. "As you rock forward, let your tummy fall into our lap as you are breathing in, and as you rock back, you're breathing out. This movement brings your awareness deeper into your body and helps to engage the diaphragm so you can feel where it is and what it's doing."

"Okay." *I don't know about this.*

Anna's previous singing teacher had certainly not used this technique. As Anna begins to rock back and forth, mirroring Moon's movements, it seems to her somehow sensual, and she feels a growing awareness of her own femininity. Not the outer dressing up kind of femininity that needs high heels and make-up and sexy dresses, but something more primal. It's bringing up a colourful mixture of feelings for Anna – some pleasing, some uncomfortable. And yet, as she continues to mirror Moon, the overwhelming feeling is good and wholesome. Like her body has always been wanting to move like this.

"Okay, now Anna, you are still chest breathing, but I'm going to help you to bring the breath deeper, okay? As you continue to breathe, in and out, keep rocking. I'm going to place my hand on your chest."

Oh no... What's going to happen to me? She can feel herself at the verge of another doorway, and the unknown is beyond it, wild, terrifying, and unpredictable.

As Moon's palm touches the skin of Anna's chest, a wave of emotion rocks through her – to be touched like this, with such care. Physical touch for Anna has always been related to sexual relationships, always with a need attached from one side or the other. This touch is so different. Anna feels the care in it, and the heat. Johannes' hands had been warm like this too. There is so much heat in Moon's hand now that it's penetrating right beneath Anna's skin, and deeper. She feels it right in the centre of her chest. *How can a hand make this much warmth?*

"Okay, Anna, now I am going to place just a little more pressure, to help your body remember, to help the breath go deeper. Keep rocking, and just let it go deeper. Let go."

But it's so hard to let go...

"You are enough, Anna. Let it go."

I can't...

With Moon's hand holding firm, it takes such effort to keep breathing with the chest, and yet Anna does, because that's all she knows. But it's not working because she can't quite take in enough air, and she feels like she's going to suffocate... and still Moon is holding, all the while whispering like a mantra, "*You are enough.*"

Without warning, Anna's body jolts into action by itself. Her diaphragm plunges down, the breath entering her lungs and reaching deep inside her, deeper than she ever remembers breathing, puncturing the ball of emotion lodged there. And to her shock, emerging on the outbreath is a deep, mournful, primal wail, the release of a long-held pain – the pain of believing for so long that she wasn't enough. Anna can't stop herself crying this time as her body collapses into sobs.

Moon places a cotton handkerchief into Anna's hands. Grateful, Anna wipes her streaming face. Moon moves both her hands around to Anna's back, holding them there over her heart, as her body cries and cries. There seems no end to it, as the warmth continues to reach deeper still, warming her chest and spreading through her whole body.

"Keep breathing," Moon whispers. "You are enough."

So Anna breathes, feeling this new, strange way of drawing in air, and all the while the waves of sadness are coming and coming, moving through her in waves apon waves.

Eventually the sobs subside, and the waves of sadness fade, leaving a tingling and humming in their wake, a kind of presence, a stillness on the other side of the storm. As Anna settles, she becomes aware again of the heat from Moon's hands, and how it is moving through her body, softening, filling the emptiness with a soft, warm light. Continuing to breathe, Anna notices how her shoulders have stopped lifting, and having let go – finally, after more than twenty years of holding – it is as if a weight has dropped off.

"Breathe that new thought right into your belly, Anna."

And so in her own softness, Anna does. *I am enough. I am enough. I am enough.*

As she breathes, she feels this thought enter her, and rest inside her, the warmth of it radiating like a little light in her belly. *I am enough.*

"There you go. You're breathing now." Moon says, lifting her hands from Anna's body and returning them to rest in her lap. Anna can still feel the warmth of the hands, as if they are still touching her.

"Does this happen a lot when you show people how to breathe?" Anna sniffles, wiping her nose again with the damp handkerchief. "I'm sorry... I've completely sodden your handkerchief."

The handkerchief is beautifully hand-adorned with little red stitches around the edges and a tiny embroidered shape of a running wolf next to a full moon. It speaks to Anna of the significance of Moon's wolf tattoo, and how it might be connected with her name.

"Actually, I haven't shown many people how to breathe. In fact, you're the first. I've heard this can happen though. There are lots of different ways people connect with their breath. Often it can come with an emotional release. It was certainly like that for me."

"Really?" Anna looks up in wonder. "You cried?"

"Cried? Ha. I wailed. I was much louder than you."

Anna begins to laugh, a laugh of release and relief, and Moon laughs with her. In this moment, Anna no longer feels separate from Moon. Moon is a sister.

As the ripples of laughter settle, Anna takes another shaky breath. "Thank you," she says, feeling more grateful than she can express, hoping that Moon can some-how feel what this means to her.

"You're very welcome."

They sit in silence for a few moments together, and Anna becomes aware again of the sounds of the festival outside Moon's tipi. All of that had faded away in the intensity of what had been happening within.

Moon arches her back and stretches her arms upwards. It's time to move.

"What can I give you?" Anna asks. "I want to give you something, in exchange for what you've done for me."

Moon smiles at Anna again, her eyes bright. "It's not like that. It's a gift for me too."

Anna looks at the soiled cloth in her hand. "Your handkerchief... I could wash it and bring it back..."

"I've got others," Moon says. "Why don't you keep it? I'd be happy for you to have it. It's good to let it go. It feels right."

"Thank you," Anna says, feeling speechless and showered with gifts, with nothing to give back in return. "Can I at least pay you for it?"

Moon shakes her head. "It's a gift, honestly. But if you want, there is something you can do. I'll say the same thing to you that was said to me when I was given some special knowledge by one of my teachers in the past. One day, when the moment comes and you see someone who needs the gift you have to give, offer it to them. Pass it on. That's it."

"Okay. I will, if I can."

Moon's grey-blue eyes are clear as she gazes intently at Anna. "You can. Trust me. One day all this will feel so natural to you, and you'll just want to share it. You'll meet someone and just know that it's your job to show them, and it will be a joy to do it." As Moon says this, Anna has a sense that Moon is describing herself.

"I'll have to take your word for it," Anna says. "Right now it still feels so strange. I mean, it feels good in a way, but I feel like I have to keep reminding myself to do it, and each time, it's like I'm using muscles I've never used before, and they kind of know how to do it, but also not, and my chest wants to just revert to the easy way."

"It takes practice," Moon says. "It's like anything. You keep doing it, and when you forget you remind yourself, and you keep doing it, and then one day, you just notice your body is doing it naturally. It really does become completely natural."

Like walking a tightrope wire.

As Anna has been listening to Moon, she realises that her chest and shoulders are lifting again, lapsing back again into their familiar shallow breathing pattern. "Oops. I think I'm going to have to remind myself quite a lot."

"It just takes attention," Moon assures her. "Just keep giving it attention and eventually you'll be able to do it without thinking. And Anna, all you ever need to do is one breath. One breath at a time. This breath. This breath is all there is. Conscious breathing will bring you into the moment." Moon lifts herself off the sheepskin to standing. "And speaking of moments, I feel like the moment has come for me to pee."

Anna tries to rise too, shakily, to follow her, but Moon rests her hand gently on Anna's shoulder.

"You don't have to get up yet Anna. I need to move, but feel free to stay here as long as you like."

Anna drops gratefully back down to the sheepskin. She doesn't feel ready yet for the world outside Moon's tipi. The emotional release has left her feeling like curling up in the softness of the sheepskins and sleeping for a very long time.

"Stay until you feel like emerging," Moon says, ducking out through the entrance flap into the bright sunlight. "You know where I am. Feel free to stop by any time."

"I will," Anna agrees.

With a light smile, Moon is off, gliding out into the sunshine of the festival.

Left to herself, Anna sits, practising her breathing, experiencing this newness. It feels like a new body, a new self unfurling one shaky breath at a time. It doesn't take too long before she gives in to the sleep that wants to take her and laying back on the sheepskins, she closes her eyes – still breathing – and sleeps.

"You are enough in all the ways in who you are
You are enough, when you think you should be more
You are enough in this moment
You are enough without atonement
I could go to the top of the mountains
To bring you back into my arms
Where you belong
Little one
And I would follow you up those cold mountains
Right to the top of your mind winds
To bring you down, home again
And oh everything is loving you
And oh everything is on your side
And you are not separate from the love inside
And oh everything is loving you

And oh everything is on your side
And you are not separate from this heart of mine
From the love inside"

from the song, 'You are Enough', by Boe Huntress

Anna wakes some time later, alone in the tipi. Someone – probably Moon she surmises – has placed a full glass of water beside her. She sits up and gratefully swal-
lows it down, having woken with a raging thirst. It is the same alive, iron rich water
she had in the Big Tipi that night – Chalice Well water. It revives her. She is touched
that Moon would care for her in this way. She crawls out the entrance flap and as
her eyes adjust to the brightness outside, she notices how crisp and vivid everything all seems, how even though the sun has passed its zenith and is now heading towards late afternoon, that things seem brighter than they had been before.
A weight has lifted off her. She reminds herself to breathe again, the way Moon
showed her and feels again this sense of a new body, breathing itself. It is as if
something has been rearranged inside her, leaving her more aware of her body,
more animal, more real.

The light raw breakfast is long gone and Anna becomes aware of a strong hunger
gnawing again, so slipping on her shoes, she lets her feet carry her down the hill,
across the Tipi Field to Pacha Mama's Cafe.

Maddy is still there behind the counter, giving her attention to the spreading of
batter. As Anna waits in the queue, her eyes roam over the blackboards out front
which list all the delicious and healthy treats on offer. At first glance the boards
look identical, but Anna notices with amusement that at the bottom of one board
is the word 'Organic', whereas the word at the bottom of the other is 'Orgasmic'.
Anna smiles at this play on words and looks up at Maddy, and suddenly she just
knows. Her eyes widen as it comes to her with absolute clarity. *Maddy is the one
who stayed with Moon last night. It was Maddy!*

With this realisation, a wave of feelings move through Anna. The first is a profound relief that it wasn't Cedar, then guilt because she doesn't think she should
feel that kind of relief about Cedar, since she has Damien. Then comes a kind of
awe, as suddenly the relationship between the two women makes more sense to
her now. And lastly, there is a kind of embarrassment, because the candles and the

bedding in Moon's tipi all paint too much of a picture in her mind of what went on last night. In an effort to think of something else before she reaches the front of the queue and faces Maddy directly, Anna searches for something else to focus her attention on. And there it is – the painting of the beautiful smiling Indian woman with the red dot between her eyebrows.

That woman probably knows how to breathe properly, Anna thinks, wondering briefly again who the woman is. But now it's Anna's turn at the front and Maddy is giving her a knowing smile. "So how do you feel now?"

Anna laughs. "Rearranged – in a good way, I think."

"Yes. Moon manages to do that to me too sometimes. That's Moon for you."

Images of the ruffled bedding fill Anna's mind again and she flushes. "Have you seen her in the last few hours?" *How much did she tell you?*

"I saw her a little while ago. She said you'd been sleeping for a while, and that it had been strong for you."

"Did she tell you I bawled my eyes out?"

Maddy grins. "Not in so many words. What went on between you and Moon is between you and Moon. She only told me that it had been transformative, and that you had begun to breathe, and that she could already feel that this had changed things for you. She seemed happy, like it had been good for you both whatever went on."

A warmth returns as Anna remembers how much care Moon had given her, the incredibly warm hands that felt like they were healing her. In her pocket, she can feel the damp handkerchief as a testament to exactly how transformative it had been. For as long as Anna can remember, she had not been one to really feel her emotions, to let herself cry. For to really cry requires an opening and a letting go, and these things are new for her.

"You ready for your pancake now?" Maddy asks.

Anna nods. "Yes please. Same again. Choccy banana."

Maddy scoops the batter and spreads it smoothly on the pan. Anna notices how graceful the movement is, and how as Maddy works, she is breathing into her belly, just as Anna had been shown. But it looks totally natural to her, as if she doesn't have to think about it. *I wonder if it will be like that for me*, Anna wonders, realising that already she's shifted back into her previous shallow breathing habit, and corrects herself.

How many times will I have to fall off before I no longer fall? She imagines what the tightrope walker might say in response to that question. *As many times as it takes*, he seems to say.

Moon's words echo again in her mind. *All you ever need to do is one breath. One breath at a time. This breath. This breath is all there is.*

Maddy flips the pancake onto a plate and adds the chocolate and banana. Anna's stomach growls noisily.

"It's too bad for Moon that she can't eat these," Anna says, accepting the plate of delicious steaming, perfectly crisp pancake and pooling chocolate.

"What do you mean?" Maddy gives Anna a funny look. "Moon does eat these... all the time!"

"But she told me she eats a mostly raw, foraged diet!"

Maddy laughs, accepting the money from Anna. "Well, that's Moon for you. She moves in many different directions."

It appears she does, Anna thinks.

"I think Moon and I share the feeling that it's best to listen to your body," Maddy says. "Not to have a strict dogma about what to do or not to do. Sometimes the medicine your body needs is a good old chocolate crepe."

Anna can't help smiling at that, inhaling the aroma of crisp batter and warm chocolate. "Mmmm. This is definitely good medicine for me right now."

"We aim to please." Maddy grins again. "And we try and make them with love, and that always seems to help."

Made with love, Anna thinks again of the kind young man at the Chai Chi Tent.

"You mean like love's the most important ingredient?" Anna asks.

"Yes! Exactly. I like that. It absolutely is," Maddy agrees.

Again Anna wonders how a person could actually put love into something, as if it were a real tangible ingredient. *But maybe it is possible,* she realises. Something had happened the other night in that tipi. Something had moved from Cedar's didgeridoo into her heart. She had felt it. It was a river of love. It was real. She could feel it in her physical body. And there was definitely something in those brownies. And Moon's hand earlier... something tangible had moved from Moon's hand into her own body, changing her.

But how do you put love into something? What does that really mean?

Anna's eyes are drawn again to the painting of the beautiful Indian woman up above Maddy's head, who seems to be smiling down at her. *I bet you know the answer, whoever you are.* She almost asks Maddy about the painting, but someone else has arrived in the queue, keen for their orgasmic pancake.

"Thank you," Anna says, moving aside.

"Enjoy!" Maddy sends a friendly smile Anna's way before turning her attention to the next customer.

The cafe has opened up the canvas flaps at one end, allowing the light to stream in. Anna carries her plate over to an empty table in the patch of sunshine. The pancake is as good as it promised to be, the crisp batter crunching in her teeth and the rest melting in her mouth, bathed in the sweet melted chocolate and banana. She feels it warming her inside, as much as the sun is warming her skin on the outside. If it's possible for pancakes to be medicine, then this certainly is.

Having scraped the plate clean, Anna steps out of the cafe and finds the same bench she had sat on before near the wishing well. Folding her hands in her lap, she closes her eyes and with the sunlight warm on her face, practises her breathing. It still feels strange, but good too. Each one takes conscious attention. It doesn't feel natural yet, but determination is ignited in Anna again – to be like the circus performers, to keep practising, like the kind gentleman with the smiling eyes had said to her.

That's the practice, see. You learn that each time your mind wanders from the present, you bring yourself back. Each time you notice. Each time you fall, you bring yourself back. Even if it's hundreds, or thousands of times. Eventually, you will discover you are not falling off so often, and you are staying in the moment for longer. And eventually, you find that you have enough presence not to fall. And that is when you know you have reached a kind of mastery. Not only of your craft, but of your mind.

I wonder if I can master my mind? Anna wonders, reminding herself to breathe again. Now, as if to test notions of presence, thoughts come fast, drawing Anna from the moment, thoughts of what she has promised to do later this evening. *The Rolling Stones with Shari and Eden.*

Shallow breathing again, Anna catches herself and takes another deep belly breath. *How easily I fall,* she thinks. As she focuses on her breathing, she begins to feel better, the panicked feelings in her body subsiding. *You only have to get up once,* the thought comes to her. *This time.*

A breeze brushes Anna's cheek. Her ears take in the swishing sounds of the little cloth dragonfly dancing in the air over the wishing well and the ebb and flow of the myriad of sounds coming from across the site, which seem to grow louder or quieter depending on the direction of the wind.

"Feel, it stirs, without, within
the air, it touches everything
Fills dark spaces, draws in light
Whispers to the newest leaves
Beats against the oldest stone

Drifts in the journey
Invites us to fly
Feel, and dream."

from the song, 'Spiritum ', by Mary and Olivia Watson

"You are magnificent." A strong, male voice breaks into Anna's consciousness. She turns toward the direction of the sound. There is an interesting venue she hadn't noticed before, just across the way from Pacha Mama's. It's a large structure, elegantly constructed from three big tipis all joined together and opened out inside. A hand-painted sign out front reads: 'Ancient Futures'. People are gathered by the entrances and sitting cross-legged on the floor within, listening intently. Without thinking, Anna stands and moves towards this voice.

Peering in through the entrance, she sees a man sat on the low stage at the far side of the venue, wearing an undyed long-sleeved cotton shirt and beige trousers, appearing very relaxed, but also alert. He looks to be physically strong, except for the wooden cane leaning against his chair. The man's dark hair has streaks of grey, but his face seems quite free of lines.

"In this life you can BE the powerful, magnificent Self you are." Arthur Cole feels the words as they move through him. "If you only knew what you are really made of, then all your fears would drop away. I am going to tell you my story – how I died, how I came to live again, and how what I saw when I died changed everything about my life."

He *died*? Anna finds this hard to believe, like so many things she has experienced this weekend, and yet, this man looks as alive as anyone she has ever met – more so, in fact. His eyes hold a light – a blazing kind of fire brighter even than Cedar's eyes, Moon's eyes or the tightrope walker's eyes, as if he really had walked through a fire himself and come out the other side, with the fire still alive and raging inside him. Anna moves through the gathering crowd so she can sit closer to the stage.

"I spent the first part of my life in the corporate world," Arthur tells them. "I lived my days 9 to 5 and sometimes more like 5 to 9... I was unhappy. A few times a year, I found some solace in the mountains near a holiday home I owned in Scotland. Up until my accident, that was the only place I ever found any peace in my life. So it's fitting in a way that this is where it happened. I had a lot going on that particular week. There was a big meeting coming up between the heads of my department, and I had to make a decision about whether to take a promotion I was being offered. It would give me substantially more money, but I had big reservations because I had seen that the company was not working ethically. I had some idea that I might try and change it from within, but this particular job would have me promoting the very thing I was starting to feel the most reservations about – this very product that I knew was endangering indigenous communities and destroying rainforest, this very product that was exploiting workers in China. Because not only were we destroying rainforest, and seriously endangering wildlife and communities, we were burning vast quantities of fossil fuel to have this product shipped to China where we were paying people very little money to assemble it and then we burned more fossil fuel to have it sent it back to us.

"So I was in this quandary. I hadn't yet learned to listen to that deeper voice inside myself. I was still stuck in fear. If I let this job go, would I get another? And there was this big promotion. Everyone around me was already congratulating me on the new job and asking me what I would do with all the extra money I'd be earning. My parents were proud of me for making something of myself. My new girlfriend – another employee at the company who I'd been fancying for some time – was behind me all the way. And yet... there was this feeling that wouldn't let me go. It was telling me there was another way, but I wasn't listening to it.

"In those moments before I slipped and fell on the mountain, I wasn't paying attention to where I was. I was worrying about what to say at this meeting. But in those moments as I was falling, I thought, 'Oh, this is it. None of it really matters anyway!' I knew I was going to die. It was a long way down, and some time during that fall, before I even hit the final ledge where my body came to land, I hit my head on a passing rocky ledge and that was it. I felt my awareness expanding outside my body, all around it. It was like suddenly I could see 360 degrees all around me. I could see every single mountain I loved so much and beyond them to the whole of the rest of the world. I could see my office, my girlfriend, my parents, and it was all SO indescribeably beautiful. And at the same time I was also watching my body fall down the mountain and then I saw it lying there, broken and crumpled in a heap. 'So this is what dying feels like,' I'm thinking to myself. And I just felt this all pervading peace, this sense that all is completely well. I felt like I was part of the mountains themselves. There seemed to be no separation between them and me, and there was no separation between me and the three climbers who were coming along this lower track, who were going to eventually pass by where my body was lying. I won't go into any details about what they found, but let's just say that there were a lot of broken bones and a lot of blood. As I watched the people going into shock and screaming as they found me and getting out their mobile phones and checking my pulse, I felt only compassion for this person I had been, who had been living this life, so concerned with all these things.

"I then felt myself drawn somehow further away from this scene. It was like people describe – passing through a tunnel, and on the other side of this tunnel, it was an experience which I can only try and put into words. It was the feeling of the most warm lovingness, of completely coming home, completely belonging. There was a sense of glowing warm presences all around me. These were my family – my soul family. Some of them were members of my biological family in this life who had died. Some of them I felt were even the higher selves of people in my soul family who I haven't even met yet in this life. And there were others I just knew, like we'd been travelling together for lifetimes and we've always known each other. And more than that, we've always been part of each other. I realised that these souls, who were part of me had always been with me, had always been loving me. My older brother, Simon, was there among them. He died when I was a teenager, and that affected my whole life up until that point. I fell into a deep depression after he died. I saw that all those times I had walked in the mountains seeking solace, that Simon had been there, walking right beside me. And here Simon was, in this place of coming home, beaming me with the most incredible love I had ever felt, and I knew that he had never left me. I saw it all. I saw that he had been one of my guides, always speaking to me of the love that I am and that I had never been alone – ever. I had always had these loving presences with me. It was as if I had stepped into the most perfect celebration with all those that I most loved, and the feeling I had was of being absolutely loved, without limit, unconditionally. And more – I could feel God, Love, Absolute Love. And I knew that this God, this Love, is not a Being outside of me or you. This Source, this consciousness of the universe, this All That Is, is in every soul around me, and every soul on Earth and even beyond that on other planets across the whole universe. I saw that I am an expression of God, God expressing this Love through me! And I could see that although God had manifested into countless various forms – into every form of life there is – that we are all part of this same Love.

"This experience has changed me forever. As you can imagine, it would have been easy to just stay in that feeling of Absolute Love and never return to this life, but then my brother said this to me – he said, 'You can choose to stay, or you can choose to go back to your life. If you go back, you will heal yourself. It will not be easy, but you will do it.' I saw what he saw – that if I went back I would be in a wheelchair for a time and then I would have to learn to walk all over again, and I would have a brain injury to heal. But I would heal these things, and if I went back,

I would be able to speak to people about what I had experienced. I was seeing the wild, free Magnificence that we all are and I knew I could communicate that to people in some way and maybe help them to see something of it too.

"So the next thing I remember, I was in a lot of physical pain and when I opened my eyes I could only see out of one of them because the other was covered with a bandage. I was in a hospital and I had been in a coma for a week. A doctor told me about my accident, and said that some climbers had found me, that they thought I had died and were surprised to find out I had not. 'There were three of them,' I told him. 'How did you know that?' he asked me. 'I saw it,' I told them.

"He didn't believe me, but I didn't mind. Then I was told that I had suffered a serious brain injury, shattered various bones in my right leg, broken a number of other bones in my body and torn several tendons and that it was unlikely I would ever walk again. I knew otherwise. That was a year and a half ago. After 6 months of being in a wheelchair, doing physio and qigong and anything else under the sun that took my fancy, I took my first steps with a cane. You can see it here. I still carry it, but I don't need it much now. I taught myself to walk again. I walk slowly, but I walk. And one day soon I know I will climb those mountains again."

"How did you heal yourself?" A woman, Janine, in the front asks.

"I saw it. I knew, because I had seen what I am really made of; that all thought is creative; all thought is a form of energy, a form of God. I saw myself healed. I saw myself walking. I knew this because I had seen it already. And this is another thing – all time is happening simultaneously, now. All future, all past, it is all now. Now this is hard to grasp for the human mind. Everything that has ever happened and ever will happen is already occurring here, now. So if you tap into this consciousness that creates all this – this consciousness that you already are – you can understand things about the future and the past. You can even affect the past and future from within the now.

"Now I'm not saying that we have no free will, because we do. Imagine that in each moment, radiating out from where you are is the infinite present, and from this point are infinite possibilities. In this place of infinite now, I saw that if I made a series of choices in this life, it was likely that a certain outcome would occur. And here's something else. This free will we have operates within a set of choices we already made – with free will – before we were even born. Before incarnation, we, as souls, set certain things in motion – a soul contract. We chose our parents and the circumstances of our birth, we chose to meet certain people in this life, to experience certain things for our soul's growth. So often without even being conscious of it, we are moving towards these soul choices; drawn or called to do certain things. This is our Higher Selves, our Wild Selves guiding us towards these things that our own souls have already chosen.

"I know my soul chose the experience of the NDE so that I could see the things I saw and remember them, and bring the story back to share with others. We are in a time in the world when so many of us are ready to wake up to who we truly are, and I felt my soul's desire to contribute in this time. You see, many souls have come into incarnation now at this particular time, because this is a very significant time in humanity's journey. So when I was offered this choice to return to my current life or to stay where I was and all that would come with that – which is more than I can talk about here – I chose to return. I knew that if I returned to my life, the doctors would tell me that I would never walk again, but I could see that I would. It was the same with the brain injury. I had to grow new brain cells, make new neural connections, but I knew I could, because I knew that all of me – my blood, my bones, my cells – is all made of God."

Anna stares at this man, amazed at these words. *Could it be true? Anna's God...* the words of Maddy drift through her mind again.

A flash on blond hair catches Anna's eye. She had been so immersed in this man's story that she hadn't seen another man come in to the tent, but there he is – the man she has been looking for in every face since that night in the Big Tipi. Cedar stands there in the sunlight, not quite stepping in, but leaning lightly against one of the wooden poles, listening. He is more casual today, in a rust red t-shirt and faded blue jeans, and with a day's worth of blond stubble on his face. She smiles to see that he is still barefoot.

"I used to be afraid of all kinds of things," Arthur continues, looking out at all these faces, and feeling a swell of gratitude that they have all come here to listen to this story. Since the accident he has lost his fear of public speaking, because there is no longer an audience separate from himself. They are part of him.

"I was always afraid of what people would think of me, afraid of failure, afraid I would lose money, lose face. Now I fear nothing. I just feel so grateful to be alive! Each day is a blessed gift, an opportunity to be joy, to experience this Magnificence that I am in a human body, and to see this Magnificence in every person I meet." He casts his eyes over the audience, all these beloved souls.

"I would like to invite you all to close your eyes now and experience a vision with me. Become aware of your breath in your body and just sit with that for a moment until you feel yourself becoming more still."

Cedar wonders whether to join in with this visualisation or not. From the corner of his eye he catches sight of Anna, sitting there with her eyes closed. *Ah*, he thinks.

So this is where you will meet her again. She seems different today – softer. Her energy has changed and expanded.

"Now, see yourself in your favourite place in the world," Arthur tells them. "Maybe a natural environment you love, a forest, a beach, a green field – anywhere you truly love – and really see yourself there."

Anna thinks back to her childhood and wonders. Then it comes to her. There was an oak tree in her parents' garden that she'd loved growing up – a great, old oak. It's still there, though it has lost some boughs in recent years. As a child, Anna had loved to sit beneath the oak's branches. She imagines herself sitting back against the old tree now, feeling the rough strength of its bark against her.

"Now, in your mind's eye, notice a path or an entrance into this place that you love."

In her vision, Anna sees the stone gate at the edge of the garden, surrounded by her mother's potted plants and ivy growing along the stone wall.

"In a moment, someone will be coming along this path. Imagine the person you most deeply dream you could be, the person you would be if you allowed yourself to truly be free, the self you would be if you could be as wild and joyful and creative and fearless as you want to be. I call this my Wild Self. But you can use whatever name feels right to you – Heart-Self, Higher-Self, God-Self, Authentic Self. You are beginning to see this person moving towards you now on this path."

A woman somewhere in front of Anna laughs out loud. "What if my Authentic Self is wearing a paper bag over its head?"

There are titters throughout the room. Anna laughs too, but out of nervousness. She wonders whether she will see anything at all.

Authur chuckles. "This is fine. Just let it be, whatever comes. But know that under that bag – if there is a bag or a mask – is that Self that you most deeply dream to be. And if you find this whole thing hard to believe, that there is a Wild Heart Self in you at all, just humour me. Imagine it as if there is. I invite you to lift off that paper bag or take off that mask and welcome your Wild Heart Self into this place with you."

"What if it's too scary to look under the bag?" The woman says, her eyes still closed. "I'm scared to see what that would look like."

"Okay. That's okay. Just do what you feel to do. This is an invitation. Remember, this person can't hurt you. This person loves you beyond measure. This person is happy beyond measure, fearless, loving, courageous, openhearted. They are the Wind and the Earth and the Rain and the Sun. What would that look like if it were true? This is who is coming towards you now."

There's nobody coming through my gate, Anna thinks, staring at the curling ivy around the wall of her vision. She wonders if her person will have a bag over their head as well.

I do want to see something, she realises, even though she is afraid.

And now, someone is coming. She can see a hazy outline of this person, approaching and opening the gate. It's a woman with brown hair – Anna's natural colour. The hair is shorter than Anna's, cut into wild, wavy layers, a little like Moon's. And she's naked and unashamed. There is no makeup on this face; her skin glows with vitality. There are fiery swirls of red and gold leaves painted at her cheekbones, highlighting her eyes, which blaze brightly with an inner fire. They are Anna's own eyes, only brighter, as bright as Moon's or Cedar's eyes, or as bright as the eyes of the man speaking onstage. They are filled with light and joy. She moves like a large wildcat, strong and supple in her body as she sits down cross-legged in front of Anna, looking her in the eye and smiling.

"This Wild Self is before you now," Arthur tells them, his voice both soft and strong. "And this person loves you, totally. This person knows you completely. They know all the things you are ashamed of – all your fears and insecurities – and they love you, totally and unconditionally."

Eyes shining, the Wild Woman smiles at Anna, as if she really does love her. The woman reaches down beside the tree and lifts up a guitar that Anna hadn't known was there, exactly like her own Martin guitar. The Wild Woman begins to strum a melody which is so sweet and deep it makes Anna want to cry and sing.

'Sing with me,' the woman says, and it is Anna's own voice, unashamed.

Anna looks into this face, bewildered. *Who am I? Am I just imagining all this?*

"This Wild Heart Self before you, this person who is all these things you'd love to be, all the things you dream you could be in your deepest dreams – this is WHO YOU ALREADY ARE."

A shiver moves through Anna.

"And if you imagine the wildest, most blissful, most compassionate and free self you can imagine... know that this is only a tiny glimpse of the magnificence you TRULY are."

A breeze brushes past Cedar's face and he opens his eyes. The others are still visioning. He is surprised at what he saw in his own. A smile curls at his lips, a reflection of the sweet one he can see on Anna's face now. *What is she seeing, he wonders, that makes her so happy?*

"What would happen in your life," Arthur asks them, "if you allowed yourself to be this Magnificence that you are?" The question reaches out across the room and vibrates in the air all around them. "What would your life look like if you allowed love to lead you rather than fear? How would it change the way you act towards other people? How would it change the way you treat the natural world around you?"

Anna takes a breath into her belly and asks herself that question: *What would my life look like if I let love guide me rather than fear?* Something is shimmering just at the edges of her consciousness, nearly visible, and the nearness of it feels bright and electric. *It would change everything*, she realises. *Everything*.

"When you are ready, bring your awareness back to this space and slowly open your eyes," Arthur says gently.

Anna flutters her eyes open and watches the man onstage sitting in perfect stillness, as he waits for the last few people to open their eyes. She resists turning to look at Cedar, but can still see him there at the edge of her vision.

"These questions changed everything for me," Arthur's eyes blaze at them all. "Because I saw that when love guided me, I couldn't engage in an action that hurt another being. And more than that, I felt compelled to help others do the same. When I was recovered enough physically, I was offered my old job back. I declined. But I didn't give up on that company. I went back there and spoke with my colleagues, as I am speaking with you now, and some of them were moved. Some of them saw that they had been asleep, and dreaming. They hadn't really seen what they were doing, how it was affecting the world, how we're all connected. It's like for many of us there's this layer of illusion, a kind of sleep. Like we're all dreaming. But when we wake up, when we remember who we are – then the illusion falls away. You realise you are the dreamer, and the dream. You know yourself as the Wild Self, and all your actions spring from this place. I call it wild because it is natural. It is your pure, natural, unadulterated, real self. This self is present all the time, we just don't usually allow ourselves to be this wildness that we are, but when we do, it is such joy! Such bliss! You are the mountains and the ocean and the sky. It is Love and Joy moving through us. It is God! And this is what I saw when I died. You are this magnificence! You are this Love! And as you experience this Love that you are, it expands the boundaries of you until you see there are no boundaries at all and it is ALL you, and you love all of it, and it all loves you, unconditionally. For when you move, it is Love that is moving you, and so all you do is authentic and guided by love and compassion.

"This is what I learned in my NDE – that I am free to be that which I already am – Joy, Radiance, Freedom, Fearlessness, Earth, Sky, Sun. And most of all, Love. And every day, I just feel this all encompassing gratitude for the gift of this life."

"I blow on these embers and I watch them alight
Inside, inside
Send this prayer on a feather and I watch it take flight
All around the world, all around the world
We create our reality
With every thought we can bring beauty
It's our responsibility
Let's make a world where the people are free
Sharpen your arrow and aim
For what you believe in
'Cause truth is what we're living
Sharpen your arrow and aim
Focus your intention
For you are the power of creation"

from the song, 'Sharpen Your Arrow', by Susie Ro Prater

I'm following Cedar up a hill. Anna watches the back of him, the easy sway of his hips as he strides up the steep grassy slope.

It had been a surprise to Anna when Cedar had been the one to approach her after Arthur's talk. She'd just worked up the courage to go speak with him when he had turned and looked right at her, as if he'd known she had been there all along, and had given her a great, warm smile. In that smile all her fear had evaporated and she had found herself smiling back. Just a boy meeting a girl. She smiles now to see the way he seems to bound up the hill, like a boy who's happiest running around in fields.

That night in the Big Tipi Cedar's eyes had blazed, had seared her, had seemed to see everything, but today it hadn't felt like that. His eyes had been gentler – questioning – and a lovely clear blue; she had been able to see that in the daylight. And he had asked her, without any small talk, *"Would you like to take a walk with me?"*

A brief thought of Damien had passed through Anna's mind, with a little flush of guilt, but she had told herself it was just a walk – even though she knows it's clearly much more than that. There had been a look in Cedar's eyes – a reason.

Anna looks up the hill towards the trees which border the silver perimeter fence. Despite all her recent trips to the gym, Anna's thighs are starting to burn, and the steeper the incline gets, the harder it is to grip in these sandals. She finds herself lagging behind Cedar.

He stops and turns to face her, sensing her struggle. "You okay?"

"I'll manage." She can hear the puff in her voice. The stair step machine had been no preparation for this.

He gives her a knowing smile. "I always find it easier to go barefoot."

"Oh, right." She slips off her sandals and tucks them into her satchel, and as she steps one foot in front of the other, feeling the grasses beneath her toes, the climbing does seem easier. Some of the grasses are tough and almost painful; some are soft, and beneath them the earth is cool. It reminds her of walking barefoot in the sauna, and how good that had felt. Suddenly, with the sun on her face, the wind in her hair and the ground below her feet and Cedar in front of her, Anna feels a wave of excited, joyful energy moving through her with such a rush that she could almost dance up the hill. She falls in step beside him, and now they are passing beneath a semi-circle of tall flagpoles, with their bright shining golden silk flags catching the sunlight in waves against the blue of the sky. It lifts Anna's heart and propels her on.

"Well that worked, then." Cedar smiles to see her there beside him.

"Seems to. I think I like the barefoot thing."

"Me too."

"I don't think I've ever seen you in shoes," Anna says, and thinks how silly this sounds, as she's only seen him twice.

He laughs. "Not many people do. I don't tend to wear them if I can help it."

"Why's that?"

"It connects me to the Earth's energy. Grounds me. Gives me strength on lots of levels."

Anna wonders exactly what he means by Earth's energy, but before she can ask him, they have arrived.

"Here's the spot."

And what a spot it is. As Anna turns to gaze out across the expanse of valley below them, she feels the catch of her breath. "Wow.... I had no idea this was up here."

He laughs again.

"I mean this view. Obviously, the hill was here..." Anna stumbles on the words. But she forgets her embarrassment in the amazement of what she is seeing. From up here, everything looks different. The festival stretches out below – first these rows of majestic purple, deep red, gold and russet patchwork flags, and down beyond them the hundreds of tall, white tipis.

What is perhaps most striking of all to Anna is the huge oak tree – right at the centre of the scene – beyond the Tipi Field and at the top of the camping field. It is the one she had noticed yesterday when she had been trying to make up her mind about the sauna, whose branches had supported the string of lights which bordered the path. It had not seemed significant then, but from here it appears so large that it dwarfs the tipis which stand in front of it, its massive canopy of green opening out in a perfect expanse – an ancient being standing guard.

From here Anna can just make out the top of the striped tent where she played her first fateful gig, and just beyond it the Park Stage, with its majestic Corinthian columns to either side of it, wound with greenery and alight with fire at their pinnacles. A band is playing there now – the sounds of soulful electric guitars sailing out over the crowds of enthusiastic people gathered. Beyond this, Anna can see past the many other big stages, past the great metal spider and all the colourful tents and extraordinary human creations right over to the perimeter fence on the other side, and beyond that out across the green fields and rolling hills to the far horizon.

Even the sounds which had felt like they were clashing all around Anna when she'd been down below now all seem smaller up here. Here the predominant sounds are the flapping of the flags on the nearby flagpoles, the rustling of the wind in the leaves of the trees just beyond the fence above them, the wind in her own ears and the pounding of her heart. Here the air is clear, and Anna can feel it brushing her cheeks and playing in her hair, carrying with it the scents of the flowers and the far hills.

"I come up here because I find it helps me find perspective," Cedar says, following Anna's gaze. He observes the look of delight on her face. *She can feel it too*, he thinks, and it pleases him. Here nature is still itself, even with all the things placed around it, like the big metal perimeter fence and all that has been created down below.

Standing here, witnessing this, Anna can feel herself part of a greater whole. In one way, it makes her feel small and insignificant, and yet at the same time, the expanse of it makes her feel her own self expand, becoming aware of herself as part of that something greater. From here she can just see the gentle curve of the Earth on the horizon.

"I can see why you like this spot."

"Yeah. I come up here a lot."

As Anna sits beside Cedar, the long blades of grass feel rough beneath the thin cotton of her dress, but the soft coolness of the Earth below feels good. She allows her body to relax into it. Intensely aware of his presence beside her, Anna reminds herself to breathe and focuses her eyes on the sky. She loves the way skies in high summer turn that wonderful, vivid blue. She is amazed by how comfortable it feels to be here with him like this – not talking, just being side by side, as if they had always done this.

"In the talk just now," Cedar says softly, "I saw you with your eyes closed and you were smiling at something."

"I was imagining my Wild Heart Self."

"Mmm. I thought so. You liked what you saw."

Anna turns to look at him. "I guess I did. I'm sure it was just my imagination running away with itself, though. What I wish, you know."

"What do you think imagination is? We are creating all of this with our thoughts and imaginations. The boundaries between what is real, and what's so called imaginary are not what most people think."

"What do you mean? That what I imagine is actually real?"

"On one level, on a subtle level of energy, yes, it is real. Thought has a vibration. And you were imagining that for a reason. Whatever it was, it made you happy, and there's a power in that. I would trust what you saw."

"In the talk, Arthur said that we already are that person – the Wild Self, or Heart-Self, whatever you want to call it, whatever we most deeply dream we could be. But the woman I saw in my imagining – it just feels like I'm so far away from being that."

"But you're not, though," Cedar says, with feeling. "Your Heart-Self is already within you. Or maybe it is more true to say that you are within your Heart-Self, because the Heart-Self contains all of this..." He sweeps his hand out across the vista before them. "You already are that. It's just about remembering it."

It still doesn't completely make sense to Anna's rational mind what he's saying, but it feels good to her. She likes to imagine that this beautiful wild woman she had seen in her mind's eye might somehow be real, and more than that, that she could actually already be her in some way.

They are silent for a time, their eyes taking in the far hills and the myriad of scenes below them. Anna remembers how she felt that night in the Big Tipi, how she had felt herself somehow connected to the whole world, truly belonging.

"That night when you played your didge... something happened to me. I felt like I became aware of all this sadness in me that I didn't know was there, and then something sort of opened up inside me, and all the sadness got... washed away, at least for a little while. I had this feeling like I was... part of everything around me, part of all the people there, part of the whole festival even."

"It feels like coming home."

Anna feels a sob rising suddenly. "Yes. That's exactly what it feels like. I felt like I'd found something I've been searching for my whole life... The feeling was there, and then it wasn't. And when it left it was almost more sad than not having experienced it in the first place."

"It was like that for me at first." Cedar turns to face her again. "I would get these little glimpses of the interconnectedness of everything, and of that feeling of 'being home'. And it would happen at random times – usually involving another person who was resonating with that frequency – but then eventually I learned some techniques that I could do myself, like the ones I do before a gig. And if I do those things, I can get close to that state, and then when I'm playing, the music and energy of the moment can flow through me and do the rest."

"So, could you tell me some of these... techniques?" Anna asks tentatively, feeling as if Cedar holds some kind of secret key.

"I can try." He takes a breath and listens inside himself. The answer is clear. "For me it starts with the breath. I gather Moon did some of that with you earlier. How'd that go?"

Anna laughs. "I cried."

"It obviously went well then." He gives her a good-natured smile.

"You could say that." Anna returns his smile. "I think I breathed properly for the first time since I was a baby."

"That's a huge step."

"Yeah. But I keep forgetting. It takes so much effort to remember."

"That's how it is at first. You forget. You remember. And then you forget and then you remember a bit more. And a bit more. Until one day there's no more forgetting."

Anna lets her eyes rest on the multi-coloured expanse below them and takes a focused breath. "So have you reached the no more forgetting part yet?"

He chuckles. "No, definitely not, but maybe I'm remembering longer than I used to. Some days I'm more clear than others. It's on the days I'm not so clear that I come somewhere like this, and tune in."

"So assuming I can learn to breathe in more than just a sporadic fashion, what comes next?"

Cedar considers for a moment. "Intention... and right use of mind."

"What do you mean?"

"It's about discernment – choosing to empower the thoughts you want to have. If there's something you want to be able to do, you put your request out to the Source – you state your intention – and something will always come back. And it will often come back to you in ways you don't consciously expect." He laughs. "In fact, that's almost always what happens for me. That's why I find it best to leave the details of how to the Great Spirit."

"The Great Spirit?"

"Or you could call it God, or Goddess, or The Universe, or Source…"

"Or The Field of All Possibilities," Anna adds, remembering Johannes had used that term once.

"Exactly."

She shakes her head. It all feels like a wild and crazy dream. *But it's real. Or is it?* Anna is beginning to question all she thought before about reality. "So how do you make an intention, then?" she asks.

"Well… for example, this morning when I woke up I said to my Higher Self, 'Thank you for helping me to experience finding clarity', and I had this strong feeling to come up here and sit on this hill. But on my way here I found Arthur's talk, and I felt moved to stop and listen. And if I hadn't followed that impulse to stop, I wouldn't have found myself up here with you now…"

"With me?"

He nods. "I felt we were… meant to have a chat. I didn't know about what. But here we are. You know how sometimes you meet someone and you just know you have business with them, like they've got a message for you, or you've got a message for them?"

Anna nods, feeling like she must know what he means. Maybe that was what she felt when she first saw him.

"So what's your dream, Anna?"

"My dream?"

"You know, when Arthur asked us what we most deeply dream we could be? What's your deepest dream?"

She takes a breath. "I don't know. I think… it has something to do with music."

Ah, so she's a musician, he realises. This makes sense. He's starting to understand something more about what he can offer her now. "What do you play?"

I don't know. Anna could answer him as she answered Alex in the sauna, but she remembers how empty it had felt to call herself a singer-songwriter then. Being here beside Cedar who is speaking so truthfully to her like this, who has already seen right inside her, makes her feels like there is no other course of action but to be as honest as possible.

She breathes a sigh. "Technically, I guess you could say I play the guitar, sing and write my own songs. But I'm starting to see that maybe I don't really know how to do any of those things after all. It's like I'm missing something, like my whole life I've been missing something."

"Ah, but that's the great moment… when you wake up and a crack appears – as the great Leonard Cohen says – where the light can get in. When you realise you don't know, it creates an openness where something new can happen."

A little seed of excitement bursts open inside Anna. "Really?"

"Yes, and even if you don't know what it is, you have the desire to know, so there's a starting point for your intention. In your case, it's a desire to… what? Find a deeper experience with music?"

"Something like that."

"So what would that look like?" Cedar asks. "You know how Arthur asked that question, what would your life look like if it was guided by love?"

Anna feels the tingle again. "Yes. I almost saw it. It feels like it's just dancing out of my reach, but I can kind of feel it there."

"So if you were going to set an intention for yourself, can you put it into words?"

"I don't know. I'll try."

They both turn their sights again to the scene below them, as if unspoken, they are both giving Anna a chance to ask and listen for the answer.

What would my life look like if it was guided by love? The judgemental thoughts arise, telling her that she is just imagining the whole thing. *But then Cedar said that this whole world is being created with our imaginations… How do I know what is guidance?* Her mind is so full of questions, remembered conversations, worries, fears.

"What if nothing happens?" she asks after a few minutes of struggling. "All I can hear are my own thoughts, and none of them feel very wise. And they all seem so loud. I can't seem to choose the right thoughts to have."

"That's the monkey mind for you. When I say 'choose the thoughts you want to have', what I mean by that is to give attention to the thoughts that give you energy, but don't give your energy to the ones that you don't want to empower. You can't stop the mind from having thoughts, that's it's nature. You can only offer it things that it can focus on – like being in the moment, like the beauty of nature, or the feel of your breath moving in and out of your body."

Anna listens to the sound of her own breath moving in through her nostrils and filling the space below her ribs, and then the feel of the release.

"What I do sometimes," Cedar shares, "is to imagine my thoughts like passing clouds, like weather. You can choose to look at them or not, but you don't have to worry about them. The thing is to let go of trying. You've asked, now just let your mind relax. Maybe let your eyes rest softly on the horizon or something else that takes your fancy. Just take the pressure off yourself, Anna. At some point you'll forget to try and that's when the answer will just drop into your awareness."

"Okay, I'll try. I mean... I'll not try. I'll try not to try." She laughs at herself and turns her attention to the great oak down below, watching the tips of its upper branches swaying gently in the rising breeze. She reminds herself to breathe deeply, becoming aware of her body again, sitting here on this ground and smelling a sweet, warm fragrance in the air. She wonders what it is – perhaps wildflowers from somewhere nearby. Allowing her gaze to roam, she alights on the billowing flags lining the hill before her, noticing how beautiful they are when the sunlight catches them and they shine gold, dancing in the wind.

I love to sing. It comes as a feeling, and now as a memory of loving to sing as a child, and more recently of the joy that had risen up inside Anna as she joined in harmony with the others in the sauna – the feeling of singing for joy, not for any objective to be achieved.

I love to feel that sense of belonging, of being home, of being part of everything.

I want to experience how these two things can happen at the same time.

Anna gasps, as these two things come together with a rush of energy through her body.

Cedar smiles. "You got something."

She feels a sense of bewildered amazement. Yes, there had been a definite, yet very subtle reply. Not from outside of her, but from within her own imagination. In her own mind's voice, as if it was whispering to her.

"I love to sing," Anna whispers. "And I love that feeling we were speaking of... of being part of everything, of feeling like coming home. And then I suddenly wondered if the two things could happen at the same time – singing and having that feeling."

Cedar feels a smile lifting throughout his whole body. "You're talking about medicine."

"Medicine?"

A shiver moves through Anna at the word. Maddy had used that word, and she too had been speaking about love – *love and medicine.*

"Medicine song." Cedar turns to her, his eyes clear. "It has the power to remind us of who we are, of our essential connectedness with one another. That's the true potential of what music can do."

"Is that what you were doing the other night in the Big Tipi?" Anna asks.

He nods. "That was the intention. I always seek to do that. Some days it works better than others. That night was special, though. It was about what everyone there brought to it. As a musician you're the one physically playing the instrument, but the energy moving in the room is about everyone who's there."

Could I learn how to do that? Anna wonders. *To make medicine music?* Johannes had told her that she had the potential to make music that could heal. *But can I? Really? How does one learn such a thing?*

"So how do I do it?" she asks. "Assuming I could."

"You can. Seeing that you want to is the first step. If you make that your intention, then you will find ways to learn the things you need to learn. The right people will appear at the right time to show you things."

Like you, she wants to say.

"So what is my intention?" she asks. "How do I... make one?"

"You already have it there... in those three things. You just have to make it a statement of intent."

Anna rests her gaze again on the shining gold flags and the curve of the Earth beyond. She takes a conscious breath again.

My intention is... To learn how to make medicine with my music. To feel joy in what I do. To experience that feeling of belonging, of being part of everything with my music.

And other things too, Anna realises with surprise. *It's not just about my career. It's about my life too! So then, my intention is to feel that in all my life. To feel free. To feel alive in my life. To have courage to walk this path.* She remembers what Arthur said about gratitude, about being grateful for the gift of this life.

The faery girl with the rainbows in her hair had spoken about gratitude too, that day at the wishing well. *You have to say thank you as you're wishing. It's called gratitude. And that's what makes the magic happen. Because you know it's already taken care of.*

Okay... Anna says this out to the far hills, to the curve of the earth, to her Wild Heart-Self... to whoever or whatever might be listening. *Thank you.* She says it silently, and it seems to fly out on the wind right across the whole festival, to the far hills and beyond, out into the bright blue of the sky. She feels a returning lift fill her body, and she can't help grinning.

"I love this!" she breathes, and realises she's said it aloud.

Cedar laughs. "Me too." Anna is a kindred spirit, he knows. There is a kinship between the dharma of her soul and his.

"What now?" she asks.

He smiles. "Relax and enjoy the ride."

She laughs because she never had imagined she might end up sitting up on a hill with a man like this, gazing out at the world and saying things like this, and how it all feels like home.

The sun has begun its descent to the horizon, swinging closer to the west, and the shadows are beginning to grow longer. Anna takes her phone out of her bag and it tells her what she already knows. It's late. If she doesn't go now, she'll miss her rendez-vous with Shari and Eden and the Rolling Stones.

She can see her old life with the old patterns of behaviour stretching like a pathway out before her, with all its promises made out of fear. But now there seems to be a junction that she hadn't seen before – a new path to take, a life lead by the heart, by love – that's just beginning to shine out before her a little more clearly. At the same time, she can see there is a part of her, like the other woman in Arthur's talk, that is still wearing a bag over its head. That part of her isn't quite ready to know what that shining path would look like, because it would mean the destruction of her old life. But ready or not, she can feel it is disintegrating already; the transformation is already happening, like an unstoppable wave. Part of that transformation is about this man sitting beside her.

"I think I have to go," she says rising. "I made a plan to meet someone. I'd really rather stay, but..."

He nods. "Well, thanks for sharing my lookout spot with me, Anna."

"Thanks for showing it to me."

And in his clear eyes, Anna sees a question answered. There is more than friendship here. Paper bag or no, there is no denying it.

"Are you playing any more music this weekend?" she asks.

"Yes." Cedar's eyes light up. "Tomorrow. Our band, Awakening the Dreamer, are playing on the One Earth stage at 10pm."

Anna's heart leaps with excitement. "I'll be there!"

They look at one another for some moments, words seeming inadequate suddenly.

"Blessings on your path, Anna," Cedar offers. "I know you'll find what you're looking for."

"Thank you. I appreciate your faith in me. And you too... Blessings I mean." She doesn't know what else to say, so she gives him one final smile before turning to go, feeling the warmth of his gaze following her as she makes her way down the hill.

Again she enjoys the sensation of the grasses beneath the soles of her feet, tough as the stalks are in some places. Here, the grasses and meadow flowers are allowed to be as wild as they naturally are.

I have to toughen up my feet, Anna thinks, *if I'm going to be doing this barefoot thing regularly.*

And with a sudden clarity, she has a definite sense that's exactly what she's going to be doing – walking barefoot right onto that shining path.

"I call upon my ancestors as I bow to the earth
I call upon my ancestors 'Come speak to me'
I ask for the wisdom of the elders and
from those who walked here before
I call to the wind and the stars and the moon,
'Come breathe through me'
I call to the buzzard and the hawk,
'Teach me to ride on the wind'
The waves pounding at my shore
teach me what surrender means
Sprit of the deer 'I call you, I call upon you'
Spirit of the trees 'I call you, I call upon you'
White Buffalo Woman 'I call you, I call upon you'
Spirit of the breeze 'I call you, I call upon you'
Wind blow through me, you remind from where I came
I am born from thee and Spirit is my name
These rivers run through me from deep within the ground
I remember this dance as the ancient drum beat sounds
Que me cura, que me guia, que me llena con la Vida.
Me cura, que me guia, poderosa medicina."
(That you heal me, that you guide me,
that you fill me with life.
That you heal me, that you guide me,
powerful medicine")

From the song, 'I Call You', by Ayla Schafer

4. Earth

"Sweet Sweet Sweet Mother Earth
Sweet Sweet Sweet Mother Earth
Sweet Mother Earth
I'm singing to a new birth
Sweet Mother Earth"

from the song, 'Sweet Mother Earth', by Praying for the Rain

The sky is full of snow. A few more steps down the dusty main track and Anna sees the source of the flakes – *The Greenpeace Field*. A fake snow machine is spurting white fluff into the air, and there are piles of the fake snow all over the ground, surrounding a fierce-looking life-sized figure of a polar bear. Three teenage boys are having a pretend snowball fight between the snow huts which are dotted about. Someone has done a good job of creating an Arctic scene here. There is even an impressive portion of an Arctic drilling ship which is doubling as a climbing wall. Greenpeace's message this year is *Save the Arctic*.

Up until now, Anna hasn't really paid attention to the stories about drilling in the Arctic; it didn't seem like it concerned her, but now she feels compelled to look closer at it, because maybe it does have something to do with her after all. She remembers hearing something on the news about how what is happening in the Arctic right now is affecting climate change, and again Arthur's talk echoes in her mind. *What would your life look like if you allowed love to lead you rather than fear? How would it change the way you act towards other people? How would it change the way you treat the natural world around you?*

Anna gazes at the snaking queue of people waiting to go inside a house-sized

Earth globe set towards the back of the field, out of which is emanating a pleasing ethereal music. Wooden boardwalks wind across the field, lined with vendors selling locally produced market fare. A man in a Save the Arctic T-shirt is rolling a huge blow up Earth ball across the bellies of several people lying flat on the ground, and they look happy about it, too.

I didn't leave Cedar on the hill to stop here, Anna reminds herself, moving on again down the main track, leaving the Greenpeace area through a giant snow white icicle-laden archway. As she thinks of Cedar, Anna feels a warm, bubbling excitement rise up inside her, overpowering the guilt about her inner betrayal of Damien, which fades into the background temporarily.

He really spoke to me. Anna remembers the intimacy of the conversation. *He said we had business together. What did he mean by that?* These thoughts create waves of confusion inside her, as two parts of her jostle about inside – the part that knows she has already fallen in love with Cedar, and the part that is holding onto the past, onto her previous life and her relationship with Damien.

Anna lifts her eyes over the crowd. Most of the people are heading the same direction – towards the Pyramid Stage, Glastonbury's largest arena. The deeper into the centre of the festival she goes, the dustier the track becomes. The dust catches in her throat and gets in her eyes and sticks to the sweat on her bare arms and legs. She glances at the sun as it slips lower in the sky, nearing the tops of the tents around her and wishes for the cool. A media helicopter swirls like a loud, angry insect above.

To Anna's right is the West Holts arena – home to one of Glastonbury's other big stages – with its rows of many-coloured silk flags, similar to the ones on the hillside. The voice of a young male songwriter with a funky band carries clearly out to the main track Anna walks along, leading her towards the heart of Babylon, Glastonbury Festival's 'downtown'.

Anna had arranged to meet Eden and Shari vaguely near the Pyramid Stage, and they had planned to use their mobile phones to find each other. After all the peacefulness of the green hillside, this feels too loud. *I don't want to be here. I don't want to meet Shari and Eden. But I have to*, she thinks, stopping by the side of the main drag. Reluctantly, she switches on her phone. It rings almost immediately. It's Shari.

"Where are you?" Anna asks, her ear pressed right up against her phone, straining to hear over the noises which seem to be assaulting her from all directions. "What burger van?" She swings around, craning her head to see. "There are three burger vans... the one near the... what? Dirty Burger? Sorry I can't hear you... No I don't have GPS on mine... Okay. I'll just walk towards the junction..."

So she walks toward the only junction she can see, deeper into the swelling crowds. A woman walks by carrying a sign reading: 'Everybody's Naughty'. It seems to Anna that even for a festival there are more than averagely high numbers of people in fancy dress here. Within her view there are faeries wearing sexy corsets, a couple dressed in full evening wear with fancy sequinned hats, a man wearing a shower curtain with a nozzle for a hat and a cheerful-looking crew of people dressed in red and white stripes with glasses and hats like *Where's Wally*. Approaching now, and moving at quite a pace through the crowds, are three young men disguised as elderly ladies grooving to the beats of the boomboxes hidden inside the wheeled suitcases they are riding.

Anna notices with distaste, the shirtless man with a beer can who has donned a fake plastic ceremonial headdress, meant to be in the style of the First Nations. Something feels terribly wrong about this. She thinks of the four banners in the Tipi Field, depicting images of four real great aboriginal Chiefs, who each offered strength and wisdom in their own ways.

"Anna! Over here!" Shari is waving wildly a few yards up ahead. Standing next to her is Eden.

Anna waves back, smiling as cheerfully as she can. *Wearing the mask again*, she thinks, but still she does it, because she can't imagine showing them how she really feels.

Eden and Shari are both clad in tiny chest-fitting Glastonbury 2013 T-shirts and short shorts. Around their necks are identical cords, dangling their backstage passes and mini programmes. Eden has a small black bag slung over her shoulder, which appears to be weighed down with some kind of alcohol.

Eden's newest hairstyle is clearly done by Shari, who owns her own beauty salon and often does Eden's hair. It's short, cropped and dark brown with a fringe over her brown eyes, which are heavily accented with mascara, eyeliner and sparkly green eyeshadow. Anna notes that Eden's make-up is even thicker than usual today. In all the five years she has known Eden, Anna has never seen her without layers of it. Now, with a sudden clarity, Anna can see something she hasn't noticed before about Eden – that Eden has no self-confidence, and even more than Anna herself has done, Eden wears the mask, too.

The moment they greet one another, Anna can see that Eden's smile is just as fake as her own. Eden leans in for the quick cursory hug that neither she or Anna really wants, her intensely chemical perfume and deodorant wafting up Anna's nose.

Eden doesn't really like seeing Anna. To Eden, Anna always seems so aloof, but since they are in the same circle of friends, Eden doesn't see a way of avoiding contact with her. And of course there is the issue of Damien. Eden has had intense feelings for Damien since the first time they'd met, and she suspects he feels the same way. But as far as Eden knows, he has never been unfaithful to Anna.

While Anna has always struggled to relate with Eden, with Shari it's different. Today Shari's makeup is much more natural looking than Eden's and she has woven her shiny blond hair into an elegant knot at the back of her head, with just a few light wisps hanging down. As Shari embraces Anna, brushing her with the fresh apple scent of her shampoo, there is real warmth in it.

Though Shari seems like a content and poised person to everyone who knows her, for Shari, beneath the surface there is a gnawing sense that she's missing something vitally important. There is a deeply buried feeling of loneliness that never seems to go away, despite having what she thought she always wanted – her own business, a circle of interesting friends and a boyfriend who her family approves of. Most of the time Shari ignores the gnawing and the echoes of that loneliness, immersing herself in the life she has created, step by step. She is only haunted on those dark, wakeful nights when the questions arise, begging an answer – *What am I missing? What haven't I done?*

Shari often wonders if her friendship with Eden is healthy for her. The dynamic usually involves her trying to take care of Eden, who she perceives as regularly going off the rails. Eden repeatedly struggles with excesses of alcohol, recreational drugs – and sometimes medicinal ones when it gets really bad – and the aftermath of the latest breakup. As challenging as the friendship is, Eden also brings something to Shari, too. It is the sense of wildness and adventure. With Eden, Shari steps out of the safe life she has created for herself, and there is a sense of danger, risk, excitement. For Eden, life is about upping the ante, upping the excitement, upping the stimulation – to feel a rush of something, to feel a sense of aliveness. Eden reaches for this constantly, and she pulls Shari along with her. For Eden, there is always a different man, sometimes two, who always initially seem to find her overt sexuality appealing, but with each of these men, nothing ever settles. Shari knows that deep inside, Eden dreams of a man who might love her for who she is and not just desire her for what she wears or what she might do with her body on a given night. Despite Shari's encouragement, Eden doesn't believe that will ever happen. She doesn't believe she's worthy of that, even though Shari often tries to tell her otherwise.

"So!" Eden chirps, "How's your festival been so far, Anna? Pretty wild here, hey?"

"Yeah. It's been... very interesting..." Anna wonders how much it is safe to share. She wants to keep all these new experiences with Cedar and Moon and the others close to her, to protect them from the judgements she is certain would come, especially from Eden. She also doesn't want any of it to leak back to Damien; she has yet to figure out how much to tell him, or indeed what will be left of their relationship when she returns.

"We've been having such a brilliant time, haven't we Share?" Eden says. "I mean, we've seen Dizzee Rascal, Sinéad O'Conner... some of the Arctic Monkeys..." She looks at Shari, pouting. "I wanted to see Portishead."

"But the Arctic Monkeys were good weren't they?" Shari adds. "And Ben Howard today – I loved that gig. And Laura Mvula before that... she was amazing... and Fatoumata Diawara..."

"And," Eden enthuses, "we get to be backstage in the performers area and it's like a whole other festival back there. I mean, there are stages and bars back there, and nice flush loos, just for the people with backstage passes." Eden casts a noticeable glance at Anna's chest and its absence of a backstage pass. "Hey, how come you don't have a backstage pass, Anna? You had a gig here."

"They don't give backstage passes to everybody who plays. There are a lot of stages here."

"Yeah. Maybe the smaller stages don't do it. It's too bad – it would have been nice to take you back there with us."

"Yeah, too bad." Anna says, with an increasing urge to turn around and run in the opposite direction.

"Hey, we're so sorry we never made your gig, Anna," Shari says, "...either of them." She is genuinely sorry, and also feels a little guilty, because she had known they would not make it back in time when they had chosen to follow Eden's lead and see another artist across the site. Eden had reminded Shari that they could see Anna performing back in Brighton any time. But now, seeing Anna's face, Shari realises that it would have been kinder to support Anna, and genuinely regrets not doing so.

"We really wanted to," Eden explains, "but we were on the other side of the festival and and we only realised at the last minute that we'd never make it back in time. And then yesterday we had to make it to see Sinéad and everything. How'd it all go?"

As Anna struggles with how to respond, she is struck by the realisation that it is going to be much easier to lie to Eden and Shari than to Moon or Cedar. There are many people she has met this weekend whose eyes are so incredibly bright, who seem to have wisdom. Anna had felt compelled to be truthful with those people, not only because she could feel they would see right through her anyway, but because she felt the truthfulness coming from them, and it was the most natural thing to return it.

"The gigs were both fine, thanks," Anna says, nodding. "You know, Glastonbury and all."

"Glastonbury... yeah, it must be amazing to play here." Shari nods back, as if she completely understands what Anna means. "Did you sell loads of CDs?"

This is the moment Anna nearly stumbles. Her mind draws a blank. There is only one thing she can think of to say – not a lie, exactly. "A truly unexpected amount."

"Wow. Amazing Anna. You worked so hard and you did it. You must be really proud." Shari smiles with real warmth, touching Anna on the shoulder.

"Yeah, you must be," Eden echoes, her smile not quite hiding the grimace underneath.

Even though her statements are accepted, Anna feels a sickening twinge inside herself. She tells herself she is only withholding part of the truth, and not actually lying, but it still doesn't feel good. She remembers Johannes' words about truth: *In truth there is liberation. To walk your path of truth is to walk the path of love.*

But if you were being completely honest, you would tell them what happened as a result of both those failed gig attempts... what you found instead... But how can I possibly tell them that? How could they possibly understand? She thinks of being up on the hill with Cedar, and making her intention. Even though being here feels so far from that joyful experience, the truth of it still rings inside her.

My intention is to learn how to make medicine with my music. To feel joy in what I do. To experience that feeling of belonging, of being part of everything with my music. .... It's not just about my career. It's about my life too! I want to feel that in all my life. To feel free. To feel alive in my life. To have courage to walk this path.

"So Anna, I imagine it won't be long till we see you up there on the Pyramid Stage, your name in lights!" Eden grins, as if making a joke.

"Not this year at least," Anna answers her, chuckling to keep it light and to hide the fact that she is starting to feel truly quite awful. The scenes playing in her mind now are all about her failure, and the miserable prospect of telling her supporters back home all about it, not to mention the fact that Shari and Eden will certainly find out the truth in the end.

"Hey! Speaking of the Pyramid Stage..." Eden looks like she is about to burst with excitement. "Can you believe we are about to see the Rolling Stones? I mean, seriously! We get to tell people we saw the Stones at Glastonbury. It's like the musical event of the year, and we get to be there!"

It is a glaring contrast between how Eden treats music and what Cedar described earlier – about how music could make you feel; about how it could heal you. *Is that what you think music is about? Just saying you saw something, like a tourist? What about how it feels? What about what it does to you?* Anna wants to yell this at Eden, but instead she smiles, feeling the stiffness of her mask. "Well, my Dad will certainly be happy when I tell him. He loves the Stones."

"I was thinking..." Eden says, getting a certain look in her eye that Anna has come to dread, "why don't we try and get right up near the front?"

"Ha. Good luck," Shari laughs. "Have you seen how many people are heading in that direction?"

Eden straightens up, making her five foot five frame as tall as she can. "Look, some of us aren't as tall as you, Share. I want to get a good view. Just stick your elbows out and your boobs forward like this... and people will let you through. Trust me, I've done it before. It works."

"All well and good for you, Ede. Not all of us have got boobs like a cattle prod," Shari says good-naturedly. She makes a joke of it, but is not really comfortable with Eden's idea.

Anna laughs at the joke, and Eden sends her a glare before effecting a laugh at herself too. "Oh... Well, at times like this they come in handy, don't they? I'll lead the train then."

So Eden sets off like the prow of a ship and Anna and Shari follow. Shari does her best to imitate Eden, but Anna simply shields herself protectively with her arms from the thickening mass of people they are plowing through. They aren't even in sight of the Pyramid Stage and yet the crowds are already like sticky porridge; tens of thousands of people are all trying to get to the same place at the same time and moving at a snail's pace. Anna's feeling of dread grows in intensity with each step further into the crowd, as she dutifully pushes her way after Eden and Shari. *What are you doing Anna? Why are you doing this to yourself?*

In her mind, she hears Johannes' words again, telling her how she always does the things she thinks others want her to do – like Damien, like her father, like Shari and Eden – but still she follows.

Finally, after all the pushing, they are within sight of the giant silver Pyramid Stage. Eden pauses for a moment, getting her bearings on the best way to proceed. Anna catches her breath and gazes at Glastonbury's elegant mainstage for a moment, the tip of its point glinting gold in the setting sun. It reminds her of the Great Pyramid of Giza, only smaller. They are still a fair distance away from it though, and from what Anna can see, the fields in front of the stage are a solid mass of crushed people all trying to be as close as they can to these rock legends, who won't even be on stage for nearly an hour.

"Come on. Let's be a little more proactive here," Eden says. "I want to get closer than this. Take my hand Share."

Without waiting for a reply, Eden grabs Shari's hand and in turn, Shari reaches for Anna's. Anna feels the scratch of Shari's long, manicured nails digging into her palm as she lets herself be dragged like a puppet, rubbing and bumping against sweaty bodies until somehow Eden does manage to get them out of the bottleneck of the trackway and into the main arena, where the crowds have thinned just enough for them to push their way even further in. Anna's body is starting to give her real physical messages now of just how not right this is for her. She wonders when Eden will be satisfied. *How far will she drag us? How close is close enough?*

"Look at that!" Shari points. "Why would anyone do that to themselves? In this heat?"

Anna laughs to see the man dressed as a giant pile of excrement. He wears a bulbous brown suit and a hat which comes to a neat little point like a brown soft serve ice cream cone. He looks pleased about it too, smiling cheerily as he has his photo taken. This man, Felix, is actually a volunteer with WaterAid, one of the three charities Glastonbury supports. He is happy to walk around the crowds in the sweltering heat dressed like shit, because with all the attention it gets him, he can speak to people about the work WaterAid does. He is seeking to educate people about WaterAid's mission – to work for a world where every person on the planet has clean water to drink and a safe place to go to the toilet. Dressing up as a giant poo helps make the point.

Felix looks up at Anna momentarily as she passes by and smiles at her with bright eyes. It stops her in her tracks. *He knows what he's doing*, she realises. *This man is trying to help people.* Anna returns the smile briefly before Shari and Eden draw her deeper into the crowd.

The man dressed like excrement is not the only one smiling. There seem to be a lot of happy people around, and a sense of buoyant expectancy. For some people here, this is the musical event of their lives – *The Rolling Stones on the Pyramid Stage at Glastonbury Festival.*

After much dodging, the three women reach the metal barriers which bar the general public from getting any closer to the stage and impinging on the VIP area. Here, Eden is forced to stop. The rectangular LED screens to either side of the stage loom large, flashing with the words: UP NEXT: THE ROLLING STONES. From here the microphones on stage are clearly visible, as well as the catwalk which stretches right out into the VIP area. Technicians work on the stage, preparing leads and guitars and checking the drum kit.

At the crest of the pyramid, just over the stage, a pair of giant multi-coloured feathered wings are poised as if to take flight. In between the wings, Anna can just make out the yellow beak and red head of the bird, in its resting pose. She has the thought that this must be a Firebird – a Phoenix – the bird that rises again from the ashes. She wonders what it is meant to do.

A sea of colourful flags wave up above the heads of the crowd, billowing in the rising breeze. There is a blue flag with a peace symbol. Another is a rainbow with the word 'PEACE'. There are various representations of different national flags: England, Spain, France, Germany. One flag reads: 'God hates flags'; one reads: 'We Love You', and another one shows a picture of the Earth.

"We should be able to see their faces from here," Eden says proudly, leaning against the metal barrier. She grins at the security man in the hi-vis jacket who stands in the vehicle-sized space between them and the VIP area on the other side.

"I want to be able to video them on my phone," she says, "to show people that I was actually here."

Anna stares at her. *This is why you made us force our way through so many people, getting bruised and brushed by so much sweat and dust? To get close enough to film your stupid video?* A fury rises inside Anna, and she really does want to scream at Eden, but she sucks it in. The resulting fatigue creates an overwhelming desire to sit down and rest. She looks down to see that the ground beneath her feet – which had once been fresh green grass – is now trampled to dust and strewn with layers apon layers of food wrappers, beer cans and something else really sticky and unpleasant that Anna can't identify and looks a little too much like vomit. It is a patch of ground Anna could never bear sitting on. She thinks again of the beautiful grass on that hill, and how blessedly sweet it had been to sit there with Cedar – how fresh the air had been; how invigorating it had felt to walk barefoot. And now, feeling light-headed an slightly nauseous she faces the prospect of standing here for hours with no hope of sitting down or taking off her shoes. On every side, the crowds press in around them.

Eden reaches into her bag and pulls out a six-pack of cider. "Well, there's nothing else to do... we could always get tipsy. It will pass the time!" Eden grins at them both. "Anna?" She holds a can out towards her.

Anna isn't a huge fan of cider in general, and getting drunk with Eden and Shari here on this patch of ground is about the last thing she wants to do right now, but her throat is parched and in her distraction with not wanting to be dragged through the crowd, she had forgotten to buy a bottle of water. Telling herself it would be good at least to hold onto something cool and wet her mouth, Anna accepts the can. It's not cool at all. It's warm.

Again, it seems there are two paths stretching out before Anna. One path is clear and bright and pulls at her, calling her away from this place to stand where the grass is green and she can feel the Earth below her feet. The other path would have her continue to stand here on these empty burger wrappers, pretending everything is fine, feeling ill and drinking Eden's cider. Anna pulls off the tab on her can. The drink fizzes, releasing an unpleasant alcoholic smell as she lifts it toward her lips.

"What's that?" Eden asks, noticing for the first time Anna's yellow wristband.

Anna stops, feeling exposed, and curses herself for not being more careful to keep the wristband hidden.

"What does that mean? Find yourself? What are you... lost?" Eden laughs at her own joke.

Find Yourself.

Find myself – my Wild Heart-Self. The wildfire within Anna bursts forth again and this time it is uncontainable as it blazes through her, flooding her body with energy. The two paths before Anna converge into one brightly shining way as she meets Eden's gaze with an expression that stops Eden in her tracks.

"No. I'm not lost. I know just where I'm meant to be. In fact, I have to go there. Right now."

She hands the undrunk cider can back to Eden, whose mouth is hanging open.

"But you'll miss the Stones," Shari says, and Anna catches a look in Shari's eye which tells her that Shari really doesn't want her to go, because Shari actually doesn't want to be here either, standing in the middle of these crowds with Eden.

"I'll hear the Stones wherever I am. I just can't stand here anymore. I need to sit down on some grass and I need to get some water." And this is the truth. As she breathes and listens to her body, Anna can feel that she is on the edge of heat stroke. "I need to go right now. I'll see you later."

"Okay, see you later," Shari echoes.

Eden manages a half-hearted wave, before shrugging and taking a swig of the can in her hand.

Free now, Anna's body propels her through the crowds. Somehow her body seems to know which way to move, finding the gaps between people and moving forward. She doesn't really know where she's going, but it feels invigorating. *I did it!* she thinks, amazed. *This is what it feels like to drive your own life!*

There is no doubt now that she will never be able to fit back into the life she had lived before she came here. There is a little cookie-cutter shape back at home in her life with Damien waiting for her to step back into it. *But I won't,* she knows. Nothing will ever be the same again. The fire is burning now inside her, and there is no putting it out. It's burning the paper bag to ashes.

Where am I? Anna wonders, not recognising any of the scenery around her and feeling increasingly like she might faint right here. There seems to be no end to the crowds, which are still surrounding her. *How am I going to get out of this?*

Just keep going. One step at a time, something inside Anna seems to say. An image comes of the wild woman she had seen in her imagining – her Wild Heart-Self. It is as if this woman is a guide within her, urging her on. *You can do it. Keep breathing, one breath at a time.*

The thought comes to Anna that if she focuses on how big the crowd is, it feels insurmountable, but if she focuses just on this step – *one step at a time* – she can do it. With each step she is that little bit closer to where she is going, and eventually she will get there. *But where am I going? And where am I?* None of this looks familiar. She moves past rows of green pit latrines, through some trees, past an upended car and through more and more people, all of whom seem to be heading in the opposite direction to her.

Blessedly, after an untold number of steps, she is through the worst of the crowds and out onto a dusty trackway that is only averagely full of people, with enough space to walk around without bumping into anyone. Anna stands still for a moment, trying to get her bearings. All she knows is that she's come out of the arena a very different way than she'd gone in. To one side of her is a sea of tents and on the other, food vendors are advertising their wares in neon lights. And as far as the eye can see, there are people and more people. The dizziness has returned and Anna remembers her need to find water.

Where am I? She asks herself again, this time with a flutter of panic. A memory comes of something Cedar had said. *You can ask for guidance.*

Okay... so where do I go from here?

Cedar's words echo in her mind: *You just have to let go of trying. You've asked, now just let your mind relax. Maybe let your eyes rest softly on the horizon or something else that takes your fancy. Remember your breathing. Focusing on the breath always helps me to still my mind.*

She can't see the horizon from here, but this is a tangible beginning. *I have to be able to see the horizon. Find higher ground.*

Not far away there is a gentle sloping rise in the hill, leading to a verge beside the trackway. That route seems to lead away from the crowds as well, so Anna takes it, dodging her way past people and food stalls up to the little patch of raised ground. From here, she lifts her eyes across the site, and in the fading light she can just make out the tops of the tipis and the coloured flags on the opposite hill, the beautiful place she had sat with Cedar. *So far away.*

One step at a time, the thought comes again, as if this wild woman inside her is still speaking – a constant, warm presence within her. *Choose a closer landmark to aim for*. Anna scans the area and having oriented herself on the site, sees something closer that she does recognise – the light and dark blue stripes of the Circus Big Top.

The dizziness reaches a new level and Anna's head is pounding, but she can see the Circus Field is not far. *I can make it there*. From there she knows her way, and can avoid the main trackways, which are still jammed with thousands of people, all still trying to get over to the Pyramid stage to see the Rolling Stones.

On the way, she catches sight of a vendor selling water and stops to buy a one litre bottle, gulping almost all of it one go. *Pace yourself Anna*, she tells herself. She packs the nearly empty bottle in her bag and carries on.

Now she is in the Circus Field, and from here, Anna knows the way, past the prayer wheels, over Bella's Bridge, past the Helter Skelter and The Avalon Inn, past Block 9 and The Unfairground until she finally joins the main trackway, and from there, it is not very far to the Green Fields.

> *"And we have always been walking through this land*
> *And we have always worn its vision like a skin*
> *The track is strongly felt, walking as before*
> *And our footsteps fit, walking as before*
> *Move to the very edge where the old world ends*
> *And something else begins, something else begins"*

from the song, 'Walking as Before', by Carolyn Hillyer [1]

She has found it – a place to rest where the grass is still green. Anna is standing before an arched tunnel made of willow, with the words 'The Healing Field' painted in bright letters on a banner above it. A willow sunflower hangs inside the tunnel and among the nooks and crannies of the tunnel are flowers and little elf-like creatures made from felt and wood. Stepping through this new entrance into the Healing Field, she finds herself in front of a previously unexplored garden – *Earth*. It

---

1. *from 'Songs of the Forgotten People'*

is blessedly calm here. The mass exodus down to the Pyramid Stage has left these upper fields much quieter than usual.

The Earth garden, like the Water garden, is woven of swirling willow withies. Unlike the water garden though, it is not a complete circle, but a semi-circle, opening to face a large, colourful patchwork bender several yards away at the edge of the green space – a venue of some kind, empty and finished for the day. Similarly to the Water area, the perimeter of this green space is bordered by healers of all kinds; they too appear to be closed for the night.

Anna enters the garden through an intricately woven willow archway, decorated with painted leaves in in earthy shades of reds and browns and purples, veined with sparkling gold. To either side of the entrance and dotted all around the circumference of the garden wall are little tiny people, made of twigs, moss and woodshavings and other natural, found objects – faeries and nature spirits. To one side of the garden, there are an abundance of plants, all edible: strawberries, kale, chard, fennel, borage, sage, runner beans, nasturtiums, and dozens of other plants Anna doesn't recognise.

On the other side of the garden are batik parasols made to look like trees, in various shades of light and dark green with small leaves of the same fabric sewn around the edges. They flutter about gently in the slight breeze. Below the parasols are handmade wooden benches, fanning out in sets of three beneath each of the three parasols. Rather than sit on the benches, Anna collapses to the ground, dizzy and shaking. This definitely feels like heat stroke. With her back flat on the grass, she kicks off her sandals and lets the soles of her feet rest directly on the grass.

Lazily, she watches the deepening sky for a while, dotted with faded pink-grey clouds, the last of the sunset. The air feels cooler now, and Anna welcomes the coolness, her skin still sticky with sweat. She closes her eyes, feeling the steady ground beneath her, the warmth of the day still held in it, supporting her. As her body is touching the Earth, it seems to Anna that there is a sense of a subtle electric current, some kind of energy flowing up into her, nourishing her.

Moon is standing on the grass outside her tipi. After her meeting with Anna earlier, she'd felt wonderful. As often happens after giving healing to someone – as she had done for Anna – Moon herself received some of that energy. She had felt happy and strong enough to go and check in with Cedar before their gig tomorrow.

All had been well until he had mentioned his time with Anna on the hill. Cedar's eyes had lit up as he spoke about her, and Moon had seen the truth of his feelings. She had tried to make light of it, not wanting to lose her wellbeing, but it was already slipping away from her as her mind left the present and her breath left her belly. Cedar had sensed Moon's feelings and out of care, had questioned her. She hadn't wanted to answer him, but because of her commitment to honesty, she had said the few words she could – *It's still too raw* – and then she had left.

On the journey from Cedar's tipi to her own, Moon had felt returning confusion and pain clenching beneath her ribs. *I thought I was free of this.* Last night she had cried with Maddy. She had released so much, and yet, so much of it is still here with her. *Perhaps it will take a little more time.*

As she has become accustomed to doing when these kinds of feelings flood her body, Moon brings her attention to her feet, to walking in the cool grass. Mother Earth is always here. Whenever Moon feels alone, she reminds herself of that. So her bare feet have brought her back here, to her own tipi, to this patch of grass, to feeling this connection to ground, to Earth, to Gaia, to Pachamama. She knows Gaia is a conscious, sentient being, who gives with unconditional love, offering her body to life, supporting the growth and evolution of humanity. Gaia is a mother in the truest sense of the word – always here, always nourishing.

Moon breathes into her belly, and on the outbreath breathes her roots down into the ground, through the layers of soil and rock. With each outbreath she is seeing them go deeper and deeper, until she reaches that deep, all pervading calm.

Thank you Pachamama, she says silently. Now, on the inbreath, she opens herself to receive that energy, feeling it rising up like a golden sap, up through the soles of her feet, up her legs into her body. A feeling of wellbeing rises with the energy, and as it does it catches the blocked pain and nudges it free. The waves of grief come and move through as the tears flow.

Maddy had helped her to do this last night, too, and so Moon finds it easier to do it again now – to witness the feelings, to be conscious with them, and really feel them, so they will flow through and not remain stuck. All the while she is breathing and the waves are moving through her and she is held by that deep Mother energy of the ground beneath her. Eventually, the waves ebb into stillness and here inside her there is a calm pool, and now an inner smile, rising up with a bubbling of joy – a feeling that here, all is well.

"*Thank you,*" she whispers.

It is the sound of a hundred thousand voices screaming that wakes Anna. The Stones have just taken the stage. A wailing electric guitar sails through the air, and voices are singing. The song is *Gimme Shelter*.

That's what I need, Anna thinks. *Shelter. It's* much colder now. The colours from the sky have faded and the clouds are reflecting the flashing searchlights from the Pyramid Stage down in Babylon. She casts her eyes around the Earth Garden. *What now?*

Though she feels slightly stiff, the heat stroke appears to be gone. Anna swigs the last of her water. *Save the bottle*, the thought comes to her. *You might want to refill it later.*

She stretches and can feel the old pain between her shoulder blades. Some months ago an enthusiastic weight-lifter had given her an unintentional knock in the back while she was working out at the gym. It had hurt at the time, but she'd been so busy making her CD that she hadn't had it looked at, and it had faded into the background of low-grade general aches and pains. It seems to be more noticeable now, though, as if her body is somehow speaking more clearly after the weekend's experiences. *Go get a healing. Well, I am in the healing area. Why not?*

But there's no point, she tells herself. *Nobody's open.* But something is telling her to look again. *Look, there!* Anna glances across the grass. There is one single lantern lit. A woman, just visible in the darkening light in her white yoga trousers and jumper is sitting at the entrance to her awning, drinking a cup of tea.

Ali has just finished eating a quiet meal and has been enjoying the stillness here after her busy day. Earlier, in the heat, thousands of people had come up here to the Healing Fields to lie on the grass, as grass had become increasingly scarce in Babylon and elsewhere on site. Many of those people had consequently come for healings, so most of the healers had been booked solidly all day.

Ali has completed more than her quota of shiatsu sessions for the day and doesn't intend to do any more. She is just at this moment considering her next move. She can hear the Stones down in Babylon and is tempted to go, but her intuition tells her it would not be the best thing for her energy. Besides, there is something else she is meant to do. She's getting that sense more strongly now, but she's not quite sure what it is yet. So she's just sitting here, listening.

This is when Ali sees the young woman in the garden who is lifting herself to a seated posture in the garden, stretching her arms up and uttering a small noise of discomfort. *Ah*, thinks Ali. *It has something to do with her, doesn't it?* Ali has the sense that she could help this person somehow. The girl is looking at her now. Ali lifts her hand and offers a wave.

Who is she? Anna wonders. Without really thinking too much about it, Anna rises and moves over towards the woman in white, if only to ask if she knows anyone who could help her. As Anna approaches, the woman rises and smiles, as if expecting her.

"Hello," Ali says kindly, with bright eyes. "Are you looking for a shiatsu?"

"I... I don't know. I guess it's probably too late for anyone here to do any healings." Anna glances around at the various tents closed up all around her.

"I could give you a session," Ali hears herself say. *Can I? I guess I do have one more in me after all.*

There is kindness emanating from this woman. To Anna she seems quite motherly; there is something soft and gentle about her. Gentleness is Ali's natural state, but she also has a deep core of strength in her, like a mother bear. It's not always been this way for Ali, but she's cultivated this strength, partly through becoming a mother herself, and partly through working with the physical and non-physical bodies of herself and others.

"What is a shiatsu?" Anna asks.

"It's physical manipulation and massage, and it also works with the body's energy pathways," Ali explains. "It helps to realign you, and it's really good for sore backs."

"Oh!" Anna breathes, amazed at her luck to have found such a person. "I actually have a really sore back right now. Do you think you could help me with that?"

"I'll do my best."

Following Ali inside her awning, Anna feels vaguely similar to the way she had felt when she had agreed to go inside Johannes' yurt.

"I'm Ali," Ali offers Anna her hand.

"Anna." Again, this hand feels different than others she has felt this weekend; it's soft, but also strong.

"Pleased to meet you Anna," Ali says, lifting the lantern back inside so that it casts its warm glow on the interior. There is a single futon on the ground, with a ring-shaped pillow at one end.

"Is there anything I can specifically help you with, Anna?" Ali asks.

"I have this pain in between my shoulder blades where someone knocked me at the gym a few months ago. And I'm feeling pretty stiff in a lot of places."

"Okay." Ali nods. "Could you just stand where you are, as naturally as you can, and I'll just have a look at you?"

Ali steps in front of Anna, casting her eyes and senses around Anna's physical body and her more subtle bodies. Anna feels mildly self-conscious as Ali's hands explore the points on her back, checking her spine and muscles, gauging her posture. It's obvious to Ali that Anna's energy is not flowing properly. For one, her posture is completely out of alignment, and the energy can only move freely up the spine and through the body when the spine is straight. Anna's neck juts out slightly and her shoulders slump forwards. *She is not standing in her power. If I could only help her to stand straight*, Ali thinks. *She would feel so much better.*

Ali can see with her mind's eye where the blocks are. As Anna had said, there is one big one right between the shoulder blades. It looks deep, but it also looks long term. It's about more than just this recent injury. She unrolls a fresh sheet of paper across the futon and pillow, poking a hole in the paper over the ring so that Anna will be able to breathe through it. "Now, let's have you lie face down on the futon, and I'll see what I can do to help with this."

At this moment, Anna's phone rings. She stares at her satchel, sitting by the entrance to the awning.

"Do you need to get that?" Ali asks.

"No," Anna says, letting it ring. She knows it's a missed call from Damien and feels a pang of guilt. She thinks again of the look in Cedar's eyes and how it had made her feel, the sense of being at home with someone. Confusion swells in her again.

She lowers herself onto the futon and places her face into the ring. It's surprisingly comfortable. Ali covers her with a blanket and Anna sighs with relief. She would pay this lady just to fall asleep here for a while. When she feels Ali's hands begin to do their work, Anna knows that she is paying for much more than that.

Ali is kneeling next to Anna, rocking along her back with the ball and flat of her hand, wiggling, massaging, applying pressure to points along the spine. It feels good, really good, but some of the points are so tender. Anna sucks in a breath.

"Too much?" Ali asks.

"It's sore there. Ooh! And there."

"Mmm. I'm already working pretty gently, but I'll try and go a bit softer if you like. Although, if you can handle it, I can get at these knots more effectively this way."

"I'll try and handle it," Anna says, her voice slightly muffled by the pillow ring.

As Ali works, the painful points become less painful, and Anna feels herself relax into it. Ali's hand is at the base of Anna's spine now, while the other one rocks its way up along the spine. With a release of tension, tingles move through Anna's body. Her body lets go of a breath.

"Good," Ali, says, still kneading. "That released off nicely." Now she's working on the other side.

This is the second time today Anna has been touched by hands for the purpose of healing. So much has happened for her since sitting with Moon this morning. It has been a whirlwind of experiences. *Did that all happen today? Breathing with Moon, hearing Arthur speak, sitting on the hill with Cedar, meeting Shari and Eden...* Her mind runs through all that's happened since she woke this morning and feels a kind of awe about it. She hasn't remotely had time to process it all.

Meanwhile, Ali is pulling and stretching and massaging Anna's back, sending her into a half-sleep, a kind of peaceful daydream with an unusual background sound-track: *Honky Tonk Woman*. When the wind is blowing this way, the sound waves carry so that it's almost as clear as if it were in a nearby field. Just over the hedge on the Toad Hall Stage a folk band is playing some lively tunes and occasionally Anna can make out some of Public Enemy from down on the West Holts Stage. There is also the nearly constant screaming – somewhere on site there is almost always the sound of massive crowds of people screaming and cheering for some-thing or someone, like the sound of a raucous never-ending football game.

Ali is now working on some of Anna's meridian points, and she's found one that's particularly in need of attention. These are the ones that are most tender to the touch. "Sorry. It's so tender there, Anna. I'm hardly putting any pressure on you at all. Can you bear it?"

"I think so."

At first it hurts, but as Ali works on that spot, just between her shoulder blades, slowly something releases. The area starts to feel warm and tingles move through Anna's body again.

Ali takes a breath. "That's better. Energy is starting to flow there now. It feels to me that you have several layers of knots here, Anna, and most of those began quite a long time before the knock you describe. I'll do my best with them, but I'd sug-gest you have a couple of follow up shiatsu sessions after the festival to get at the deeper layers. I can't get them all in one go. It would be too much for your body."

Anna would reply, but she finds she has lost the power of speech, and is drooling through the hole in the pillow where her face sits. She hasn't been this relaxed in a long time.

"I'm not just working with your physical body, Anna. I'm also working with your meridians," Ali says. "There are a number of them which have been blocked and were flowing the wrong way."

"My what?" Anna manages to mumble. She has vaguely heard that term before, maybe in the context of a window in a Chinese medicine shop in Brighton.

"Meridians are your body's energy pathways. You've probably heard of acupres-sure or acupuncture, right? Well the acupressure points are points at the ends of the meridians. If you put pressure on those points it can help rebalance your energy. I've managed to get most of them flowing more smoothly. There's still some work to do, but you'll feel a lot better after this."

Ali presses into a point on Anna's foot.

"Ow!"

"Sorry, Anna. I'm hardly pressing here either. The point is tender because it needs work too. I'll try and be as gentle as I can." In a few moments, the pain passes, and with it, Anna feels something relax inside her again, with another wave of tingles and a release of breath. Her whole body begins to soften. She drifts off again into a half sleep, wanting to stay on this table for hours, feeling this cared for, feeling this loved.

All too soon, Anna becomes aware that Ali has stepped away from the table. It feels strangely like Ali's hands are still on her body, still working the 'points' as she called them.

"Take your time, Anna," Ali says softly. "There's no rush."

But I don't want to move, she thinks. *I wish I could just stay here and sleep.*

"Try wiggling your toes and fingers, and then rolling over onto your right side," Ali suggests.

Some minutes pass before Anna feels able to move her toes. She wiggles them, feeling them somehow more an integral part of her body than before, and her fingers too. Eventually she urges her eyelids to open and rolls over onto her side, gazing lazily through a gap in the awning to the dark world outside.

I don't want to go back out there.

Finally, with effort, Anna hoists herself to sitting. Her head reels.

"Whoa."

"Go slowly, Anna. You might feel light-headed for a bit. I've released a lot of tension."

Anna waits for a moment for the dizziness to pass. It doesn't.

"Here. Have some water. That will help."

Anna accepts the cup and gulps it down.

"Another?"

Anna nods. Ali refills her cup.

"Thank you." The dizziness is passing a little now.

"You're welcome," Ali says with a smile. "You needed it. When you have a lot of energetic work done, your body needs extra water to help metabolise all the changes. I would suggest drinking more water for the rest of the evening. Also, take it easy tonight. I would suggest for instance, that you don't do any wild dancing, just for tonight. Give your body a chance to adjust."

Anna nods. "I don't plan on doing much else, tonight, to be honest, except sleep."

"A good plan," Ali agrees.

As Anna rises from the futon and stretches out her arms, she notices with pleasure that the pain between her shoulder blades is almost completely gone.

"Wow. I feel so much better. Thank you."

"You're welcome." Ali smiles. She can see the change in Anna; so much is flowing that wasn't before. But not everything – not yet.

"Before you go, Anna, can I show you something quickly?"

Anna nods.

"It's your posture. The energy is not moving as well as it could because you're sort of hunched forwards. Your spine is not straight. Can I show you what it feels like to be straight?"

"Okay."

With the changes that have gone on in Anna's body during the session, Ali knows she will be receptive to this now in a way she wouldn't have been before. Ali places one hand on the top of Anna's back and the other on her belly, shifting her until she feels the moment when the energy aligns, where her neck becomes straight.

Anna's eyes widen as she feels something in her spine shift into place, and with it, an energy moving through her body.

"There. Feel that?" Ali asks.

Yes! It feels really good. But she knows she can't hold this position on her own.

"You feel kind of... joined up, don't you? Like suddenly there's something connected that wasn't before?"

"Yeah. That feels different."

"Imagine it like there's a silver thread running up through your body, up through the crown on your head, lifting you up."

Anna imagines this in her mind and feels her body straighten even more.

"So, that's your body in proper alignment. That's something else you can look into, Anna. There are other things that would really help you, like Alexander technique, or even something like Kundalini Yoga or qigong." Ali lets her hands go.

"Oh, I think I lost it again." Anna feels her body return to its habitual stance.

"Yes. You let yourself go as soon as I took my hands away. It's like that. Your muscles are used to holding you the other way. You have to retrain them – and you can."

Like breathing, Anna thinks. *Like thinking. Like so many things.* She feels overwhelmed suddenly at just how many things she seems to need to practice. This whole time she's been forgetting to breathe properly too. "I've got so many things I've got to learn... to practice. I don't know if I can manage anything else. I can't even do the other things I'm trying to do yet."

"That's fine, Anna," Ali says, encouraging. "I felt guided to share this with you, but everything comes in its own time. You're right that you can't focus on too many things at once. If you want to truly embed something and make a change, you need to give it time and focus. They say that it takes three weeks for the brain to rewire itself to change a habit. It can also take weeks for muscles to change their habitual patterns. Maybe it was just about putting it in there in your awareness so that one day you'll meet the right teacher, and maybe something will click for you about this. You just have to take it one step at a time."

"I'll try." The next step at least is clear. "Do you happen to know where the nearest nice loos are from here?"

Ali smiles. "Well there are a surprising number of quite nice loos, for a festival. The closest are probably the WaterAid African Pit Latrines. You'll find them a pleasant surprise."

Ali directs Anna to their location, just up in the next field, King's Meadow.

"Thank you for the session," Anna says, handing Ali a £20 note as a donation. She's pleased to actually be able to pay somebody this time. It doesn't seem much for what Ali's done for her, but it's what she can manage.

"Thank you," Ali says, accepting the money with gratitude. For Ali, money is a form of energy, and is also made of love. She receives it as such.

"I haven't felt this good... at least my body hasn't for... well, since I don't know when."

"Well, you're more in your body now," Ali says. "and that will always feel better."

Walking away from the awning, Anna can feel her body in a new way. It feels more supple, more real. She's more aware of her bare feet on the grass, the sway of her hips as she walks, all the parts of it moving together in space.

"We're nurtured by the water
Guided by the sun
Freedom comes from where we are
And what we belong
From the Earth we come and will return
like the seeds of evergreen"

Ali's directions lead Anna out of the Earth area and through *Fire*. There is a circular garden made of willow withies here in Fire too, decorated with fiery-coloured fabrics. In the centre of the garden is a large fire pit, casting light on the faces of the people gathering around it, who are all singing a heart-felt rendition of the Beatles anthem, *Love is All you Need*. They are lead by an energetic band – known by some as The Lost Padres – who even though the sun has gone down are still wearing their daytime costumes – the fiery guitarist in a faded yellow suit jacket and dark grey newsboy cap, the quicksilver fiddler in a fantastic Hawaiian shirt and straw hat, the bright smiling accordion player with a black fedora and an equally fantastic Hawaiian shirt, and the able double bassist keeping a foot-stepping rhythm from under his own straw hat. Many of those around this fire circle have been here with the band since well before the sun went down, and will be staying here for some hours yet.

Having sung the Beatles to the full, the Padres kick off with another song which Anna recognises. Its clear the others in this circle know this song well too, as they all jump in, singing along with gusto to the chorus of *Your Love Keeps Lifting Me...* and somehow managing to all be in tune, as if they have practiced together for years – which in fact, some of them have. Many of those around this circle have been singing these songs with the Padres in these fields for more than twenty years now. In these healing fields and beyond the Padres are much loved for their infectious versions of cover songs that bring joy wherever they go and their tireless ability to perpetuate that joy for hours. They are as much an integral part of the multi-coloured patchwork fabric of this festival as anyone could be, and in all their years of singing in these fields, they have made them a brighter place. And now the circle of people are all clapping as they sing out the Padres' own addition to the song, "*Your love is a healing thing... your love is a healing thing... your love is a healing thing... your love is a healing thing...*"

Anna is tempted to stay and be immersed in this jubilance for a little while longer, but the litre of water she drank earlier needs urgent addressing. Not far along, at the junction where the Fire quadrant meets the main dirt and gravel track, there is a giant heart made of swirls of woven willow, nearly as tall as Anna, and just beside it is an upright piano, surrounded by a crowd of people all singing *American Pie*. Above the piano, giant paper lanterns glow.

Stepping onto the main track, Anna notices a number of attractive cafes, of a different calibre to most of those down in Babylon. There is an *Indian Thali Cafe*,

The Buddhafield Cafe, which sells wholesome vegetarian curries, burgers and salads, and the *Chai Shoppe*, which specialises in falafels and chai.

Anna can feel her body's hunger too, and reminds herself to come back and eat something. Just before her is the gate into the *King's Meadow*, and guarding the gate – just as Ali said there would be – are two serious harvest goddesses, underlit by lanterns to either side, which make them look even more severe. She stops to take in the sixteen foot tall goddesses with a kind of awe. They are made of wood planks and straw, with greenery winding up around their bodies, woven with seed heads and flowers. Atop their heads they hold platters of the abundant harvest. To Anna it seems as if their faces are staring stoically down upon her, as if in judgement, as if they are saying, *So what's your harvest? So what have you grown this year?*

What have I grown? She can't help laughing at the image in her mind of a field, with a thousand stalks in it, each one growing a shining CD, with all her carefully polished tracks on them. She shakes her head. *Well, that crop failed.* She thinks of that first gig that brought her here to Glastonbury, and all that has lead from it. *Perhaps one crop has to fail,* she realises, *before you realise that you wanted to grow something else.* She thinks again of her intention up on the hill with Cedar. *What will I grow now?*

Drawing closer to the two goddesses, Anna gazes up at them with a sort of reverence. She is reminded of a scene from a film she loved as a child – *The Neverending Story* – where the hero, a warrior-child by the name of Atreyu, must pass through a gate guarded by two giant, golden sphinxes, eyes closed in rest. Only one who knows their own true worth may pass through the gate unharmed, and should the sphinxes see into a person's heart and find someone who believes they are unworthy, the closed eyes would open, releasing lasers of destruction and a fiery death. As she moves to pass through the gate, Anna wonders at the truth of her own worth. Moon's words echo in her mind: *You are made of Love... You are a Goddess!*

Anna laughs at herself for feeling that little tremor of childish fear as she passes between the two regal goddesses, as if she really were about to be judged and destroyed, as if these structures of wood and straw and seeds could actually see into her and pass judgement.

Having made it through the Goddess gate unscathed, she joins the queue at the WaterAid toilets. On her way in, she is handed a small bucket of water by one of the attendants.

What do I do with this? Then she sees. As people leave their respective cubicles, they empty the water onto the cement floor of the latrine, washing it clean. Anna steps into a free cubicle, closes the wooden door, and notices two things simultaneously: one, that it really is quite clean and that surprisingly, it doesn't smell; and two, that there is no toilet, only an elongated hole in the cement – shaped for purpose, with two slightly raised platforms on either side for her feet. There is clearly only one thing to do.

As Anna squats, she's reminded of those rare times walking in nature – mostly as a child or teenager – when she would relieve herself by the shelter of some tree, and now natural the position feels. Standing up, she swishes her bucketful of water over the floor and exits the stall, feeling much better. After washing her hands with one of the bars of natural soap left at the taps, she drops a donation into the bucket held by a kind-looking young man in a WaterAid T-shirt who offers her a smile of thanks.

She then braves the Goddess gate again, in search of her body's next need – a hearty meal. The lights in Babylon still flash down below, and the Rolling Stones are still going strong, along with the thumping and booming of dozens more other smaller stages. The screaming has escalated now, so that it now sounds to Anna like there are about ten football games going down below her in that city of lights, along with whistles, keyboards, electronic dance music and anything else one could image that might make a sound. She can feel it coming up through the ground, vibrating in the cells of her body.

The wind is whipping up too, as it does in the evenings when the mist rises up in the valley, creating currents of cool air. The multi-coloured flags along the track flap against their poles, while the larger flags above the cafes billow in waves.

Which one? Anna wonders. Immediately, her eyes are drawn to the flag with a Buddha's face on it, flying atop the Buddhafield Cafe. The blackboard out front shows a picture of a peaceful meditating figure and surrounding it are examples of their wholesome fare with a drawing of a pink heart, as if to say *we make our food with love too.*

Anna has had minimal experience with Buddhism, preferring until now to steer clear of anything that seemed remotely religious, as a result of many Sundays spent on hard church pews during her childhood. She got the idea then that religion of any kind was dogmatic and judgemental. As far as Anna had been concerned Buddhism had fallen under that category. But now, standing here, witnessing the scene of openness and warmth before her, something tells her this is different and that maybe some of her ideas have been wrong. She is drawn in by the inviting atmosphere, with its colourful streams of fabric decorating the ceiling of the white tent, the cosy rugs and bamboo mats on the floor and all the brightly painted low round, wooden tables, each surrounded by coloured cushions for sitting on. She moves quickly to the front of the queue and is greeted by a pixieish young woman with dark hair coiled up in a bun on top of her head.

Becky is attempting to put into practice the loving compassion and mindfulness that is part of Buddhist practice. All those who work here at Buddhafield have this intention. At regular intervals a bell is rung – or in this case, a singing bowl is struck – so that the note rings out clear and strong, as a reminder to be present and mindful, and to be loving with whatever you are doing and whoever you are with. Becky sees Anna and gives her a smile. For Becky, Anna is the only person here, because she's the one that's here now.

"What would you like?" Becky asks.

At that moment a fellow co-worker hands a colourful plate laden with a rainbow assortment of cooked and raw vegetables over the counter to the person ahead of Anna.

"I'll have some of that, whatever it is," Anna says.

"Which salads would you like?"

Anna selects a lovely purple one made of grated carrot and beetroot and a green salad. "Thank you." She accepts the plate, which is made of real ceramic, and collects some metal cutlery on her way to where the tables are. She marvels that they actually have real cutlery and plates here, but realises that it fits with the ethos of the place. They don't want to add anything to the landfill. *They must have dedicated washer-uppers here*, she observes.

Becky herself is now trading places with one of her fellow workers at the washing up stand. As she puts on the gloves and scrubs the first plates she is treating this too as a meditation in action. The intention here is to treat every action in this way.

Anna spots a spare table and settles herself on one of the cushions around it. She notices the music on the sound system. Somehow even though it's quite softly played, it manages to create its own cosy atmosphere and all the other sounds outside don't seem so loud in here. It's a young woman's voice, lovely and clear, singing, "*Mama Kita Makaya.... Mama Kita Makaya...*"

Ah... it's the song Nina Marshall sang, Anna realises. *This must be Carrie Tree's version*. She listens for a moment.

"*There's a quest on my heart... I love this ground...*"

Anna remembers her food and digs into it. It is as delicious as it looks. *Definitely made with love*, she thinks, reminded of Kai's brownies and Maddy's pancakes.

Having eaten very quickly, Anna wishes perhaps she had savoured the flavours a little more. But still, she feels good and nourished. As she scrapes the last bit of sauce with her fork, a piece of paper on the far side of the table catches her eye.

She almost doesn't bother with it, but something makes her reach over and pick it up anyway. It's a brochure the colour of light green leaves, with the word 'Buddhafield' written on it. Next to that word, in smaller letters is 'Fire in the Heart'.

Anna reads these words again. *Fire in the Heart*. Something tingles across her skin. She thinks of the little fire that she had felt burning inside her own heart since that night in the Big Tipi, since something had been awakened in her. *Maybe there is something to this Buddhist thing after all.*

She opens the pamphlet and reads: *Members of the Buddhafield Sangha are drawn to nature as the primary context for life and practice, not unlike the original followers of the Buddha. The natural world offers us a direct experience of living interconnectedness and beauty, and thus the opportunity to develop profound wisdom. We are inspired to live simply and lightly on the land… Living in connection and community with each other, we aspire to include all of ourselves, integrating work, play, Dharma practice, and our economic needs. We endeavour to be receptive to our own and others' experience, to communicate in truth and harmony, building a Buddha-land for the benefit of all beings.*

She flips the brochure over and looks at the back of it. At the top in large letters is a quote from the Buddha: '*Loving kindness is freedom of the heart, it glows, it shines, it blazes forth*'. The words seem to call a warmth to Anna's own heart. She tucks the brochure into her satchel.

The Stones are now doing their greatest hits. Anna recognises *Brown Sugar*. Something is pulling her now to listen – at least to these ones. So with a warmth in her belly, she steps back onto the main track, out into the Glastonbury twilight.

Shari is glad she stayed. She had been feeling similarly to Anna earlier and had wished she could have just followed her out of the crowds. Actually though, the gig has been incredibly exciting. Eden often draws Shari deeper into things than she would naturally go and it takes her to the edge sometimes. In the end, this one has been good. The combination of being lightly tipsy on Eden's cider and the wild, infectious enthusiasm of the crowds has drawn Shari into the frenzy of it. And there is Mick, in his tight black clothes and black fur robe, close enough to see the features of his face and the tilt of his head as he powers out the vocals. The screen behind him is alight with flames and the more than hundred-thousand strong crowd are singing along with frenzied devotion to *Sympathy with the Devil*.

Shari sings out too and it feels good. Nobody can hear her and she's singing at the top of her lungs. And now to the delight of the screaming crowds, the great bird at the top of the Pyramid Stage comes to life, lifting its head and raising its colourful wings to the sky, as if it could take them all into flight with it.

But where to go to listen? Anna asks herself. Immediately, an image comes into her mind's eye of those benches back in the Earth garden. She passes by the willow heart again, to where the people crowded around the pianist are still going strong, this time with Don McLean's *Starry Starry Night*.

Only a few paces along, in the Fire Garden, the Padres have shifted gear. The accordion player has now swapped his accordion for a ukulele and is leading the other instruments and chorus of voices around the fire in one of his own songs, a rhythmic chant. "*When we get what we want... without even trying... And it's no more than we need... truly then... we'll live in a Heaven on Earth...*"

Anna is struck by the synchronicity of the words, because in the gaps between the phrases of the chant, almost like an echo, she can hear the words of the Rolling Stones moving in waves up through the air from Babylon. They're singing one of their greatest classics. *You Can't Always Get What You Want...*

It is strangely as if the two songs are being sung together, as if what is happening down there with the thousands of people by the Pyramid stage and what is happening here in this small circle of people in the Fire Garden are not separate, but somehow part of the same song. "*When we get what we want... without even trying...*" the voices around the fire circle rise in harmony, while at the same time, a hundred thousand voices are thundering down in Babylon to *You Can't Always Get What You Want...*

And here they sing, "*...And it's no more than we need... truly then... we'll live in a Heaven on Earth...*"

Anna pauses for a moment, tempted to stay here by this warm fire with all these people who look truly happy and this band that seems to naturally incite joy, but something is tugging her onwards, to a place where she can sit and really hear these last couple of the Stones' greatest hits.

She stops at the junction where the Earth quadrant begins and peers into the quadrant. It's dark in there now; the garden is only a dim silhouette, among the other dark silhouettes of the tents and tipis and other things bordering the area.

Anna shivers a little, having not brought enough layers with her. It seems to be the trend here, sweltering in the days, extremely cold in the nights. She contemplates forgetting the Stones and going back to that other warm fire when something stops her. *What's that?*

There is a glow emerging from the tents bordering the Earth area. A small fire appears to be moving through the air. Anna can just make out the subtly illuminated glow of a figure, carrying this light. The glow disappears for a moment as the person carrying it sets it down behind the plants in the garden. Out of the darkness, a single candlelight rises up through the air again, and now a second one. From where Anna stands it is as if these tiny lights are twinkling stars or faeries. The lights seem to dance as they find their way across the garden and settle around the edges. Mesmerised, Anna moves towards them, stepping through the archway to the garden, now lit by two little candles to either side.

The leaves edging the parasols flap restlessly in the wind. Anna finds a seat beneath the middle parasol and watches the floodlights down in Babylon radiating up and bouncing off the clouds as the song reaches its climax.

Anna can see the softly-lit face of the woman who bends to the tray as she lifts more of the glowing jars and carries them around to the little nooks and crannies of the garden. It feels magical to Anna – as if the very stars are settling around her.

The woman seems familiar to Anna. There is something in the way this woman holds herself that reminds Anna of her dear friend, Carolyn – perhaps the only dear friend she had before coming to this festival – who she hasn't seen now in years. Perhaps it is this that makes Anna feel a fondness for this woman with the lights; she moves like Carolyn, with a quiet assurance.

At last there is one light left on the tray. The woman lifts it up and scans the space around her, looking for the last place that wants a candle. Seeing Anna sitting there, Michelle moves towards her, placing the glowing jar on the grass beside her.

"A little light for you," The woman, Michelle, says to Anna, offering her a smile through the darkness.

"Thank you," Anna says softly. For even though the candle can't possibly actually make her physically warm the light somehow does make her feel warmer inside. "This garden is beautiful. Did you make it?"

"I'm just one of a group of people who helped create the space. I did very little of the garden actually, but tonight I felt moved to light the candles. Everyone else has gone down to see the Stones and I thought it would be nice for them to come back to the garden lit."

"You didn't want to go down?"

Michelle turns her head to face the flashing lights down in Babylon. "Ah... yes and no. My little one is asleep in camp and someone had to stay. Besides, I didn't really fancy the crowds."

"I know what you mean," Anna says, wiggling her chilled toes in the grass. "I didn't fancy the crowds either, but unlike you, I actually went down there anyway – against my better judgement; it was a mistake." *Or was it?* she wonders. Maybe it had all been part of a necessary process, because it had lead her to that experience of finally driving her own life, of making her way to these green fields, of meeting Ali, of passing through the Goddess gate, of having a wonderful meal and being here in this garden with these magical lights.

"Or maybe it wasn't a mistake after all," she says softly, "because I ended up here."

"Overall, a much better place to listen to the Stones," Michelle agrees. "You can still hear all the words, especially when the wind blows this way."

The two women are quiet for a moment, listening to the final chorus of the song. Gazing out at the glowing sky over Babylon below, Anna marvels again at the strangeness of the purple, green and orange light reflecting off the clouds. She thinks about the words of the song. *Do we always get what we need? Is that true?*

I really want to be warm. Anna shivers again, as the chill of the night moves deeper inside her. It's in her bones now – one way or another she will have to leave this spot soon – but she is determined to hear the end of the Stones' set. The wind rises sharply again, whipping at her hair and making the leaves on the parasols rustle and dance above her.

The song finishes and the audience roars their appreciation with an enthusiasm bordering on hysteria. Anna shivers again, sucking in a shallow breath of frigid air. Michelle hears the sound made by the young woman beside her and notices she is dressed only in a light summer top.

"You must be freezing."

"You could say that," Anna replies. "I'm probably crazy to sit here in this temperature wearing this... but I promised myself I'd hear their set to the end."

"This must be nearly the end." Michelle turns her gaze to the flashing sky. "I think they've done all their other greatest hits now."

The first guitar chords rise up over Babylon for *Satisfaction*.

"Oh, except this one..." Michelle says. "I'll be right back."

Anna watches the woman lift the empty tray and disappear in between the tents. A few moments later she returns with two fleece blankets and offers one to Anna. "Here. This might help."

Anna accepts the blanket gratefully. "Thank you. I think you might have saved me from hypothermia."

"You're welcome. Not really summer temperature is it? Something about this valley. The cold mist rolls in at night." Michelle settles herself on the bench beside Anna and wraps her own blanket around herself.

"Perhaps the last song was right," Anna suggests. "Perhaps we do get what we need. I needed to be warm, and this blanket arrived." She's not really warm yet, but the fleece blanket has stopped the most violent of the shivers.

Michelle nods. "It feels right to me. Like maybe... I'm kind of just working this out myself... but maybe our souls draw things to us. Like we might not know it's what we need consciously, and maybe our egos think they want something, but it's our soul – our heart, whatever you want to call it – that draws the deeper things to us, for our growth. Does that make sense?"

"I think so," Anna says. She's not quite sure, but it intrigues her, the way this woman is talking.

"Someone once said to me that this song they're playing now is like the song of the ego," Michelle says.

"What do you mean?"

"It's like... the ego part of us can't ever be satisfied. It always wants more and more, like trying to fill a black hole... but that's its nature – to believe it's incomplete."

Anna remembers something Johannes had said like that. "Earlier in the festival someone said to me that the ego is like a kind of illusion, making people forget who they really are."

Michelle nods. "I've heard that too. You know, that makes me think of an experience I had tonight when I went to the Peace Dome."

"The Peace Dome?"

"Mmm. It's just up in King's Meadow. It's where the Peace Flame is kept. If you have a chance to go there I would really recommend it – it's a very special place. Tonight, before everyone left, I had this feeling that I wanted to light the garden with the Peace Flame, so I went to the Peace Dome to get it. I sat with the flame in the central mandala and the most amazing thing happened – I felt like my ego self just stepped back. For a moment, I felt like I became aware of myself as the part of me that's not controlled by the ego, that knows it's made of love... It was like being with the Peace Flame called me more into the truth of myself, into love, if that makes sense. It's hard to explain the feeling."

"I think I know what you mean," Anna says, remembering the night in the Big Tipi, when she had felt herself expand, and how it hadn't been her little 'I' self anymore. It had felt like she was seeing with eyes of a self that knew it belonged to everything.

"When I carried the flame back in my little lantern," Michelle explains, "it felt like I was carrying this presence with me. And I can feel it here now, in this garden – it's in every single one of these lights."

Anna feels a wave shiver through her, and this time it's not about the cold. *Yes, I can feel something too.* She makes a note to herself to find this Peace Dome.

The Phoenix at the crest of the stage is in full flight and Shari is on a high. It's nearly too much for her and her throat is sore from all the singing, but she is with it right to the end of the climactic finish, belting it out with the rest of them. And now, to the euphoric delight of the crowds, the giant heart right below the Phoenix is coming to life, blasting out living fire. From behind the great bird's wings, the sky erupts into a blaze of fireworks. As the song finishes, the voracious screams of the crowd are echoing on and on with increasing fervour. They cheer their love and gratitude for a full four and a half minutes.

That resonance carries across the whole festival site; even in the Earth Garden the feeling of excitement and devotion is contagious. But Anna can feel it is time for her to get properly warm somehow. Even with the blanket, it is really necessary now. It's been quite a while since she'd felt her toes in these sandals.

"Thank you for this." Anna rises shakily from the bench and offers the blanket back to Michelle.

"You're welcome. Nice to meet you."

"You too."

Michelle watches the young woman's figure disappearing into the shadows, and smiles to herself. Something about this conversation has inspired her to make some notes for the book she's writing; something about the heart, and love.

Where to find heat? Anna feels so shivery now she can barely concentrate. As she rubs her icy hands together, she catches sight of the yellow band on her wrist: *Find Yourself.*

Of course! Where had she been the warmest of all this whole weekend? In the sauna at Lost Horizon. She wants that heat, as intense as possible. *But it's late. Will it still be open? I can only hope...*

The promise of the sauna keeps Anna's numb feet pumping up the track, back again between the harvest goddesses. After another brief and shivering visit to the WaterAid loos, Anna cuts across King's Meadow towards the exit on the other side. This is a faster route to the Tipi Field. Before she reaches the end of the meadow, she catches her first sight of the Peace Dome, silhouetted against the twilight sky. There is a small entrance on one side of the large geodesic dome, which opens into hexagonal shaped garden. From within that entrance, hundreds of flickering lights dance. *The Mandala*, Anna recalls the words of the woman in the garden. Though it attracts her, she reminds herself of the warmth of the sauna, praying again that it will be open.

I'll come here tomorrow, she promises herself. She pushes on, through the exit up the track and past Pacha Mama Cafe into the Tipi Field. A band called *Baka Beyond* are playing a fusion of Celtic and African music in the Ancient Futures venue where people are dancing to the voices in harmony and the percussion and guitar melodies. Anna is drawn in by this music, which sounds it belongs in a rain-forest. But again, she is so cold she can only carry on toward her destination – heat.

She moves past the central fire and towards the beacon of the lanterns which light the entrance to Lost Horizon Sauna. To Anna's profound relief, she can see now that there is still someone there – a young man in a woolly hat – just stepping towards the canvas entrance flap, as if to close it.

"Are you still open?" Anna asks, breathless.

Rory stops what he's doing – which is closing up for the night – and looks up at this young and very cold looking woman in front of him. By the light of the lanterns he can see the desperation written all over her face. He had just decided this very minute to close up, as it is now past midnight and he has been looking forward to his post-shift sauna before going to bed. But when faced with a person so clearly in need...

He gives her an understanding smile. "For you, yes. You just squeaked in. I was just about to bring the board in and close up for the night. Go on in. Once you're in you can stay as long as you like."

"Oh, thank God." Anna lets out a breath she didn't know she'd been holding. She wants to cry she's so relieved. "Thank you so much."

"You are most welcome. Enjoy." He lifts the curtain and Anna steps through the gap.

The scene that greets her eyes is one of firelit gentleness. An open fire burns brightly in a central firepit out on the grass. Naked bodies are silhouetted in the firelight. On the opposite side of the fire, relaxed faces shine in the glow of the flames. One man strums a guitar. They all appear completely at home here, naked beneath the stars and the clouds and the cool night air. The sauna yurt smokes with its beckoning heat. It has lanterns lighting the entrance way. The doors slam themselves as people leave the sauna, the steam rising off their bodies into the night air.

To Anna's right another fire burns welcomingly in the chill-out tipi. This fire too has several people around it. Some are seated and some appear to be sleeping. There is one person Anna doesn't see in there, as he is sitting on the other side of the fire. Cedar is nearly ready to go to bed, for he knows he must rest and garner energy for his gig tomorrow. He has been sitting here by the fire in the chill-out tipi for some time now, in a semi-meditative state, contemplating the events of the last few days and trying to allow them to move through his mind and heart. He thinks of Anna and of Moon. He thinks of the woman he made his promise to in the vision, and feels her smiling with twinkling eyes at him, saying, *Just be happy. Be in your flow. All is well. I do not hold you to anything that is not in your highest good.*

Once in the changing yurt, Anna can't get her clothes off fast enough. Stepping out naked into the night, most of her skin feels numb with the cold and she's shivering uncontrollably. She makes a beeline for the sauna. Inside, people are chanting *Aum*.

As she closes the inner doors behind her, the blessed heat hits her frigid skin with a blast. Surrounded by the womb-like dark and heat, she is embraced by the sound as it resonates all around her body.

Aaaaaaaaaaaaaaaaaooooooooooooooouuuuuuuuuuummmmmmmmmm...

Aaaaaaaaaaaaaaaaaooooooooooooooouuuuuuuuuuummmmmmmmmm...

The orange fire is visible through the cracks of the wood burning stove, lighting Anna's way to a spare seat. She doesn't worry this time about not having a towel to sit on. She just allows the heat and sound to permeate deeper, until finally the heat reaches deep enough inside her to warm the bones and return the feeling to her toes. Her body finally stops shivering and becomes still. With the stillness, her listening settles and she is drawn further into the chant, as if it is coming from somewhere within her.

Aaaaaaaaaaaaaaaaaooooooooooooooouuuuuuuuuuummmmmmmmmm...

She hears the others breathing in turn around her and reminds herself to breathe too. She had been forgetting to breathe with her diaphragm in the cold. So now remembering, she draws her breath down again, back to her belly, feeling the still strange movement of her diaphragm as the moist air is drawn in and released. As she breathes, her body relaxes still more. The hum of the Aum is resonating inside her now, part of her. Now as she breathes, Anna feels her mouth making the shapes of the sound, and with the next outbreath she is singing it too, from a deeper place that she has ever sung before. She listens to the voice rising out of her on this deeper breath and is surprised. *Is it mine?* It's more full, more rich, more resonant than before. She is an observer of this body making this sound, feeling the pleasure in it as the resonance moves through her.

Aaaaaaaaaaaaaaaaooooooooooooooouuuuuuuuuummmmmmmmmmm...

The chant moves into stillness and they all sit together, eyes closed and quietly breathing, feeling the hum of the *Aum* still in the air and in the ground below their feet. The hum of the Earth.

Sweating at last, Anna can feel the call of her body for water, and to be clean. She steps out into the night air, feeling the delight of the contrast of the crisp air and the heat still held in her body. She watches the steam rising from her skin as she makes her way to the drinking cask, where she pours water into the communal cup and drinks.

Still steaming, Anna steps into the showers and gasps as the cold water takes her breath away. But it feels so good to be clean – to wash off all that sweat and dust. And as she runs her hands over her face, Anna realises she is washing off too, the mask she put on earlier – the meticulously applied make-up, put on for the benefit of Shari and Eden. It feels so good to let it all go.

Shivering again, Anna switches off the water and makes her way back inside the two doors of the sauna. She stands in the centre of the space, right in front of the wood-burning stove, breathing consciously with her diaphragm and letting her eyes adjust.

He sees her before she sees him. He tries not to look at her too closely, but from the corner of his eye, he catches sight of the rise and fall of her belly as she breathes. Cedar smiles to himself. Such a thing to meet her again here – unclothed. He moves his awareness to his heart centre and to his own breathing to stop his thoughts from straying where he would rather they didn't stray.

He closes his eyes now, but he can still feel her presence only a few feet away from him. He hears her move to sit on the opposite bench, and as she settles herself there, hears her release a soft breath of relaxation. He feels the moment her eyes are adjusted enough to notice him there across from her and hears the catch of her breath. He opens his eyes and hers are staring right back at him, her lips parted as if caught in half gasp. He nods to her and smiles, lifting a hand to say hello. She smiles back, glad that the dim light of the yurt is hiding the flush of her cheeks. *Breathe Anna. Breathe.*

Of all the places to see him again – here, naked. She tries not to look, but her peripheral vision shows her more than she means to see: he is wearing only the black the white bone carving on a black cord around his neck and his two wristbands, same as hers.

When Anna opens her eyes again, Cedar appears to be meditating. She watches his face, and feels her own heart ache with a new feeling of wanting. *No!* she tells herself. *This isn't allowed.*

Someone ladles a spoonful of essential oil water onto the wood-burner. The already moist air fills with scented steam. The heat intensifies. It's definitely the sexy blend.

The sauna is beginning to feel almost too hot for Anna. She closes her eyes again and tries to focus on her breathing to try and calm her racing heart and other bodily reactions. It helps a little.

"I saw that dragon you were talking about, over in King's Meadow."

Anna recognises the voice that's speaking – it's Saffi, who first showed her around the sauna. Anna also recognises the woman Saffi speaks to, for it is the same goddess woman with the extraordinary dreadlocks who had swirled the fabric around the sauna yesterday.

Dragon? Anna wonders. *In King's Meadow?* She doesn't remember seeing one there.

Cedar opens his eyes and glances over at the two women briefly and smiles. He knows the dragon they are referring to. He usually pays the dragon a visit at least once during the festival.

"And what did you think of it?" Ella asks, breathing deeply.

"Amazing. The way it sits there, in the trees, with the water all around it. I swear it was real. I mean, that eye – it's like it's really looking at you."

"Did you touch it?" Ella asks.

"Touch the eye?" Saffi raises an eyebrow. "Why?"

"Well, I was told that if you touch the eye, you'll receive a vision."

"A vision? Of what?"

"Of whatever's in your highest good, I guess. Like for me, I had a question in my heart, and when I placed my palm against the dragon's eye, I saw my path, and I saw how the energy around me was part of that path, and how everything was. I saw how I fit into all of it. Then I knew what I was supposed to do."

"Wild... I'll have to try that."

Me too. I'll have to find that dragon, Anna thinks.

I must take time to visit the dragon, Cedar thinks to himself. He had not heard that story about receiving a vision when you touch the eye, but he knows how it works when you ask a question of the heart and remain open to receive the answer.

Perhaps a giant dragon eye could help with that process, he muses. There certainly is a power in it. Meeting the dragon for Cedar is always about remembering that dragon-serpent energy within himself and his connection to the lines of energy within the earth.

Some time passes and Anna hears movement across from her. Without opening her eyes, she knows Cedar has left the sauna. She feels his absence with panic. *Do I go after him? To speak to him? Naked?* She feels pulled by two fears: one that she will lose her chance to see Cedar if she doesn't follow him, and one that she will see him and where that might lead. *And what will he think of me chasing after him? Who am I to him anyway?*

You are enough, the words echo inside her again. Again she feels that little fire flaring up inside her. *Go! Go now!*

Out again in the cool of the night, which now seems brighter than before, Anna casts her eyes across the grounds. She can't see him. *Perhaps he's gone.* She walks to the water cask and drinks from the cup again, feeling a confusion of both disappointment and relief.

He isn't gone. Cedar emerges from the shower, wearing a sarong over the bottom half of his body like a towel. Seeing him so close and now covered, Anna feels dreadfully exposed and her eyes cast about for anything she might fling over herself in the next five seconds. And there it is – a partially used towel someone has left in a heap by the water cask. Trying not to think too much about who might have used it before her, she grabs it and flings it around herself, finding it reasonably clean, though damp from the dew of the night.

Cedar feels compassion for Anna as he sees her there, hastily wrapping the towel around herself and looking up to face him with her sweet gaze, but he has decided he will not allow a certain flow to happen tonight, even as he feels the urge in his body to do otherwise – even now, after the cold shower. Even if his Promised One might bless it and release him from his vow.

"Goodnight Anna," he says to her. "I'll see you tomorrow." His eyes smile at her warmly and she feels a flutter inside at what she sees there; it is a mirror of what is in her own heart. And yet, she can see he has no intention of stopping. Again, she reminds herself of her promises to Damien back home. *Just as well, because even if Cedar does stay, nothing is going to happen tonight. It wouldn't be right.* She tells herself this, even as there is another voice in her asking, *Why see you tomorrow, why not now?*

"Tomorrow?"

"Our gig."

"Oh! Of course. Yes. I'll definitely be there."

He smiles again. "Good. I'll see you then. Goodnight."

"Goodnight," Anna answers, feeling her mouth saying these words she doesn't want to say.

With a final smile, he turns and disappears too quickly out into the night. Anna stares at the empty space for a while, willing him to reappear.

Cedar wouldn't have found it so easy to walk away from a situation like this last year, but the work he has been doing on himself this past year has given him the strength now to do what he feels is right, even though he recognises there's a part of him that would jump at this opportunity to share more time with her, to allow wherever it would lead – and he knows full well where it would lead. *And no*, he tells himself. Even if only for the reason that he has to conserve his energy for the gig tomorrow. He has learned in the past that sex after gigs is exhilarating. Sex before gigs is a bad idea, because it leaves him energetically depleted in some way and unable to do the work onstage. Still, just outside the entrance to the sauna Cedar does stop, pausing for a moment to witness the sensations in his body which are willing him to go back inside.

I do not hold you to anything that is not in your highest good. The words his Beloved had spoken to him in his dream ring again in his mind. *If she is real she would bless it*, he knows. And yet, this is about more than just his vow. *Think about your energy and what will be able to happen at the gig tomorrow night if you conserve it.* Holding this thought, he moves his body forward and walks himself straight back to his tipi.

When he doesn't come back, Anna lets out a shallow breath and turns her eyes to the chill-out tipi. Suddenly she feels very tired, but she has no desire to return to her tent. *And besides*, a little voice in her head chimes, *he might still come back*. But really, she knows he won't.

She hurriedly dresses and returns to the fire inside the tipi chill-out space. There are two people lazing next to the fire – a young man and woman – dressed, but hair still dripping wet from the sauna. They both look up and offer a smile of welcome as Anna approaches, but neither one speaks.

Anna finds a spare dry cushion near the warmth of the embers and curls herself up on it. There's a blanket nearby, which she draws around her. In the confusion of feelings she no longer cares whether this blanket has been used by others. In a way it's comforting that it has. It smells of woodsmoke and incense. She closes her eyes, feeling the desire to sleep settling around her and just as she is about to drift off, there is the murmur of voices across the fire as the man and woman whisper to one another in soft tones.

"Your heart didn't wash off in the sauna," the young man says to his friend.

Anna notices how the young woman has a red heart painted on her cheek with the word 'Syria' inside it. She'd seen quite a few people with painted hearts like that around the festival and had been wondering about them.

"It seems to have grown on me," the young woman answers. "It's sort of become part of my skin now. I must have painted about a hundred of these on people today."

"So how is it working for Oxfam this year? I really loved stewarding for them a couple of years ago."

"It's been really amazing. Everyone's super friendly, and the whole experience has been kind of an eye opener."

"How so?"

"I never knew about all the work they did for people." She shakes her head. "I guess I've been in my own bubble about it all. Like I had no idea that the conflict in Syria has forced five and a half million people out of their homes, and there are more than a million people living as refugees! A million people! Can you believe that? I just can't comprehend it, really. You start to see that they're regular people, just like you and me – teachers, musicians, families..."

The young man nods. "And you know it's going to get worse before it gets better."

She stares at him. "Really? I'm surprised to hear you say that, Andy. You of all people. You're always saying we have to think positively... that our thoughts matter. And if we don't think positively, how could we carry on doing what we're doing? We have to know all this energy we're putting in makes a difference."

Andy nods. "Of course... if we want to continue to have energy for things, we have to feel we're making some kind of progress in some way. If want to change the world, we have to be able to see it getting better. If we want the conflict in Syria or anywhere else to end, we do have to look to our thoughts – they're so powerful. But I feel like there's a bigger picture here too, Kells. I just have this sense about it – that this is a wake up call for the world, like climate change is. This will become one of the catalysts for a global awakening. I have a feeling it won't be just a million refugees in the end – it could end up being ten times that many before it's through."

Kelly stares at him, open-mouthed. "How can you say that? Surely people will stop it before it gets to that point."

"I'd like to think they would, but I'm not so sure, Kells. I have the strongest feeling we're at a critical turning point for the consciousness of humanity, and that it may take something of massive global significance to touch everyone at the same time, so that humanity as a whole will be put in touch with their hearts and start to wake up, and feel their connection with one another. Until enough people wake up to their hearts, war and suffering in the world won't end."

Kelly is silent for a moment, staring at the fire. "So how much is enough then? How many people do you think have to wake up for all that to stop?"

"I don't know." Andy shakes his head. "But it feels like it's already happening. It's like there's this wave, and it's growing. And we can be a part of it consciously, by helping it grow bigger and move faster, or we can sit back unconsciously, and be swept up by it in the end. For me, I want to be a conscious part of it."

Kelly nods. "Me too, but I guess the question I want to ask is... how? How do we become conscious parts of it?"

Andy rests his gaze in the fire. "Intention. By making the choice to wake up, however we can, by becoming conscious in each moment, in each act. Every act of love makes a difference. Every act of love makes the world a little bit more loving."

"I like that... Every act of love makes the world a bit more loving. I guess that's all we can do."

"And imagine – imagine if every person in the world made a commitment to do that, how quickly the world would change? How quickly everything would change."

"Yeah, and it's like a ripple effect," Kelly agrees. "Each act of love affects others and maybe helps them to act a bit more lovingly."

"It starts with ourselves, too," Andy says. "Acting with love towards ourselves. Ending the violence inside our own minds and hearts towards ourselves, because the world out there and the world in here are really the same thing."

Anna is not really meaning to eavesdrop, but can't help listening. She thinks of the thoughts that she had been having about herself, of not being enough, of being worthless, and how Moon had shown her she could turn those thoughts around to *I am enough*.

Kelly nods. "That makes so much sense. I'm so hard on myself. I think I do violence to myself in my own head every day without meaning to."

"Yeah, me too, but then I try and remind myself to think differently. There are so many ways we can be kind to ourselves. And then when we do that, it is so natural to be kind to others. Like, if we could really learn to love our bodies and feel grateful for them – how amazing would that feel?"

"Yeah, that's one of the hardest things to do. I feel like my body and I are at war with each other most of the time."

Anna knows how that feels. She thinks of all her trips to the gym and how none of it was ever enough. How every time she looked at her body in the mirror, there were always faults to be found.

"Imagine if you could really love your body," Andy says. "Really bless it, and feel grateful for all the amazing things it does for you. This is your only body in this life. It's such a gift, and it's only our thoughts that make us feel differently about it."

Kelly looks up at Andy and gives him a knowing look. "You've been reading your books again, haven't you?"

Andy chuckles. "Mm. Jack Kornfield and Byron Katie, most recently."

"Maybe I'd better borrow those books from you sometime." Kelly sighs. "Well, I guess if I really want to be loving with myself, I'd better put myself to bed. I've got an early shift tomorrow."

"Doing what?"

"I'm part of the morning crew doing a sweep of King's Meadow."

"Nice. I remember doing that. It's kind of satisfying isn't it? You arrive to this blanket of rubbish all over the ground from the night before, and you leave this clear swathe of grass behind you."

"Yeah, but it would be nice if people didn't shit it up in the first place. You wouldn't believe the things people leave behind."

"Oh, yeah. I would."

"They even call it 'sacred space' on the map," Kelly says. "And yet, some people treat it like their toilet. I don't understand it."

"And they're probably treating themselves the same way," Andy whispers.

"Yeah, they probably are," Kelly agrees.

"You know what that makes me think of?" Andy runs his hand along the ground beside him. "How this earth is actually part of our bodies. You know they say on an energy level it's all connected, but science tells us that too. The cells in our body all completely change every seven years. The air we breathe becomes part of our bodies... and the water we drink... and the food we eat. And then when we die, our bodies become part of the soil. It's all connected."

They are both silent for a while. The fire crackles its last flame and relaxes into red glowing embers.

"On that note, I'd better go and take care of my body," Kelly whispers after a while. "Goodnight, Andy."

"Yeah, I should too. Goodnight then, Lovely."

They embrace and Anna's eyes flutter open to see the young woman leaving the tipi. Andy's eyes meet Anna's for a moment and he smiles. She returns the smile sleepily. The fire has nearly gone out and she shivers a little, drawing the blanket around her more tightly and reaching for another one nearby.

Watching her, Andy turns to pick up a small log from the pile of wood behind him and nestles it onto the fire, blowing gently so that the fire leaps to life again. Anna closes her eyes again, enjoying the renewed warmth and watching the play of firelight on the inside of her eyelids. After a few moments, she hears the rustle of the young man across from her rising and the slight movement of air which flickers the flames as he follows his friend out into the night.

He'd made up the fire just for her – a gesture of kindness. *Every act of love makes the world a little bit more loving.*

"Thank you," Anna whispers to the empty space where the young man had been.

Maybe I could just rest here a while, she thinks, wrapping the blanket more closely around herself, curling her body into a ball for warmth, as the flickering orange light dances through her closed eyelids.

"*And we know this now,*
This earth is our body
And this water's our blood"

from the song, 'Water', by Carrie Tree

In her dream Anna is walking across King's Meadow towards the woods. *This is where they said it was*, she thinks. It's dark. She feels afraid. There are some partiers still awake around the circle of stones, but it feels to Anna like they are in another world, like she could walk right by them and they wouldn't see her. She remembers her wish to be brave, and feels that flaring of fire inside her, driving her forward. Yes.

She follows the gentle slope of the hill down toward a wooded area, passing through a gap in the trees. As she enters the woods, everything is illuminated as if lit by a full moon from above. But Anna knows the waning moon is not shining now. This is an ethereal light. Bathed in this light, Anna has her first sight of the dragon.

Overhung by branches, the dragon coils in rest. The stream that borders the field and runs down the hill moves through the giant creature and becomes a waterfall from her open mouth. The scales of clear quartz along her body and the rose quartz spikes along her spine glint in the light.

Barefoot, Anna steps into the pond which surrounds the dragon, placing her hand on the cold, stone scales. The dragon herself seems to breathe under her hand and the trees seem to breathe all around her. She moves up along the body of the dragon until she faces the eye – the huge, penetrating, red crystal eye – with the circle of white quartz shot through its centre like a staring pupil, flashing at her as if it knows something. She shivers, afraid again.

Her energy is your energy, a voice says. *What you fear is your own power, your own energy.*

Cedar stands naked before her, his whole body painted with multi-coloured light. In the place just below his navel is a great, golden sun, its rays radiating out across his belly. Another sun shines pink at the centre of his chest, seeming to extend beyond his body like great wings. Between his eyebrows is a smaller shining sun, this one radiant in hues of purple and violet, colours dancing across his eyes.

Three suns, Anna thinks. She looks down at her own body to see that she too is naked and painted with swirls of gold and orange. The water at her feet glistens in the light, making undulating patterns on her, like living fire.

Are you dreaming too? she asks him.

We're all dreaming. We're dreaming all of this, he says, moving through the water to stand beside her. He looks up at the overhanging trees, which are still glowing with that same ethereal light.

Why is everything glowing? Anna asks.

Because it's all energy, Cedar explains. *Everything is made of light.*

Even me?

You, me, everything.

Even the dragon is glowing. The dragon seems to be alive. Anna shivers again.

Everything is alive, Cedar says. *The Earth and all she creates is alive. There are lines of energy running through the earth – energy pathways. This is Dragon energy. Dragon energy is also the energy that rises like the serpent up our spine. It is lifeforce energy.*

What does that have to do with me? Anna asks.

Everything, Cedar whispers. *If you touch dragon's eye, you'll see.*

Anna reaches forward to touch the red crystal and...

...opens her eyes.

There are birds singing. It's dawn. The remnants of the fire are just embers now, smouldering quietly. It's cold. The sounds around the festival have quieted now, all except for one last incessant beat, far across the site. The resident blackbirds, tits and thrushes who have taken refuge in the trees up above the Tipi Field are singing the dawn chorus. Drowsily, Anna lifts herself from her cushion. *The dream...*

She struggles to hold onto the details of the dream before it fades, the feeling of it: Cedar, his words, the paint, the dragon, the sense of light. She holds this preciously in her mind, clinging to the details she remembers, etching them into her memory. *It felt so real...* Half-awake and walking through the dawn, this feels to Anna as surreal as her dream. The image of that gold and orange paint on her body returns, and how it had danced like fire. Everything in her dream had breathed, had been alive.

The central fire in the Tipi Field is still lit. Anna stops briefly to warm herself by it. For the first time since she's passed by this fire, there is nobody else here. For a few moments it is only the crackling of the fire, the singing of the birds and the images moving through her mind from the dream. *In the dream Cedar said something about lines of energy... a serpent. It had something to do with me. What was it?*

In the hazy blue of dawn's first light and the sweet freshness of the air, she recalls the Aum – its resonance still humming inside her. She doesn't mind going back to her tent now. Even the public camping field is peaceful. She flashes her wrist at the two sleepy stewards manning the gate of the Artist and Crew camping area and after visiting the portaloos, crawls into her tent. The feeling inside sustains her, even as she curls up – fully clothed and shivering – inside her slightly damp sleeping bag. As the shivering begins to subside, Anna wills herself to return to that dream of the dragon and Cedar, to see what she was meant to see when she touched the dragon's eye...

> "She's wild, she's wild, she's wild in her body
> And it's for her, it is her
> It's for her own connection.
> She's Fire, she's Fire, she's Fire in her belly
> It's for her, is her own
> She knows her beauty
> She has green dragon eyes"

from the song, 'Green Dragon', by Boe Huntress

5. Spirit

"Man seems
Spirit is
Man dreams
Spirit lives
Man is tethered
Spirit is free
What spirit is man can be"

from the song, 'Spirit', by Michael Scott* [1]

Anna wakes to the sounds of the festival in full swing all around her. Feeling hot, she kicks off her sleeping bag and lies there for a moment, watching the play of midday light on the top of her orange tent. She doesn't remember any other dreams but that first one of the night. Struggling again to recall the dream, she gently pieces it together in her mind. *The dragon... Cedar...*

There's nothing for it but to go there, she decides. *Right now. See if any of it was real.*

As she dresses, Anna feels a bubbling of excitement about what she might find there and about seeing Cedar later tonight at his gig. She lifts her satchel and her phone drops out – still switched off.

Damien. Without even checking, she knows he's called. It's been more than 24 hours since she last sent him a message, and that will feel like a long time to

---

1. *Dizzy Heights Music Publishing, Ltd. All rights administered by Warner/Chappell Music Ltd.*

him. So much has happened since then. Switching on the phone, she finds several voicemail messages and worried texts from both Damien and Shari. Taking a deep breath, Anna dials her home landline number, hoping that it will be the answerphone that picks up.

"Anna! God, are you okay?" Damien answers, his voice higher pitched than usual.

"I'm okay. Why wouldn't I be?"

"Because you didn't answer your phone, and when I tried to call you later the phone was switched off. So I called Shari to see if she'd heard from you, and she told me that you'd left right before the Stones started, looking like you had heat stroke or something. And then you didn't reply to any of my messages."

"Oh." Anna feels dumbstruck for a moment that all this worrying has been going on about her. "I'm fine. I mean, I did feel like I was getting heat stroke, so that's why I left."

But you know it was more than that. She remembers the fire and the liberating feeling of driving her own life, of being on her own path. *What happened to that?* She watches herself putting on the mask again, even as she can feel the little flaring of fire inside her that speaks of her heart's truth.

"But you're okay now," Damien confirms.

"Yeah."

"Okay." He breathes a sigh of relief. "But Anna, why didn't you answer your phone? And then why didn't you check your messages before you switched it off? You told me you would leave it on. I don't know what's going on."

Anna feels her heart heave. *What am I doing to him? But I can't tell him. I can't. Not until I figure all this out.*

"I'm sorry, D. I was just having a shiatsu and so I turned it off, and I guess I forgot to put it back on."

"You were having a shiatsu? Why?"

Because I needed healing. "I had a sore back."

"Since when?"

"I don't know. A couple of months ago, I guess. I told you that a guy knocked into me at the gym."

"You didn't tell me he hurt your back, though."

There's a lot I haven't told you. There's a lot I haven't shared. "I guess we were a bit busy at the time with the CD and everything."

"If you'd have told me I could've given you a massage or something. I could've helped you."

Anna's body releases a sigh. "You probably could have." *Could he?* Anna knows more went on with Ali than just a back massage. Ali had realigned some energy in Anna. She had done something that was about more than just the physical body.

"Maybe when you get back." Damien's voice is strained.

"That would be nice." Anna tries to keep her voice light. *What will be there when I get back? What will be left of my life?* It feels as if the ground is shifting below her feet and nothing is as it was anymore.

Damien sighs, as if giving up on something. "Well, what's done is done. Have you called Shari, by the way? I'm guessing not because your phone has been off. She's been trying to get ahold of you. She seemed kinda worried about you. At least you could give her a call and set her mind at rest."

"Okay," Anna says, feeling herself growing smaller as she relents, feeling the shackles of her old life getting a grip again. "Sorry D."

"Okay. I just wish you'd called me sooner."

"I should have. You're right."

"So what are your plans today?"

My plan was to visit the dragon, and to see Cedar play. "To see some music, I guess," Anna says neutrally.

"Well, try and stay out of the big crowds if you can. I don't want to be kept up half the night worrying about you again."

"I'll do my best. I should go. I haven't had breakfast yet."

Damien sighs again. "Well, try and take care of yourself. And call me later, okay? You will call me later, right?"

"Yes. I'll call you later."

"And call Shari."

"I will."

"I love you."

"I love you too." Anna says the words because she knows that not to say them would make things more difficult, but right now it feels as if something has shut down inside her; the words feel hollow as they come out of her mouth. To say *I love you* with an absence of love feels like a deep betrayal of not just Damien, but herself. *But I do love him,* she tells herself as she hangs up her phone. She drops it into her satchel, switched on.

The tent feels too hot. Anna rips open the zip, breaking the catch. Poking her head out of the tent, she can see hundreds of people moving by in the camping field and up on the trackway into Babylon and the green fields. They all look so busy, so intent, as if they all have somewhere wonderful to go.

What do I do now? Anna thinks of the dragon and her dream, and it all seems like a silly fantasy now. The empty ache in her stomach is back, making her think of food. Rather than heading up to the Tipi Field for one of Maddy's lovely pancakes – even though that's what she'd like more than anything – Anna visits the Artists and Crew canteen, where she finds a coffee with milk and two sugars and two pain-au-chocolats. They sit heavily inside her.

She steps out back into the sunlight and wonders whatever can be done with the day. It feels barren to her, even the thought of Cedar's gig. She doesn't know how to face him, or any of the others. *I'm not like them*, she thinks.

The words of Johannes come to her again – a reminder. *You are the same as that person you think is better than you. Exactly the same.*

Not so sure about that, she thinks.

You are enough... it echoes softly inside her, and Anna imagines the face of her Wild Woman – her Heart-Self – smiling at her. It feels like a dream belonging to somebody else right now, a fanciful imagination, just like the dragon.

I should call Shari, Anna tells herself, but she doesn't want to speak to anyone, or to have to answer any more questions. So instead she just sends a text.

Hi Share. Hope the Stones were good. Sorry I had to go. Feeling better now. Hope you're both having fun. X

Yesterday, feeling the invigoration of driving her own life, Anna had felt so much energy. *How did I get back here? To this? And where do I go now? How do I stop feeling this pain?* An image comes into her mind of the healing area and Johannes, who seemed to have so much faith in her. *Maybe he could help me understand all of this.*

On her way, Anna passes through the Permaculture area again and stops by the Rainbow Wishing Well. She remembers her wish at the Pacha Mama wishing well – to be brave.

Ha, she thinks. *That didn't last long.*

But even so, as she runs her hand along the rough, warm surface of the well, over the mirrors reflecting the sun's light, she feels a desire to make a wish here too. Reaching into her pocket, she finds a twenty pence coin. She drops it into the water, whispering, "I wish I knew what I was supposed to be doing... I wish..." Then she remembers her intention on the hill, and how the girl with the rainbows in her hair had spoken of gratitude, and how it's gratitude that makes the magic happen. An image of the girl's smiling face and knowing eyes comes into Anna's mind's eye, and she can almost hear the girl laughing and saying, *See, I knew you'd be back! I knew you really believed wishes could come true.*

"...Thank you..." Anna says softly. With this comes a surge of emotion, because suddenly, surrounded by these trees and bathed in the dappled sunlight, it feels like there really is someone or something listening.

"Thank you..." she whispers again. "...for helping me... to remember. Whatever it is I am meant to remember." A wind rustles the leaves, making the sunlight dance over the mirrors on the well.

You are here.

This is what the little arrow on the map says. Anna had tried to find Johannes, but he hadn't been at his yurt and all his bookable slots for the day were taken. With a heavy step, Anna had traipsed back here, to the place where the four quadrants of the Healing Area meet, as if from here she might know where to go.

From this centre point, she looks around her at the entrances to each of the four quadrants. Suspended over the entrance into the Earth area there is a willow sphere; above Water, a mermaid; above Fire, a rainbow sun; above Air, a pair of white wings and a purple heart. Her attention is drawn to the only quadrant she hasn't yet explored: Air.

At the centre of Air there isn't a garden like there are in the other three quadrants. Instead there is a beautiful mandala made from long grasses, seed heads and pine cones with an elegantly whirling wind-spinner at the centre, and beyond this is a giant three-dimensional Star of David, constructed from long tubes of bamboo and suspended from four upright bamboo poles. It hangs just high enough that a man could stand and stretch his hands up underneath it without touching it.

There is a person sitting in meditation just below the bottom point of the star. Jonas sits here each day beneath the Star of David because he believes it has the power to harmonize his being. He knows that even though it sits in Air, it is actually the symbol for Quintessence, or Spirit, and like the symbol which matches it at the Peace Dome, it brings him peace; it brings him back to his centre.

The sun lights the man's face and Anna watches him for a moment. He looks so utterly tranquil. A soft smile curves his lips and his hands are in prayer pose in front of his heart.

How do people find such peacefulness? Anna wonders, but then remembers feeling moments of true contentment herself over the weekend. *How do I feel that way again?*

Around the Air circle, there are nearly every kind of meditation and yoga one could hope to find at a festival: qigong, Buddhist meditation, an intro talk for Transcendental Meditation, Tantric yoga. At the far side of Air there is a large, rectangular tent full of people doing the tree pose, and here, next to where Anna stands, is a huge and colourful bender, housing a Kundalini Yoga workshop.

"*Ong Namo Guru Dev Namo...*" the people in this tent are chanting.

Those in this workshop know that this mantra is about connecting to the awareness of the Higher Self.

Ong Namo Guru Dev Namo....

Ong Namo Guru Dev Namo....

Even though she doesn't understand the Sanskrit words, the chant still weaves its way through Anna, bringing her a sense of calm. She listens for a few moments before deciding that she doesn't really belong here with all these people who look so peaceful. On her way out of Air, she passes a large workshop space, made out of another huge and colourful patchwork bender. She's about to pass it by, but something makes her stop and look again. On the chalk board outside the bender are the words: *Connecting with Your Divine Centre.*

Anna peers tentatively into the space, which is surprisingly spacious inside and is already quite full of participants.

"We're just about to start if you'd like to join us."

Anna turns to see a gentle-looking Japanese woman with very kind, deep brown eyes standing beside her. The woman is clear-faced and seems quite young to Anna, but the smile lines at her eyes indicate someone older. The woman is shorter than her, slightly built and dressed very simply. Immediately, Anna feels drawn to the kindness and warmth radiating from this person.

This is for you, something in Anna seems to say. At the thought of taking the workshop, a flutter of excitement and energy lifts through her. Surprised, she finds herself nodding back to the woman. *Why not?* she thinks. She has no other plans, and it could be interesting. "Thank you."

The woman grins at Anna brightly and then steps back into the tent, making her way up to the front. She sits perfectly still, with her spine absolutely straight, reminding Anna of a little female Buddha waiting patiently for everyone else to settle themselves.

Stepping inside, Anna observes the other participants around her. Many have brought things to sit on and are making themselves comfortable in a similar cross-legged position to the woman at the front. Anna finds an empty space at the back, so that if the workshop gets too strange she can discreetly make her way out. She does her best to get into a comfortable position on the mat, but the ground feels hard.

"Here's an extra cushion if you like." The male voice sounds familiar. Anna looks up and sees a face she recognises. *But from where?* Then it comes to her. This is the same softly-spoken man who had been sitting beside her around the fire in the Big Tipi the other night, who had smiled so warmly at her. His eyes seem to be just as bright today, and he is wearing the same t-shirt he wore that night, with the circle of fire on it. She can see the words '*Awakening the Dreamer*' which are written in faded letters across the bottom. *Cedar's band!*

"Oh! Thank you." Anna smiles. "That would be great." She isn't sure whether or not to mention the other night, or whether he even recognises her.

Accepting the cushion, she positions it under her bottom. The man kneels beside her, as if he wants to say something to her. He seems nice, but Anna is not sure if she wants him to sit with her. It is the same feeling that has come up so many times for Anna – the idea that when a man is friendly, it means he wants something. But of course, she reminds herself, she had met so many kind men and women at this festival and they had not wanted anything from her. They had genuinely been offering something.

"I remember you from the tipi the other night," he says.

"Yes," Anna nods. "I recognised your shirt." She feels silly for saying this, because it is his bright eyes that she recognises too, and that easy, open smile which he is giving her now.

"I'm Paul," he holds out his hand to her.

"Anna." She returns the handshake and is glad to find it warm but not sweaty. These hands again feel different from other hands she's met at the festival. They are soft hands for a man, softer than Ali's even. The fingers are long and slender.

"Pleased to meet you properly, Anna," Paul says. "And by the way, if you don't mind me saying, the best way to sit with the pillow is like this..." He shows her the way his cushion is folded so that it lifts the base of his spine. "If you place it under your sitting bone and elevate the base of the spine, your back will have more support."

"Oh, thanks," Anna says, adjusting hers similarly. "You're right. That does feel a lot better."

"I hope you enjoy the workshop," he says, rising. "I'd be happy to answer any questions afterwards if you have any."

Why? Why would I ask you questions? Anna wonders. *That's a little presumptuous.*

She feels somewhat relieved when he steps away and doesn't attempt to sit beside her after all. But now she experiences a wave of foolishness for her thoughts, because she sees that he is not only just not sitting beside her, he's not sitting beside any of the other workshop participants either. He is seating himself cross-legged on a second cushion up at the front of the dome, next to the lovely Japanese woman.

He's leading the workshop? Anna gasps to herself. *This softly spoken man?* Anna never would have pegged Paul for the kind of person who would sit up at the front of the room and have something important to say. She is more intrigued by him now.

It is true that self-confidence has been one of Paul's challenges in life, but after he discovered the teachings which he is about to share today, he found a way to be centred and to feel the core of strength within him, to shift himself from a state of fear to a state of lovingness. In this way, he is able to stand up in front of people – something he never could have done even two years ago.

Anna can feel Paul's presence from where she sits. She finds it strange – he is such a different kind of man from Arthur who had such a strong physical presence, but something about the way he's standing there feels the same.

"Welcome," Paul says, holding his hands in prayer position at his heart and smiling brightly to everyone. Anna is surprised by the quality of his voice. It's intrinsically soft, yet somehow it has enough strength to carry right across the room.

"Thank you all for being here today. My name is Paul, and this is my partner Luwen."

His partner? Now Anna sees. This is a couple who have come to teach a workshop together. Paul was clearly not hitting on her. He was only trying to help.

Luwen nods her head and smiles, her hands in prayer position also.

"Together we're going to share with you what we know about connecting with your divine centre," Paul explains. "We both come from slightly different yet complementary backgrounds. First I would like to share a little of my story – how I came to be here with you today. Two years ago, I had a dream. It showed me that there are three stages when it comes to working with energy.

The first stage is when we're unaware of our energy and how we use it, and how the energy of those around us affects us. In this stage, we draw on the energy of others, and unconsciously allow others to draw on our energy. We can be easily swayed and affected by the vibrations of energy that move around us."

Something tugs inside Anna, a vague awareness that this is where she stands.

"The second stage," Paul continues, "is when we become self-sufficient with our energy. We learn to connect to our own source, and are able to raise and sustain our own energy, therefore maintaining our own energetic vibration in whatever situation we find ourselves in. In this state, we can consciously work with energy, affecting the vibrational energy fields around us in a positive way.

"I was told in my dream that I had reached the second stage. I was able to increase energy in myself, maintain my energy and also benefit the energy fields of those around me in a positive way. But the main guidance from the dream was this: It was time for me to move onto the third stage. The third stage is where we share what we have learned with others. We embody that wisdom and we help others to learn how they can sustain and raise their own energy and in turn share that positive energy with others. In this way, we can create an energetic ripple effect which spreads throughout the world. And this is why I am here now, offering this workshop to you. I never thought I would stand up in front of people and offer workshops, but here I am.

"I am fortunate that Lu is not just my partner in life, but also a gifted teacher. She has been working with energy for more than twenty years. Together we developed this workshop to try and give you the best of both of our backgrounds. Over to you Lu."

Luwen stands. Her presence is every bit as strong as Paul's, and in some ways stronger, even though she is much shorter and more slightly built than he.

"This workshop is about connecting with our divine centre, in my tradition what we call 'the Hara'. Hara is a Japanese word, which translated literally means, 'the centre'. It is also said to mean 'sea of energy'. In the Taoist tradition that Paul follows, this same centre is referred to as the *Lower Tantien*. So you may hear these terms used interchangeably throughout the workshop; they mean the same thing. The Hara is our centre, both energetic and physical. It is located 2 to 3 inches below the navel, or three finger widths below the navel, just inside our body. It is the same point that is referred to in Kundalini Yoga as *The Navel Point*. According to the founder of Kundalini Yoga, Yogi Bhajan, this is the place where the 72,000 nadis, or energy pathways that run through the body begin. When we create a strong Hara – in other words, making our cup strong, as they say in qigong – we increase chi and create health and wellbeing in our body."

Chi. There's that word again. Anna wonders what it really is.

"Chi is lifeforce," Luwen continues, her dark eyes bright across the room. "Chi has been described as the activating energy of the universe. It is an electrical type of energy animating and flowing through everything. It both creates our body, and also determines the health of the body. Chi is the essential life force not only of our bodies, but of the body of the Earth below us, and also the bodies of the planets, the sun and the stars above. Chi energy is what brings us vitality and strength. It flows through us in many ways. The more chi in our bodies, the healthier and happier we are. Chi is what flows through the hands of healers."

Like Ali. Like Moon. Like Johannes, Anna thinks.

"Chi flows through us, and through all living things on earth. The Hara is the centre of our energy, and when we are connected with this centre, chi builds in our body and flows through us and through all our actions in the world. It brings us calm and balance. It literally centres us."

Anna lifts her hand to her abdomen as Luwen is doing, wondering if there really could be such a wondrous thing inside of her, a centre that could do all of that.

"Children naturally come from the Hara," Luwen explains. "They are born centered, connected to the world around them. When we were first born, we were this way too, once. But for many of us in the Western world, when we developed our minds, we lost touch with this centre. We began to live our lives by the dictates of our minds, rather than by the intuitive, centered body knowing that comes from the Hara. Many indigenous cultures around the world are more connected with this centre, living in balance with the world around them. In the Western world, most of us have forgotten how to do this. But the good news is that we can easily bring ourselves back to centre through simple meditation practices, some of which we will share with you shortly. Before we do that, Paul will explain to you about some different forms of chi we will be referring to."

Paul turns his attention to the group, smiling. "According to the Taoists, we are given a reserve of chi at birth – what is called '*Original Chi*'. As we go through life, this reserve can become depleted, and so we find ways to replenish our chi and bring more chi to flow through our bodies from the world around us. I work a lot with Earth Energy. You can draw this chi up from the earth and it will ground you and give you energy. In fact, we are all doing this now by sitting directly on the earth. We are allowing her energy to flow into us, to balance us."

Anna thinks of walking barefoot on the hill with Cedar and how good that had felt. Her attention shifts to the ground below her, to where her feet are resting. She removes her sandals and places them beside her, wiggling her toes on the mat, feeling the strands of grass poking through from underneath.

"Gaia, or Pachamama – our Earth – she is conscious," Paul tells them. "She is a being of love. She is offering her body to us, giving us nourishment. And when we ask, her energy will flow into us, and can heal us."

Anna stares at Paul. This really does sound like a wild fantasy, something she would have imagined in her games as a child. *The Earth a living being? With consciousness?* And yet as Paul speaks these words, there is a palpable wave of energy moving through Anna's body, as if she had always known this. She wants to believe him, to believe in a world where even the Earth below her feet is something that can hear you, and respond.

"Another form of chi I would like to speak about is what some call '*Heavenly Chi*' or '*Cosmic Chi*'. This is chi drawn from the celestial bodies like the Moon, the Sun and other planets and stars beyond our solar system. You might think this is fanciful thinking, but you truly can breathe in the energy of the sun and the stars. They have an energetic resonance – a consciousness. Many aboriginal cultures I have come across speak about a Father Sun. Just as they see the Earth as a conscious, sentient being, so too the Sun. It may be hard for us to grasp, but all stars and planets have consciousness. Our sun is not just a ball of fire. It is conscious. Fire itself is conscious. In fact, all the elements are."

Really? This almost seems too much for Anna to believe, except that Paul is speaking about these things in such an earnest way that she can't help wanting to believe him. And there is a a lifting of excitement inside her, as if this is only the beginning of what she might discover about the true nature of reality.

"Really, though," Paul continues, "as we speak about different forms of chi, of course, at the deepest most fundamental level, all energy is one. There is no real separation between any kind of lifeforce energy, but as we work with it as human beings, it can be useful to recognise the different forms energy can take."

The shit bucket needs emptying. Cedar accepts this as a necessary part of his Glastonbury routine. It means not having to regularly visit the portaloos or pit latrines, but it does mean a hot trek with a sloshing bucket full of his own excrement across the fields to the African Pit Toilets every two days. Today he is finding it harder to be Zen about this particular job.

He didn't sleep well last night. He had lain awake, his body protesting his celibacy. He had refused to give himself release, wanting to save that energy for the gig the next day. So in the end he had gotten up and walked around. His feet had lead him through the twilight of the Glastonbury night to visit the dragon.

As he joins the queue at the African Pit toilets, Cedar's eyes move to the gap in the hedge at the far end of King's Meadow, and recalls how he had sat in the early morning hours with the great stone creature. He had taken off his shoes and approached the eye of the dragon. *Vision*, he'd thought, as he placed his open hand against the red crystal.

For a while he had just stood there, listening and breathing. He had felt himself growing more and more still. The sounds all around him had become like his own breath. He felt how the energy of the earth below him was flowing through this stone where he held his hand, and that if the earth was alive, so was that stone against his hand. He had stayed there a long time.

Something had occurred to Cedar just before the sky had begun to lighten with the coming dawn. It was about the lines of energy running through the earth – Pachamama's own meridian pathways – and how some people call these dragon lines. How the very line which runs right through the centre of Glastonbury Tor and runs up through Avebury to Suffolk and around the world is known by the Australian aborigines as *The Rainbow Serpent*.

His eyes had widened as he'd remembered being told once that the festival site itself had been consciously placed directly above this energy line, with the Pyramid Stage standing at the very centre of it all. That very line, The Rainbow Serpent, could even be running through this very spot. *Had the people who'd made the dragon known this?*

Yes, he'd surmised. *They must have known.*

Then he had remembered what he often did when visiting the dragon – that dragon energy is also that energy which rises like the serpent up the spine, the energy he had begun to experience more strongly over the past year – *Kundalini*. Placing his awareness on that energy, he had felt the stirrings of the dragon again within himself.

"Any questions so far?" Paul asks.

A woman up near the front raises her hand.

"Yes?"

"What about Kundalini energy? Where does that fit in with all this?"

Paul nods. "We won't be working with Kundalini here, but it's a good question, and relevant. Lu, can I hand this one to you?"

"Of course. Kundalini energy is that spiritual energy which for most people in the world at this time, lies dormant at the base of the spine. It is a coiled serpent energy, and when awakened it travels up the central energy pathway – *the Sushumna* – up through one or all the chakras, until ultimately it rises up through the crown and brings samadhi or nirvana. When this happens it is called *Kundalini-Shakti*."

Kundalini? Anna wonders. *Shakti?* She hasn't heard these terms before.

"You've felt it?" The woman, Heather, asks.

Lu nods. "Yes, occasionally. I found it began to awaken on its own as I grew more adept at working with the subtle energies of the chakras and prana. But we do not deliberately encourage people to try and awaken it, especially on their own. Kundalini-Shakti will naturally happen when a person is energetically ready. If you are interested in working with Kundalini, please ensure you work with a qualified practitioner, because when you are working with this kind of energy – though it can be incredibly powerful and life transforming – without guidance, it can, in some cases, be dangerous."

"How?" Heather asks. "I mean, isn't spiritual energy good?"

"For some people, if too much generates in the head and they don't know how to ground the energy, it can create things like hallucinations, dizziness or a feeling of being spaced-out. Sometimes it can lead to depression or mental illness. Some people lose their connection with the physical and aren't able to function properly. Also these kinds of energy can overload the meridian system if the system is not prepared for it. Like a short circuit."

"I know a story of a woman," Paul explains, "...a friend of mine, who started to have experiences of kundalini awakening, but she was not grounding herself properly and she got very carried away with it all, with these experiences of divine, ecstatic love and feeling herself part of everything. She alternated for a while between these states of extreme bliss and states of deep depression, until finally it became too much for her, and she realised that she needed to focus her attention on her physical body, to give herself nourishment physically. She realised that being grounded and earthed in this physical reality is essential for any spiritual activity."

Lu nods. "So this is why being grounded when working with energy is extremely important. Working with the Hara itself is inherently grounding. So there is not a danger that we will become disconnected from physical reality through breathing into our centre. It brings us more presence, more body awareness. It is possible when raising chi energy in your Hara that you may feel an excess of chi. If this feels uncomfortable, physical-energetic movements such as qigong or yoga can be extremely helpful. You can also use your mind to direct the energy flow back into the Earth. But generally, we find that increased chi in the Hara brings us wellbeing, presence, increased physical energy and vitality. Are there any other questions?"

"Is the Hara a chakra?" a red-haired man named Brock asks.

Lu smiles. "Good question. Paul will you answer this?"

"Of course. Yes and No. It depends which tradition you are speaking of. It is my feeling that the chakra system as described in Yogic philopsphy and the Tantiens as explained in Taoist teachings are actually separate energy systems, but they are working intimately together. It is said that the Tantiens are major energetic storage mechanisms, whereas the chakras are energetic vortices, which are not about storing energy so much as about giving out or drawing in energy."

"But I'm still confused," Brock says. "In Kundalini Yoga, they speak of the Navel Point, which I understand is located exactly where the Hara, or Lower Tantien is located. Yet they say it is a chakra."

"They do," Paul agrees. "The energy systems in the body are complex and multi-layered, all working together in harmony. It is difficult really to separate them out and say that they each do an independent job or are even separate things. It is all working together. What I do feel clear about is that when we are working with the Navel Point, we are also working with the Lower Tantien. As we mentioned before, Yogi Bhajan teaches that this is the place where the 72,000 nadis, or energy pathways originate, radiating out throughout the whole body to the hands and feet, as well as through the crown. Lu and I work with this idea a lot, about how our energetic centre connects with every part of our physical and energetic bodies."

A white-haired woman named Elizabeth who sits near Anna lifts her hand. "Excuse me, but I'm relatively new to the idea of chakras. Would it be possible to explain them?"

Lu nods. "Of course. Would everyone like an overview of the chakra system?"

There are various murmurs of agreement throughout the space.

Thank you, Anna thinks, grateful. She doesn't really know what chakras are either, but she recalls the way both Cedar and Johannes had spoken of a subtle heart, and how she had begun to feel something there at the centre of her chest – a new warmth. *Perhaps this is a chakra?*

"As Paul mentioned before, chakras are energetic vortices." Lu's eyes seem to alight with fire as she speaks about these things. "The word 'chakra' literally means 'wheel' or 'vortex'. Chakras are swirling energy centers which are part of our subtle energy bodies. They are a bridge between these more subtle bodies and our physical body, bringing in chi energy and giving out chi energy. There are numerous chakras in our bodies, especially if you count the ends of the meridians as chakras, which some people do. And there are also those on the fingers and in the centre of the palms. In the tradition I follow there are seven main chakras, which run up from the base of the spine, from your tailbone to the crown of your head. They open on the front and the back – except for two. The first of those is the Root, or Base Chakra."

Lu's two hands hover over her pelvic area. "This chakra is about connection with the earth – physicality, sexuality, groundedness. It is connected with the point in the area around the base of the spine. The Root Chakra opens downwards – a great spinning vortex at the base of our spine – which connects us to the earth below. When this chakra is in balance, we literally feel rooted, safe and happy in our bodies."

Lu moves her hands up to rest just below her navel. "The next chakra, which opens on the front and back, is called the Sacral Chakra. It can can also be called the Womb Chakra in women or the Spleen Chakra in men. This chakra is about creativity, sexuality and nurturing. It is where we once drew our nourishment from our mothers when we were in her womb. When this chakra is in balance, we feel nurtured and nurturing and creative. We also feel centred because the Hara also resides here, within the sphere of the Second Chakra." Lu holds her hands here for a moment, allowing her words to settle in before laying her palms on the place just below her ribs.

"Above the Sacral Chakra is the Solar Plexus Chakra, which is about action, personal power and the will of the individual consciousness. It is also about joy and radiance. Some people call this the Sunlight Chakra. It is about energy in the world, action and will. When this chakra is in balance, our will becomes connected with a greater will, a deeper, more connected body and heart knowing."

Lu moves her hands now up to the place at the centre of her chest, where Anna had been feeling her subtle heart. "This is the Heart Chakra."

Anna places both her hands over this spot. *The Heart Chakra.* It's true then; this heart she has been feeling is, in fact, a chakra.

"The Heart Chakra is about unconditional love," Lu explains. "This is the love centre. It is the point where the three lower chakras and the three higher chakras intersect. This is the meeting place between the physical world and the subtle worlds, some might call the *divine worlds*. It is through the heart that we may access these higher levels of consciousness and bring them into the physical world. The Heart Chakra corresponds to the Middle Tantien in Taoist teachings. Because of this, with the heart we have both the capacity to raise and store energy and also to give out and receive it."

Lu moves her hands up to her throat. "This is the Throat Chakra. It is about communication and creative expression. It is the flowing of who we are expressed in the world. It is our authentic truth, our voice. When we express ourselves creatively while maintaining our connection to the Hara centre then all that we express will have authenticity and truth. It will be connected."

Anna lifts her hands to her own throat. *Creative expression. Authentic truth.* She thinks about how it has been so hard in her life to speak her own truth, but that for the first time yesterday she had been able to be honest with Shari and Eden about how she felt, and it had given her so much energy. This morning she had not spoken her truth with Damien, and it had resulted in a massive loss of energy. *In truth there is liberation.*

"This is the Third Eye Chakra," Lu says, touching the spot at the centre of her forehead between the eyebrows. "It is about inner sight and intuition. It is literally an energetic third eye which enables us to see more deeply and more intuitively. This is why we see people wearing a bindi in this spot. It is a reminder of this inner sight, of the vision of the Higher Self."

In her mind's eye, Anna sees Maddy's blue bindi and the red dot between the eyes of the Indian woman whose painting smiles down on everyone at Pacha Mama Cafe.

"The Third Eye is also connected with the Upper Tantien, which is located in the same area," Lu explains.

She lifts her hands now so that they hover just at the crown of her head. "The Upper Tantien is also connected with the Crown Chakra. The Crown Chakra is about pure consciousness and connection with our spiritual selves. Like the Root Chakra, the Crown Chakra does does not open to the front and back; it actually opens straight upwards, connecting us to the heavenly energies, to Heavenly Chi. We may work with this chakra only when we are fully grounded through the Root Chakra, fully connected with the Earth beneath our feet. Which brings us neatly to the first of our meditation visualisation practices – grounding."

Cedar steps out from the shower at Lost Horizon, feeling much better. As can happen when you try and empty a full bucket of excrement into a narrow hole in a concrete latrine floor, it can become rather messy, especially when you get splashback. The toilets function well for single use, but they are not really designed for two days worth to be dropped all in one go. That's why Cedar had worn his wellies; it's the only time he ever uses them at a festival. Standing here beneath the oak in the sauna gardens, he closes his eyes and enjoys the feel of the breeze against his wet skin and the damp grass beneath the soles of his feet.

This is when he opens his eyes and sees them. Moon and Maddy are sitting together on the grass at the far end of the garden, unclothed as usual. But this time something is different. They are facing one another in a way that suggests intimacy, as if the world contains them alone. They've always been close, but there is something new in Moon's gaze – something Cedar recognises. Moon had looked at him often that way in the past... after they had made love. His eyes widen as he understands. *Ahhh. Well. So that's how it is.* He had known Maddy's sexual preference for women, but he had not foreseen that her friendship with Moon would develop in that way. Moon is moving on, and Cedar is happy for her. Even so, a hint of grief contracts his body at the thought. *Yes, there is still some letting go to do.*

Suddenly aware he is there, Moon lifts her gaze towards him and their eyes meet. Cedar smiles and nods. Moon nods too, her face serious. Both women are watching him.

I bless you both, he thinks, and he means it. He doesn't want to disturb them and is about to go, but Moon gently squeezes Maddy's hand and rises, moving across the grass towards him. She reminds him not so much of a wolf today, but more like a panther, supple and cat-like as she approaches.

Stopping a few feet away, she regards him. So, *does this change anything?* her eyes seem to ask him.

We are still soulmates, Cedar offers the thought to her, unspoken. *And I still love you. I always will, wherever our paths lead us.*

"All well for tonight?" Moon asks.

"All well."

"Good." She offers him a smile now.

They both know that this gig is not going to be like anything they've done before.

"Let's begin by standing up and moving our bodies around," Paul instructs them. "If you haven't got bare feet already, I suggest you remove your shoes now."

Anna is grateful for the movement. Her legs are already going numb. She wanders barefoot over to the grassy bits around the edge of the tent, touching the grass with her toes.

"Where you are standing, feel the soles of your feet connected to the ground below you. This is your mother – Pacha Mama, Gaia. She nourishes you. She gave birth to all of us. We are not separate from this Earth. We are part of her. As you touch the Earth with your feet, you are touching the mother that gave birth to all of us."

For Anna, the idea of Mother has had its challenges. While things had been fairly easy with her father, with her mother has not always been the case. At times her mother could be nurturing, and she had always known her mother loved her, but there was also always a sense that she wasn't living up to something that she should be, that she had failed in some way. And now Paul is asking her to treat this Earth below her feet like a mother?

But there is a part of Anna – this deeper self she is beginning to feel – that knows what Paul means. She'd felt a sense of it up on the hill with Cedar of touching something wholesome, of true nourishment.

"I find it works best to stand comfortably, with knees slightly bent – in a qigong pose, if you will." Paul demonstrates. "Allow your spine to straighten, like there is a cord is running up through it. This helps the energy pathways to flow more easily."

Anna does her best to imitate Paul's stance. In this position, she is reminded of how good it had felt when Ali had held her back straight. *Joined up.*

"Now," Paul explains, "we can direct energy by the use of two things: breath and thought or intent. Breath is Spirit; the word 'Spirit' literally comes from *'spire'* – to *breathe*. With our breath, in the physical body we are bringing in oxygen, but for the subtler bodies, the breath is drawing in chi. We can assist this process through using the power of our thoughts. Many of us think of our thoughts as having no substance, but they do. They are a subtle form of energy that has an instant affect on the subtle energy bodies. So in this way, you can actually breathe chi energy into your body through using your thoughts to visualise where you want it to go."

Really? Anna finds this amazing. *Thoughts have substance? Thoughts are just thoughts, aren't they?* But she is beginning to suspect now that reality is of a completely different order than she'd previously believed – utterly more meaningful and mysterious. She remembers something Cedar said on the hill – *We are creating all of this with our thoughts and imaginations. The boundaries between what is real, and what's so-called imaginary are not what most people think.*

"So, take a deep breath now, deep into your belly, and on the outbreath, breathe your energetic roots down into the Earth. Imagine you are a tree, with roots extending deep into the ground through the soles of your feet. With every outbreath, see them growing deeper and deeper. Go as deep as you feel to go. Some people like to imagine their roots extending all the way to the fiery centre of the

Earth. Some like to extend their roots just a few feet down, until they feel that still, calm place in the soil and rock layers just beneath us. Do what works for you."

So Anna breathes into her belly, feeling grateful that Moon has already taught her how to do this. With the outbreath she tries to imagine these roots Paul is speaking of growing out from her feet, but can't really feel anything.

Paul gives them all a knowing look. "If you can't feel anything tangible at first, don't worry. Just keep seeing it in your mind. What you imagine in your mind over time will eventually become a real sensation you can feel. This is because your thoughts are affecting your subtle bodies and our subtle bodies are completely interconnected with the physical body. Thought energy collects together and builds... the more you think a certain thought or collection of thoughts, the more that manifests in the physical world – whether inside or outside of your body."

Extraordinary, Anna shakes her head. Really wanting to feel something, she continues to imagine roots growing from the soles of her feet, twisting and diving down below her. Still nothing. But persevering, there is just a hint of something now. *Yes, I can feel it!* She has a sense of the cool of the ground below her. It feels solid and strong.

"And when you have reached that place you feel is deep enough, when you feel that connection to Earth, you can draw this nourishing energy up through your roots. When I do this, I always thank Mother Earth for her energy. For as we said before, Pacha Mama is a conscious, sentient being. You can speak to Mother Earth and she will hear you, because she is alive and she is part of you."

Can you really hear me? Anna wonders, her awareness in those roots, listening below her to what she had always imagined was just soil and rock, without any conscious awareness. But since being here this weekend, everything seems different. *Could there really be someone there? A great being holding all of this? Being a mother to everyone and everything?* It feels an awesome idea to Anna, and yet there is a sense of a deep pulsing response, a warmth below her feet.

Thank you Mother Earth, Anna whispers softly, *for... your energy*. She waits for a moment, and feels it again – a definite sense of a something – a deep, pulsing warmth, tingling in the soles of her feet.

"Now, in your mind's eye," Paul instructs, "see a light – I use gold, but you can use whatever colour comes to you most naturally – see this light, rising like a warm nourishing sap up through your roots, up through the soles of your feet, up through your body which is like the trunk of the tree and out through your arms and hands and fingers and the top of your head, which are like the branches of the tree. You are a fountain of living light, and this light is coming from deep in the Earth, from the deep nourishing energy of the Mother."

As Anna imagines this light rising up through her like golden sap, it feels somehow as if this pulsing warmth truly is rising up through her body. *Oh!* And now the tingling is not just in her feet; she can feel it in the palms of her hands, and the sensation is growing.

"Some of you may feel your palms start to tingle," Paul says. "This is the energy moving through you."

Anna imagines now that her veins are filled with this sap-light, and it is pouring through her and running out her hands and fingers, like the branches of a tree. For some reason the image of the rainbow girl she'd met at the Wishing Well comes into her mind again. Anna feels like a child now herself, with a growing sense that magic truly is possible, that there really could be magic all around her.

"That was interesting." Moon sits back down on the grass in front of Maddy, watching Cedar's figure as it disappears back out into the Tipi Field. A small smile curls at her lips. "He knows."

Maddy nods. "Is that so bad?"

Moon looks up to see the warmth in Maddy's green eyes, and the dimples brought out by her smile. She knows that as unexpected as this all is, and while it still doesn't make sense to that part of her that dreamed of conceiving a child with a man, that this is good. It feels wholesome.

"Not so bad," Moon says. "Good, in fact. Very good." Her body hasn't felt this strong and whole and full of energy for a long time. There is a freedom in her heart, and each time she feels the warmth there in the centre of her chest, it makes her want to sing out loud for the joy of it.

This is being in love, she realises. And it's not just being in love with Maddy, it's a love which seems to reach beyond that and encompass the earth below her and the sky above and the sunlight that seems to shine out from right inside her.

"We will do a meditation now which will help us to connect with this energetic centre within us, our Hara, the Lower Tantien," Lu explains. "We draw much of this from Zazen Buddhist Meditation practices."

"With some adaptations of our own," Paul adds.

"You may do this lying down," Lu tells them, "or standing or sitting comfortably. Ensure you are in a position where your diaphragm has free flowing movement."

Anna chooses to remain sitting. She is feeling grateful for both the cushion and for Paul's suggestion of how to sit with it.

"Now, become consciously aware of your breathing, of the inbreath and the out-breath. Do not try and force it, just observe," Lu instructs. "Allow your body to breathe into your belly with the diaphragm breath, this natural breath that we knew how to do as infants. This deeper breath helps us connect with our centre. If anyone finds they are having trouble with abdominal breathing, put your hand up and Paul or I will come around and see you."

Lu and Paul step quietly around the space, observing people as they breathe, helping where necessary. Anna half-expects one of those being helped will burst into tears as she had done with Moon, but it doesn't happen. Grateful for Moon's help with her own breathing, she reminds herself again to bring the breath deeper.

"With each outbreath, imagine you are letting go of whatever no longer serves you," Lu says, passing by Anna. "Let go of any tension you are holding in your body."

Anna feels the holding in her shoulders again and lets them drop, returning again to the deeper breath.

"Now, when you are ready, close your eyes," Lu says, joining Paul at the front. "Continue breathing consciously, observing your breath as it flows in and out. If any thoughts come, or you drift away from the awareness of the breath, just gently bring your awareness back to the breath, to the slow, deep breath in and out. Again, don't force the breath, just allow your body to breathe, gently and naturally, the way it was meant to breathe."

Eyes closed, Anna can hear people breathing all around her. She observes her own breath, the new, more animal feeling of her body breathing this way.

"When you feel that you are comfortable in this breath," Lu continues, "bring your awareness to this centre point, three finger-widths below your navel and just inside your body. This is the Hara. Place your hand there now, and feel your breath drawing right into this place and expanding in all directions. Feel the rise and fall of your hand as you breathe."

Anna places her hand just below her belly button and attempts to make her breath go to this place. It takes focus, but she does manage to do it with some success.

"Again, don't force it," Lu says softly. "Just allow it to go there. This is where the natural diaphragm breath goes. It is about bringing our awareness to this point, and connecting it to the breath. As you are breathing, feel a sense of gratitude, of thankfulness, for this energy you are bringing into your body."

Lu observes them breathing for a minute and then lifts a Tibetan prayer bell from the ground beside her, ringing it gently. "Now, you may slowly open your eyes." She casts her eyes across the group. "Were people able to feel a sense of this centre in your belly?"

Some are nodding.

Not sure, Anna thinks. *Maybe.*

"As we breathe in," Paul explains, "we are breathing in chi – from the earth, from the air, from the sun, from the natural world around us. Imagine that you are breathing in this light, the energy of love that permeates all things. As you breathe in this light, see it entering you and going deep into your core, filling this centre with glowing light, like a giant shining sun. When I am consciously breathing in this way, with each breath in I am thinking 'Thank you'. This can really change how you feel about breathing. You are breathing in gratitude. With each breath in, we feel this sense of wellbeing increase, we see the light at our centre glowing brighter and brighter. And with each outbreath, you can give back this love to the world around you."

You can give this love back to the world around you. The words send a shiver through Anna's body, as if meant for her.

"We're going to try something now," Paul says. "To begin with, choose some part of your body, let's say your arm. Lift it up in front of you as you normally would and see how that feels. Hold it up until you feel like putting it down. You can even move it around if you like."

Anna lifts her right arm in front of her and wiggles her fingers a little. It's not long before the movement feels boring and a little tiring so she drops her arm back down.

"Okay," Paul instructs, "now I would like you to imagine there are golden threads connecting all of your fingers and the palm of your hand to this core of light at your centre. Now when you move this same hand again, keep your awareness in your Lower Tantien, and feel the movement beginning there, travelling down these golden threads which have their culmination in the movement of your hand."

So Anna breathes into her belly and tries to see the sun shining there, and the golden threads extending to her fingers. *Okay, start the movement from my centre. And now as she moves her arm... Oh! That does feel different!* It feels fluid, and suddenly quite exciting, as if this movement is the only thing there is. She watches her fingers, each one the end of a golden thread, waving in front of her.

"How was that experience? Does anyone want to share how it was for them?" Paul asks.

"Kind of trippy," a man named Miles speaks up from the back.

Laughter erupts from various points in the room. Paul chuckles. "I know what you mean. It might be surprising to some, but in my experience the kinds of highs you get from working with energy are far more satisfying and longer lasting than any drug."

As the laughter quiets, Brock lifts his hand again. "It made me move slower and it made me want to keep moving my hand, whereas the first time I found it boring."

Paul nods. "Anyone else?"

"I felt more energy in the movement," Heather joins in. "It felt really joyful. It wasn't just a hand movement. It felt like it was a meditation."

"That's how it can be," Paul agrees. "Any time you remember, you can turn any action, any activity you are doing into a meditation, coming from the centre, from the Tantien in our belly. Then that action becomes authentic and filled with energy."

"As you build energy in your Hara – drawing it in from the earth and the world around you – " Lu explains, "you can use your thoughts to direct this energy to your chakras, and since the chakras also act as energy output mechanisms they are capable of directing energy out of the body to the world. In this way, we can consciously send it out through one or more chakras to people, plants or other living things or give it back to the Earth herself."

Anna tries to digest this. *Energy output mechanisms?*

"In our last meditation, we spoke about breathing in the love from the world around us into our centre, and on the outbreath giving back that love to the world. When we breathe out, we are using our thought and intent to see that light flowing out through our Heart Chakra. The chakras each have their own tint, to make a colour analogy. If you want to give out the energy of unconditional love, you direct chi through the Heart, and so it becomes Heart Energy."

Heart Energy! It is as if something jolts through Anna's body as the pieces fall together for her in a way she doesn't fully comprehend. When the man at the Chai Chi tent had said that they put love into their food, she had wondered what that meant. She had thought love was an intangible thing.

Love is the most important ingredient in anything...

But perhaps it is not so intangible. *Perhaps love is connected with Heart energy.* She feels that lift of affirmation inside her with a rush of energy through her body.

"I have been blessed to experience musicians who can do this," Paul says, and he smiles as his eyes flick momentarily to Anna, for they both know who he is referring to.

"Some musicians have learned to direct energy through the Heart Chakra as they play, so their music becomes infused with love, and this radiates out to all those who listen to it."

A tingle moves across Anna's skin again. *Maybe this does have something to do with me after all...* Suddenly she knows with absolute certainty that this is what Nina Marshall was doing in her gig. This is why the audience had responded the way they had.

"And this is what Lu and I strive to do here in this workshop with you," Paul explains. "Standing here on stage right now, I am breathing into my belly Tantien, seeing the light at my centre expanding, and on the outbreath I am sending out that light through my Heart Chakra to all of you. In this way, I am not closed down by fear, which in the past I always was. I used to get terrible stage fright. The thought of giving a talk would make me feel physically sick. But when I learned these techniques for bringing myself into a vibration of love through giving Heart Energy, that all changed. When you are in the vibration of love, there is no place for fear."

Anna's eyes widen again. *This makes so much sense now. I've always been afraid on stage.* She can see it now. *No wonder it never worked...*

"Does anyone have any other questions?" Paul asks.

Brock lifts his hand again. "So, let me get this straight – Heart Energy is chi that flows from the heart, and Earth Energy is chi that flows to us from the earth, and Cosmic Energy is chi that flows to us from the sun and the stars and other planets?"

"That's right."

"So where does Original Chi come from? Is this generated in the Hara?"

Paul shakes his head. "This is chi energy we are born with, and it is not new; it is part of the already existing universe. We are made of the same stuff as the stars. Original Chi is connected to everything in the cosmos; we perceive it and experience it as being a reserve within us as an individual at birth, but it is part of the universe's energy. Our centre is the centre of the universe. Each of us has a universe within our belly. This is where it all begins."

This is where it begins. Anna has images of stars and planets and galaxies expanding from her in all directions. *How could it be?*

"Each of us are the beginning of the universe?" Brock asks. "How is that possible? Isn't there only one centre of the universe? God knows where that is."

Paul smiles. "There is only one centre, and we are all part of it. It's all infinitely connected. My centre is your centre. Your individual awareness perceives the centre within you, inside your physical and energetic being, but your centre and my centre all come from the same place."

Anna stares at Paul, bewildered. It doesn't make any sense to her mind.

"The mind is incapable of comprehending infinity," Paul says, as if hearing Anna's thoughts. "But you can experience it. For when you connect to that which is infinite in yourself, you connect with the infinite in everything. The rational mind can never know what the heart knows. Through the consciousness of the heart, we can feel our connection to one another and the world around us. Through the heart we can understand that our centre is not separate from the centre of the person next to us."

They are silent for a moment, contemplating this. Anna lets go of trying to understand.

Cedar sits in the sun in front of his tipi, wearing only his sarong, feeling the pleasing heat of the sun. It's good to be clean – at least physically. Emotionally, it is not so simple. He brings his awareness to his breathing, catching the scent of woodsmoke from the central fire riding on the air. He has a vague recollection that Paul and Lu are running their Hara workshop right now. He had thought he might go there and support Paul energetically – as Paul had done for him the other night – but with everything that has happened, he had forgotten.

Still, I can send some energy from here.

Cedar closes his eyes, and seeks to centre himself. He does his usual grounding practice and then in honour of Paul and Lu, decides to do the meditation practice Paul taught him.

It occurs to Cedar as he closes his eyes that he has been working so much in his Kundalini yoga practice with this chakra in his belly – the Navel Point. He's been doing a lot of *Breath of Fire*. He's also been working regularly with the Third Eye point in his meditations and yoga practice, and working a lot with the connection between the two.

But there are three centres, he reminds himself. Paul, who has been much more into qigong than Kundalini yoga speaks more in those terms. Cedar remembers how Paul often referred to the three Tantiens.

There are three, it comes to Cedar again. *Three. Of course!*

The Middle Tantien is the one he had been neglecting up until this weekend. He had felt it on the hill, as he gave energy to the tree and felt his heart expanding. *You are Love.* That had been the key that had opened everything up. He had been able to access that love again in the Big Tipi, when he had played his didgeridoo and the music had been deeper than ever before.

The Heart. He holds his hand over this place and feels the waves of emotion still moving through him. He witnesses a little contraction inside his solar plexus as he thinks of Moon. Then there are the confusion of feelings about Anna, and also his promise to the Beloved in his dream mixed with his body's desire, which seems to be making itself felt more urgently recently.

The Heart. It always has to come back to the Heart. Love transforms fear, he reminds himself. *Always. Love brings us into the present, where all is well.*

Cedar realises he is doing a lot of thinking about love, and not very much meditating with it. So *let's do something about it,* he tells himself, returning again to his breathing. It seems harder to be still today, harder to focus.

He breathes again into his Lower Tantien, until slowly he begins to feel that sunlight building in his centre. With each breath, he imagines the fire at his heart growing brighter. Into his mind's eye comes an image – unbidden – of his old friend Noela, and her particular form of healing magic.

I should find Noela. Cedar makes a note to himself to seek her out this afternoon. *After my meditation,* he reminds himself, returning again to the breath.

> "I'm gonna start right here
> Stop the war in my heart
> Stop the violence to myself
> I believe in love, I believe in love, I believe in love
> I believe in love, I believe in love, I believe in love
> As the strongest force there is
> As the strongest source that there is"

from the song, 'I Believe in Love', by Boe Huntress

"This is a gift we can give," Paul says. "It all comes together in this final meditation. We invite you to close your eyes. As we did before, let us observe the breath as it goes into the belly, naturally and gently allowing the body to breathe as it was meant to breathe. Now imagine as you breathe that you are breathing in the energy of love from the world around you. See the sunlight at your centre growing brighter, feel the energy building there. Again, don't force the breath. Just let it come naturally and observe it."

Anna feels her own forehead relax. It's becoming easier.

"As we did before, use your thought and intent to see this energy of sunlight flowing back to the world around you through your Heart Chakra. It is a giving back, a blessing. Sometimes when I do this, I begin to feel a sense of increasing warmth in my heart. With each breath in, we are fanning the flames of that fire, and it grows stronger."

The fire in the heart. Anna thinks of the little fire in her heart that at times had seemed to flare up and at times to be only embers, smouldering gently.

"Now," Paul continues, "at the climax of the inbreath, become aware of this fire burning in your heart, this great shining light, and feel it flowing forth, as a gift back to the world around you. Give it as a blessing to the others in this room."

The words of the Buddha come again into Anna's mind.

Loving kindness is freedom of the heart, it glows, it shines, it blazes forth.

"Choose someone or something now that you love," Paul instructs. "This way you will be able to feel the amplification of that love. You could try this another time with someone or something you find harder to love, but for now choose someone or something you already have strong feelings of love for. It could be something in nature. It could be a person or even a group of people. Or you could choose Mother Earth herself. When you ask yourself '*who do I love?*', what is the first image that comes to you?"

Who do I love? Anna wonders. It only takes a moment before Cedar's face flashes into her mind. *But what about Damien? Surely I love Damien too.* She feels a contraction in her body at the thought, as if she should be loyal and choose him, but she doesn't feel like sending energy to Damien right now. Besides, he had not been the first person that had come into her mind. With these thoughts, her breath has gone shallow again. Anna consciously brings it deeper again.

"When you have chosen this person or thing," Paul says, "ask that they receive whatever is in their highest good. In your mind, as you breathe in, see the light glowing at your Hara, and on the outbreath, see this light of love flowing out from your heart to whatever or whoever you are focusing your attention on. This is a warm, soft energy. Heart energy is chi energy which moves through the filter of the heart, which is about unconditional love. The Heart Chakra is our bridge between physical reality and spiritual reality. Through the heart incredible things are possible. Love is a power which is beyond anything, because ultimately love is all there is. By consciously working with love, you are working with the most powerful force in this universe. The reality is that there is no separation between you and the thing you are loving."

Cedar's face shines in Anna's mind again. She imagines this energy of love reaching him wherever he is.

Freedom of the heart, it comes to Anna. It feels so good to allow herself to love Cedar. She remembers now how she felt that night in the Big Tipi, when she had not needed anything from him. She had felt part of everything. Love had been inside her then, and love is inside her now, knowing there is no separation between her and the one she loves.

An image of Anna comes to into Cedar's mind so strongly that he opens his eyes and stares ahead of him, almost expecting to see her standing there in front of him. He can feel her presence, though she is clearly not physically here. But he can feel her heart, this sweet heart that has been opening up since they'd first met. This soul friend.

The confusion in his own heart clears as he realises, *It's okay to let myself love her.* And as he breathes, feeling this awareness in his heart, he feels the energy of that love flowing forth freely to her, knowing he needs nothing from her. *To love her in this moment is enough.*

The prayer bell is now ringing, signaling that the workshop is coming to an end.

"Very gently and slowly open your eyes," Paul says. "You may find it helpful to wiggle your fingers or toes, or to stretch or move your body."

Anna moves her fingers, still feeling the golden threads connecting them to her centre. Slowly fluttering open her eyes, she tries to wiggle her toes, but both legs from the knee down have gone to sleep. She rubs them gently, feeling the pain and tingling as the blood begins to move freely through them again.

"Now that you have felt your centre," Lu says softly, "you can always return to it, whenever you remember. You can eventually bring this awareness into all your activity, whatever it may be. For all activity that comes from the Hara and from the heart is coming from authentic truth, from connectedness, from a place of compassion. So whatever it may be – be it walking, dancing, playing music, or even speaking – all of it can come from this place of loving and centered awareness. You will find that through maintaining awareness of your centre and of your heart, you are not drawn into the same ego dramas. You are literally no longer knocked off centre. Or if you are, you can remember to bring yourself back to a state of being present, authentic and loving even in challenging situations. Through this awareness, we find the challenges in our lives begin to transform."

Anna thinks of her life back home with Damien in Brighton. *If I can learn how to do this, maybe I can transform my life back home.*

Yes! Something inside her seems to say, as a flash of energy moves through her at the thought. *I can transform my life!*

"From this awareness," Lu continues, "whatever action we make in the world is connected and centred, coming from the truth of our deepest selves, from that self which is connected to everything else. And the more you do this practice, the more it will become integrated into your life. The more it will become your natural way of being."

Like breathing, Anna thinks. *Like walking the tightrope.*

"Thank you all," Lu says. "This brings us to the conclusion of our workshop."

"And if you would like more information on longer courses we run, please come and see us," Paul adds. "Thank you all. Namaste." He bows his head slightly, holding his hands in prayer position at the heart.

"Namaste," Luwen echoes.

"Namaste," some of the people around Anna murmur in response.

Namaste? What does that mean? Anna wonders, rising from her seated posture and shaking out her stiff legs again.

"Thank you, Anna." Paul nods to her as she steps past him on her way out. He's setting out fliers on a small table by the entrance.

"Thank you," Anna says. "That was... enlightening. Maybe I'll take one of your fliers." She reaches down and collects a pamphlet with the words *Heart Fire* written across the top.

"I wonder if I could ask you...what that word Namaste means?"

"It means the divine in me honours the divine in you," Paul replies, his eyes sparkling. "Namaste Anna."

The divine in me honours the divine in you.

Anna smiles, "Namaste to you, too." As she says it, a child-like wave of delight flutters through her.

> *"You have God*
> *Look at me with earnest eyes*

And feel the truth in your heart
Feel the sound around you
And feel the source within
See the smiling faces that surround you
Look into them and see who you are
See the smiling faces that surround you
Look into them and see who you are
Feel compassion in waves
Feel compassion in waves for who you are
Feel compassion
Feel this is who you are"

from the song, 'You Have God', by Maya Love

As Anna steps away from the workshop space, feeling the radiance of the sun on her face, she notices that the world seems different again – more real, more vibrant. She finds the nearest water point in the healing area and fills her bottle. She drinks the lot, then fills it again and packs it in her satchel for later.

Now she is at the centre of the four quadrants again. *You are here.*

So where to now? She no longer feels the need to find Johannes. She can tell by the angle of the sun that it was a long workshop. Feeling the call of nature, she makes her way to the African Pit Latrines, passing again between the two giant harvest goddesses. This time she imagines they don't look so severe. She can almost see a slight upward curve to their lips, as if they know what she is beginning to discover. She doesn't really even fully understand it herself yet, but something is happening to her – something wonderful.

After an uneventful visit to the loos, Anna buys herself a satisfying falafel in a pitta bread from the Chai Shoppe and sits on the bench out front to eat it. As she nibbles one of her olives, she can hear the pleasing sound of many voices raised in song heading up from Babylon along the main track, in the direction of King's Meadow.

"One by one everyone comes to remember…
We're healing the world one heart at a time…"

Now Anna can see the approaching choir – at least twenty strong – men and women both, beautifully dressed in shades of crimson and red and marching joyfully down the centre track as they sing Michael Stillwater's *One By One* together in sweet harmonies.

"*One by one everyone comes to remember…*

We're healing the world one heart at a time…"

Many of them have their faces painted with red flowers, hearts and spirals. Some wear red feathers or flowers in their hair; some wear hats and evening gowns. All the faces seem to shine as they sing out with such passion.

"*One by one everyone comes to remember…*

We're healing the world one heart at a time…"

Those who have joined the *Shakti Sings Choir* have done so for many reasons, but one of the biggest is that it is an experience of joy and it brings joy to others. It is a gift they can give back to the world. They sing with the intention of opening hearts through music, and helping people to feel more connected to one another and to the Earth through song.

They stop their march just in front of the Chai Shoppe, and begin to sing in rounds, their harmonies rising and falling in waves of connected sound. People walking by stop to listen.

"*… We're healing the world one heart at a time…*

We're healing the world one heart at a time…"

Some of those people who have stopped to listen are now joining in with the song. Anna can't help smiling. She feels the pull inside herself too; it's contagious, this joyfulness. Having finished her falafel, she stands and steps out into the track to join the gathering crowd, feeling a lightness inside her as she allows her own voice to rise up with them. It feels so good to sing this way.

"*One by one everyone comes to remember… we're healing the world one heart at a time… one heart at a time… one heart at a time… one heart at a time…*"

As the final wave of sound comes to rest, Anna joins in the chorus of applause. The choir are smiling their gratitude, and are now moving on their way up the track between the harvest goddesses and into King's Meadow, singing Nick Prater's *Open Your Heart*.

"*Open up your heart… and let the river of love flow through you…*

Open up your heart… and let the river of love flow through…

Love is like a river… flowing through your heart…

Love is like a river… let it flow… let it flow… let it flow… let it flow…"

From where she stands, Anna can see one of the green fields she has not yet explored – *Green Crafts*. Attracted by the green grass, the small colourful windmills atop poles and the unusual nature-based creations, she takes that path. There are wood carvers, blacksmithing, pottery throwing, basket weaving, stone carving, a group of people making willow dragonflies, timber frame house building, wooden bowl making, woodwork swords and magic wands and other interesting sights. She is most intrigued by the iron age axe throwing.

I might give that one a miss... she thinks. But there are clearly a lot of festival-goers up for that experience, she can see by the queue.

Feeling a sudden urge to make something, Anna contemplates joining in a basket making workshop. There is a woman with a long, white braid who appears to be running the workshop, who looks up and smiles warmly at her. Anna returns the smile, and is about to go in when her attention is drawn to a crew of people sitting by a nearby fire. They are all focused intently on whatever they are making.

Catching Anna's eye, a strong looking man with a wild brown beard and equally wild but friendly eyes, waves heartily. "Come make a spoon!" His enthusiasm is so infectious, Anna moves toward their circle of three men and two women. Four of the people are all talking and joking with one another while they work the wood, but one of them – a woman across the fire with curly brown hair – is working quietly. She looks up at Anna and smiles a welcome before returning intently to her task. Anna watches the woman for a moment; she is so focused. Each movement of the knife seems like it is taking all her attention and has a grace to it.

This is Layla's preferred meditation practice. She finds it hard to sit still and meditate, but working with wood is something that just feels right to her. She gives her full awareness to each and every stroke. She gives her love to it, loving whatever she is making into existence. With each movement, she feels the energy in her body guiding her, guiding the shape that she makes.

Joey, the strong bearded man, introduces himself and hands Anna a pleasingly-shaped rectangular chunk of wood, a chisel and a small knife. He shows Anna where to start; how to chip off the first larger pieces and when to begin the finer shaving off of the wood, bit by bit.

"There's a spoon in there," Joey says. "See it in your mind. As you remove layer after layer, you release the spoon. The spoon already exists, see."

Layla looks up and smiles. "Ah... but surely the truth is that there is, in reality, no spoon."

The others around the circle chuckle; they've seen *The Matrix*, too.

"Ah... that is the divine dichotomy," Joey grins. "There is, and yet there is not."

So Anna begins, trying to see the spoon in her mind. And slowly, slowly, something is happening. Somehow it is deeply satisfying to feel the spoon take shape in her hands, the curls of wood shavings gathering at her feet. As the last shaving falls, Anna gazes at this thing in her hands that she has made. It's not the straightest spoon in the world. *But I made it*, Anna thinks, pleased. She's never made anything out of wood before, and to her, this spoon has a certain rustic beauty.

Joey gives Anna a piece of sandpaper and she rubs her creation smooth until it almost shines and her fingers can slide across it without encountering any rough edges.

"Give it a few coats of oil once you get home," Joey instructs. "Then you can use it. There's nothing quite like eating food with a spoon you made yourself. Next best thing to eating with your bare hands."

Finished her shift for the day, Sorrel is free to wander about the festival. She's a little tired now, after several hours of helping people to weave willow baskets and flowers, but she doesn't want to miss the spectacle that's happening right now in the Circus Field. Anything that involves lots of people working together to create something positive appeals to Sorrel.

Despite the long hours each day and the soreness of her fingers, Sorrel has loved being here at Glastonbury. She's met so many interesting people, and she's managed to keep up with the rest of the crew – some of them, like her granddaughter Rose, who are more than 50 years younger than she. Even Rose, who knows Sorrel's strength of will and impressive agility for her age has been surprised at how much her grandmother has been able to do.

When the spare ticket had come up for the basket-weaving crew, Rose had tentatively offered it to Sorrel, knowing her grandmother's interest in such things. Rose and the other members of the crew had been concerned about whether the older woman would be able to keep up with her shifts, but Sorrel had been adamant that she could do it, and she'd been right. Her cheerfulness and energy have lifted the morale of the whole crew, and she's kept up with the youngest of them. Nobody can believe that she is nearly eighty.

"It's the qigong," Sorrel tells them.

As she passes by Block 9 with its smoking buildings, Sorrel shakes her head, amazed at the extraordinary things people create. As a whole experience, Sorrel has not been disappointed by her first Glastonbury Festival. In all her eighty years, she has never seen anything like it. The noise has been a bit much at night, especially as their camp is not far from The Unfairground and Shangri-La. Sorrel hasn't bothered going to places like that. The young people seem to love them, though. But she has very much enjoyed visiting the *Left Field* stage – as she had earlier today – to listen to political speakers like Tony Benn. Over the years, Tony Benn has been one of Sorrel's greatest political inspirations, in the way he reminds people of their courage and of the power of many coming together to take action for a common goal.

Sorrel checks her little map, looking for the Circus Field. *Yes, it's just up ahead*, she sees. Just beyond Bella's Bridge. She approaches the little stone bridge which arches over a stream and heads towards the row of large metal prayer wheels on the other side. She'd seen wheels like this travelling in Tibet years ago. They have a Sanskrit mantra on them, and it is said that when you spin the wheel it has the same effect as if you say the mantra aloud or quietly to yourself. Sorrel knows it is best to spin the wheel with conscious intent, so as she runs her hands along the rounded metal of the wheels, she pays attention to the feel of the raised letters under her fingers, embossed in gold paint and whispers the mantra to herself.

Om Mani Padme Hung.

Om – symbolising the body, speech and mind of the awakened Buddha, and also said to be the sound of the earth, *Mani* – meaning the heart, the jewel of love, *Padme* – meaning lotus, and *Hum* – meaning indivisibility, or one consciousness.

The jewel of enlightenment is in the heart of the lotus.

Anna is not consciously following the woman with the long, white braid and straw hat, but she has kept a steady pace with her all the way from the Green Crafts Field. She had seen the woman earlier, helping people to weave baskets. She had looked up and had smiled at Anna with such warmth that Anna had almost gone to make a willow basket on the basis of that smile alone, had it not been for the enthusiasm of the wooden spoon makers.

After completing her spoon, Anna had decided to head towards the Circus Field, to see if she might be delighted by more acrobatics, or maybe see the gentleman tightrope walker again. As she had set off down the track, she had noticed this same white-haired woman walking up ahead of her, with a purposeful stride, as if going somewhere important. Anna had been struck again by this long white hair, loosely braided down to the middle of her back. There is also something interesting about the way the woman is dressed – not like a grandmother – in slim-fitting denim overalls and a straw hat with several colourful bands on it. She seems to stand out from the crowd, somehow a little brighter than those around her.

As Anna passes through the field of Avalon, she hears Sir Bruce Forsyth delighting crowds on the Avalon Stage. She stops for a moment, listening to the laughter of the audience and wondering whether to stay here instead of going to the Circus Field. But from the corner of her eye, she can see the white-haired lady disappearing off into the crowds and without really thinking, Anna carries on in that direction, wondering if she too is heading to the Circus Field. She watches the older woman stepping over the little arched bridge and pausing at the row of metal prayer wheels. The woman seems to whisper something as she runs her hands along the wheels, making them clack and spin, before carrying on into the field ahead.

When Anna reaches the wheels herself, this time she doesn't worry about the hands that have touched them before. She reaches out her own hand and runs her fingertips along the metal wheels, making them spin and feeling the roughness of the metal symbols carved into them as they move under her fingers. She now sees the symbols written on them, and wonders at their meaning.

They were right, Sorrel thinks. It is quite extraordinary. In the centre of the Circus Field, some people are constructing a life-sized model of *St. Michael's Tower*, the monument that stands on top of *Glastonbury Tor*. This is to be the tallest cardboard building ever created. Sorrel moves closer, watching the synchronised movements of the people surrounding the tower as one man shouts, "One, two, three, UP!" and in one perfectly coordinated movement, the existing structure is lifted while another level is pushed into place at the bottom. The cardboard is fastened with strong tape and the whole movement starts again, like a dance. Sorrel loves to see how all these people – most of whom she imagines have never met one another before – are joining together to create something so special. It is a thing that could never be made by one person alone. It is only by working together as a group that they are able to make this extraordinary thing. *Power in numbers*, Sorrel thinks.

Her attention is drawn to a young woman who is standing not far away from her, looking equally amazed by what's happening here. Sorrel recognises her. *From where? Ah, yes.* She had seen this girl up in Green Crafts. They had smiled at one another. The girl seems to know Sorrel is looking at her and turns her head towards her, making eye contact. Sorrel smiles at her again and the girl smiles back.

Sorrel takes a few steps towards her. "Quite something, isn't it?"

"It is," Anna replies. The tightrope walker had used the same words, and Anna recognises a similar light in these eyes too.

"Do you know what they're building?" Anna asks.

Sorrel nods. "It's a life-sized replica of St. Michael's Tower." She gazes up at the structure, already towering above them.

"What's that?"

"It's the tower on top of Glastonbury Tor."

"Oh. I've never seen that."

"Well if you think this is something, the real one is quite something else. My granddaughter Rose always makes her pilgrimage there before and after the festival. She took me up there this year, and I tell you, it is a sight. She told me that I would like it there, because it's a powerful heart place. And she's right, it is."

"Is it?" Anna asks, a shiver moving through her in the heat. "Why is that?"

"Rose says that Glastonbury is the Heart Chakra of the world. She says the lines of energy intersect right at St. Michael's Tower, just like the meridians on our own bodies, and it makes a chakra – a spinning wheel of energy. She says that's why it's a powerful place for the heart. You can bring in the energy of love or send it out. Me of course, I don't know about these things really, but I trust my granddaughter. She seems to believe it, and that's enough for me. And I really did feel something standing up there, I must say."

Sorrel can believe that the Earth is alive, and that it would have meridians too. *Why not?* Sorrel has been working with her own body's energy pathways in her qigong practice, and it makes perfect sense.

"And perhaps that's why this festival is such a powerful thing," Sorrel realises. "It's near such a place of power. It's a good place to bring in energy for changing things."

Maybe so, Anna thinks. Glastonbury certainly has been a powerful experience for her, and yes, many things have changed.

They watch the next row of the cardboard tower slot into place. It looks to be about twenty feet high now. A woman in a neon high-vis vest is calling out and beckoning to them, "We need more people!"

Sorrel turns to Anna. "What do you say? Shall we join in?"

Anna's eyes widen at what this older woman is suggesting. *Is she strong enough?*

But now Anna sees the mischievous sparkle in the older woman's eye. *This woman knows what she's doing*, Anna realises, and she feels in herself a desire to be part of this creation – to put her energy into making this extraordinary thing.

"Why not?" she agrees, feeling herself pulled by this flow that seems to be bigger than her, drawn into place beside the older woman within the circle of more than thirty people now around the base of the tower.

"Are you going to be all right lifting this?" Anna asks.

Sorrel smiles. "I'll be just fine, dear. There are power in numbers, and I know my limits." She does, and she's not afraid to push them; Sorrel has done that a lot in her life. But she knows she has to be a little more careful now than she used to be. At nearly eighty, her will sometimes exceeds what her body wants to do. That being said, she knows that if she is listening to her body and applies the qigong 70% rule – *never exert yourself beyond 70% of your capacity* – she tends to do all right.

Sorrel had come to practices of meditation and qigong fairly late in her life. It was the increasing frequency of the passing of friends and loved ones that had brought the reality of Sorrel's own mortality home to her. Sorrel was not ready to die and had felt that something critical was missing in her own life. Her perceptive granddaughter Rose had suggested qigong, and Sorrel had taken to it like a house on fire. And something has been happening lately for Sorrel as a result of her practices. She has ceased to be afraid of death. She has ceased to be afraid of very much at all.

"I'm Sorrel." Sorrel offers her hand to Anna.

"Anna." As she takes the woman's hand in hers, feeling the veins and the thinness of the bones, she expects to feel frailty. Instead, she feels strength. These hands have a vitality in them, and they seem to exert a heat, very like Moon's hands – perhaps even more so. *She'll definitely manage*, Anna realises.

"One, two, three, lift!" the woman in the hi-vis vest calls out. In one coordinated movement, the whole of the top of the tower lifts several feet off the ground and the next layer is shoved neatly into place. People get to work taping up the gaps between the boxes.

"I love this," Sorrel says. "All these people working to create something amazing together."

Anna nods. "It is amazing."

"This is the power of collective action," Sorrel says, with a fire in her eyes.

Anna observes how tirelessly Sorrel lifts her share of the building, and feels the strain in her own arms. But then she remembers the Hara workshop from earlier and decides to try Paul and Lu's golden thread technique.

Breathing into her belly, Anna sees that light expanding from that place – from her Hara – like a giant sun. And with each lift, she feels the movement beginning from this centre, extending through the golden threads to the tips of her fingers. To her surprise a new energy floods her body, making each movement no longer a strain, but more like a dance. Anna finds herself laughing with Sorrel for the joy of it, as the tower continues to grow.

Until it is done. The final foundations slot into place. Anna notices now how there are long ropes attached to each of the four corners at the top of the tower, holding it upright. Sorrel and Anna and the others step back to observe this masterpiece. All around them people are cheering their congratulations.

They've done it. They have made the world's tallest ever cardboard building. It seems as if the whole field is holding their collective breath as they witness this more than fifty foot structure towering over them. Though it is only made of cardboard, there is a majesty to it, as if it is calling the spirit of the real St. Michael's Tower to this very place.

"They say there are angels at Glastonbury, like the angel this tower is named for," Sorrel whispers. "And it feels like they are here too."

A breeze ripples through the crowd. *Angels?* Anna had heard angels mentioned in her mother's church, Arch-angels like Gabriel and Michael. Even Anna's old friend Carolyn had spoken of angels, but until this moment they had seemed to be just a story to Anna. Now though, with a shiver moving through her, Anna wonders if perhaps angels might be real after all, like so many of the other seemingly magical things she has experienced this weekend.

The wind increases in intensity, catching the top of the tower. It begins to wobble. "Stand back!" The people in the hi-vis vests are calling, and the crowd moves back. It's time for the tower to come down.

Amidst the delighted cheers, the cardboard St. Michael's Tower gracefully bends and falls to the ground, seeming to move in slow motion, until it is no longer a tower, but a very large pile of cardboard boxes.

Without anyone saying anything, the crowd around Anna jumps to action – all those who have helped to build it and almost all of the spectators in the field – as if they have all heard the same inner call, all rushing forward, climbing and jumping like children up on the huge pile.

"Come on!" Sorrel cries, moving forward. Anna can't help laughing at the sight of this older woman in overalls climbing on the hill of boxes and jumping up and down like a child, helping to crush up the mass of cardboard.

Creation, and now destruction, thinks Sorrel. But in itself this is creative too. Sorrel can see that these people needed an invitation to let go, and be child-like and free again. That really, they all want to jump and dance and laugh with abandon.

Sorrel can see this in Anna too, in the delight on her face as she puts all her energy into jumping onto one huge box, squishing it down. She looks up to Sorrel with a grin, her eyes shining.

When the frenzy has calmed, Anna and Sorrel step back to catch their breath.

"Well, I haven't had such fun for a long time," Sorrel laughs, with tears in her eyes.

"Me too," Anna says, and she means it.

"You know, Anna, you remind me quite a lot of my granddaughter, Rose. I have a feeling you two would get on well. You've both got a sweet strength to you. I have a feeling you'll both do things to help change the world for the better. And you'll do it with love, I feel. With heart."

"Thank you," Anna says.

And so with lightness in their hearts, they step forward now to help the crew gather up the crushed boxes and put them into the recycling bins.

"May you walk the path of truth
May you give it all your worth
May you rise every day, even stronger
Friend to the earth.
May you walk the path of truth
May you give it all your worth
May you laugh every day
May you stay a friend to the earth"

from the song, 'Friend to the Earth', by Chris Ellis

After all the excitement in the Circus Field, Anna feels her body's need to sit down and rest. Remembering how she had found that peaceful spot in the Earth garden to sleep yesterday – *was it only yesterday?* – she heads back to the healing area. Unlike the quiet of last night, this time the Earth quadrant is completely full. The whole expanse of the green grass is covered with people lounging in the sun or making use of the patches of shade created by the parasols, flags, tents and large sails which decorate the area. There is also some lovely shade cast by the large and colourful patchwork bender – *The Healing Area Music Space* – which is up and running with live music. It's something quite wonderful too.

One of the musicians is a youthful-looking man with blond hair and clear blue eyes, whose nimble hands are dancing over what looks like a small silver spaceship sitting in his lap. He is tapping it lightly at various points on the rounded metal surface, releasing a resonant sound like nothing Anna has ever heard before. Beside him is a sparkly and bright-eyed faery violinist with flowing brown hair. An aura of nurturing and warmth surrounds this woman as she plays one of the sweetest melodies Anna has ever heard. She moves closer to the duo and settles into a patch of shade, made by the large Tibetan flags flying above.

"Anna Leigh, isn't it?"

Anna turns towards the familiar male voice. It's the young man with the nice dreadlocks from the Chai Chi Tent, looking relaxed and stretched out in the sun.

"Oh! Hi." She smiles back at him cheerfully, pleased to see him again. "I meant to ask you your name before."

"It's Kai." He offers his hand and she accepts the warm, energetic handshake.

"You got some time off?" Anna asks.

Kai nods. "My co-worker Alice sent me off. And she was right, I needed a break. Plus I really wanted to see Miniature Universe. I love these guys."

"Miniature Universe. Nice name."

"Yeah. It always makes me think of the universe inside my own belly. It seems like it's tiny, but it's actually infinite. It's like the divine dichotomy. We're human and yet we're infinite at the same time."

Anna laughs. "I seem to be hearing these kinds of things a lot today."

"It must be what you need to hear then." Kai smiles.

The exact right teacher will appear... Anna remembers Johannes' words, and thinks about how many kind and wise people she has met over the weekend, and how these meetings have changed her.

She turns to face Miniature Universe and listens to the dance of the two instruments, feeling the lift of joy inside as if her own spirit is rising and dancing with the music. As she watches the couple in their effortless creation of this music which seems to move right inside her and dance in her very cells, Anna imagines they do know about this great shining sun in their bellies, that they do know the universe begins in the centre of themselves. She imagines that the faery violinist has golden strands stretching from this centre of the universe inside her to the tips of her fingers which are making the bow dance. The bow itself seems connected to the one playing it, as if part of her own body.

I wonder if guitar playing and singing could be like that, too. And with a rush of energy through her body, Anna knows it can. *Just as the movement of lifting the cardboard tower had gone from strain to joy, perhaps it could be the same with my music.*

Anna sits there, eyes wide open, digesting this for a moment, the glimmers of understanding crystalising inside her, as the light shining on her own creative path grows brighter. Something is humming inside Anna now, with the possibility of it all. After a while, her thoughts quieten as the music draws her again into its magical soundscape. She settles into this feeling of contentment, here with the Tibetan prayer flags moving above her and this music around her, and the ground holding her from below. The dance of the two instruments rises in intensity and Anna is taken into a kind of trance, riding on waves of this resonance. She doesn't want the music to end, but eventually it does. All across the grassy expanse, people lift their hands to clap. Having moved so deep into the music, it feels strange to clap, but Anna does so, gently.

She lets out a breath and turns to Kai. "Do you know what that thing he's playing is called?"

"It's a hang," Kai answers. "They're pretty rare, and they seem to have a kind of healing magic to them – at least when they are in the hands of a sensitive player, who can bring some heart to it, like these guys are doing."

Anna watches Miniature Universe packing up their instruments and speaking to the people who have come to buy their CDs. There's still a pang inside her to see how other musicians are managing to sell their CDs, but she is starting to understand something more about it now.

The next performers are arriving. They are the same band of jubilant musicians who were playing in the fire garden last night, wearing the same hats and the same fantastic Hawaiian shirts.

"What are you up to now?" Kai asks Anna, rising from the grass. "Can I buy you a chai?" He tilts his head towards the little yurt cafe set up beside the Music Space. Anna hadn't noticed it before, but it is an attractive little place. The cafe itself is a small white yurt with an open wooden door where a small queue of people are waiting to order. In a semi-circle around the yurt are several rustic hand-made wooden benches. Upright planks of wood nailed to the the benches support strands of Tibetan prayer flags, which are strung between the cafe and the venue and are still waving pleasantly in the wind overhead. At the centre of the benches is a small pond created from a little paddling pool with a solar-powered fountain in it, filled with shiny stones reflecting the sun's light.

"How about I buy you a chai?" Anna asks. "It's my turn really."

"I will gratefully accept," Kai grins. "Thank you."

"I would have thought you might be sick of chai by now," Anna says as they join the end of the queue at *Cafe Kailash.*

"Nope. I have to love it, remember. That's my job. And besides, these guys make their chai with love too. And the chocolate slices here are pretty damn good. They also give all their profits to ROKPA, a charity which helps people in Tibet." He gestures towards the image of a smiling Tibetan woman on one of the information boards next to the yurt. Anna's gaze settles on some of the words written there: *ROKPA is a Tibetan word meaning 'to help' or 'to serve'.*

To serve. With a flutter inside, Anna remembers what Sorrel had said – that she would do something to help the world to be better in some way, and that she would do it with love.

"To serve," Kai echoes, as if reading her thoughts.

"You seem good at that," Anna grins.

Kai shrugs. "It just feels better to the heart that way, you know."

Anna nods, as if it almost does make sense to her now. She remembers the moment she had stumbled into the Chai Chi tent, and what a haven it had been. "Hey... I wanted to say thanks again for everything the other day. I was..." She catches sight of the words *Find Yourself* on her Lost Horizon wristband. "...Lost. I guess that's a good word for it. I was pretty lost."

"So have you found Anna Leigh Mayes yet?" Kai asks, smiling at the yellow wristband. He has one too.

Anna laughs and shrugs. "Maybe some small piece of her. I dunno. Maybe a glimpse. Maybe I'm starting to wonder if I'm even Anna Leigh Mayes at all. Do you know what I mean?"

Kai nods. "I certainly do. Like you start to see yourself as being more than just an individual person. Like there's something bigger going on."

"That's it. Something so big I don't even know how big it is. I don't even know where to start."

"How about starting with a chai and a chocolate slice?" Kai grins.

As they reach the front of the queue, an attractive young woman with long and partly dreadlocked sunshine blonde hair greets them with a cheerful smile through the open door of the yurt.

"What can I get for you?" she asks.

"Two chais and two chocolate slices please," Anna says, returning the smile.

The young woman turns to a man who Anna notes must be her father, for he has the same bright smile and sunshine blond hair – which in his case is neatly dreaded and tied in a thick knot on the top of his head. He turns towards the huge chai pot steaming on the camp stove behind them and begins to ladle out two mugs of chai.

On both sides of the man's black t-shirt are quotes from the Dalai Lama, inscribed with white letters. On the front it reads: "*Be kind wherever possible. It is always possible*" and on the back – "*Remember that NOT getting what you want is sometimes a wonderful stroke of luck*".

Anna smiles. *Maybe so.* Before she had come here to Glastonbury, she had been convinced that her deepest wish was to be discovered and make a success with her music. That had seemed like the most important thing. But if that music industry man had arrived and handed her his golden business card and she had sold dozens of CDs – would all the amazing things she had encountered this weekend have happened? Would she have ended up in the Green Fields searching for more gigs and instead finding them, discovering something so much more important?

They carry their mugs of chai and chocolate slices to a clear patch of grass in the sun, out of the way of the crowd of dancers who have materialised in front of the Lost Padres, who have launched into a highly energetic version of *Brown-Eyed Girl*, to the delight of the dancers moving about on the grass who are singing along at the top of their lungs.

Anna takes a bite of the deliciously sweet chocolate slice with its base of crunchy crumbling chocolate biscuit. The chocolate is melting in the heat and she licks it off her fingers. "You're right. These are amazing. Yours are better, though."

"Couldn't say." Kai wipes a smear of chocolate off his lip. "These are definitely made with love, though."

"Definitely."

Anna sips the sweet milky drink and her contentment deepens.

"Did you ever find those gigs you were looking for?" Kai asks.

Anna laughs. "No. Well... I did something pretty dumb actually... I found a gig, but my god, was it ever the wrong gig."

"What was wrong about it?"

Anna feels the contentment start to slide away as the memories of her most recent gig fill her mind. "It was the wrong place, the wrong PA, the wrong songs. You know, during that gig, I realised I don't even like my own songs anymore. I don't believe what I'm singing about, so maybe I won't actually even sing them ever again. And I've managed to saddle myself with a whole box of CDs of this music. I can't even face that one yet. I don't know what I'm supposed to do anymore. It's like this festival has turned everything upside down. I don't even know if I'm a songwriter anymore... I don't actually know what I am." She feels like crying again as she remembers all that she had worked for, and how none of it seems to mean anything now. And here Kai is looking at her with those understanding eyes again.

"But here you are, Anna," he says. "Isn't this an amazing moment for you? Because this is not knowing. You're suddenly open... so you can be filled with something new."

Anna stares at him. Cedar had said almost the exact same thing on the hill.

"And oh yeah," Kai adds, "you're going to write some songs... and they're gonna be awesome."

"What makes you say that? How do you know?"

"I dunno." Kai shrugs. "A hunch. I can see you're opening up. You're starting to have a sense of something greater than yourself, and that can only lead to the creation of something amazing. 'Cause you're on the path now."

Am I? Could I be? She thinks again of the glimmer of light she had seen shining on her path, a sense of what could be possible. *Maybe so.*

Anna stares at the last few bits of chocolate slice crumbling in her napkin. "But where does it all lead?"

"Here."

Anna picks at a crumb. "Here? In my crumbs?"

"In everything – Grass. Sky. Music. Chai. Anna. Kai."

"You're a poet." Anna smiles. Speaking with Kai is lifting her spirits again.

"Only when I don't try." He grins again and lifts himself off the grass. "I better be getting back. Nice to see you again, Anna Leigh Mayes. Thanks for the chai."

"You too."

She watches the sway of his dreadlocks as he makes his way off towards the centre, and through Fire.

Back again at the African Pit Latrines, Anna waits in the queue for the young person in a WaterAid T-shirt to hand her a bucket of water.

Two women join the queue right behind her. They are both intoxicated and smell strongly of alcohol. Anna moves ahead as much as she can to give herself some space, but the two women unconsciously move forward too, filling the gap. They begin to argue about what to do next. One wants to go to the Park Stage; one wants to go to The Other Stage – and the latter is getting progressively more upset about it.

"You said…" she points a shaky finger at the other woman. "You said you wanted to see them. You can't go back on me now. Not after everything I've done for you this weekend."

"What have I done for you?" The first woman is bewildered, stumbling.

"No, you're drunk! I said, it's what I've done for you!" The other woman is nearly yelling.

As the woman's irritation with her friend grows, so Anna's discomfort increases. This queue seems much too long now. Her anxiety about Damien begins to return. She'd promised to call him later – which is pretty much now. *And what will I say to him?*

By the time she reaches the front of the queue, Anna is a completely different state of being from the one she arrived in. Squatting in the privacy of the loo, she feels an overwhelming urge to cry for all that's been happening, for all that's changing, for the sudden loss of her earlier feeling of wellbeing. It has happened a number of times this weekend – a feeling of happiness would arise as a result of something she was experiencing, but then without warning it would just disappear and she would be plunged back into where she was before, except that it feels worse for the contrast.

A vague memory of what Paul had said about energy moves through her awareness – how in the first stage you can be swayed by the energy of others. You can deplete them, and they can deplete you. She thinks of those women in the queue and how being next to them had felt so uncomfortable. She had felt fine before standing in the queue, and now she feels awful. *Had their presence had anything to do with that?* But despite this passing awareness, Anna's thoughts are spiralling downwards, like the hole she's crouching over.

In her mind, the stories are beginning again, which include the imagined painful conversations to come with Damien, and the questions about how she could ever really change anything about her life. Were all the things she had experienced here really real or were they just a festival-induced fantasy? *And what about Cedar?* In the confusion of feelings, the judgemental thoughts come, asking her why someone like Cedar would be interested in her anyway. The thoughts make her feel smaller, just as she imagines that her life back home will do. She flings the contents of the bucket over the cement floor and watches the water swirl down the hole, splashing at the bottom, which is not so far below now.

Stepping back out into King's Meadow, the griping hole is back, clawing inside Anna with a vengeance, aching in its familiar way. She has a sense of just drifting, of being lost again. *How could I have fallen so far?*

You fall and you get back up again, she can hear the tightrope walker saying.

But it doesn't feel like she can right now.

Breathe, a soft voice inside her seems to whisper. *Remember to breathe.*

Her breaths have been shallow since she first began feeling that discomfort in the queue, and after that it has been a vicious circle. The shallow breaths are drawing her more and more into a state of panic. Anna casts her eyes about frantically for something to help her in this moment, to help ease this pain. Her gaze lands on the stone circle in the centre of the field in front of her, and she frowns at the layers of rubbish strewn around it – trails of beer cans, cigarette butts and thousands of nitrous oxide canisters embedded in the ground. *How can people do this?* She thinks about the young woman she had overheard last night around the fire, who along with other Oxfam volunteers would have swept this field clear of rubbish only this morning. Yet, already it is filling up again.

Anna accidentally steps on one of the small silver laughing gas containers. It's hard to walk through this field without standing on one. She can spot a dozen or more from this spot where she stands. *The things people do*, she thinks.

To escape from the feeling of emptiness, the thought comes quietly. These are the same feelings of emptiness that are creeping back in for Anna. She knows them well.

Out of habit, she reaches for her mobile phone, knowing with a creeping sense of dread what she'll find there. As well as a message from Damien, there are two new messages from Shari. She remembers her promise to Damien that she would call Shari and knows she must do that before she calls him. Something in her is strongly rebelling at the idea. *But I have to. I don't have a choice.*

You always have a choice, a softer voice inside seems to say.

Taking a shallow breath, she dials Shari.

"Anna! Thank God. Are you okay?" Shari's voice sounds strange to Anna – thinner, worried. There's something else too, that Anna can't quite place. Hearing the concern in Shari's voice, Anna feels a little guilty for delaying the call.

"Yeah. I'm okay." Anna listens to herself saying these false words. "I... I think it was heat stroke."

"Well at least you're okay." Shari lets out a shuddery breath. "I'm so glad you called, Anna. It's really not been one of my better days."

"What happened?"

"Oh. Eden and I sort of... spectacularly of fell out, I guess you could say. And now she's just gone AWOL."

"AWOL? What do you mean?"

Shari releases a frustrated sigh. "Oh, she met up with this guy last night at the bar backstage, and she's completely convinced about this one. I've seen this so many times with Ede. He's not the one, clearly, but she can't see it. She's blinded by the fact that he's with one of the bands and so this guy can get her in to meet so-and-so and etcetera and etcetera. And she wanted to be alone with him, because she thought she had a better shot that way at... I don't know... ingratiating herself with him in her particular Edenish way. She refused to accept what I was telling her, because I care about her... God knows why I try... but still. So when it was clear I was running a losing race, I said fine, go, have fun. And so she did. And now... I'm..." Shari's voice trails off. *On my own*, is what she can't say. *Lost*. For Shari, it was fine being in this exciting place with Eden – wonderful, bizarre fun at times. But on her own, Shari feels overwhelmed by it all.

In the silence that follows, it's clear to Anna what Shari wants of her.

I can't. Please don't. Don't ask me to give up the rest of the day, because I won't have a choice but to do it.

You always have a choice. This softer voice has momentarily faded into the background as the louder thoughts descend on Anna's body, weighing it even more heavily than before.

Shari is keeping her voice as light as possible so that Anna won't know how much this really matters to her, but Anna can still hear it loud and clear.

"So, I was wondering what you're up to this evening, and whether you want to go see some stuff with me? Mumford and Sons are playing on the Pyramid Stage and Cat Power is on the Park Stage. Do you fancy seeing either of those?"

"Sure. Sounds good." Anna hears herself accepting, all the while crying inside as she watches herself crawl back behind her mask, and despising herself for it. *What are you doing Anna? What about Cedar? What about your promise to him that you would be there tonight?*

They arrange to meet in an hour, at 8pm. Anna gauges it's just enough time to make her way back to her tent, have a good cry, get changed and put the makeup back on her face. Mustering her usual cheerful voice, she feels like a fraud. "Okay, see you then."

The phone is a dead weight in her hand, but Anna knows there is one more call she must make. She doesn't know if she can face speaking to Damien right now. *But I have to set his mind at ease*, she tells herself.

Hi D, got plans with Shari tonight. Should be fun. Look forward to seeing you tomorrow. Love you xx. She sends the text and it doesn't feel good. *Do I really look forward to seeing him?* She had not known what else to write. It's what he would expect her to say, and to not say it would arouse suspicions that something might be up.

But something is up, she knows. *Something is definitely up.* She doesn't want to face how that could impact her life with Damien right now. She drops the weight of the phone into her satchel and crouches down, because suddenly it feels like all her energy has dropped out of her. She feels physically sick.

You won't see Cedar tonight, the thoughts swirl in her mind. *Maybe not ever again. You can't pretend anymore that this is your life. That you could be like these people. That he could be interested in you.*

Dizzy suddenly, Anna just wants to curl up somewhere, but the ground below her is so littered and trampled that there is nowhere to sit down and she doesn't want to cry here. Further up the field is a large oak tree with nice roots for sitting on, but there are already a dozen or so people smoking and drinking beneath it.

The dizziness intensifies and the thoughts are coming hard and fast now, pushing the tears ever closer to the surface, creating that familiar ball of constriction in her throat. *You were deluded Anna. Cedar could never love you. You're giving yourself up, like you always do.*

As the thoughts snipe at her, pushing her deeper into that despairing place she knows so well, something happens for Anna. As she had before, she becomes a witness to herself hunched over in pain and fear. She becomes aware of herself as an observer, as both the person suffering and also something else – something observing the suffering. And somehow Anna manages to have the thought to ask for help, to call out to someone or something, to that love that she felt that night in the Big Tipi, to that feeling of warmth in the heart, to her own Wild Heart-Self.

Please! Help me!

Breathe, the message comes again. *Breathe into your belly.*

And so Anna breathes, using her mind to see that sun in her centre. She can't feel it at all.

It's not working.

Just keep breathing. One breath at a time.

So she does, and the breath becomes a lifeline. With each breath, the little ember inside Anna's heart seems to glow a bit brighter, and a little brighter still, bringing with it all the held tears.

Not here. I can't cry here.

Through blurred vision Anna looks up and sees it – a gap in the hedge, just as it was in her dream. She knows exactly what's in there.

Anna has the sense of being in a dream again, of rising and stepping forward like a sleepwalker, following the slope of the hill downwards into an improbable oasis of lush greenery. Graceful willows and mature ash and beech trees overhang the lush waterplants, buttercups, ferns and mare's tails. It is so like it was in her dream; she feels as if she's been here before. The sound of running water is all around her and at the centre of it all rests the extraordinary dragon.

The sun dips towards the opposite side of the valley, casting just enough light through the trees to dapple the dragon's curling stone body in a golden pink glow. One of the chunks of rose quartz embedded in the spine of the great, 80-foot dragon sparkles as the light catches it. Anna moves closer. The dragon does seem to be alive and to breathe – as it did in her dream – even with all its scales of broken stone and the mosses growing between the cracks. Its elegant wings fold across its back as it crouches on great, curled forelegs with phoenix-like claws. The long tail winds like a serpent, coiling at the tip around a young ash tree – which had clearly seeded itself there long after the dragon was built, as it is cracking the stone with its growth.

Surrounding the dragon is a man-made pond, muddy with clay and bordered with rocks. It's fed by the stream coming from the hillside above, which trickles down into a small waterfall, splashing into its own little pond before running down to surround the dragon and move through its body, ultimately cascading out through the gaps in the great stone teeth of the dragon's open mouth.

The magnificent dragon's head is the most breathtaking of all – from the tip of its long snout to the ends of the fin-like ears fanning out behind it, it is encrusted with small chips of quartz and is longer than the length of Anna's body. And the eye – that blood-red stone eye – shot through with a circle of white quartz is a staring pupil, seeming to look right inside her.

The earthy ground beneath Anna's feet is muddy, made so by the water dripping over the edge of the dragon's pond and by the numerous feet that have stepped in and out of it. Feeling a strong urge to be barefoot, she takes off her sandals and steps into the cold, refreshing water. Despite the heat of the day, it's cool here in these woods. She moves towards the dragon, the soles of her feet connecting with the clay bottom of the pond, the mud squishing between her toes. Reaching out her hand, she strokes the cool stone scales of the dragon and the soft, moist mosses, remembering her dream – something about touching the eye and seeing.

Silly girl, she tells herself. *It's only made of stone and crystal. It's not really alive.*

Cedar's words from the dream come back to her again and she shivers. *Everything is alive.*

Paul's words from the workshop echo in her mind too – *The Earth, she is alive.*
She is sentient.

And this stone and crystal is part of the Earth, Anna thinks, a tingling moving through her body.

In order to reach the dragon's overhanging head, she steps out of the pond onto rocky outcroppings which drop down into a stream several feet below. Balancing carefully on the slippery rocks, Anna runs her fingertips closer to the eye, stopping just before she reaches the outer edge. The giant, curved red marble is larger than the size of her open hand and is perfectly rounded, partially overhung by a regal stone brow.

What does this have to do with me?

Everything. If you touch the eye of the dragon, you'll see…

She reaches out her hand and rests the flat of her palm against the cold crystal of the eye.

Will I really see anything?

A part of her very much wants to believe that she could. The cool on her palm, the feel of the water splashing gently onto her feet from the pond above alerts her to her body. She feels the shallowness of her breathing and opens to the belly breath again, allowing it to plunge deeper, and now again come the welling up of tears. This time she lets them come, streaming down her face to join the waterfall below.

Who am I? The question arrives in her mind. Who am I really?

A goddess! Moon's words come back to her.

And Arthur's words too – *You are the mountains and the ocean and the sky. It is Love and Joy moving through us. It is God! You are this magnificence! You are this Love! And as you experience this Love that you are, it expands the boundaries of you until you see there are no boundaries at all and it is ALL you.*

A shiver moves through Anna.

If you imagine the wildest, most blissful, most compassionate, free self you can imagine… this is only a tiny glimpse of the magnificence you truly are.

An image comes into Anna's mind again of the woman she saw in her vision – the Wild Woman with the painted face – and how in her dream the paint on her own body had seemed to glow like fire.

She breathes again, seeing the sun in her centre and feeling how that centre reaches its golden threads to every part of her. How the movement of her finger-tips which touch the stone begin from that place in the centre of her belly. *Where the universe begins.*

If she allowed her body to move – to be authentic, as Paul had said – where would she go now? *What would my life look like if it was guided by love rather than fear?*

Okay, lead me.

For a moment, nothing is happening.

But now she realises it's not nothing. What's happening is here, all around her – in the gold of the sunset reflecting off the water and making patterns of light on the rocks, in the smell of the wet earth, in the sounds of the breeze rustling the beech leaves. She looks again at the dragon's great crystal eye and realises that she has been shown something after all. Or perhaps reminded of something.

A feeling of gratitude wells up inside her.

Thank you, she whispers, to the Dragon, to the woods around her, to the Earth below her feet.

"*Only love only love only love can reach me now*
Circle round circle round circle round Spirit of light
Call me home call me home call me home my guiding ones
I am here I am here I am here to listen to your songs
Within the shadow
In the centre only love
Inside this shadow
I am the centre only love
Behind the shadow
In the darkness only love
I am the shadow
I am the shining light of love"

from the song, 'Beneath the Shadow', by Susie Ro Prater

Anna's feet are moving now. She doesn't know exactly where they are going, but when she imagines the threads of golden light and the movement beginning from her centre, it feels like her body wants to walk this way. In this direction there is the artist's camping area, but it doesn't feel like that's where she's going.

The Tipi Field?

No. Somewhere else.

Her eyes alight on the large white geodesic dome at the far corner of King's Meadow. *The Peace Flame.* The sun is dipping just behind the dome now, casting it in silhouette.

As Anna moves closer, she can see the light coming from within it. She stands before the entrance to the hexagonal garden which opens into the dome. At the centre of the garden, supported by three wooden poles, hangs a massive three-dimensional copper star, inside which is suspended a large and ornate lantern, containing a church candle burning with a surprisingly bright flame.

The Peace Flame, thinks Anna, remembering the words of the woman from the Earth garden.

I want to go in, the awareness comes.

But you can't go in there, the fearful voice rises up in answer. *Remember your promise to Shari. You only have just enough time now to go back and put on your make-up.*

Put on my mask, thinks Anna. *I can't let Shari down.*

But her feet don't want to go that way. She feels frozen to the spot, aware of these two simultaneous pulls inside her – one driven by fear, and the other powered by love. It is the diverging path before her again, and only one way shines with light. Through the entrance of the dome the flickering lights of a hundred candles dance their invitation.

Anna hears Johannes' words again in her mind – *Fear contracts. Love expands. When a thought is in alignment with Love, you feel flow and expansion in your body. You feel energy. A message from your Heart may come in the form of a picture in your mind, or it may be a feeling that translates into words in your mind. Whatever it is, it will give you that feeling of energy. Just notice your body, notice how it feels.*

But I promised Shari. I can't let her down.

The answer comes as a soft, loving whisper inside her, that fills her with warmth.

What if my deepest, truest path is also the deepest truest path for Shari? She remembers what Johannes had said: *When you listen to the deepest guidance of your heart, it will always guide you on the path of the highest good. So your actions will be the right ones for you and for those around you, because we're all connected. When you follow your deepest calling, you are following that which is connected to*

the whole, therefore connected to the deepest calling in others. We are not indepen-
dent of each other. It's all one.

The candlelight flickers and seems to grow brighter in the great bronze lantern, and without thought, Anna moves into the garden towards it. It feels like an echo of her own heart's fire, calling her. The closer she moves to the flame, the stronger her own inner fire burns.

Inside the garden, she feels held. A sense of peacefulness settles around her. She has made the right choice. It doesn't make sense to her head, but that doesn't matter. There is a bubbling of energy in her body, of aliveness, of what she may discover here.

At the entrance to the dome itself there is a little laminated sheet with an image of a bright candle against a dark background, explaining what the Peace Flame is all about. In the fading light, Anna can just make out the words:

> *"The Peace Flame was first lit from the atomic fires of Hiroshima in 1945 and has been kept burning ever since as a symbol of remembrance, forgiveness, transformation and unity.*
>
> *In 1945, after the atomic bombing of Hiroshima, a man named Tatsuo Yamamoto collected some of the embers from the devastation. His grandmother then kept the fire burning on her Buddhist altar, before which she prayed every day, morning and night. It was a flame of love for her family who had died in the nuclear holocaust.*
>
> *Thirteen years later, a newspaper reporter, hearing of the long burning flame, wrote an article about it in the daily press and in 1968 a "Peace Flame Monument" was inaugurated. Since then, the flame has been carefully maintained as a symbol of protest against the testing and deployment of nuclear weapons and as a powerful symbol of peace.*
>
> *Countless other flames have been lit from it so that the Peace Flame now burns all over the world. The Peace Flame has been burning in Glastonbury for 9 years now.*
>
> *In the Peace Dome, we work with sacred geometry, sound and silence to create a universal sacred space for people to sit with the flame, to meditate and pray, and to light their own Peace Flame.*
>
> *The central Merkabah is a "Star Tetrahedron" or three dimensional Star of David which symbolises the balance of heaven and earth and is also said to be the divine light vehicle through which we can connect with higher realms of consciousness.*

Please come in and enjoy the space.
Every evening at dusk there is a lighting ceremony.
All are welcome"

Anna gazes again at the lantern in the centre of the garden, suspended within this beautiful metal structure. It is a great copper star. From where Anna stands, it appears to be six pointed, made from two great triangles superimposed upon one another. But as she moves around it, she sees that there are many points and many triangles. It is the same shape as the bamboo Star of David she had seen hanging in the Air quadrant of the healing area.

She considers the words she's just read. *Said to be the divine light vehicle through which we can connect to higher realms of consciousness.*

Those who created this garden are the same people who are lighting the candles within the Peace Dome now. They know that the six pointed star is a symbol of Spirit, or quintessence, the fifth essence. In Alchemy, when the symbols for Water, Fire, Air and Earth are superimposed upon one another, the six pointed star is the resulting symbol. It symbolises the totality of all. When all comes together at the centre, there is Spirit, the Spirit that breathes all things.

There has been an invocation here – an invitation by those who care for the Flame – inviting what some might call angels to be here, to bring their energy of peace and healing. The Peace Flame itself has an angel responsible for it, and wherever the Peace Flame lives, that angel is present, bringing with it stillness and peace.

There is small sign at the entrance: *Please remove your shoes before entering this sacred space.* Anna removes her shoes and steps just inside the entrance onto dry grass. There is a sweet and spicy fragrance of burning incense that intensifies the feeling of entering a shrine. With a sense of awe she notices the palpable feeling of peacefulness intensifying around her softly like a mantle. This is a sacred space.

Even though the sounds of the festival are still audible in here, they seem to be farther away than before. Another, stronger energy is holding this space, filling it, enveloping it and embracing all those who enter. Suspended from the centre of the dome is another massive copper star tetrahedron, containing a similar large and ornate lantern with a brightly burning flame inside it.

Below the hanging lantern, a hexagonal shape is cut out of the grass, revealing bare earth, apon which a luminous six pointed flower design – created entirely out of hundreds of tiny burning tealights – shimmers and dances before Anna's eyes. Surrounding the dancing lotus flower are large chunks of rose quartz, set amongst more church candles and tealights. The candles are still being lit slowly and with great care by two women and one man.

The candle lighting ceremony, Anna realises. She observes how reverent these people seem to be as they light each new candle, as if they know that every single one is special, because every single one holds the energy of the Peace Flame. Their faces seem to shine, as if reflecting back the light of the flame.

Anna feels herself drawn into this sea of living light. A circle of straw mats with little blue cushions on them surround the shining centre as if the whole space was created to be a mandala. As well as those who are lighting the candles, five other people are here, sitting around the circle with their eyes half-open, meditating and praying quietly. Anna follows the circle around to find an empty mat and sits cross-legged on one of the cushions.

So what am I supposed to do here? she wonders, gazing around at all the others who appear to be so serene. She is aware of the other voice inside her – not yet quite stilled – which is reminding her of the time and of her promise to Shari.

Just breathe, the softer, gentler voice seems to say again. *Breathe in that light at your centre.*

And so she does. It comes to Anna that the light before her is a mirror of the light inside. With each breath in, the mandala of light in her own centre grows brighter, fanning the flames of fire in her own heart.

The fiery lotus flower seems to transform itself before Anna's half-closed eyes. She can see a shape there now – a figure, like a mirror image, sitting cross-legged in the flames. It is her Heart-Self. The woman's face is painted as before, radiating with orange fire and light and she is fearless, boundless, free. Her shape shimmers in the dance of the glowing lotus flower. The wild woman smiles at Anna with warmth and understanding.

A memory comes to Anna of her conversation with Cedar up on the hill: *Your Heart-Self is already within you. Or maybe it is more true to say that you are within your Heart-Self, because the Heart-Self contains all of this. You already are that. It's just about remembering it.*

And from within the fire, Anna watches her Heart-Self rising and moving towards her as if to embrace her, closer and closer until the woman's body merges with her own, infusing Anna with light and shining from within every cell of her body. With a rush of energy, she sees her centre blazing like the sun, magnificent as the lotus flower. The filaments of light radiating from her heart suddenly appear to Anna like the mane of a lion, or the wings of a dragon.

She is me! Anna realises. *She is not who I will be one day in the future. She is me right now! She is me and I am her.*

With this thought, an energy of expansiveness, of lightening, floods through Anna's body and she knows it must be true.

She knows what to do now.

Anna sees Shari before Shari sees her. Shari, not knowing she is being watched, has her guard down for a moment. Her shoulders are slumped and not held high as usual. Shari had practised being a model in her younger years, and Anna has never before seen her without that posture – until now. Shari looks smaller, lonely. Anna is nearly beside Shari before Shari notices her.

"Anna! God, you startled me. Wow. You look different."

Anna knows it's true. She never went back to her tent to change and put on her make-up, and the fire blazing inside wouldn't be quelled this time. She can see herself reflected differently in Shari's eyes.

"I mean, it's in a good way," Shari stammers. "Just... oh. I don't know. Sorry. I'm a bit of a mess." Shari leans forward and embraces Anna, and Anna holds her for a moment, feeling this unusual fragility in Shari.

This is more than just about Eden. Shari holds back the tears that suddenly want to rise up, brought on by the surprising warmth of Anna. It is surprising to them both, for Anna realises now that there is a real desire in her to help Shari feel better and that she genuinely does care for Shari.

"I could really use a good distraction right now," Shari says, her voice cracking a little. "What do you think? Cat Power or Mumford and Sons?"

"They're both good... but I've got a better idea." Anna's eyes twinkle. "How about Awakening the Dreamer?"

On their way to the One Earth Stage, Anna shows Shari some of the sights in the Green Futures field. Shari and Eden had not once been to any of the green fields on any of their adventures. Shari is experiencing unspoken disappointment about missing both Cat Power and Mumford and Sons, but she doesn't want to be on her own. In an effort to distract herself, Shari points to the house made of tetrapaks.

"Ha, the Tetrashack! That's funny."

It's grown since Anna saw it last – by quite a lot. It has subsumed two and a half more days worth of used tetrapaks from across the festival. Now it's more of a Tetra-palace.

At this moment, one of the most stunning women Anna has ever seen steps out onto the path in front of them – a faery, to be exact – but the like of which Anna has never seen, at this festival or anywhere else. She is a tall dark-skinned woman of African descent, wearing very little in the way of clothing, but painted a lot. Her top is bare, and at her heart is a giant swirling sun, streaming swirls of gold and pink across her breasts and beyond, moving round her ribs and rising up over her shoulders to meet a pair of intricate and similarly coloured faery wings. Stars and moons decorate her belly and surround her navel.

The only actual physical garments the faery-women wears are a very short faery skirt, made from torn fabrics in shades of green, gold and pink, and a brown faux-leather faery belt with large pockets hanging on each hip. Striding out from beneath the skirt are muscular and shapely legs, which are also painted with swirls like a helter-skelter in gold and light pink, which on closer inspection turn out to be dozens of tiny stars, hearts and moons. This woman is a work of art. Her feet are bare, and her nails are also painted with tiny celestial objects. The woman's hair is no less a work of art – in long black twists, it is woven with gold beads and threaded with shimmering gold thread. Some of the woman's hair is tied back princess style, with the rest flowing down past her shoulders in unkempt wild black and gold sparkles. And her face – at the centre of the woman's forehead, again in gold, is a starburst, with offshoots of light radiating from her eyes and across her cheeks.

Anna and Shari both stop walking, and just stare.

"Wow," breathes Shari.

Anna is speechless.

Noela gets that familiar feeling in the heart when she comes across the next person she's going to paint. It's a kind of recognition, for what happens between her and those she paints is a kind of communion, and she usually feels it a moment beforehand. She smiles at the two women, who have the kinds of looks on their faces she often gets walking around the festival.

Noela is a healer of a kind – in her own way – and she works mostly within these green fields, where more often than not, nakedness is not just accepted, it is honoured. Besides, she knows her breasts are a work of art, and Noela's aura is such that nobody would dare to question her on the matter. She seems to Anna like a faery-warrior.

"Would you ladies like your faces painted?" Noela asks, cheerfully. "It's all by donation."

Images flash into Anna's mind of her Wild Heart-Self, and of her dream and how her body had been painted in those swirls of living light.

Yes! Yes I would!

"Uh…" Shari tries to suppress a nervous giggle. "No thanks." Though secretly, she is very tempted. Shari too is imagining herself painted like this, and the image is so tantalising it scares her. She has to laugh, because the the idea of it is so at odds with how she sees herself. Yet, a part of her really does want it – a lot – but Shari is used to suppressing her more raw urges, and this is no exception.

But I do want my face painted, thinks Anna, looking back at Shari, and wondering if she might change her mind. But no, the indecision Anna saw pass across Shari's face a moment ago is gone now. *So you can't have your face painted*, the familiar voice in her head tells her. *Shari doesn't want to, so you shouldn't either.*

This results in instant contraction throughout Anna's whole body. She notices it and wonders, *Is it true? Really?*

What would your life look like if it was guided by love? her Heart-Self is whispering.

Noela's eyes twinkle at Anna.

"Thanks anyway," Anna hears herself say, feeling the energy in her body becoming heavier as she fights with herself, held by her past beliefs about not being enough.

Noela hears Anna's words, but she doesn't believe them. The feeling in her heart is still here, the sense of connecting with a person she is about to have business with. Still, she smiles, accepting it. "Well, if you change your mind, I'll be around. Enjoy your festival." After giving the two women a wide, knowing grin, Noela saunters off.

Anna stares after at the woman's retreating figure, and notices that even across her lower back are more of the same intricate and beautiful designs.

Wait! Don't go! I do want to do this! I really do!

But you can't… Not with Shari here… and Shari would never do this… These are the old thought patterns, the ones that tell her she must not follow her own urges, because they are not good enough, because she must follow what others are doing, so she can be accepted.

But I want to have my face painted! It is exploding inside her now, a dam bursting. And this time it is different.

"Wait!" Anna hears herself cry aloud.

Noela turns around slowly and grins her fantastic bright smile back at Anna, with a look that says, *Well done. I was wondering how long it would take you.*

Shari, open-mouthed, is shocked at Anna's outburst. In her experience, it is unlike Anna to act impulsively. But then it occurs to Shari that there is something different about this Anna.

"Actually, I would like my face painted," Anna says, standing taller. She reminds herself to breathe into her belly, and it feels better.

"You do?" Shari asks, her own desire reawakening in the face of Anna's courage.

"Yes, I do. Do you mind waiting?"

Shari opens her mouth, unsure of what to say, and shakes her head. "Sure."

But Shari does mind. She doesn't want to just wait. She wants her face painted too.

"I'm Noela." The faery woman holds her hand over her heart in greeting.

Anna echoes the gesture. "I'm Anna, and this is Shari."

"Pleased to meet you, Anna and Shari."

Noela leads them both to some wooden benches set beneath the cluster of tall wooden flag poles, their rainbow flags flapping against the tops with a tap tap tap against the pale grey-blue of the darkening sky.

Anna sits opposite Noela, heart pounding. It feels right, but also frightening. Again, as when Anna had stepped out naked for the first time at the sauna, she feels a sense of doing something forbidden, something wild. The last time she had her face painted she was a child, and back then it was nothing like this – nothing like the intensity of these eyes on her right now.

Noela reaches out with the tips of her fingers, gently holding the sides of Anna's face. This is the moment Noela breathes in and opens her heart, asking for help from her guides and Higher Self to bring through whatever is in the highest good for the person she is working with.

Noela has a special gift, as everyone does – a dharma, a way to serve, to bring her whole heart to something. This is what she loves to do. When she paints a person, she is painting an expression of the person's own unique beauty. Though she knows all people are at their essence the same, on levels closer to human understanding, she experiences the expression of divine love in each one reflecting light in a unique way. As she paints someone, she is letting the heart energy flow through her heart, through her hands. To Noela, each person she works with is the most beautiful person she has ever met. They are God. And so is Anna. Noela smiles, because she sees it now; she sees the light, and the energy begins to move in her. She reaches into one of her side pockets and draws out her small set of face paints, her healing tools. They are made of natural pigments – faery brand.

As Noela begins, a stillness falls over Anna, a sense of being completely cared for. She closes her eyes and drifts into a meditative state, surrendering to the feel of the wet brush gliding across her cheekbones, the brush kisses at the edges of her eyes, Noela's nimble fingers, so sure and soft.

It's such a pleasing experience, Anna falls deeper into a kind of a trance. The wetness of the brush tickles her forehead between the eyebrows, drawing her attention to her Third Eye Chakra – the centre of intuition, deep sight and conscious awareness.

Shari takes a sharp inbreath, gasping a barely audible, "Wow, Anna."

Noela sits back on the bench, releasing a breath. "There. It is done."

It takes Anna a moment or two before she can slowly flutter open her eyes.

"Anna you look... amazing!" Shari's eyes are wide.

"Have a look." Noela draws a little round mirror out of her left faery pocket and offers it to Anna. Lifting the mirror to her face, Anna hears a gasp of awe emerging from her own lips. *Is this me?*

Gazing back at her is an image of her own fiery Wild Self, in gold and orange and white, with flecks of teal blue. The starburst at Anna's Third Eye radiates with filaments of light in all directions in gold, orange and white ascending over her eyebrows. At the outer edges of Anna's eyes, above her cheekbones, are swirls of colour – leaves and flecks of teal and aquamarine accentuating the colours of fire. Her eyes seem to glow brighter, and are shining back at her.

"It's... wow."

"Yeah, it is," agrees Shari.

"Thank you Noela." Anna shakes her head, still hardly believing that this face in the mirror is real. "I keep wondering if this is really me."

"This is you," Noela says with absolute conviction, "A most beautiful woman – a goddess."

"I want my face painted too." Shari's voice carries a conviction Anna has not heard before.

"With pleasure," Noela grins.

With one arm around Anna's shoulders, Shari snaps a selfie of them both with her mobile phone. She plans to upload it to her social media to show Eden what she's been missing, but the two women review the image and are both struck silent. It is a new version of Anna and Shari.

Anna recalls the delight in Shari's face, the moment she had been offered the mirror and had seen what Noela had done, as if it had given her permission to free some part of herself. Shari's face paint is softer than Anna's, in pinks and whites and purples, with tiny flowers, hearts and swirls dancing across her upper cheekbones and at the edges of her eyes. A tiny purple lotus flower opens at Shari's third eye. This is Shari's gentle power, made visible through Noela's hand and heart.

"Don't post it," Anna says, knowing with a sudden certainty that this is what Shari intends to do.

"Why not?"

Because I'm not ready for anyone back home to see me this way. Not yet. "I kind of just want it to be for us, right now."

Shari shrugs, slightly disappointed. "Sure, but we do look pretty gorgeous, Anna."

"You're right, we do." Anna does feel beautiful tonight.

"I kind of never want to wash it off."

"I know what you mean." Anna nods, feeling the pinch of knowing that a time will come when she must. But that time is not yet.

They are outside the venue now, and it is already packed. Lanterns strung up above the entrance are brightly lit and inviting. Large paintings of trees, mushrooms and other plants intermingled with various instruments adorn the inner walls of the tent. The images have all been highlighted with white and neon colours which reflect back the black light placed around the venue, giving the impression of glowing lines of energy. It reminds Anna a little of the magically-lit up forest in the film *Avatar*. As they pass beneath the rows of shining lanterns and step into this world, Shari's facepaint begin to glow, and Anna knows hers must be doing the same.

The stage is set, ready for the band to arrive. Along the back of the stage is a large, earth-red fabric with a fiery mandala in the centre and the words: 'Awakening the Dreamer' across the bottom. The bright yellow flames sewn into the centre of the mandala glow in the black light. Large cut-out wooden oak trees flank either side of the stage and are painted with bright colours and similarly glowing veins. The effect is of a stage set in a magic woods.

Up until now, Shari has been reserving judgement on why they had to miss her two favourite musical choices. But after the facepaint, and now standing here in this extraordinary venue, surrounded by hundreds of people who all seem to be glowing, she is willing to give Anna the benefit of the doubt. Intrigued by this new, fiery Anna, Shari wants to know more. The crowd's anticipation crackles in the air around them. It is going to be a special night.

There are an interesting array of instruments laid out across the stage: a drum kit, a djembe and a kahon, a guitar, a bass and violin. But in pride of place is the impressive-looking didgeridoo with a bird carved into it, resting on its stand in readiness. Anna has met that didgeridoo once before, and the memory of it moves now through her body again.

Out of sight from the audience, Cedar and Moon are going through their pre-performance preparations.

Moon stands barefoot out on the grass behind the stage, breathing into her belly and breathing out into the Earth. With each breath out, she imagines her roots reaching deeper until she can feel the calm of the Earth's hum below the soles of her feet.

Thank you Pachamama.

As she opens herself to receive this energy, it is a golden sap rising up through her roots and out through her hands and heart. She feels herself shifting into a state of present-moment awareness, a state of being Moon knows will enable something to happen tonight that is not driven by her own personal ego's needs and fears.

Not far away, Cedar is deep in his own ritual. He has grounded himself and connected with the Earth in a similar way to Moon. He has chanted *Ong Namo Guru Dev Namo* three times silently to himself – feeling the movement of his tongue against the roof of his mouth with each syllable – to connect him to his Higher Self, to the Guru within. Then he had done Breath of Fire, one of his Kundalini Yoga practices, which wakes up his senses more fully and brings him into a heightened state of awareness. Now he is breathing into his Lower Tantien, breathing in the energy from the world around him – from the Earth and Sky – with a sense of gratitude. On the outbreath Cedar reminds himself to give the energy back as a blessing. *This is the key*, Cedar is realising.

Breathe gratitude into the belly; breathe out a blessing of love through the Heart.

He breathes this way for a few moments, and as has been happening for Cedar in recent months, he begins to feel an energy rising up from the base of his spine. With this awakening energy, a sweet bliss is rising up through his body, igniting in his heart. His awareness expands and he can now feel the audience inside the tent too; they are part of him, and loving them all, he is ready.

May the energy of love flow through this music. May I be in service of the whole, for the upliftment and good of all.

Alex is the first one to jump onto stage, to excited cheering and clapping. He waves, giving them all a cheeky grin. After Alex is a man Anna assumes must be Ed, who heads for the bass guitar. Next is Moon in her bare feet, wearing a sleeveless knee-length dark green dress. At the sight of her, the excited cheering jumps up a notch. They clearly love Moon and Anna can see why. She shines, and it's not just the black light either, which highlights the patterns of white moons embroidered along the lower edge of her dress. A crescent moon is painted in dark blue and silver on her left cheek. Two feathers – one small hawk feather given to her by Cedar, and one buzzard feather she found herself – hang clipped into her wild hair. The medicine pouch sits nestled at the centre of her chest. Again, Anna wonders what's in there.

Moon stands in front of her microphone and casts her gaze over the audience, taking them all in as a whole. She is grateful to see Maddy there at the front, with love shining in her eyes. Maddy had said she would be sending them all energy from there in the audience. Moon knows how much difference this can make to a performer onstage, when they are not the only ones holding the energy of what comes through.

Like a sudden breath of wind Cedar arrives on stage, and the cheering reaches a new pitch. Anna's own breath catches as her whole body pounds with the rush of seeing him so close, and like this!

It's like the dream! Three suns!

Cedar had his own meeting with Noela earlier. Knowing the effect of the evening's lighting in this venue, he had invited Noela to paint his body in her own unique way. In the place of the Third Eye is a white star, rays of yellow and gold shining over Cedar's eyebrows. A starburst of living fire radiates from the centre of his chest, in gold and light green, visible through his open tan-coloured waistcoat. Swirls of that fire move in tendrils down his bare arms, over the tops of his hands and out to the tips of his fingers. A third sun emerges like a sunrise around Cedar's navel, just above his belt where his eagle feather is hanging. He and Moon standing there together on the stage – the whites of their eyes gleaming bright in the black light – make quite a pair.

"Wow," Shari breathes. "Who is THAT?"

Anna says nothing. She can't – there are no words.

Cedar moves to his place onstage and holds them all in his vision. Like Moon, Cedar has shifted into that right-brained state where the vision becomes peripheral; everything is in soft focus as it takes in the whole. He can sense Anna is here somewhere, but he's not entertaining the part of himself that's glad she is. He wants to be in service to the whole, not the individual self, not his primal attractions. For the moment, he is succeeding. He gently and deliberately lifts his didgeridoo from its stand, drawing it toward his lips, softly and with intent. There is a moment's pause as he listens, waiting for the energy to move him.

Like thunder, it comes and shocks them all into alertness. It is more than the deep rhythmic thrumming Anna had experienced in the Big Tipi that night. It is that, but more, bigger, and amplified. It is Cedar let loose.

Awakening the Dreamer are starting with this song for a reason. At first, when audiences come to a gig like this, usually their ability to listen is dented by the sheer number of things happening on site. Their energies are often dissipated and tired. Many have come directly from Babylon. This first song draws all the energies in and plays to the chaos, like the Pied Piper. If the band had begun with a gentler song, people wouldn't have been able to listen so deeply. The musicians know that here, at this point in the festival, they have to first speak to the chaos, to the disparate energies, to the stray thoughts. To draw all of it in with this wildness, focusing it here, now.

Anna is in a whirlwind, her own thoughts blasted out in the waves of sound. Moon's voice is a primal wail. The bass accentuates the deep pulse. The drums beat fast and steady.

Until it all stops. There is only this silence, filled with everyone's listening.

Into this clearer space, Cedar plays a single sustained note on his didgeridoo. Anna feels it right in the centre of her chest, as if Cedar is right here in front of her, didging her heart again as he did that night in the Big Tipi.

From the corner of her eye, Anna can see the look of shock on Shari's face as she is being put in touch with a part of herself she is not used to feeling. Even Anna, who has been put in touch with her heart several times over this weekend, is stunned by the intensity of the vibration right here at the centre of her chest.

How is he doing this? she wonders.

Moon and Cedar know that everything has a frequency, even a chakra. This particular note is designed to resonate with the Heart Chakra, and if it be in their highest good, to bring all those who are listening right here, to this place, to an increased awareness of their hearts. The intensity of the resonance is so strong that Anna can hardly breathe. It's almost too much, but as she gives herself to it, she can feel her awareness shifting from her head to her chest, to the pulsing in the heart. A heart beat note.

And just as it feels that it really will be too much, there is silence again. Out of this silence comes a clear note, sounding out – Moon's voice. It rushes up through Anna's body, tingling all over her skin.

You can do that with a voice?

It is Moon's heart that is singing, calling to the song in the hearts of all those who listen. She is drawing the voice up from deep in the Earth. For Moon, it is the Earth herself singing, and this is why it is so pure and so raw. Moon consciously focuses this energy through her Heart Chakra, so that it becomes infused with Heart Energy. This is how she can do this without fear. This is how she can bring herself into a state of love onstage.

Moon knows that it is partly thanks to Maddy that she has been able to open her heart again, that she is able to do this at all. Even now, Moon can feel Maddy is helping. There in the audience – as she said she would be doing – Maddy is focusing energy though her own Heart Chakra and directing it to all the musicians on stage. Receiving this energy, the ones on stage are then able to give it back to the audience, thus raising the collective Heart Energy in the room even more. Paul and Lu are in the audience somewhere too – Moon had seen them earlier – no doubt doing the same thing. Though they are not on stage themselves, those who listen and consciously give their energy to what is happening are every bit as much a part of the music as those who play it. *Or are played*, the thought comes to Moon.

The sweetness of Moon's voice fills Anna. As the song reaches its crescendo, moving in ecstatic waves through Anna's body, in comes the pulsing rhythm of the didgeridoo, and now Ed's violin, and now the beat of Alex's drums. This song has a sweetness and an urgency to it. Having been touched in the heart, those who listen feel the music in their bodies too, and it is moving them all. Anna has never felt this way before – having music inside her like this. It feels more than good; it's euphoric.

The thought comes to her – *What if I did what I was shown earlier in the workshop? How would my body dance then?* Breathing into her centre, Anna allows the movements of her body to begin from this place, travelling through all the golden threads out to the tips of her fingers and toes. Feeling something shifting inside herself, Anna observes with awe how the music is now beginning to dance her body, rather than the other way around! *What an extraordinary feeling!*

A memory comes of Cedar playing his didgeridoo in the Big Tipi, and how it had seemed then that the instrument had been playing him. She hadn't understood it at the time, but here, being danced by this music, Anna is beginning to understand how music can play a person, and the joy of that surrender.

Something in the room shifts again. The beat intensifies, becoming faster. It's trance now. With this beat, a deeper sense of presence takes them all. Anna feels a new primal aliveness in her body – everything is vivid; everything is here. She remembers the moment her Wild Heart-Self had risen from the flames in the Peace Dome to merge with her body, and how she had felt herself one with that wildness. That same wildness is alive in her now, moving her body with total abandon. It is freedom this letting go, this letting love flow. There is no guilt here, for this is love that needs nothing in return, only to give of itself, and in the fullness of that it is overflowing.

Moon is singing, "*You are the sun, you are the fire, you are the flame burning within... You are the sun, you are the fire, did you ever wonder... where the universe begins...*"

And as she sings, Anna finds her own voice rising out of her body. This is the feeling Anna had as a child, singing to the trees for no other reason but the expression of joy moving through her. The beat pulses her and she is the wild creature, the dragon, the goddess. She is part of the moving sea of all these beautiful souls around her – each one somehow completely connected to her – through her heart and the universe in her belly. Anna can see now that the golden threads extend beyond her own physical body and are dancing with the golden threads of all the others in this sea.

"*You are the sun, you are the fire, you are the flame burning within...*"

This is the moment Cedar notices Anna. He hadn't recognised her with the face-paint, but now he sees her – so radiant, so free. In this moment he knows he loves her. He loves them all. In this state, he can see the energy of the room and it's alive, alight with colour and light and fire. There are non-physical beings present too, giving their consciousness and love to what is happening here. He can almost see them at the edges of his vision. He can certainly feel them, for they have been invoked and the air is potent with their presence.

There are those in the audience who are now holding up their outstretched palms towards the stage. Cedar has seen this happen sometimes. It's spontaneous – as the energy builds there is a feeling of wanting to give it back, of gratitude. Like a wave, more and more people are raising their hands and offering their love.

Observing how her own hands are spontaneously lifting to face the stage, Anna wonders whether she could feel this way when making music herself. A resounding YES! rushes through her. *This is what I am meant to do!*

She doesn't know how to do it yet with songs, a voice and a guitar, but right now the how of it doesn't matter. Her path is shining out in front of her.

"*Your glowing soul is a flaming fire*

Have courage to dance within your flames
Oh spirit never tires to whisper the sound of your name
Just follow the light of your soul
For you shine so bright, Holy Spirit, beautiful soul
Just trust in your light. You know your way, you're coming home"

From the song, 'Follow the Light', by Ayla Schafer

"Anna... wow. That was... amazing!" Shari's face is glowing as they walk through the Tipi Field towards the fire where the band is gathering. The stars sparkle above them. Someone has lit a fire outside the Big Tipi in a large fire pit with wooden benches surrounding it. The band's instruments are being taken to their safe lock-up, but Cedar is keeping his didgeridoo with him. This is his most special instrument and he never lets it travel with anyone else. He places it softly beside him on the bench and smiles warmly up at Anna as she arrives, gesturing welcome.

Anna can hardly believe that they have been invited here to be part of the band's after-gig gathering. In Anna's satchel is Awakening the Dreamer's CD – she and Shari had both joined the queue to buy one after the concert. Alex had been the one selling merchandise, and when Anna and Shari had reached the front, he'd broken out into a huge grin to see them both.

"Anna! Nice to see you! And your friend." He'd given Shari an appreciative nod.

Shari had turned to Anna with a look of surprise as if to say, *You know these people? Personally?*

"Shari, this is Alex. Alex, Shari."

"Nice to meet you." He'd shaken Shari's delighted hand.

"You too," Shari had enthused. "I think you're my new favourite band!"

Alex's face had flushed with pleasure at this, and then he had invited them to come back to the Tipi Field with the band, to share their fire. So here they are, and here is Cedar, eyes warm and bright in the reflection of the firelight, seeming genuinely pleased to see her.

"Anna and Anna's friend, welcome." He raises his hand in greeting.

"This is Shari," Anna introduces them. "Shari, this is Cedar, Moon... and everyone else." Anna nods to the two she hasn't met yet, Ed and a petite, raven-haired woman she assumes is Ed's girlfriend by the way she is leaning against him.

"This is Ed, and this is Rae," Cedar introduces them. They smile in greeting. There is a cheerful friendliness in Rae's open face. Ed seems more reticent.

"That was amazing!" Shari looks around the circle with adoration. "I've seen so many gigs this weekend on all the big stages and they were good, but none of them made me feel like that!"

Cedar smiles and nods gracefully. Many people have said words like these tonight. Sometimes he finds the overwhelming praise difficult, because the more he serves the moment and lets love flow through him, the more the love rushes back towards him from the audience. Most of them seem to think that he, Cedar himself, did the thing that touched them so deeply, but he knows that he was only a small part of what went on. There are always many other energies at play – angelic and otherwise. He was only serving the music as best he could, being a kind of channel for it. They were all creating it together.

In the face of this intense gratitude and enthusiasm from the audience (a high proportion of whom are women), Cedar has to remind himself that this is not personal. That he by himself did not do that thing that happened tonight. He can still feel his ego there, trying to puff itself up with the praise, but he keeps reminding himself to do the thing he was taught: *When the gratitude and appreciation comes towards you, send it on to the Source, to that Love that came through and brought through the music, to the Great Spirit, to Pachamama. Give it back, let it flow through. Be a conduit for both the music, and for the praise of it.*

Moon is sitting on a bench across the fire from Cedar. She lifts her eyes from the flames and offers a smile to Anna. Anna can't read her expression. *Is it welcome?*

Moon is full tonight with many emotions. She is glad to see Anna though, and wonders who it was that invited her here. *Was it Cedar?* Moon feels just a tiny pang at the thought but lets it go. She appreciates the paint on Anna's face and the new spark of life that seems to be with her tonight. A flash comes to Moon of a golden animal – a lioness. *She's beautiful.* Moon wonders briefly whether Cedar will find Anna that way too and then shakes her head and takes a breath. *How quickly the thoughts come back in.*

For Moon, the moments following a gig are not always easy. She notices how for Alex, the post-gig always involves food – large amounts of it. For Ed, many things. Similarly for Cedar, but for Cedar – especially in the past – it had often been about sex. He would take the energy built up from the performance and channel it into physical lovemaking. For a long time she had done that with him. *But no more.*

The experience of stepping off stage has become more complicated of late.

Tonight she was able to experience the joy and exhilaration of serving the collective, of allowing the energy of the Earth to move through her. In those moments she'd fully given herself to the music and the moment, she'd felt herself part of everyone in that tent and beyond. At moments, the thoughts in her head had ceased altogether in the bliss of that trancendence. But tonight, stepping offstage and being Moon again has felt particularly challenging, because there is a vulnerability from having opened herself to so many, from having been part of so many energy fields – some of which she can still feel resonating on as people bring their sense of joy out into the greater festival with them, reliving their experiences in their minds and hearts. Moon reminds herself to close down her energy centres just a little more – for they have been so open onstage, more open tonight than ever before. There seems to be a protection onstage, as the performers invoke their guides and intend the highest good for all, entering willingly with the audience into a shared communal experience. But Moon knows that if she remains that open after a peformance, she can be easily overwhelmed by the energies of the world around her, especially here at a festival like this. Cedar seems to find it easier to move between energy fields, as a result of his various practices. In the past, meeting with Cedar after a gig had been one way to integrate it all. *But no more.*

Cedar looks up, reading Moon's expression. *Well done you,* he beams this to her. *And THANK YOU.*

She receives the spirit he is trying to convey and offers a smile in return. *You too.*

There is love and friendship here. Moon is pleased to still feel it between them and knows that it will never end. Even with everything else going on, they had managed to serve the moment together, to *Be In Love* onstage. After all that has happened, the experience of performing together tonight has been even deeper than before. And yet, she can still feel the question inside her about whether they will be able to do this long-term.

It comes now to Moon – an unbidden vision – of two paths diverging, like streams changing their course, both destined for the same sea, and on a deeper level never really separate, though on the surface they may meander far from one another. It brings with it a bittersweet knowing that their two paths which have been so intertwined for years – the closeness of which has brought them both so much growth and healing – has served its purpose for now.

At this moment, Maddy arrives with a large tray of goodies from Pacha Mama Cafe: a large pile of chocolate crepes on a paper plate, several slices of spelt carrot cake and some raw chocolates, as well as a stack of paper cups and a large flask containing chai.

"Goddess!"Alex raises his arms and bows to Maddy. "Our hero."

Maddy laughs, amused by the gesture. "I think we should be bowing to you all, really. You were all the Gods and Goddesses tonight. This is just a small offering in thanks." She places the tray down on one of the benches and Alex dives in, helping himself to a crepe and a handful of raw chocolates. Moon doesn't want to eat yet, but she accepts a cup of hot chai from Maddy and sips it slowly. Cedar likewise.

"Everyone in that room was," Moon says aloud after a moment. "Gods and Goddesses... We should all bow to ourselves and each other really."

"That's kind of a physical impossibility, though, isn't it? Bowing to yourself?" Alex asks. "I mean, it doesn't really work..." He proceeds to demonstrate this, bottom in the air, resulting in a chorus of laughs from around the circle.

How good it feels to be around this fire! Anna thinks, laughing along with them. Shari is having a good time too. Anna wouldn't have pegged Alex for Shari's type, especially when she has Evan back home, but there is a definite look of appreciation there in Shari's eyes.

Anna's thoughts turn to Damien, and to what going home will mean. It doesn't mix well with her good feelings. She doesn't intend to betray Damien, but she doesn't want to think about him right now either, because that world and this one don't seem to belong together. But then a thought comes to her like a faint whisper: *Perhaps the worlds are not so far apart as you think...*

Shari laughs, tickled by something Alex has said. Anna smiles to herself. *And Shari is here, and I never knew that could happen. So maybe there is hope for the rest of my life too. And tonight, I am here. Tomorrow is tomorrow. Tonight I'm going to enjoy it for all it's worth!* Something in Anna knows this is a very important night in her life, and it's definitely not over yet.

There are now eight around the fire: Cedar, Alex, Shari, Anna, Maddy, Moon, Ed and Rae. The plate of goodies is making its way around the circle and as it arrives at Anna, she gratefully accepts a cup of chai and a chocolate crepe.

Shari tucks into her crepe, chocolate dripping down her chin. Alex offers her a crumpled up napkin, which she accepts, laughing at herself as she wipes her face.

"There really is no way to eat Maddy's pancakes without getting food all over yourself," Alex says, demonstrating this deliberately with his own pancake in a cavalier manner. "They are so good, you just want to cover yourself with them."

Maddy laughs. "I've never seen them used that way before, but it might well be something to try."

"You know, it might," Alex nods, emphatically miming a sign in the air with his hands. "Chocolate pancake therapy... £10.50... or... £12 with cream... Pacha Mama would be the most popular cafe in the festival."

"God these are good," Shari says between bites. "Or maybe I should say 'goddess' they are good!"

"They're made with love," Anna hears herself saying this aloud.

"I can totally believe it," Shari replies. It occurs to Anna what a different way this is to be speaking with Shari. Shari hasn't even remotely balked at a phrase like *'made with love'*. Not only that, she seems to understand it.

Tonight Shari has had her heart opened, and she too can feel the love that is present here, still flowing in the hearts of those around the fire. The fire crackles with life, sparking with the energy of all those around it.

"That was the best gig of my life." Rae speaks what they are all feeling.

Anna nods, the magic of the music still humming through her body. She still feels like she's dancing.

"I knew you guys were good," Rae continues. "I mean, I've heard you lots of times, but tonight something just shifted up a gear. Or ten gears! I don't know, I just felt like my heart completely expanded!"

There are murmurs of agreement around the fire.

"That's love for you," Cedar says, his eyes meeting Moon's. Here, by the glow of this fire, Cedar can see how Moon has grown. Something has shifted for her too, this weekend. She's stepped into her power in a new way on stage; it was a true joy to be with her up there. Tonight they could hold and focus more energy together than they ever had before. The audience felt it too.

Moon turns her gaze to Maddy, and Cedar sees what passes between them. *That's love for you*, he thinks again, knowing that he and Moon won't be sharing their usual post-gig time together tonight. But it feels okay. It feels right. He can see that he is having to let go of a certain thing he'd drawn from her. She had been right about that.

But what will be in its place? He realises that maybe it's not about integrating the experience with another person, so much as integrating it within himself. *And maybe it's about the collective too, about all of us.* His eyes move around the fire, stopping briefly at Anna. He knows this night still has something to do with her.

She has surprised him this weekend. She'd been so blocked when he'd first met her, and yet she had opened that night in the Big Tipi; she'd been ready for it. Then they had shared those special moments on the hill, and then again in the sauna when he had known without a doubt that she felt something for him too. She had been dancing through his thoughts all weekend, and then dancing with such freedom before him at the gig. And now here she is with this incredible paint on her face, revealing something more of herself. She is beautiful to him, and not just in the way that all people beautiful when Cedar is managing to live in his heart and love everyone unconditionally. There is something utterly more personal going on here; he has to accept it now. *But what does it mean?*

"I think for me," Rae speaks out again, "something really kicked in about three songs in. I mean, it was powerful before that, but during that song – the one about the heart... whoa... I just... something happened to me. I really can't explain it. I felt like something took me over."

"It's trance," Cedar says. "If done with the right intention, it can shift people into a heightened state of awareness."

"It's the same experience I get when I listen to someone playing a Native American medicine drum," Moon adds. "When they're doing it from a loving place of presence and honouring. And that's really where the song comes from. It's about feeling your heart for the first time. The moment you first have that experience of awakening."

Awakening, thinks Anna. *It feels like that's what's been happening to me. Awakening. Like I've been asleep my whole life. And then I heard Cedar and Moon playing in the tipi that night, and something in me woke up. And it happened again tonight.*

"I used to go and listen to trance music when I was younger," Alex joins in, "but it never made me feel like this. Awake is a good word for it. I didn't know trance music could be like that."

"Depends where it's coming from," Cedar says. "If it's conscious trance, and into that state you bring the intention to heal, it has that power. There are some kinds of trance which can lead you deeper into numbness. It's all about the intent behind it, what's driving it. I know I'm not always perfect at it, but whether it's trance or anything else, it's always our intention with our music that we are serving a higher purpose, as best we can, that it be a vehicle for love to flow through and bring people whatever they most need."

"I always feel like when we get to that song, my drumming suddenly gets really good." Alex chuckles.

"It does," Moon says seriously. "I mean you've got skill, Alex; you're a good drummer. But tonight you made that shift with the rest of us, and we all locked into it and the music just carried us. When you shift into that state, it's easier to get out of your own way."

"That's a good way of describing it. Getting out of my own way. I think I must be in my own way most of the time." Alex laughs again at himself.

"Most of us are," Maddy says. "Until we're not."

"Until we're not?" Alex raises an eyebrow. "And then what happens?"

Maddy shrugs. "Enlightenment, I guess."

"Enlightenment? What is that anyway?" Alex asks, thinking of the Van Morrison song.

"It's waking up," Cedar says. "That's the awakening. It's arriving in the moment, knowing yourself connected to everything. It's living in a state of constant love."

"You speak like you've been there," Rae says.

"You mean here," Cedar grins.

"What?" Rae asks, confused.

"Enlightenment is about being here, not there."

"Oh, right," she laughs, "I get you. So you're speaking from experience? Are you enlightened then?"

Cedar chuckles softly to himself. "No. But there have been a couple of peak spiritual experiences I've had which I know have changed me and have helped me to be more present and not get taken away by my thoughts like I used to. But my ego still does manage to get a grip sometimes. There are parts of my shadow I still haven't integrated." He looks up at Moon, who is offering him a wry smile. He knows what she's thinking, and returns the smile. Tonight all of that feels okay.

"It's like that for most of us," Moon says. "A gradual process of awakening."

"But there are some who just seem to be born enlightened," Maddy offers. "Like Amma."

"Who's Amma?" Alex asks.

"She's the hugging mother," Maddy says, her eyes lighting up. "You've seen the painting hanging at Pacha Mama's?

Alex nods.

"That's her."

That's her? Anna realises. *That's the name of that beautiful smiling Indian woman with the red spot between her eyes? Amma.*

"I remember hearing about her," Rae says. "Doesn't she hug like, thousands of people a day or something?"

"Thousands?" Alex asks.

"Yes," Maddy says. "She's hugged literally millions of people around the world. She travels around, doing something called 'darshan', and people queue up for hours for a hug."

"God, she must get tired." Alex lets out a breath.

"I wouldn't think so." Maddy shakes her head. "She's a conduit for divine love. She is totally in the present, totally in love with each and every person she's hugging. I've felt it. I had one of her hugs in London a couple of years ago. I was in a strange place in my life at that time, and when Amma embraced me, I felt like all that strangeness fell away and I could see myself clearly. Because to Amma I was love, and the love flowing through her showed me that. She was like a mirror of me. It completely opened my heart, and it's like... that experience taught my heart what was possible. So even if I don't feel that all-encompassing love all of the time, still I remember it and so I'm always moving towards having that feeling again."

"That's how it is with resonance," Cedar says, thinking of his own heart, and how it has been opened more this weekend; how through that opening, things have gotten so much deeper. *You are Love* – the words he'd sung out on the hill that day dance through his consciousness. He is understanding more of what that means in a real sense now.

"The heart is where it all integrates," he says aloud, his realisations crystallising for him as he speaks. "The divine and the earthly realms come together in the heart." He sees something so clearly now. He had been struggling to integrate his physical life with his spiritual life. *But it comes together in the heart. They are not really separate at all.*

Moon looks up, smiling to hear this. She had said very similar words to him many times, but she knows that until a person comes to a truth in their own way, they never really know it. Cedar meets Moon's gaze and nods, *You helped me to see that.*

"You hear about these people who spontaneously become enlightened at some point in their lives," Rae says, "like Eckhart Tolle."

"Or Byron Katie," Maddy adds.

Moon nods. "And all those cases, according to their books, it was serious emotional pain that was the catalyst for their awakenings."

"It's often like that," Cedar says. "The most challenging, painful times can be the blessing in disguise that cracks us open." He looks up and meets Moon's eyes again.

"So you're saying pain is good?" Alex says. "Who needs hugs then? I need to find me a good spanking."

Laughter erupts again around the circle.

"Spank me to enlightenment, sweetie!" Alex chortles, offering his backside to the fire and spanking himself heartily to another explosion of laughter.

"Well, I suppose that could work," Maddy grins wryly, "If you did it with love."

"Here's another service Pacha Mama could offer," Alex points out. "Free spanking with every pancake."

"With chocolate on top," Moon adds.

Maddy gives her a look.

The laughter feels good and as it fades into silence, the energy moves back to the fire, to the aliveness of the flames, leaping and crackling, and the swirls of smoke dancing higher.

"I loved what you said at the end of the concert," Shari speaks up. "About sending the energy out across the world. I actually saw it happening. It was amazing."

Anna stares at Shari, surprised to hear her speaking in this way, expressing the very thing she herself had experienced. In those moments after the band had finished their encore and the audience was still crying out for more, Cedar had approached the microphone and asked them all to send the positive energy that had gathered there on this night and to send it out across the world, for the good of everyone. And like a wave, Anna had felt it moving outwards from that tent, rippling on and on, out across the festival and beyond. She had felt her connection to the whole world in that moment.

Here now, in this circle, by this fire, Anna turns to look at her friend, this woman who she had judged so many times, just as she had judged herself. She hadn't really known Shari at all, just as she hadn't really known herself. Suddenly, with their faces lit by firelight, an image flashes into Anna's mind with a corresponding rush of energy throughout her body. Shari sitting here before her is a mirror image of herself, just as her Heart-Self had been in the candlelit mandala of the Peace Dome. *Shari is me, too!*

"That was a moment," Cedar agrees. "There was so much heart energy vibrating there in the room, it felt like it wanted to fly out across the world, and go to where it could be of most good, to add together with the wave of awakening that's happening."

"Mmm," Moon nods. "I see it like that too – a great wave of consciousness, rippling out, touching everybody."

"I've heard people say this is the Time of the Great Awakening," Maddy says. "The time of the hundredth monkey."

"The hundredth monkey?" Alex asks. "What's that?"

"There was an experiment done," Maddy explains, "back in the fifties with monkeys on a Japanese island. The monkeys were given sweet potatoes covered in sand. They loved the potatoes, but they didn't like the sand. One of the young monkeys learned how to wash its sweet potato and discovered how much nicer it tasted. So it taught its mother and the other young monkeys, and they taught their mothers and so on. Apparently, the story goes that once a critical mass was reached – say 100 monkeys – then all the monkeys on that island had the knowledge and the ability to wash their sweet potatoes. But not only that, monkeys on other islands and on mainland Japan also knew how to wash their food. They say it's like that with becoming conscious as human beings..."

"So when enough of us wash our potatoes, so to speak, we'll all become enlightened?" Alex asks.

"That's exactly what I'm saying." Maddy gives him a look. "When enough of us reach a critical mass of awareness, of living in our hearts, of living with compassion for other beings, then whole world will shift."

A shiver of energy moves through Anna.

"So how many monkeys are there in that sense then?" Alex asks. "Like, what if I am that hundredth monkey, and if I can become enlightened – or wash my potatoes, if you will – I could be the saviour of the whole world!"

Maddy laughs. "It's my sense that we're very close to it. The question is, do we just carry on with our lives until this great wave of awakening washes over us and takes us with it or do we actively become a part of that awakening with our intentions and our thoughts so that we can speed up the process?"

"The sooner the better, for the planet," Rae says, "...and for the people in Syria and everywhere else in the world who are suffering."

There are nods around the fire, many thinking the same thoughts: *How many more species will become extinct? How high will the sea levels have to rise? How many more wars will have to happen?*

"And that's one way we can contribute as musicians." Passion is ignited in Cedar's eyes. "I think I'm only just beginning to see what my path with music is really about... How one of the most powerful things a performer can do onstage is to be part of raising the collective heart energy of the group through the shared experience of music – to have that intention – and then consciously give that energy back to the world, to wherever it's most needed, to help humanity reach that critical mass of heart energy."

Anna feels like an electric bolt is jolting through her body. *Yes. Me too! But how?*

"So if it came down to one simple thing..." Anna leans forward, the question burning in her heart. "...one thing that you could say to someone who asked you, about how you do THAT with music... what would you say to them?"

Cedar looks up and smiles at her. "The way I see it is that it comes down to two things on stage – presence and love. You may not be consciously thinking 'I am going to make spiritual, healing music now', or even be consciously aware you are working with energy, but if you can bring total presence and love to what you're doing, that transmits to the people. It's whatever can get you to that place of love and of being in the moment onstage – 'in the zone' as some performers say. And the performers who can do that, whether they are consciously trying to or not, will be making a kind of medicine music."

"Like The Band," Ed says, poking at the fire with a stick.

Anna's eyes widen. *The Band?* They're speaking about her father's favourite music here in this context?

"Yeah. Exactly like that," Cedar says. "If you've ever seen film of those guys performing live onstage, like in The Last Waltz, you can see they are lit up with energy, totally present, giving themselves to the music. They're tapped into something. It's alive, and that's why it's so powerful. And they're listening to each other. Listening in the moment. That's how you know what to play. You're not thinking about it. You're in that state of loving openness and *listening*."

Anna travels back again in her memory to those times riding in the car with her father, and how when they listened to The Band together, her father always seemed happier. *Come to think of it, so did I.* It was as if for those moments, everything was fine. The music that had done that.

"So," Anna speaks again, "I have to find whatever it is that gets me into that state of loving openness and listening on stage?"

Cedar nods. "And then when you find what works for you, you'll be able to stand up there on stage and be in that resonance, and if others are open to it, they will start to resonate with you, like the way a guitar string resonates with a note that's struck beside it."

"I think it's like that with anything you do in life," Maddy says softly. "Whether it's art, or writing..."

"Or making pancakes..." Moon nudges her. *Or making love.* The unspoken words hang in the air for those who can sense them.

Maddy smiles, flushing a little as she catches Moon's meaning. "Anything. I think it works with anything you do. You bring presence and love to those things – whatever actions you're making in the world – and that transmits to others. And in these little ways we have an effect."

"Every act of love makes a difference," Anna says the words aloud, remembering Andy, the kind man who had made the fire up for her in the sauna chill-out tipi. "Someone said that to me recently."

"Exactly," Maddy agrees.

Shari shakes her head in amazement, feeling overwhelmed by it all, by the possibilities of what these people are saying, that a person really could live in this way. *Could I give something positive to people when I cut their hair?* Shari wonders, *Could I love them even?* She'd never thought of that idea before. The possibility of it brings a flutter of excitement.

"There's something else, too," Cedar says. "It's got to be about service. It's not about what you get for yourself, but it's about what you can give. To make true, healing medicine, you have to be able to serve – selflessly, unconditionally."

"But isn't that what love does anyway?" Maddy asks. "Because love is selfless, if it's real. Maybe love covers it."

"Maybe it does," he nods. "Maybe it does."

An image of Kai comes into Anna's mind's eye – Kai who genuinely didn't seem to need anything in return for what he was giving to people. *This is what Love does. Love is the most important ingredient in anything. It serves.*

And the thing that niggled at Anna that moment in the Chai Chi tent, the thing she couldn't quite put her finger on about selflessness, crystallises for her now. *This is what I never did*, she realises. It comes to her here in this heightened state, for she can hear the whispers of her heart more clearly. *I was always making music with a view to what was in it for me. That's where I went wrong.*

"And the thing is, you give without needing anything, but you get everything. That's where the joy is – in the moment, in the giving," Cedar says.

Anna realises she has found something tangible after all – a step on her path, a step in the direction of love.

> "Dance to the beat of your wild heart
> Feel your feet on the bare ground
> Catch the breath of a new dawning day
> This is what it is to be human
> This is what it is to be here on Earth
> This is what it is to be connected
> This is what it is to be living our lives
> Eye to eye, hand to hand
> Heart to heart, we live we stand
> We are the power that catches the wave
> That turns the slave inside us all
> Into a wild wild heart"

from the song, 'Connected', by Shannon Smy

At some point well into the early morning hours, people begin to drift away from the fire. The first to go are Ed and Rae. Rae is falling asleep on Ed's shoulder, so he helps her to rise, and with heartfelt goodnights they had off to their tent.

Next it's Shari's turn. She doesn't want to go either, but she's just turned on her phone and there are several desperate sounding texts from Eden, whose grand plans have not worked out.

"I better go and see how Eden is. I have this feeling she might need me right about now," Shari says to Anna. "As much as I'd love to stay here all night." Shari has particularly been enjoying Alex's company. She looks over at him and sees that he doesn't want her to go either.

"Do you want me to walk you back?" Alex asks. Anna can see this is more than just chivalry; he has taken a shine to Shari, and Shari seems genuinely pleased with the attention. Anna doesn't know how this bodes for her relationship with Evan back home, but for now, none of that matters. Shari's eyes twinkle as she accepts his offer. "I'd really appreciate that. Thank you."

Shari turns to face the rest of the group around the fire. "Thank you so much everyone – for tonight, for the music and the fire. For everything."

Cedar nods and smiles. "You're welcome."

Shari leans over to embrace Anna with a new warmth. "Thank you, Anna...Thank you so much for inviting me into this world of yours."

"You're welcome." Anna hugs her back, returning the warmth. "It's your world too."

"See you back in Brighton." Shari rises from the bench, followed by Alex. She gives a final wave as they step away into the night.

The space between Anna and Cedar is now open. The only others remaining around the fire are Maddy and Moon, who sit opposite them. Moon takes Maddy's hand and squeezes it. There is a message in that which both Anna and Cedar can see. It is time for them to go.

Moon steps around the fire and places her hand on Cedar's shoulder, holding it there for a moment. *Thank you*, the gesture says. *And it's okay. Whatever you need to do is okay with me.* With a quick glance between Cedar and Anna and a wry smile, Moon whispers, "Good luck Charlie."

Cedar knows exactly what she means. He can feel it himself. There is a part of him – a very human part – which knows that soon he will be left alone around the fire with Anna, and that's where the challenge will really begin for him. He shakes his head and smiles back at Moon.

"Only you can get away with that... Rachel."

And so here it is, Moon's previous name spoken aloud too. It is as if by bringing these names here, in a lighthearted way, they are welcoming these former selves into the fire, no longer seen as separate from who they really are.

"Good night Anna," Moon says. Maddy waves.

"Night," Anna waves back.

Moon turns and follows Maddy through the darkness between the tipis.

And now there are two, Cedar thinks.

He kneels by the firepit and places another log onto it, to do something physical to ground him in his body, to help him with the feelings that are arising. He kneels there for a while, just watching the flames. Neither one speaks. The fire crackles again and sparks, the smoke swirling. The air fills potent, filled with the thoughts unspoken, the questions in both hearts.

Cedar can feel his body's need to sleep soon. It has been such a high energy night, and of course he had slept little the night before. And yet at the same time, there is a palpable electricity moving through his body at the nearness of Anna, and the sense of something still unsaid, or still un-done.

What is it? he wonders.

Anna's heart is almost bursting with where she is, with the music of the night and the inspiring conversation. And now, the nearness of this beautiful man.

"I like your paint by the way."

Anna flushes at the compliment. "Thank you."

"I can feel it's been quite a festival for you, Anna. And me too, for that matter."

He hears her utter a soft sigh, and in that sigh he hears his own dilemma, and knows she is feeling the same way. They could return to his tipi now. They could just do it. It would be so easy. *And would it be so wrong?*

Across the site, another electrified beat begins, with the fervour of late-night partying still going full tilt as festival-goers make the most of their final night. The volume seems to shift up a notch and Anna can feel the sub-bass frequencies thumping beneath her feet. Her own heart seems to race faster, as if keeping time.

I can't betray Damien, she tells herself. *I mustn't. It would be wrong.*

She remembers how breathing into her centre had helped her before to do the right thing. But in this case, the more she breathes into her body, the more she feels what her body wants to do.

Cedar pushes another log closer in. The fire crackles.

To distract herself, Anna looks for something else to talk about, to break the silence that is so filled with all they are not saying to one another. "It's so loud, all the sounds. I've been finding the noise a bit overwhelming. I mean, I didn't used to, but I suppose something's happened to me this weekend, and now I just wish it would all be a bit quieter."

"Mmm," Cedar nods. "I've felt that way about it before, but I've learned something about when you fight things. What you resist persists. There's a flow, and we're part of it. If you're straining and trying not to experience something that's happening, a big part of your discomfort – maybe even all of it – is about what's going on inside of you, your own thoughts, and not what's out there."

And as Cedar says this he realises he is speaking for himself too, for the struggle he has been putting himself through this weekend about not allowing things to flow between himself and Anna. He takes a breath. *So how do I honour the flow and still keep my vow?* he asks himself, staring hard into the fire.

"But it's so... there's just so much of it," Anna says, talking about more than just the noise. And he knows it too.

"I've got something that might help."

"Earplugs?" Anna asks, trying to make a joke, to lighten the intensity of what's happening here.

Cedar chuckles. "No. Infinitely better than that – a change in perspective." He lifts up his didgeridoo bag and unzips it, pulling out his beautiful cedar instrument.

"Are you going to play?"

He shakes his head. "Not me. Them." He gestures out into the dark and the noise of the Glastonbury night.

Anna doesn't understand, until Cedar lifts the instrument into the air, holding the flared end towards her. "Listen. Put your ear to the didge, and tell me what you hear."

She leans in. "What am I supposed to be hearing?"

"Lean in. Closer. You'll hear it."

So she leans, and all of a sudden it's here – the whispering melody of all the sounds of Glastonbury Festival. But here, through the didgeridoo, they are singing one song – a beautiful, breathy, whispering song where all the dissonance becomes one harmony.

"Wow," Anna breathes. "It's beautiful."

"Now listen again to the sounds out there." He lowers the didge and they listen together. She can still hear it. It's a version of the same song she'd heard through the didge, louder and far less subtle, but still the same.

"Oh... I see what you mean."

"Sometimes it's just about shifting your perspective."

"Thank you. I'm sure I'll rest easier tonight." But as she says this, she knows she doesn't want to rest well tonight. She doesn't want to rest at all. She wants to stay beside Cedar and she wants this night to never end.

Cedar places his didgeridoo carefully back in its cover and zips it up. "My body is telling me I need to sleep soon."

"Yeah. I guess I should too." *Please, let it not end yet.*

"Do you have far to go to get back to your tent?" Cedar asks.

"I'm camped just beyond the public camping field, in the crew and artist's camping."

Cedar can read her face, how with every fiber of her being she doesn't want to go back there now. He doesn't want her to go back either. He takes a breath and listens, and it comes to him. *So maybe there is a way, after all.*

"I could offer you a place to sleep in my tipi, if you like."

The blankets are steaming. They are handwoven and beautiful, in simple earth tones. The scent of damp wool is mixed with something herbal and the musk of Cedar's scent. But Anna doesn't mind, because this is Cedar's fire, and this is the only place she wants to be right now.

It had been cold when they'd arrived, the fire having long gone out. The dew had fallen and the air inside the tipi had grown very cold, as it does in the early morning hours in the valley. Cedar had swiftly kindled a new fire and had lifted the blankets onto two chairs to warm the damp out of them, and the pillows too. The two buckwheat pillows propped up on the other side of the fire smell subtly like toasting grain.

Cedar's tipi is sparse, more so than Moon's. His clothes are folded in a simple cotton bag and his toothbrush and comb are set out on a small wooden table. There is a simple food preparaton area to one side, with one pan, one pot, two bowls, two mugs and a kettle.

And of course there is the bed, made of sheepskins and blankets. Cedar had explained that he always tried to sleep as close to the earth as possible, and on natural fabrics. Because of the damp, though, he had accepted the necessity of having a ground sheet beneath his bedding.

He had offered Anna the use of his make-shift loo – a bucket with sawdust, sheltered in a little lean-to behind his tipi, complete with a pleasing view of the stars.

Returning now himself, Cedar closes up the tipi's entrance flap and joins Anna by the fire.

How would Moon feel about me being here? So many times before it must have been Moon sitting here with him. But then Anna remembers the look in Moon's eye earlier and her wry smile when she had said goodnight. *Charlie, she had called him. Is that his name?*

Cedar fills the heavy-looking kettle with water from a large plastic bottle and places it directly into the flames. He runs his fingers along the fabric of the blankets. "Almost there. It won't take much longer to get the chill out of these. It will be much nicer to sleep in them after this."

Sleep? Anna thinks. *Will we really sleep? Is that really why I'm here?* On one level, her body is telling her she should sleep. It's been a huge day. But her body is also telling her something else too, and every time she thinks about that something else, she tells herself *no*. Because of Damien, and the promises she made to him. But her life back in Brighton feels like another life belonging to someone else. After all that has happened this weekend, she feels like she could just give up all of her old life and dive whole heartedly into this new world of heart and fire.

"Licorice tea okay?" Cedar asks. "It's a good one for calming you before you sleep, and I know we both got a bit chilled." *And perhaps we both need a bit of calming*, he thinks to himself, seeing that look again in Anna's eyes.

"Sounds good."

Cedar breaks a handful of licorice sticks into the pot and lets it steep for a few moments before pouring them each a mug.

"Thank you." Anna accepts the drink, inhaling its spicy sweetness.

They drink their tea in potent silence, watching the flames dance, each wondering what will happen when their mugs are empty.

"Moon called you Charlie." Anna breaks the silence.

Cedar's lips curl into an amused smile. "Charlie. That's the name I was given. Charles Pemberton. It's a long story. Cedar is a name that came to me in a dream – a medicine name. All words, all names have a resonance. What you call yourself is a powerful thing, and at that time in my life I felt like Charlie wasn't me. Cedar held the energy of who I wished to become, of who I imagined I was."

"Your Wild Self?" Anna asks.

"Yes, I guess you could say that. But I wasn't balanced, Anna. I dove into this world of spiritual seeking, and I banished Charles Pemberton from my life. Moon used to say he was part of my shadow, and she used to goad me with the name sometimes. She knew it was something I didn't want to face and so therefore it was holding me back. You can't just shut off parts of yourself you don't like. Becoming a whole person is about integrating all of yourself, loving all the parts of yourself. Moon helped me see that."

"So that's why she called you Charlie tonight?"

"Yes. She knows I have been struggling with... integrating the different parts of myself. In particular, the spiritual and the physical... the sexual."

At the word sexual, heat flares through Anna's body. *What are you saying?* She catches a look in his eye just before he turns his gaze back to the fire. He stares at it intensely, as if searching for an answer.

"Can I tell you a story Anna?"

"A bedtime story?"

He chuckles, looking up. "Not exactly. A story that will explain something to you."

"Okay."

"A little over a year ago, the band went on tour to America. As you probably know, there was a time when Moon and I were partners, in more ways than just with the band. We had been together intimately for a number of years by that point, but I'd been feeling like something wasn't right and I needed some space. And I had this idea that I wanted to walk out into the desert in Arizona and go on a vision quest. So I did. I found a place to camp and I fasted for a few days, and I meditated and I dreamed. And on the night before I returned to Moon, a vision came to me – the strongest vision I've ever had. It was a dream, but it was so vivid. I saw myself onstage, and I saw my energy dissipating in all directions. I saw that every time I had sex with a women, I was depleting my energy, and I also saw that I was feeding a need in myself for acceptance. That was the Charlie Pemberton in me. I hadn't wanted to accept that he was there, but in reality, those things I had suppressed were affecting everything I did in subtle ways, and sometimes not so subtle ways. I saw that even with all my spiritual practice, I had actually been lonely for a long time, and I hadn't realised it. I saw that I had been using sex to try and feel better about myself, but I never really felt okay. It was like that with Moon. We were both on a spiritual path and we tried to make sex part of that. We were trying to meet each other, to experience unity through sex. But we were always missing something..." And now Cedar can see what it was.

"The heart," he whispers. "It's funny, you know. It should have been obvious. I knew it was important, but I was focusing so much on the higher centers, and on clearing my energy bodies, that I had sort of forgotten to consciously bring love into it."

"I went to a workshop today about that."

He looks up suddenly, catching her eye. "Paul's workshop?"

Anna nods.

"So you understand what I'm talking about then?" he asks, a smile playing out on his face.

"Yes. It feels like this whole weekend has been about that for me. About finding my heart and discovering what love really is." As she looks up again, she sees it reflected there in his eyes. *Love.*

"Can I tell you the rest of the story?" he asks. It feels more relevant than ever now.

"Of course."

"The dream showed me that I have a deeper path, and it showed me that if I could learn to channel my sexual energy, I could be a vehicle for even more healing onstage. And not just onstage, but in my life as a whole. I knew that I had to stop having sex until I could make the sexual act a truly sacred act, something dedicated for healing and service. In the same way I saw that I needed to do this with my music. As soon as I realised this, in my dream I was suddenly back in the desert. My body was still asleep, but I was aware of myself dreaming; it was a lucid dream. I heard these tinkling bells, and there was this path leading out into the desert from the fire. I saw the figure of a woman walking towards me – a beautiful, dark-skinned woman with long black hair. And I knew without any doubt – more than I've known anything before – that she was my wife. She had come to meet me in my dream. She told me she was waiting for me, that she would not have sex with a man until it was with the man she was going to have children with. With all of me and all of the guidance I trust in me, I knew that I was that man. And I knew without a doubt that one day we will meet in the physical... and we will have a child together."

He looks up at Anna, seeing the way her body is tensing in the firelight. Still, there is more to tell.

"In that place between sleeping and waking, I could still feel her presence with me, and I gave her my conscious vow. I vowed to abstain from sex until we were together in the physical, and during that time I would conserve my sexual energy and use it for the good of the whole, channel it into healing. The following morning, I walked back out of the desert and I found Moon and told her my dream. But I only told her half of it – the first half. I thought the last part would only hurt her, unnecessarily. She was devastated enough to learn that I wanted to be celibate, but she accepted it because she understood what I'd been trying to do with my life. As much as she hated the idea, she also honoured my vision. But she didn't know the whole story, and even though I made it clear to her that she shouldn't wait for me, she did wait for me. She never let it go. She thought I would eventually finish with being celibate and come back to her. I didn't see that by not being honest with her, I allowed her to continue believing that. And this weekend, she confronted me about it. She asked me if I'd had enough of celibacy yet. She came to me full of sexuality, challenging me with it. And I knew I finally had to tell her the whole truth."

Ah, Anna realises. *That was the day I met Moon. That was the look I saw in her eyes.*

He glances at Anna. "But this is not about Moon. I'm sharing this with you because..."

Anna feels a breath heave through her body as she understands. "Because you want me to know why we can't..."

"Yes."

"I should tell you something, too," she whispers. Cedar has given her his honesty, and she owes it to him to do the same. "I have a boyfriend. I live with him back in Brighton. Or at least I did before I came here."

"Ah. I wondered. I felt something."

"But I don't know what will be left of that life when I go back. I feel like my whole life is... not what I thought it was. Before I came here, I thought I was going to marry this person, and now I feel like it's a life belonging to somebody else. I mean, I do love Damien. I do. But so much has happened and I don't know how to go back."

"I understand." Cedar nods. "You've changed, and now when you go back your life there will change too, and you don't know what will happen."

"Yes, and it scares me. I don't know what I'll say to him. Or maybe worse, that I'll somehow lose all of this."

"Do you know what I'm learning do when I'm scared of something?" Cedar says, reminding himself of this as he speaks.

"What?"

"You give love to it."

"Give love to it?"

"Yes. Fear is an absence of love. It's easier said than done sometimes, but if you can find a way to give love to the thing you fear, then it transforms it. Like fire."

Anna stares at him, the firelight flickering on her face, pieces dropping into place. "I'm afraid of how much I want to be with you," she whispers, surprised at her boldness.

"You know there's a part of me that feels the same way, Anna. I know you. Our souls... we're... connected. Can you feel that?"

"Yes."

She can feel the intensity of his gaze and doesn't trust herself to meet his eyes. She doesn't want to make it more difficult for either of them. Instead, she focuses all her attenton on the simple beauty of the rough clay mug in her hands, rubbing the well-worn handle with her thumb. *Think of Damien,* she reminds herself. Even with everything that's happened this weekend, he is still there at home waiting for her. *And I don't want to hurt him.* But still, there is a feeling inside her – in both her body and her heart – which is speaking about the rightness of this, of being here now with Cedar. *What does it all mean?* She sips the last of her tea carefully.

Cedar is silent for a moment, considering. He regards this woman sitting by his fire and feels the sense of incompleteness. This is not just about allowing Anna to share his tipi, to share dreamtime. There is something more; he can feel it. *But what?*

Their mugs are empty. Anna sets hers down by the fire and sighs, feeling the calming effects of the tea and the settling of her body after the high energy of the evening. "I guess it's time to sleep then."

"I guess it is," Cedar echoes, touched at the look he sees in Anna's eyes. He has never been so close to breaking his vow as he has been tonight. It has taken – and still is taking – every ounce of his willpower to hold firm to that promise. *And the night's not over yet.* Again, Cedar questions himself, and the dream. And bubbling up again comes the knowledge that if the woman from his vision is real, she would wholeheartedly bless whatever is in his highest good. *What is in the highest good?* he wonders, his eyes lingering over the contours of Anna's painted face, shining golden in the firelight.

Cedar returns their mugs to a little washing up bowl by his table before checking on the bedding. Running his fingers along the blankets, he nods, satisfied.

Anna watches him carefully lifting the bedding from the chairs and arranging it on their sleeping place. She moves over to join him on the bed, her heart still racing, despite her telling it to stop. *Because nothing is going to happen. You are only going to sleep.* But even sleeping next to Cedar feels like such an intimate thing. *To share dreamtime*, as he had said on the way here.

As she kneels beside him, looking questioningly at their bed, Cedar feels an overpowering compulsion to hug her, to hold her and let her know it's okay, to somehow lift the confusion from her. *Give her some heart energy*, it comes to Cedar. This is something he can give her freely.

"Good night Anna," he says softly, opening his arms to her. She lets herself be enveloped by the embrace, feeling the physicality of his arms around her, with a deepening sense of wellbeing. It feels like coming home. She closes her eyes, resting her cheek against his neck, feeling the strength of his chest, the rise and fall of his belly as he breathes against her. It reminds her to breathe deeper, too.

She can smell the musky, herbal scent of him, the sweat of the evening's performance still on his skin.

"You are Love," he whispers.

You are Love. The words resonate inside Anna.

In her mind's eye she recalls the moment in the workshop when Paul invited them to give heart energy to someone they loved. Anna knows now with a sudden awareness – a rising warmth in the heart – that this is exactly what Cedar is doing with her now. In this warmth, all worry and concern about what they should or shouldn't do dissolves. She feels totally held, totally loved. This feeling of warmth, of being home is enough.

It shines with a clarity for Anna, as she realises this feeling of closeness, of feeling someone else's heart, is something she has never experienced before when being intimate with a man.

Sex can be medicine too... like music. An act of love!

In the past for Anna, sex had always been about what she wanted to achieve, what she wanted others to give her – acceptance. She had tried to please men, to give them what she though they wanted, because of what she ultimately wanted. She can see how the desire for acceptance and validation had always been the underlying force driving her actions in all the parts of her life. *I don't want to do that anymore.*

Earlier, during the workshop, when she had practised sending heart energy to Cedar, it had felt so sweet – it was a feeing of giving love without needing anything in return. It was more than enough; it had completely filled her. And it was the same at the gig tonight – the love had flowed through Anna, filling her until it was overflowing. She gives that energy of love back to him again now. But this time, he is right here with her – his belly next to her belly, her heart next to his.

Cedar can feel what Anna is doing and the knowledge that she is giving him heart energy too touches him so deeply that he feels his heart expanding even more. Intensifying in equal measure, is the heat in his loins. Heart energy – he is surprised to find – is an extraordinary aphrodisiac. But at the same time, the more he stays with an awareness of the heart, the less he needs to do anything about this rising sexual energy. He just stays with the awareness of the growing sensations.

Breathing again into his belly, Cedar draws up the energy of the Earth, the energy of love from the air and the ether around them, and breathes it back out through his heart to hers. *Let it be for her highest good.*

Again the dragon energy in Cedar is waking – the serpent, Kundalini. It has done this before for Cedar, a number of times. It happened earlier tonight during his performance, as the pranic energy had begun to rise up the spine. And now as it did then, it brings with it that feeling of sweetness beyond measure and a sense of light rising up from his Base Chakra, through the Sacral Chakra and up through the Solar Plexus to the Heart.

Something new is happening this time, though. It hadn't happened in the gig. It hasn't happened ever before for Cedar. This time, the pranic energy is rising higher. He can feel it moving through his Heart, expanding it even more and now rising up to his Throat Chakra and tingling in his Third Eye as the golden warmth fills his whole head and moves upwards... and now the tingling of the Crown as it opens... to the deepest peace and bliss he has ever known.

And now, something else extraordinary is happening – the ojas is rising. It begins as a warmth at his Root Chakra, intensifying with each conscious breath.

Stay with the heart, the reminder comes when he is distracted by the growing sensations. As he focuses again on his heart and the breath, the ojas slowly rises higher, following the pranic energy upwards. With it, the sweet nectar of love and wholeness floods through Cedar's whole body. He offers this energy of love to her.

In synchrony, the warmth in Anna's own heart grows stronger. As it does, there is a sense of expansion at the centre of her chest, as if this subtle heart has grown larger than it was before, as if it now holds more capacity to love and feel compassion for others. In this place, she can hear Cedar's heart more clearly, how much his vow means to him. In so loving him, it matters to her too. She knows now that she will help him to honour it, that loving him truly is enough.

And now, without warning, a surprising energy begins to build in this place between her legs – this place she wants to find a new name for. It has been a place she has felt ashamed of throughout her whole life, a forbidden place. But now, with this wildness still in her body, she can feel the power and the sacredness of this opening, this place of birth, this place where the Root Chakra is opening downwards and connecting to the energy of the Earth below. And the feeling of exquisite pleasure – even though he is not physically touching her there – is not just on the surface, but right deep inside her, connected to her very core.

What are you doing to me? she wonders, bewildered at what is occurring inside her. The sensation is building, like an ever expanding wave, the petals of a lotus flower, humming and vibrating and opening, tingling all over her skin as her body's senses awaken.

She tries to focus on keeping the pleasure of the feeling, but as she does, it diminishes. So she reminds herself to breathe again, remembering that it is not about what she can get for herself, it is about giving. And it is about gratitude, for the gift of this moment. *Breathing in gratitude, breathing out a blessing of love from the heart.* As she does, the energy intensifies again, seeming now to travel along these golden threads of light which begin at her centre, tingling to the edges of her physical body and beyond.

Cedar can feel something profound is happening for Anna; that as his own dragon energy rises, it is stirring hers, and though Anna is not yet ready for her own Kundalini-Shakti experience, like the strings of a guitar they are both vibrating; the resonance of his bliss is singing hers into being, and it's the sweetest song Anna has ever known.

Let go, the soft, warm voice of her heart whispers. *Let love carry you.* Giving herself to it, the opening deepens, and the warmth in her heart becomes so big now it's filling her to overflowing. She is vibrating, tingling and ringing with song.

Cedar is swaying her gently, allowing his body to move naturally as it does sometimes when the Kundalini spirals up the central energy channel, a gently twisting, rotating dance. And as he moves, Anna is moving with him in the dance; it is dancing them both. It is the dance of two Heart-Selves meeting, two bodies dancing to the same song, remembering that they were never separate.

Love making love.

They are sitting on the hill overlooking Glastonbury Festival. Cedar is playing his didgeridoo beneath the stars, which are sparkling alive above them. The resonance thrums inside Anna, as if he is playing her very cells and they are dancing to it.

Stretched out across the valley below them are two hundred thousand fires – each one like a sun shining up from below, reflecting the stars above. Each of these fires is a person. Each one like her, is a glowing light. Anna can see that the trees too are shining; every plant, every living thing, even the rocks all have a light. It is all alive. It reminds her of a giant version of the candlelit lotus flower mandala in the Peace Dome.

As Cedar plays his didgeridoo, the glowing lights themselves seem to be dancing to the music. The sound seems to come from inside her and all around her. And now, just on the horizon beyond the trees where the stone dragon sleeps, the first rays of sun are coming up over the hill, catching Cedar's face, and reflecting in his eyes. It is a new day.

Turning to face one another, Anna is awestruck by the beauty of this soul before her, by the love shining in these eyes.

"I'm home," she whispers. But as she says this, Cedar's face shimmers and changes, and it is Damien looking back at her now, his face in shadow.

"What are you doing here?" Anna asks him, frightened suddenly as the world around her seems to darken. She turns to run, to try and find her way back to the place of light she had been in before, but the shadows are pressing down on her from all sides. There is nowhere to run. She feels the certainty of love she had found slipping away in this blackness. *Worthless*, the darkness taunts. *Worthless*.

Then she can hear Cedar's voice again, whispering. *Give love to the thing you fear. Fear is an absence of love. Just as the light is you, so too is the shadow. Dark and light are two sides of the same thing.*

Anna gazes more deeply into the shadows before her, facing them. *Worthless*, they say. *You are alone.*

I am enough, Anna says back to the shadows. *I am love.*

The thought seems to echo out from her, rippling on and on into infinity. And now in the darkness she becomes aware of a point of light. It is coming from the centre of her, and the more she looks at it, the brighter it becomes. As she breathes into this point of light, it grows brighter still. She can see herself now, shining out in the darkness as a radiant glowing star, visible only because of the darkness around it. She continues to breathe the thought of *I am enough* right inside her, until it is a fire blazing at her very core. *I am enough. I am love.* Breathing out, she offers that love to the voices in the dark, which have now grown silent.

And now, suddenly, she can see there are other points of light beginning to shine out in the darkness. Countless other stars, twinkling and shining brightly throughout the universe. They are the most beautiful lights Anna has ever seen. Some are close and some are far away, but all are glowing with this same magnificence. Multi-coloured filaments of light radiate from every star, reaching out into the infinite universe, touching everything. They are born of a love that yearned to know itself. Each star is made of the same light, but as these stars individuate themselves, experiencing what it means to be a star in the universe, they each reflect the light in their own unique way. There are some which shine more red, some more blue. Some are green, gold, purple, orange or a combination of colours, every colour of the rainbow. And there is a harmony of song, each shining soul singing their own note in a great symphony of stars, an interwoven tapestry of light, of which she and everyone else is an integral part.

As Anna looks closer at the stars nearest to her she recognises the colours. There are Cedar, Moon, Maddy, Alex, Shari and all those that had been around the fire. There are Johannes and Sorrel, the tightrope walker, Kai and all the other wise and interesting people she has met at the festival. And there are all the musicians whose music has touched her over the weekend. And there is Eden, too. Her star shines just as brightly as all the rest. And of course there is Damien. His star is before hers now, reflecting his own uniquely beautiful colours. And though they are not the same colours as hers, they too are magnificent to behold, with as much beauty and grace as any other star. How had she missed the beauty of this soul when it was right in front of her?

Anna becomes aware now of a warm presence on her right side. It is Cedar, sleeping soundly beside her as they share dreamtime. She can still see the beautiful expression of his own colours as his Heart-Self sings that song it was born to sing.

Someone is playing a song nearby. It's a sweet, stirring guitar melody. It's so familiar, like a song Anna always wanted to write. She opens her dream eyes and lifts herself to see that the fire at the centre of Cedar's tipi is burning brightly again. A woman is sitting across from Anna on the other side of the fire. Her earth-brown hair hangs down across her face, swaying as she plays. She wears no clothing, holding only the guitar in front of her. Her fingers are moving with such grace across the strings it is as if they are dancing too. Anna wonders if this is Nina Marshall, but as the woman lifts her head Anna sees the facepaint. It is the paint she herself is wearing, and the face is her own. It is her Wild Heart-Self.

The woman smiles at Anna. *I love you*, her eyes seem to say. *I accept you, just as you are. You are me, and I am you.* The woman's eyes reflect the light of the fire, and seem to be themselves a light radiating.

The woman begins to sing with a voice that lifts from the very core of her, a voice so familiar, and so deep, and rich. It is a voice in many ways like Moon's, but also unique – a sound that sings to Anna's very heart.

"*There's a medicine I can bring...*" the woman sings. "*It begins with love... and love can sing...*"

Anna listens, wishing she'd written that song.

The more the woman sings, the more Anna can feel the song in her own body, moving through her in waves, and it feels like the voice is coming from inside her own chest, from her own heart.

The woman stops playing and looks up at Anna. "This is your song." She holds out the guitar towards Anna. "Here... it's yours."

Anna opens her eyes. She is looking up at the inner peak of Cedar's tipi. Through the opening at the top she can just glimpse a slip of blue sky.

It was a dream, she realises.

There's a medicine I can bring... She searches for the words of the song. *It begins with love... and love can sing. I did write that*, she realises. *It is my song.*

I wonder if I can write the rest of it. She imagines her Heart-Self smiling at her, as if she knows Anna was always meant to write that song. She doesn't know how she'll do it, but she knows she'll try. And somehow, this morning, it all seems possible. So many things seem possible after last night. The whole weekend has been one magical, extraordinary journey. She knows now that whatever happens, life will never be the same again.

She can see from the corner of her eye that the pillow beside her is empty. Cedar is gone.

But the pillow is not completely empty. There is an exquisite feather sitting there, brown and cream coloured, with flecks of white. It is the feather that Cedar had hung from his belt that night in the Big Tipi, and last night when he had played. Last night, he had still been wearing it as he held her.

She rises to sitting and lifts the feather in her fingers, twirling it, careful of the soft downey parts at the base of the shaft. It's an eagle feather. It's small, but she can feel this is what it is. *Why did he leave it here?* She can't imagine he's left it for her. *Could he? And he can't have gone without saying goodbye.*

Coming from all directions are the sounds of transience, of the vehicles now allowed on site, the sounds of people taking down their tipis. It's Monday. People are going home. This thought creates a wave of panic in Anna's body.

Outside the open flap of the tipi Anna can see the sun is shining. *He can't have gone far,* she thinks. *Surely.*

She pads across the tipi and peers out the entrance. With relief she sees Cedar sitting there in the sun with his eyes closed, cross-legged in meditation. He wears knee-length beige shorts and no shirt, his bone pendant resting across his bare chest, which still shows the streaks of painted fire radiating from his heart, over the rising sun at his navel. The Eagle tattoo is there on his arm, in quiet flight, his hands resting palm over palm on his lap. Anna smiles to see him this way – with his hair uncombed and slightly wild – the way a lover would see her beloved the morning after. *The morning after what?* If someone asked her whether she had made love with Cedar, she would say yes. If someone asked her if they had had sex, she would say no. Yet both are true.

Had she been unfaithful to Damien? Anna thinks of that beautiful shining star she had seen in her dream. Damien's star. Yes, she has to admit. *What you do with your energy matters, perhaps even more than what you do with your physical body.* She has shared a deeper energetic experience with Cedar than she has ever shared with another human being. She can see now that she must go back to Damien and bring him the truth of her heart, and accept the consequences, whatever they may be. For as Johannes had said, *In truth there is liberation. To walk your path of truth is to walk the path of love. Only in truth can we have a real, shared experience with others.* And this is what her Heart-Self is calling her to do, to walk a path of open-hearted, loving connection with others.

Quietly, so as not to disturb Cedar, she walks carefully around the tipi to the lean-to toilet. From here she can see just how many empty spaces there are now in the Tipi Field, with lighter-coloured circles on the grass as the only reminders to show what had once been there.

As she returns Cedar cracks open an eye.

"Good morning." An affectionate smile lifts the corners of his lips. "I was just doing my morning meditation."

"Don't let me disturb you."

"It's okay. I've just finished." His eyes move to the feather in Anna's fingers. "You found it."

She lifts the feather and twirls it in her fingers. "Yes. You must be moulting." She grins at him.

He laughs. "It happens. Sometimes you gotta let things go."

Anna's face is serious now. "But it's the feather you wear when you're performing..."

"It was, but I don't need it now. It was clear to me when I woke this morning that it wanted to come to you."

Anna moves across the grass and sits beside him, quietly holding the feather in her hand, the most precious object she has ever been given. "I don't know what to say."

"It's my way of saying thank you, Anna. For what happened last night. For the gift you gave me."

"The gift I gave? But it was you..."

Cedar shakes his head. "It was both of us. You were giving Heart Energy too – I could feel it – and that made all the difference. I had an experience last night which changed me, Anna. This morning, I'm seeing the world with new eyes. The things I was afraid of are just gone. Gone." He lifts his hands, and his eyes twinkle. "I just feel peaceful. Like no matter what is happening, has happened, or could possibly happen, all is well."

"It changed me too," she says softly. "I don't think I even know how much until I go back..." She looks up at his smiling eyes. *I'm afraid to go back. What if I lose all this?* Yes, the fear is still there. And yet, she can feel the fire burning in her heart which tells her that she will go back, and she will do her best to bring her heart and her truth to her life there. She had faced the darkness in her dream and out of that something extraordinary had grown.

"Thank you," she whispers. "It will help me to remember."

Cedar smiles. "I also wanted to give you this feather as a blessing for your journey. I know you will find what you are seeking, Anna – in your life, and in your music. Because if you can do with music what you did with me last night, you will find your medicine song."

It begins with love... and love can sing...

"Maybe I'm already beginning to..." Anna whispers, twirling the feather in between her thumb and forefinger again, watching how the tiny strands of white catch the sun's light and seem to shine. "Maybe I'm just catching a glimpse of it."

Cedar stirs the pot with a wooden spoon. He's making them porridge over his fire. "It's grounding," he says, "on a day when people are getting ready and travelling home."

Through the open flap of the tipi, Anna watches a green car with a trailer pull up nearby. A man gets out and begins the process of packing up his tipi. Her own process of leaving is inevitable today. It is only a matter of time. One bowl of porridge.

Cedar rinses out the two clay mugs they had used the night before and fills them both with water from the large plastic bottle.

Anna gratefully accepts the mug and gulps down the contents. This is more than the usual morning thirst. Without her having to ask, Cedar refills her cup.

"It's this amazing water again," she says finally, placing her empty cup down beside her.

"Chalice Well."

"That's it. Where do you get it?"

"The well is just on the edge of Glastonbury town. We always stop there on the way to and from the festival. It's just below the Tor."

"Oh!" Anna says, thinking of the great cardboard tower that she had been part of erecting in the circus field. "I've never been there. To the real one."

"If you have time, stop and visit it on your way home. You can see it for miles as you approach. It's a tall narrow hill with a monument on top. But it's so much more than that. It's place of great power, a place where great lines of energy meet."

"Like a chakra," Anna whispers.

Cedar nods. "Exactly."

"A woman I met yesterday told me that Glastonbury Tor is meant to be the Heart Chakra of the world."

"I've heard that, too, and it feels true to me. If the main chakras in our body are formed by the intersection of major meridians, which create vortices of energy, so the intersection of powerful earth energy lines – Pachamama's own meridians – would create similar vortices of energy, albeit on a much larger scale. Thus, a chakra. And like our own Heart Chakra, Glastonbury Tor feels like a place of power where energy can be brought in or sent out. I've been told that the overguiding energy of that place around the Chalice Well and the Tor is Love – Christ Consciousness."

Anna stares at him, shocked to hear someone speaking of Christ here in these fields. "Christ?"

"Some people think Christ has nothing to do with earth-centered living," Cedar says. "I used to think like that, but I am discovering that Christ Consciousness is not about religion, Anna. It's about Love. And I've come to see that all these things are not separate either. Christ and the angels like Michael, and the realm of Spirit, and the realm of the Earth elementals, of Fire, Water, Earth, Air, the plant devas, all of this. They are made of the same thing we are, Anna. They are made of Love. It's just Love in different forms. That's the way I see it anyway."

"I like the way you see it."

Cedar spoons out some porridge into two wooden bowls and offers one to Anna. "It's quinoa flakes with chia seeds, pear and honey. One of my favourites."

"Thank you." She accepts this food that Cedar has made her with his own hands gratefully. They carry their bowls back outside onto the grass and eat in silence. As Anna enjoys the warm, sweet porridge, she watches the man with the green truck removing the outer canvas from his tipi, leaving the bare bones of the structure standing.

She thinks of her life back in Brighton. "What if it all gets destroyed?"

Cedar places his empty bowl down on the grass and turns to face her, his eyes clear. "What if it does?"

As the meaning of his words filters through to her, it creates a window in her mind's eye, to that possibility. *What if it does? For out of the darkness a new light can be born.*

"Destruction and creativity are two sides of the same thing."

"Just like light and shadow," Anna says softly.

"Exactly. You can't have one without the other."

Anna watches the man nearby walking the lashing rope back around the tipi poles, so now they are only loosely laid against one another, ready for dismantling. Soon Cedar will be doing the same thing.

It is time to go. They can both feel it.

"It's time for me to meet Moon," Cedar says. "I told her I'd help her with her tipi. And we have to coordinate the next bit of our journey."

"I should get going too."

Anna sees the tenderness in Cedar's eyes as he opens his arms to her. She hugs him back, feeling the strength of those arms as they wrap around her again. This time they are the arms of a friend. Anna reminds herself to give some Heart Energy again, and feeling the warmth returning to her heart, knows he is doing the same.

"Thank you, Anna."

"Thank you, too."

"We'll meet again. I can feel it," he whispers.

"How about tomorrow?" Anna says, joking.

He squeezes her more tightly and laughs, catching her joke, and also listening to the part of her that wishes it were true. "You know, if that is where our paths lead us, it would be a joyful thing."

He brushes the hair from her cheeks and lifts his hands to the sides of her face. Gently, he leans in and kisses Anna in that place just between her eyebrows. With all they have experienced, this is the most intimate physical touch they have shared.

"You are Love," he says softly, and Anna sees herself reflected in his eyes.

"Namaste," she whispers.

"Namaste, Anna."

A circle remains. Two circles in fact, one inside the other. Moon kneels on the grass in the centre of the larger circle, where her tipi once stood, feeling the warmth of the sun on top of her head. Before her is a round hole in the ground where the fire had been, with most of the ash now cleared away. Beside Moon are the pieces of grassy earth that she had lifted to make the fire at the beginning of the festival. One by one, she places the pieces back in, five in all, like a puzzle fitting neatly back together. She crumbles bits of the dry earth so that the cracks fill in again. So much has happened here. So much has changed.

Cedar has gone to get the van. He had helped her take down the poles, as was their custom. But today, something had felt different. He was different. *Perhaps we both were*, Moon muses. There had been a new light in Cedar's eyes. A new, gentle easiness. Some old pain has left him, and Moon is glad for him. She wonders briefly whether it has anything to do with his evening with Anna last night. He hadn't said anything about it, but Moon had had the strongest sense last night leaving them alone by the fire that their night was far from over.

But it doesn't matter, she tells herself. While there are still vestiges of the grief still to move through, she can see now that she was never meant to conceive Cedar's child. It was a fantasy she had let herself believe. Something has shifted inside, and now the world feels new with possibilities again. She is free to dream a new dream.

Moon opens her medicine pouch and tips out the contents into her hand. There are three seeds left.

When you wish to give a gift back to the earth, to express your gratitude, plant one of these seeds in that place, and give thanks. Those were the words of the woman who had given her the seeds. Special seeds. Blessed seeds.

Moon selects one seed and returns the other two back to her pouch.

With her finger, she opens one of the cracks of Earth and gently places her seed inside. She smooths the earth over it again and holds her hands there, feeling the cool grass beneath her fingers and giving the seed energy.

"Thank you," she whispers. "Thank you Pachamama. Thank you for the blessings of this life."

She reaches for her last bottle of Chalice Well water and tips what remains over the dry ground, an offering to new life.

Anna looks out for the beacon. Maddy had said it would come into view about now. She flicks her eyes again to the map Maddy had drawn for her on one of the Pacha Mama Cafe napkins when she had gone to say goodbye. She fingers the napkin as she drives on the road leading away from the festival. But not back to Brighton. Not yet. There is still one stop to make.

Beside her on the passenger seat are Cedar's feather, Moon's handkerchief, the wooden spoon she had made and Awakening the Dreamer's CD. There are also two chocolate brownies from the Chai Chi tent. After seeing Maddy, Anna had gone to say goodbye to Kai. He had been suitably impressed by her facepaint, and had insisted she take the brownies for free, as he was packing up and they were extra.

Next to the brownies is the plastic water bottle she had saved, waiting to be filled. Before her, on the horizon, is Glastonbury Tor.

"We came down from the hill of dreams
Bernadette, mother earth and you and me
Through Carraroe, down the wildwood side,
blinding our eyes in the shallow seas
Drank fire with the king of the blues,
plugged in to the medicine way,
took a long last look at Crazy Horse
Push now for a golden age
I just found God
I just found God
I just found God where He always was
Found myself on the roof of the world
just-a-waitin for to get my wings
Strange angel in the changing light
said Brother you forgot one thing
My heart beat from the inside out
So lucky just to be alive !
Can you tell what I'm talking about?
Any day now the sun's gonna rise"

from the song, 'Glastonbury Song', by Mike Scott (The Waterboys) *[2]

Anna reaches the lane Maddy described, the one that skirts the base of the Tor and runs between two sacred wells, the *Red Spring* and the *White Spring*.

On the left side of the lane is a long stone wall, so high that only the green tops of the trees in the garden beyond are visible. On the right is an unusual stone reservoir building, with a little stone courtyard out front filled with people who have

2. *'Glastonbury Song' Words and Music by Mike Scott © 1993, Reproduced by permission of SM Publishing UK Limited, W1F 9LD*

clearly come directly from the festival. Some are drumming, some are smoking. Trees and hedgerows line the sloping hill around it.

Anna drives past them and finds a space to park further up the lane, beneath overhanging ash and sycamore trees in full leaf.

Bottle in hand, she strolls back down the lane, looking out for the water point Maddy had described. To her right is a tall, wooden fence which hides most of what is beyond, but the tantalising tops of lush, green trees speak of the life that dwells there. Maddy had spoken of the beauty and tranquility of the Chalice Well garden, and of the majestic stone Lion's Head within, where the sacred, healing waters flow from the Lion's open mouth. Anna had known she would not make it before the garden closed, so Maddy had told her about a special drinking water spout on the outside of the garden wall, where pilgrims may come and receive the water, where it flows freely.

She finds it beneath the boughs of the overhanging yew and laurel trees, pouring from the mouth of a tiny stone lion's head. Mosses and lychen grow up beneath it, nourished by the water. On the wall to the right of it someone has pasted words in clay over the stone of the walls: *Love One Another.*

Love one another, Anna thinks. *Christ said that.*

Now she realises that this phrase doesn't mean what she had thought it meant all her life.

Love one another as yourself. As yourself. Because they are you, and you are them.

She remembers what Cedar had said about Christ Consciousness being the overguiding energy of this place. A wind rustles in the leaves overhanging the wall, and Anna feels a little shiver. There is a sense of presence here.

Yes, I can believe it, she thinks. *I can believe in things I can't see.*

She bends to the water flowing from the little lion's head and washes her hands in it. It's cold, but so fresh. It feels good. She cups her hands and brings the water to her lips. And it's so alive! If she had thought the water they had drunk that night in the Big Tipi was special, this is even more so, flowing straight from the source.

Maddy had explained that there is a healing power in this water. That all the intention over the many years, the prayers, the power of the earth's energy in this place have all contributed to the potency of this water. And those who believe in the power of it receive this power, and even those who do not know about it often still feel something.

Anna drinks deeply, feeling the coolness right inside her, awakening and enlivening. A feeling of reverence comes over her as kneeling, she watches the water pouring down from the spout and through the metal grate below her, meeting an underground stream.

I will not forget, she vows.

She bends her head under the flow of water, letting it run over her and over her, feeling herself renewed, cleansed. Lifting her head, she runs her hands through her dripping hair, feeling the water splashing down her dress. She feels like dancing here in the lane. The world feels new. Full of possibilities.

As she fills her empty bottle, Anna can feel the presence of another pilgrim waiting for their turn. Before stepping aside, she cups her hands and takes one more drink of the life-giving water.

Thank you, she whispers to the well and to the Spirit of this place. *Thank you.*

She takes the path that winds up the steep grassy hill to the summit, and there rising above her on the crest of the hill is the real St. Michael's Tower. The cardboard replica she had helped to raise at the festival had been nothing compared with the majesty of this ornately carved stone structure, which seems itself to be alive with the energy of all those who have travelled here over the years to pay it homage.

If Anna had felt reverence gazing up at the cardboard version, the real tower evokes a sense of true wonder, as if perhaps angels really do reside here. Anna feels a tingling of excitement running through her body as she climbs the path towards it.

As her thighs burn, she remembers walking barefoot up the hill with Cedar, and kicks off her sandals, carrying them instead. Now she is bounding up the steps, not minding the little stones under the soles of her feet as she moves step by step, higher and higher. She passes by some sheep, grazing on the hillside.

Approaching the summit, Anna can hear someone is playing didgeridoo inside the tower. Her heart beats more quickly for a moment, but even before she sees the man inside, she knows it's not Cedar. Still, the sound is hauntingly beautiful and resonant inside the tower. Rather than go inside, she sits at the edge where she can see the view out across the fields of Avalon.

Who am I? This life is not what I thought it was.

Everything seems somehow more beautiful than before. Even the blades of grass seem to have a quality of light around them. The sun is golden on the horizon now, casting the stone of St. Michael's Tower in a rosy glow. Windows on some of the houses below sparkle like fiery gems across the valley reflecting the light. Anna watches the sun as it begins to dip behind the farthest hills, feeling the dew as it begins to fall. She knows she will have to go soon, but not yet.

As each little streetlight flickers on below her, Anna remembers her dream of being on the hill, how each fire she had gazed down upon on had been a human being, each one a radiant light, reflecting the stars above. How every soul in the universe had been born from the same light. How that same light shines from every plant, every stone, from the Earth herself.

Anna's heart fills with a sweet gratitude for this journey. She doesn't understand it all yet. Far from it. It feels like it's only just the beginning. Breathing in the sweet scent of the evening right into the centre of herself, she offers it back with her love, out across the hills and beyond. With a breath of wind, comes a returning lift, a sense of magic, *the love that is in all things.*

It's all one song.

Sitting here on the peak of this hill, with the wind in her hair and the lights below her, the curve of the Earth on the horizon and feeling herself part of it all, her heart is singing.

"There's a medicine I can bring
It begins with love and love can sing
It's the heart of everything
It begins with love and love can sing
Whatever you do, whatever you make
Begin with love, it's your medicine
Whatever you do, whatever you make
Begin with love, it's your medicine song"

from the song, 'Medicine Song', by Anna Leigh Mayes

Acknowledgements

There are so many people who have given their love to the creation of *Medicine Song*.

Firstly I thank **my dear family** on both sides of the Atlantic, for all your love, patience and support. I truly could not have completed this book without you.

I am deeply grateful to all those who gave their time to the reading of the many drafts, offering me their honest critical feedback and insight which has made the book so much better: my generous and wise parents **Joe Truscott** and **Ginny Lovick,** my aunt and author **Brenda Carre**, my dear friends **Robin Gillmor, Sarah Price, Rosie Toll, Vanya Green, Delagh King, Mac Macartney** and **Brian Boothby** and most especially my sister **Amanda Truscott**, an author whose courage in publishing her own book *Creative Unblocking* inspired me to do the same and who has been here for me every step of the way.

Many thanks also to authors **Lucy H Pearce** and **H.P. Carr** for all your generous advice and support. Also to those other dear friends and musicians who read various drafts and offered their insights and help: **Domenic DeCicco, Shannon Smy, Martin Wilks, George Borowski** and **Mary Watson.**

My sincere gratitude to all those who gave me permission to write about their inspiring creations: **Simone Kay** (*Rainbow Wishing Well*), **Ray Brooks** (*Glastonbury Water Dragon*), **Bernadette Vallely** (founder of *Shakti Sings Choir*), **Ali and Chenma** (*Cafe Kailash*). Thank you also to the three venue staff at Glastonbury Festival who allowed me to depict their likenesses and to all those who gave me their kind permission to invent fictional staff and use their real-life venues as settings for fictional events: to **Katy, Giles, James, Carl** and **Anna Moon** (whose similarity in name to my main characters is completely coincidental) and to all the staff at **Lost Horizon Sauna;** to **Anna** (whose similarity in name to my main character is also coincidental) and to everyone else at **Pacha Mama Cafe;** to **Stevie** at **Ancient Futures;** to all the dear **Healing Area Music Space** team and to **Tim, Sophie and Sarah** and all the others who have given their love to creating the **Peace Dome.**

A special thank you also to the **Chalice Well Trust.**

And to all those who offered their advice on various sections of the book: author and chirologist **Johnny Fincham**, voice and breathwork coach **Sandra Smith**, shiatsu practitioner **Sebastian Deans** and qigong and t'ai chi master **Cos Stephanides.** Also thanks to **Charles** for looking over the NDE scene for me.

My deep thanks to the visionary artist **Dorrie Joy** for dreaming the beautiful cover image with me, and to my dear friend, wise author and artist **Glennie Kindred**, for allowing me to use her drawings of the elements.

My gratitude to all those who created **Glastonbury Festival** with their love, for it has been one of the places that has offered the most opportunity for growth and transformation and has given me some of the musical highlights of my life: **Leonard Cohen, The Waterboys, Coldplay, Xavier Rudd** and so many others (many of whose lyrics appear throughout the pages of this book).

And finally, my heart-felt gratitude to all those whose financial support during the crowdfunding campaign enabled the publication of *Medicine Song*. This book would not be here right now without your generous help.

The Patron Sponsors: **Joe Truscott, Ginny Lovick, H. Schroeder, Suzie Mumme** and **Howard Stanley**. And all the others who gave their generous support during the crowdfunding campaign, in alphabetical order: **Jennifer Aikman, Emrys Baird, Theodore Best, Carolyn Bidgood, Ali Blackburn, Sue Bolshaw, Beth Brockett, Sylvia van Bruggen, Adley Bruneau, Rachel and David Calder, Hollie Pita Carr, Brenda Carre, Charles Cox, Liz Day, Mal Darwen, Sebastian Deans, Sarah Donald, Sarah Dunseath, Suzy Edwards, Red K Elders, Peter Ellis, Paul Fitzgerald, Anne Gastaldo, Robin Gillmor, Jason Glover, Nat Goldthorpe, Patsy Gormley-Steele, Vanya Green, Kris Hansen, Edwina Hayes, Melanie Heap, Andrea Helm, Nadine Hermann, Jennifer Howarth, Gray Jordan, Jeneanne Kallstrom, Mike Kennedy, Vincent Kennedy, Imran Khan, Delagh King, Helen Krause, Kathleen Lapeyrouse, Isabella Lazlo, Kendra Lovick, Laurene Lovick, Keith Lyon, Mac Macartney, Marion McCartney, Olivier Maxted, Anna Meynell, Alina Mihailova, Margi Molyneux, John and Jane Mooney , Nina NW, Sara O'Brien, Anita Parry, Samantha Piercy, Sarah Price, Melanie Purdy, Arne Radtke, Laila and Mathew Risdon, Steve Riva, Tracey Sanders, Ayla Schafer, Gail Scoones, Megan Selby, Shannon Smy, Cos Stephanides, Dave Sturt, Rosie Toll, Amanda Truscott, David Truscott, Kevin Urbanski, Lara Waldman, Robin Watson, Sue Weaver.** My thanks also to the sponsors of the Book Launch in Norwich, **Rainbow Wholefoods** and **Anglia Print**.

Most of all, I thank my beloved husband **Chris** and son **James**, who have lovingly given more than I can possibly begin to express in words here.

This book is a true collaboration and has grown to find itself through the heartfelt contributions of so many people. I thank you all from the depth of my heart.

Musicians and Songwriters

My heartfelt gratitude to all the musicians and songwriters who have allowed me to use excerpts from their songs throughout *Medicine Song*. I have chosen lyrics from songs which I have personally loved and been inspired by over the years. Please support the work of these wonderful artists, who make the world a better place through the gift of their music. For direct links to their websites visit: **www.medicinesong.uk**

Brian Boothby: www.brianboothby.co.uk
Peace of the Action, E.P.N.S.

George Borowski: www.georgeborowski.com
Chant

Tina Bridgman: www.tinabridgman.com
Cradle, Stars in Your Soul

Domenic DeCicco: www.twinarrowsmusic.com
Seeds of Evergreen

Chris Ellis: www.christopherellis.co.uk
Friend to the Earth

Robin Gillmor: www.myspace.com/robingillmor
Hearts on Fire

Carolyn Hillyer: www.seventhwavemusic.co.uk
Walking as Before

Boe Huntress: www.boehuntress.com
You are Enough, Green Dragon, I Believe in Love

Maya Love: www.mayalovemusic.co.uk
You Have God

Lost Padres: www.myspace.com/thelostpadres

Miniature Universe: www.miniatureuniverse1.bandcamp.com

Nick Prater: www.susiero.co.uk/nick-prater
Open My Heart

Susie Ro Prater: www.susiero.co.uk
Phoenix, Sharpen Your Arrow, Beneath the Shadow

Praying for the Rain: www.twinarrowsmusic.com
Light is Fire, Sweet Mother Earth

Ayla Schafer: www.aylaschafer.co.uk
Tracking, I Call You, Follow the Light

Mike Scott/The Waterboys: www.mikescottwaterboys.com
This is the Sea, Spirit, Glastonbury Song

Seize the Day: www.seizetheday.org
Child of the Universe, I am Dust, No One's Slave,
Big Big Love (Ali Blackburn), Mother Earth Chant

Shakti Sings Choir: www.shaktisings.org

Shannon Smy: www.shannonsmy.org
Connected

Michael Stillwater: www.innerharmony.com
One By One

Carrie Tree: www.carrietree.co.uk
Mama Kita Makaya, Perfectly Cast, Water

Mary and Olivia Watson: www.oliviaemmawatson.com
Spiritum

Martin Wilks (Lost Padres): www.musicmartin.uk
Heaven on Earth

Author's Note

This novel takes Glastonbury Festival 2013 as its setting and many of the physical elements depicted in the book are drawn directly from life. However, this is a work of fiction. Names, characters, businesses, events and incidents are either the products of the author's imagination or are used in a fictitious manner. Any resemblance in appearance or name to actual persons (except in the cases of those who have given me permission to use their names or likenesses, and where I have described officially programmed performers), is purely coincidental.

I have written about many different energetic techniques and meditation practices here in this book which have had a positive impact on my own life. I do not claim to be an expert in any of the techniques described, so if you would like to explore some of these things further, I would advise seeking the guidance of a trained master practitioner.

If you are interested in the work of artists mentioned or in any of the teachings or techniques I have written about, you can find some of the real-life inspirations for the book on the *Medicine Song* website.

www.medicinesong.uk

May love guide you on your path.

Namaste

Worthy Causes

Glastonbury Festival supports three main charities. To find out how you can get involved, visit their websites:

www.oxfam.org.uk

www.wateraid.org.uk

www.greenpeace.org.uk

To learn more about these and Glastonbury Festival's other Worthy Causes visit:

www.glastonburyfestivals.co.uk/worthy-causes/

About the Author

Celeste Lovick was born on the west coast of Canada and now lives in Norfolk, England
with her husband Chris and their son James. During the summers, Celeste may be found
with her guitar in the green fields of various festivals around the UK. As well as being an
author and songwriter, Celeste is also a home-educator and reiki practitioner. She has
released five solo albums of original songs and one collaborative album called *Dreaming*
(2010) with Chris Ellis. *Medicine Song* is her first novel.

www.celestelovick.com
www.medicinesong.uk

Also Available from Sheltering Tree Books and Music

Dreaming CD; Celeste Lovick & Chris Ellis; Sheltering Tree Music, 2010
original songs with voices and guitars

Piano Improvisations CD; Chris Ellis; Sheltering Tree Music, 2009
improvisations on a steinway D at Dartington Hall

Chris Ellis Acoustic CD; Chris Ellis; Sheltering Tree Music, 2007
original songs with voice and guitar

In This Time CD; Celeste Lovick; Sheltering Tree Music, 2007
original songs with voice and guitar

First Reflection CD; Chris Ellis; Sheltering Tree Music, 2003
instrumental guitar and piano

Listening CD; Celeste Lovick: Sheltering Tree Music, 2002
original songs with voice and guitar

Tread Softly CD: Chris Ellis; Sheltering Tree Music, 2001
original songs with voice, guitar, piano and band accompaniment

Digital albums **Travelling Home** (2009) and **Inside is Outside** (2018)
are available for purchase here: www.celestelovick.bandcamp.com

Lightning Source UK Ltd.
Milton Keynes UK
UKHW041141201118
332641UK00001B/191/P